HUGH HOLIDAY

Richard Straws

Hudson MacArthur Publishers

Hugh Holiday is a work of fiction. Names, characters, places, and incidents either are the product of the author's imagination or are used fictitiously. Any resemblance to actual persons, living or dead, events, or locales is entirely coincidental.

Published in the United States by:
Hudson MacArthur Publishers, Inc.
PO. Box 1008
Gouldsboro, PA 18424

Printed by:
IngramSpark

ISBN 978-0-9675946-2-0
Ebook ISBN 978-0-9675946-3-7

Cover design: Rod Cameron

Chapter 1

The images kept coming, vivid and binding his senses, fading and replaced by the next, each as graphic as the one before, each sending Hugh spiraling through the emotions he had experienced. The bloody scene in the kitchen hovering in rich but ghastly detail, supplanted by the cop frantically breaking in the back door, displaced by his flight through the neighborhood, succeeded by the two cops questioning him.

It was a Sunday like no other.

The old man wasn't the one who'd made the 9-1-1 call. And he wasn't a particularly observant eyewitness. Just an eighty-two-year-old taking his dog for an evening walk in the late-spring air. But, he'd seen the stranger enter the property; he'd even talked to the stranger. More importantly, he was the only person close-at-hand when the police arrived.

The rising wail of the siren transfixed the man as he eyeballed the patrol car speeding down the tree-lined street and stop just fifteen feet away, at the curb of the property with the yellow house. He reeled in the leash of his cocker-spaniel, which until this point had been entertained only by an occasional squirrel. This quiet, suburban community of upper-middle-class homes, just a ten-minute walk from the man's own neighborhood, was an unexpected site for developing police action.

Officer Oren Taylor, big and lumbering, unfolded from the driver's seat of the patrol car and approached the old man. Twelve years on the Pittsburgh police force had drummed into Taylor a fair helping of caution and common sense. He wanted the lay of the land, and his first consideration was to ask the old-timer if he'd heard anything in the house or seen anyone enter. His slighter, more harefooted partner, Officer Bill Scott, wasn't so guarded. Unlike Taylor, Scott was sure a crime had been committed; his first act was to rush toward the house, unfastening his .40 caliber pistol as he neared the front door.

The yellow house at the center of the action was a relatively modest Victorian and three stories only if one counted the attic floor evident from the small street-side window. A long, eighty-foot pathway of close-fitting stepping stones extended from the sidewalk to the house, bisecting a well-trimmed lawn. Built on one of Pittsburgh's many hills, the property was elevated, necessitating seven steps on the street side of the pathway. At the far end, three more steps led onto a porch that wrapped halfway around the right front of the house—the same side as the blacktopped driveway that ran back to a separate garage. Tall hedges bookended the property, masking it from more spacious homes on either side.

With its light yellow color framed by a beautifully manicured flower garden of petunias, marigolds, yellow trilliums, and tulips, the house seemed the epitome of tranquility.

That was until the front door cracked open a little and a hand grasping a white cloth suddenly appeared, vigorously wiped the doorknob and doorbell, and withdrew inside.

The old man watched as Taylor's eyes were drawn away, pivoting to the house, where Scott was trying to open the now-locked door. Frozen mid-sentence, Taylor left to join his partner, who by now had thrown the full force of his shoulder against what turned out to be quite a solid, hardwood obstacle. It had not budged. At all.

Scott, visibly frustrated, crossed the porch to the right side of the house and jumped to the ground, warning the approaching Taylor to stay at the front entrance while he checked the rear.

Save Scott's barked orders, the evening was quiet. Only the flashing of the police car's strobe lights, left on after the siren had been silenced, contrasted with the seeming peacefulness of the neighborhood.

That would soon change.

Less than a minute after Scott had leapt from the porch, the stillness was broken by the thrice-repeated sound of glass shattering in the back of the house. Taylor reacted quickly. His shout of "Police! Open up!" was followed in short order by a front kick, as he drove his heel into the door just below the doorknob. The frame splintered only slightly. He kicked once more, more determined, more forcefully, with his heavy bulk, and with a side kick. The frame fully splintered, revealing a thin but solid gold-colored chain that held but swayed in the narrow opening between the door and frame. Another savage blow and the door violently swung open.

Taylor entered warily. He had not seen the enigmatic hand and wasn't quite sure why Scott felt such urgency to get into the house. The 9-1-1 call had been about a man forcing entry and a woman's screams. But no confirmation of a physical attack. And everything seemed quiet now.

As Taylor watched spellbound from the shattered doorway, his partner, silent and coiled-spring alert, like a leopard in pursuit of an antelope cut off from the herd, half-sprinted into sight from the opposite side of the house, gun drawn. Taylor continued to stare, riveted by the theatre unfolding, as Scott, moving quickly, saying nothing, glanced into the dining room off the left side of the entrance and, finding it empty, suddenly dashed, two steps at a time, up the wide and slightly curving wooden staircase that connected the first and second floors.

Taylor retraced Scott's movements and entered the kitchen. The backdoor stood ajar, broken glass scattered on the hardwood floor. And immediately Taylor understood the exigency of the situation.

On the floor of the kitchen lay a woman. Under other circumstances, Taylor would have ranked her as one of the most attractive women that he'd ever seen in person. Long, radiant, lustrous black hair partially concealed a lightly tanned face with high cheekbones, large eyes, full lips, smooth skin. The blouse, light sweater, and short skirt complemented more than obscured the classic hour-glass figure with long legs.

But these attributes took a distant second to Taylor's first impression: it was that she was quite observably dead. A long kitchen knife lay near the woman, with the body and knife both enveloped in a crimson puddle. Red droplets, like a surrealistic blood splatter painting, sprayed out as far as the entrance where he was standing. He realized he was standing on someone's blood.

For a minute, Taylor took in the morbidly mesmerizing spectacle; he had never been among the first at the scene of a homicide. And this was obviously a homicide. He admired Scott's quick reaction and instincts. In a moment he would join Scott in his search for the killer. But, for now, he would check for vitals, call this in, and mobilize backup.

The response was rapid. In less than twenty minutes the police were swarming the property and neighborhood. After all, this wasn't the Homewood or Hill districts of Pittsburgh; this was a well-to-do area. And the victim wasn't a nameless drug dealer.

The raven-haired victim was Megan DuPont, a woman with M.D. and Ph.D. after her name, a professor at The MacArthur Medical College and—despite still being in her mid-thirties—

internationally recognized in her research specialty of medical genetics. But it would be the added bonuses of her being strikingly beautiful and with distant ties to scions of the well-to-do Du Pont family that would ignite a media frenzy and make the crime tomorrow's front page news in both Pittsburgh's *Post-Gazette* and *Tribune-Review* and picked up by media outlets coast to coast.

This was when the old man could finally give his statement.

In his defense, he had only spoken with the stranger for a few minutes. And it had been dusk. And since the 9-1-1 caller who'd reported the woman screams that Sunday evening was nowhere to be found, he was all the police really had as a eyewitness.

But the old man's details were sketchy and uncertain. He did know the stranger was a white man. Size? Not sure. "Bigger than me, I suppose," said the man, who still thought of himself as six feet tall but was now closer to five-ten. Age of the intruder? Well, maybe somewhere between eighteen and thirty or maybe into his early thirties. Color of clothes? Don't remember. Wearing a jacket? Think so. Hair color? Eye color? Don't recall. Tattoos? Don't remember. Facial hair? Some kind of facial hair, but not sure if beard, mustache—both? Or maybe just five-o'clock shadow? Could he provide a description to a sketch artist? Not a chance. How about identifying him in a lineup? No way.

But he had seen the stranger enter the property. That much was certain. He had watched the man walk ahead of him and go up the stepping-stone pathway to the house. The hedges had prevented seeing him actually enter the house, but he certainly hadn't come back down the pathway to the sidewalk.

And the old man did have one other key observation. The stranger was British, or at least had a clear and fluent British accent. And he was well-spoken.

The police fanned out. Within a ten-block radius they found several men fitting the general physical description, but none with a British accent. And most with solid reasons to be in the neighborhood. One didn't offer a coherent reason. If he had one, the officers couldn't get it out of him: he had a major stuttering problem. But no hint of an accent. The officers, compelled by their urgent, exciting task to find a murderer, and deciding he was a waste of time, let him go on his way. But not before recording the name and address from his license.

Chapter 2

Hugh Holiday was the man with the stutter. He was also the fluent speaker with the British accent.

The old man was right in that Hugh was bigger than him. Indeed, he stood six feet two inches tall and actually was somewhat stocky—not obese as he was throughout middle and high school and most of college, but still rather broad at the shoulders and a good 220 pounds. He also was between eighteen and thirty years old, so the old man had that right. He was twenty-three to be exact.

If the old man had paid close attention during the encounter, he might have identified some mild pockmarks on Hugh's chin, which were battle scars from some quite severe teenage acne. However, this would have required careful observation and ideally under the glare of the midday sun; at any rate, the scars were largely obscured by the five-o'clock shadow Hugh sported at the time of their chance meeting. Overall, Hugh's difficult high school years notwithstanding, he was now a handsome young man, with alert blue eyes, ash blond hair, strong chin, and a toned body with erect and almost soldiery posture. He also had a captivating and broad smile that displayed what one might call perfect teeth. A woman would be quite drawn to him as a potential boyfriend to flaunt — that is, up until he opened his mouth to speak.

The stutter was a real part of his life; it was not contrived. For as long as Hugh could remember, stuttering had been a constant reminder of his outsider status in society. And it was severe and total—involuntarily repeating syllables, consonants and words; prolonging vowels; and frequently characterized by gaps where nothing came out. At times, his struggle to start speaking, lips pursed together, would suddenly be punctuated by an explosion of sound. And unlike almost all with the disorder, Hugh spent years without any good, stutter-free episodes.

His parents, perhaps well-meaning at first, perhaps not, had exacerbated the situation to the *n*th degree. As he'd heard his parents telling the neighbors one day, Hugh had been a reluctant early talker, barely verbalizing even in his third year, and when he did speak it had this tell-tale stutter. They didn't realize until he was ready for kindergarten that he wasn't growing out of it. In the parents' version, they were great martyrs, taking little Hugh to a speech therapist, then a psychologist, at great financial cost, but no solution could be found.

But if their initial concern had been for the boy, he soon grew to understand that he was supposed to be the child they could proudly brag about to others, but proved just an embarrassment to them. The psychologist had allayed their fears that Hugh was intellectually disabled; indeed, he was evaluated as being particularly bright and with spatial abilities off the chart. Nonetheless, his condition only got worse as he got older. And finally, his parents, whether overcome by financial stress or marital stress or frustration at their only child being a burden and humiliation to them, lost patience. Stern, testy admonitions to "not be so scared," "speak more clearly," 'enunciate!" and the like just made the situation progressively difficult until verbal communication became a near impossible task.

The daily stress of his parents' lives paled in comparison to Hugh's. Elementary school classmates considered him dull-witted. Middle school students made him a target for their barbs. High school classmates, with his added youth obesity and acne, considered him socially undesirable to be seen with.

Adding to his problem was the name with which his parents had so unpresciently encumbered him. The name "Hugh" turned out to be a particularly annoying challenge for him to pronounce. When newcomers would ask him his name, his difficulty in getting it out made it seem like he was saying "you," and his repeated efforts to clarify would lead some to give up and walk away embarrassed, concluding that he was mentally challenged. The addition of his last name led to initial confusion that he was called "Holly," a moniker used to mock him from middle school onward.

But, despite the first impressions he created, Hugh was actually quick of mind. And he remained ever hopeful. Against his parents' advice and without their support, he applied for college and financial aid and enrolled in Pittsburgh's Duquesne University. For dread of the inevitable discussions, Hugh never verbalized to his parents his ultimate goal: medical school and eventually medical or psychological research.

His dream of a medical profession proved illusionary. His 3.9 GPA in his biochemistry major, despite being disadvantaged in those classes that required oral presentations and graded discussions, certainly qualified him for a serious review by medical schools. So did his great MCAT score above the ninety-fifth-percentile. And he managed to find volunteering positions to add to his resume. Most applicants with similar credentials would have found placement in a medical school somewhere.

But recommendations and interviews were his downfall. His collegiate recommenders, as nice as they were to his face, no doubt carefully couched their language to imply he wasn't a good candidate. They would have been too wary of liability to mention the word "disability," but surely an unenthusiastic letter that referenced shortcomings in communication ability was unassailable. He got only one interview—West Virginia University School of Medicine—which he figured was because they were one of the few schools that didn't look at recommendation letters before granting interviews. The interview itself was a disaster, his stuttering made worse by the heightened tension of this being his only shot, and the fact that it wasn't even a one-on-one interview, it was two professors at the same time. He didn't even get a waiting list offer.

Hugh did consider himself fortunate to get a job in his field. The Pittsburgh Bioscience Center for DNA Diagnostics had an impressive sounding name. But it was just a young start-up operation, where clients came to seek information about their ancestry, or paternity issues, or, more rarely, whether they had a predisposition for a certain illness. The Center shrewdly and economically farmed off their work to The MacArthur Medical College. Hugh's job was to take the samples to a Dr. Megan DuPont, pick up her lab results, and write up the detailed report for the client. By design, the oral presentation of the results fell outside his orbit.

Three weeks prior to the death of Dr. DuPont, this was Hugh's life. Living alone in an apartment in Pittsburgh, sixteen blocks from his parents' home. Commuting by bus daily to and from work. Struggling paycheck to paycheck, hindered by the student loans that took a good chunk of his salary. Interacting with people more via nods and gestures and a computer keyboard than verbally. All with only one friend in the entire world, a roommate not so ironically named Holly.

And Holly was a real bitch.

To be exact, a bichon frise breed of dog. She was fifteen pounds of white gentleness, alertness, and intelligence, and, although still only two years old, very well-trained thanks to the time that Hugh had to spend with her. Her main problem, Hugh found out, was that she didn't like to be left alone during his long hours at work. Fortunately for Hugh, Holly was such a peaceful, obedient, quiet dog that his elderly next-door neighbor, who lived alone, welcomed the dog's companionship most days while Hugh was at the Bioscience Center.

****

Unlike the stuttering, the British accent, spoken with fluency to the old man, was contrived and a new development.

Its acquisition began with a single word—and a personal tragedy.

The tragedy was the shocking death of both Hugh's parents, the result of a car accident as the two were enroute to the North Carolina coastline for a vacation. For four days Hugh suffered in silence, emotionally flooded with memories of their times together and poignant regret that he was never able to be the son of his parents' hopes. On the fifth day, enveloped with grief and loneliness, he embarked on a trip, traveling aimlessly to the west in a rental car, granted the time by his boss, a kindly man who added a week to the two-week vacation Hugh had coming. Hugh journeyed with only Holly to comfort him. He knew he could do worse in a choice for a traveling partner: bichons frises, equipped by nature with a merry disposition, were prized historically as companion dogs by sailors on long voyages.

The single word? "Accusatory." Just one of eight thousand words on a CD that Hugh chanced upon at a music store on his first day out of Pittsburgh.

It was on the second day, just outside of Indianapolis, when Hugh popped the CD into his car's player. A comedy compilation by a British troupe, Hugh thought it might lift his spirits. But through the first four skits, Hugh found himself barely engaged, the humor unable to break the suffocating melancholic state into which he had fallen.

The word that finally pierced his withdrawn state of consciousness came early in the fifth skit. Heard out of context, the word perplexed Hugh; it sounded so unfamiliar. He paused from his reverie to repeat the word in his mind. He still couldn't comprehend what was being said. He replayed the portion with the word.

And then he understood. And smiled. A quite ordinary word, really. It just didn't sound like anything he was used to. Instead of the "ah-cus-sah-tory," it sounded like "ack-Q-za-tree," with the second "a" pronounced like the letter. His fog lifting, four times Hugh ran the CD back to hear the word, finding its curious pronunciation as amusing as the way it was being presented for comedic effect.

Then, in a spontaneous moment, Hugh verbalized the word, mimicking the British comedian's strong accent and uniquely deep voice, husky yet silky.

The word flowed from his lips flawlessly.

"Ack-Q-za-tree."

Hugh chuckled. He said the word again. It came out seamless once more: no pauses, no repeated syllables, no prolonged vowels.

One stutter-free word by itself was not unusual. True, Hugh's stuttering was singularly severe and bedeviled him on nearly every phrase of every sentence—but not every word. But "accusatory" was another case. Hugh struggled with every variation of accuse: accused, accuser, accusingly, accusation, accusatory. Generally, he got no further than "ac-ac-ac" before he gave up. It was among several sets of words he tried to avoid.

After his second repetition of accusatory, Hugh laughed loudly. Holly, curled up on the passenger seat, looked up at him quizzically, head cocked. Hugh said it three more times in quick succession, now loudly articulated toward Holly. At the rising volume of Hugh's voice, Holly jumped up from her spot and put her paws on his leg, her mouth open, wide eyes staring at his face. Over and over Hugh repeated the word, delighting himself and Holly with each flawless rendition.

Hugh continued playing the CD, now engrossed. Soon he heard and tried another British word that sounded odd to him, "privacy," affecting again the low voice and accent of the comedian. It was another from a set of difficult words. Similar outstanding results ensued. He tried it again, theatrically adding for Holly what Hugh speculated was the comic's head-tossing mannerisms. Flawless.

"Privacy" had been a word that carried a particularly foul memory for Hugh: an altercation with his father who tried to rouse Hugh out of his room and then had reacted with scornful mocking when Hugh butchered this word as he used it alone and explosively, without the softening of a preceding "I'd like some...." P-p-p-pri-pri-PRIVACY," he had blurted.

But now, the word flowed, although sounding very different to his ears.

The CD was doing more than cheer Hugh up: he was experiencing an uncommon high of sheer delight, with Holly bounding around the passenger seat, understanding only that her owner was happy, and so she was happy.

The next peculiar sounding word Hugh tried was "garage," using the identical affected low voice and strong inflection. And with the same results. Another difficult word, one in which typically he repeated the initial "g" four times or more. A word that he avoided while growing up by just pointing at the garage. But now: another success.

Had someone passed him on the highway, the driver might have thought Hugh quite batty, having such delight on his face as he was speaking to a dog. A dog that in turn was jumping up and down and running in circles on the passenger seat, pausing only to look at Hugh with mouth wide open, as if caught in mid-bark. But Hugh would have been quite oblivious to the attention of others. He was in the right lane on the interstate, lost in another world.

Hugh let the CD continue but complemented it by his own search for British pronunciations using his phone. New variations of difficult words came in short order: debris, advertisement, vase, zebra. All sounding odd; all coming out flawlessly in his accented, affected manner.

And then Hugh found he could mimic entire British sentences from the CD. Smoothly. Unbroken. The long elusive stutter-free episode.

Perhaps he should not have found this so unusual. Such experiences weren't exactly unknown for others with similar afflictions. Hugh was aware that some with stuttering conditions find they can sing without difficulty, or act on stage without a hitch. Marilyn Monroe had been taught to use a breathy voice. But Hugh had never been able to sing, not even "Happy birthday to you," without attracting embarrassed stares or throwing everyone out of sync, and thus he would just mouth the words. Being stutter free through adopting this accent? This was revolutionary for Hugh: the unraveling of the structure of DNA on a personal level, the transition from telegraph to radio, the first heart transplant.

Had he missed the word "accusatory," the opportunity might have passed. Had it not been an unguarded moment, distracted by grief and the highway, Hugh's conscious mind might have brought out his insecurities and told him "you can't do that." But Hugh's conscious mind was distracted, the chance was seized.

At hotel stops, Hugh streamed British TV shows and movies and looked up and rehearsed common British phrases. He digested instructional videos comparing British and American pronunciations. He learned to drop "r"s where the British dropped the letter, and keep "t"s that Americans tended to drop, and use a soft "t" where the British kept it strong. He learned to round his lips more for the British "o" in words like "hot," where Americans would lower their jaw and draw out the letter as an 'ah" sound.

Over his three-week trip, Hugh became the personification of a strongly accented British man. Initially, efforts at communicating went no further than with Holly: "I say, good chap, you are a bloody good listener for a dog. Have you had your vitamins?" Hugh was delighted by even this level of stutter-free communication, and Holly's excitement about Hugh's joyful talkfest was unmatched reinforcement. Holly accepted every experiment, every trial with equal enthusiasm.

But soon, as Hugh's confidence rose, he was branching out his experiment at gas station stops and with hotel clerks. Then, driven as well by fear of losing this new found talent, he began addressing strangers in parks and fast food establishments, store clerks in malls, and ultimately anyone with whom he came in contact.

Hugh had no idea what dialect of British English he was using at any particular time, whether it be the Queen's English or cockney or that of Dorset or Cornwall or Lancashire or Liverpool. Or even of Scotland or Wales. For all he knew, he was mixing them all up. It didn't matter to him: as long as he was mimicking a British accent and using a deeper voice than normal, it was working. Indeed, with the low, almost silky voice and the slow and measured pace that he employed while in character, he sensed that his speech not only sounded very natural, but pleasant. And self-assured. Engaging.

More and more, his command and confidence grew. True, he reasoned, if he actually ran into someone from Great Britain, his lack of knowledge of the island would leave him exposed. He knew little of England and less of Scotland and Wales. He knew that his perhaps unique blend of dialect might be perplexing to someone from the island and might even be taken as mockery.

But what if it were? He was now freely speaking. And he surmised he could always say he was from some other part of the British diaspora. From Sidney. Or New Zealand. Or India. Or even Newfoundland. Or just that he just learned the dialect in an international school or picked it up from living among expatriates in America.

By the time Hugh was ready to return to Pittsburgh, his British persona had become second nature. Indeed, at times he was unsure whether he'd even remember the American way of enunciating particular words like "garage" or "water" or "vitamin."

He did remember. Any hope that his previous habit of stuttering was a thing of the past was regularly dashed during his occasional reversions. To his chagrin, should he be caught off guard by someone when he was lost in thought, and he failed to transition into his assumed personality, Hugh would find himself with the same stuttering way of speaking that he had used for his entire life. That, it seemed, had become an indelible part of his being.

When Hugh finally returned to his hometown, he arrived with newfound hope. And with a plan. He was sure that Dr. DuPont, with whom his job put him in regular personal contact, would be particularly surprised by the British English accent he now sported.

Chapter 3

The big man had finally arrived.

As he strode onto the scene at the DuPont house, curiosity allowed the cops to take a peek; prudence dictated such be short. They quickly buried themselves back into their jobs. Dusting for fingerprints. Collecting samples for lab analysis. Taking photos. Looking outside the house for footprint impressions; examining blood splatter inside. Like politicians at a funeral who spot a camera, any lighthearted banter promptly turned serious. The last thing any of them wanted was the attention of this particular officer—an officer who would respond with asperity to any sign of ineptitude or inertia, the latter often drawing the customary, loudly growled "Get back to work! You think this is happy hour?"

Lieutenant J. P. Kelly had just such an intimidating reputation. For one thing, he was physically imposing. He stood six feet six inches tall without shoes, at least 280 pounds, with wide shoulders, a thick neck, strong chin, and close-cropped dark brown hair, without a hint of gray. His piercing hazel eyes were unyielding and could be unnerving. It was a feature of which he was well aware and made sure not to obscure with sunglasses as much as possible. Perhaps this was the same reason that he didn't sport any facial hair, to better expose the stern countenance of his face, which evinced a controlled anger seething below the surface.

Kelly's mannerisms were every bit as striking as his physical features. He had strong command presence: when he walked into a room, it was understood by all that he was in charge. Command presence permeated everything about the man. His pressed uniform, always polished badge, well-groomed appearance, and clear, unwavering voice all signified the quality. His confidence and fearlessness, the way he held his body, all embodied the same.

It didn't matter if he was on duty or off, in uniform or out. Where others might speed up when crossing a street as to not inconvenience traffic, his measured gait indicated to drivers, even in his street clothes, that this was someone worth patiently waiting for. Restaurant patrons and store customers, when frustrated by slow or inconsiderate service, sometimes found themselves grumbling under their breath that this person was treated with so much more respect than they by the waitresses and salespeople. Hell, he had been known to have his coach-class ticket upgraded to first-class for free just by asking at the airline counter, without once flashing a badge or letting anyone know he was a police lieutenant. Command presence.

As part of the Investigations Branch of the Pittsburgh Bureau of Police, Kelly had risen through the ranks not just because of his command presence and innate intelligence. He also had an uncanny ability to expeditiously find the perpetrators of crimes and then quite literally scare them, and sometimes trick them, into revealing incriminating details. Particularly he liked to tower above seated suspects, effectively using few words and letting his silence between questions unnerve them and unlock their lips. Keeping what he knew close to the vest, he masterfully would guide the unwitting suspects to the point where Kelly could tangle them in their own webs of deceit. When Kelly was asking questions, even the innocent felt guilty, like they needed to unburden their souls of transgressions.

The force of Kelly's personality could be just as intimidating with subordinates as with suspects, and his arrival to this particular crime scene was ripe for his wrath. But most of his anger was directed not at the cops taking the lead at the scene now, men and women who were from his Homicide Squad out of police headquarters. He was seething about the officers out of the Northumberland Street Police Station that had been among the first to arrive.

In Kelly's view, which he shared with all the subtlety of sledgehammer meeting nail, those Zone 4 officers had already fouled the situation up. Big time.

One could only pity the investigator tasked with reporting to Kelly about the questioning of the old man, how the old timer had been asked if he could identify the perpetrator in a lineup or help an artist sketch his appearance. Kelly's face had simultaneously expressed several distinct emotions—most of which could be described by words starting with the letter "D." Disbelief. Disappointment. Disapproval. Disturbed. Disdain. None of the expressions could be described as "delighted." The controlled anger seething below the surface had quickly transitioned to barely restrained anger erupting above the surface. If he hadn't already, the hapless messenger soon understood the problem: the old man's "no," as part of a police report, would be all a defense attorney would need to shred the old man's testimony should he later concur on the perp once in custody. Except the hapless messenger understood it conveyed in much more colorful language and with some imagery he would've preferred not etched into his brain cells.

Then there was the issue that the officers had sent out an alert to look for a man with a British accent. "Why the *hell* was this part of the description?" he had bellowed to those within earshot. "Any jackass can assume an accent." To Kelly's further disbelief, this description even went out in a BOLO to neighboring law enforcement agencies.

The presence of the press was yet another major irritant. That the press were there was hardly surprising. But Kelly was rankled that the reporters, as evidenced by the shouted questions, seemed to have secured quite a few specifics—none cleared by Kelly.

To top off the ineptitude of those early on the scene, the scouring of the area for the murderer had started way too late for Kelly's liking. Only the patrolmen Scott seemed to have started an early search of the neighborhood. But now his absence from the crime scene for over an hour, unavailable to report to Kelly, became just another in the list of vexations that Kelly didn't keep bottled up. For the officers in Kelly's path, the initial excitement of being at the scene of a high-profile murder quickly transitioned to an array of far less pleasant emotions.

Hugh Holiday looked out the bus window. *What had just happened?*

Earlier that evening, he had been the epitome of a young man with grand expectations. But nothing had worked out the way expected. His plan had been simple: tomorrow, he would show up at the office for the start of the workweek and unveil his remarkable breakthrough. His boss would be delighted. So would his co-workers. Although he had few others to inform, or who would even care, he could tell his neighbor who watched Holly. And Dr. DuPont at The MacArthur Medical College.

From then on, it would be a British accent exclusively. Every day. Every hour. Every occasion.

Hugh's entire world had opened up, bright and wondrous. Medical school might yet be a possibility. He could find opportunities to shadow physicians to build his resume. He could take some evening courses at Pitt. And then he could reapply to med school with better recommendations in hand. And girls. Yes, that sphere would surely open up as well.

Although not really British, and he might seem phony to many people, he could now communicate facilely, pleasantly—finally. There might be missteps and some reversals, but clearly he was onto something phenomenal. *If only my father and mother could see me now. They'd be so proud.*

The unraveling had started with the call on his cell phone from Dr. Michael Faccon.

The Dr. Faccon. The chair of the Department of Surgery at The McArthur Medical College. TMMC researcher. Surgeon, Professor.

Hugh's job at the Bioscience Center placed him in regular contact with Dr. DuPont, never with Dr. Faccon. Hugh had not met the man. But Faccon was a nearly mythical character at the medical college. Everyone knew of him; everyone had an opinion. Hugh had once heard a graduate student, Zach, describe a particular business survival skill using the phrase "he who talks is he who meets the reaper." This warning apparently didn't apply to those at the medical college—they freely shared their views on Faccon, even with an outsider like Hugh.

Many used glowing adjectives: brilliant, ingenious, gifted, rich, handsome. But the critical assessments were just as indelible. Arrogant. Cold and condescending and abrasive to his subordinates and colleagues alike. Notorious as a womanizer, discarding wives like he did girlfriends, paying alimony to three women while he was yet in his late 40s. (*How does that work?* Hugh had thought when he first heard of the three divorces. *Do you give half your salary to your first ex-wife, then a quarter to your second ex-, and then one-eighth to the third?* He had chuckled with the memory of the late comic Robin Williams dubbing alimony as "all the money.")

The fateful call from Faccon came late Sunday afternoon. It came but a few hours after Hugh had arrived back at his apartment from returning the rental car and dropping its key in the after-hours drop box.

The conversation was largely one way. Faccon did the talking; Hugh listened. The words were those of a request; the tone that of a command: Faccon needed Hugh to pick up an express mail package at the surgeon's house and to bring it right away to his lab at the medical college.

Faccon explained that Dr. DuPont had given him Hugh's number and was sure Hugh would be willing to bring it. Faccon made it clear he didn't have anyone available to bring the package. He couldn't leave the lab. The contents in the package were essential to the research in which he was engaged. Hugh would be reimbursed for the trouble.

As quizzical and out of the blue as the request was, Hugh entertained only one possible response. Faccon was the medical college's big shot. And his authoritative tone led Hugh to an unstated, but inescapable undertone: "Do this or maybe we reconsider whether we should be analyzing samples from the Bioscience Center."

But the excitement of getting a call from the big shot himself also buoyed Hugh with a more upbeat thought: *Maybe, just maybe, this could be an inroad toward getting a med school recommendation, just the ticket to reapply. Maybe even to getting into TMMC. After all, it is who you know…*

And so Hugh didn't hesitate in saying yes. Other than the hesitation involved in the response being a stammered "y-y-yes." For from the moment he answered the out-of-the-blue phone call with an unguarded "h-hello," Hugh had debated whether to reveal his new persona to Faccon. Whether to surprise Faccon with his smooth British accent. Whether to begin the process of impressing him. That is, of course, should he get an opportunity to say more than "uh huh" during Faccon's monologue of directions.

In the end, Hugh decided this wasn't the time nor the means. Not over the phone. Not in a rushed conversation. Not during his first contact with the man. Especially since Faccon was without doubt expecting a stutterer given Hugh's reputation, and the fact that DuPont had supplied his number. It would all be too confusing. It would require too much explanation.

Maybe, he thought, *when I show up at Dr. Faccon's laboratory to deliver the package. Maybe then. If I get a chance to speak in detail…*

The thought brought a smile to his lips.

And then, just as suddenly, the conversation ended. Two minutes at most. An urgent request, an address given, and Hugh agreeing to go right away.

Hugh put on his dark-blue jacket. A favorite possession, it was lightweight, but high quality. Worn partly to make the journey comfortable in the cool spring evening; worn mainly because Hugh thought it would make him more presentable when he delivered the package to Faccon.

He then checked two apps on his phone. One, rarely used, showed available taxis cruising near his location. One, frequently used, showed bus routes and times, including a real-time bus tracking function that allowed him to know where the bus was and its expected arrival time.

In the end, Hugh opted to take the way with which he was most comfortable. The bus trip itself didn't take long. It had been but a few minutes away, and there was only one brief changeover.

Indeed, the outing started out very enjoyable, even for someone scarcely back from a trip. The weather was pleasant. The area where he disembarked was tree-lined and beautiful. There was the smell and sights of spring in the air. Hugh even met a friendly old man on the street whose dog seemed to take a fancy to Hugh, probably due to the lingering smell of Holly. And for the first time since back in Pittsburgh, Hugh used his British accent, delighting the old man with a brief "chin wag" before moving up the block ahead of the pair.

The chat was brief because, after all, Hugh was a man on a mission. The sooner he got the package, the sooner he caught a bus to TMMC; if he dallied too long, he just might be forced to take a taxi.

The pleasant outing began to come off the rails as soon as Hugh reached the house.

It was nothing major at first. Just some incongruities. Things that didn't fit with Hugh's preconceptions. The petunias and marigolds and yellow trilliums and tulips? The flower garden so beautifully arranged didn't in itself signal an enduring feminine presence at the house of the bachelor Faccon. Hugh's own father was a hobby gardener. But the small gardening gloves left on the stairs of the porch? Clearly those of a woman. Accentuating these were the women's boots on the porch at the top of the steps.

And then there was the small, two-foot-diameter round table on the porch. Someone had taken care to add a tightly fitted tablecloth. A tablecloth with a very feminine floral pattern. On top of which was a box of flowered tissues.

None of these observations fit smoothly with the reputation of Faccon as single and macho and dating a new woman every week.

For a moment, Hugh considered that he might have gotten the address wrong, an odd occurrence for someone with a near photographic memory. Or, perhaps it had been Faccon who had made a mistake in his own directions? *Given wrong directions to his own house?*

Hugh scrutinized the house. It appeared empty, sounded quiet. There was no car in the driveway, no lights shining through the windows. Certainly the dusk provided enough illumination to see reasonably well outside the house, but it would have been uncomfortably dim inside without lights.

As a precaution, Hugh rang the doorbell. No one answered. He looked under the doormat. There was the key exactly where Faccon said it would be. He shrugged and entered the house.

Hugh had not even completed the process of shutting the door when he was further rattled by the feeling of something not right. For, even in the faint light, he discerned a very feminine décor. And then there was the magazine on the coffee table. *InStyle*. A women's magazine. And not one picked up from a grocery store display: it had an address label. In the dim light, Hugh had to bend closer to read the small print; it was the address of where he was now standing. And a woman's name. Megan DuPont.

None of these observations made any sense. Faccon clearly had stated that it was his home. Yet, everything he had seen so far was consistent with this being a woman's house and, more than that, quite obviously DuPont's. Hugh couldn't think of any reason why Faccon lied about whose house Hugh would be entering. Or why, given that it was her house, DuPont wouldn't have called with instructions to enter. It was equally inconceivable that Faccon and DuPont were cohabitating. As if the rich, playboy Faccon didn't have a house of his own. As if DuPont, who had made no secret of her distaste for the man, had decided to go halfsies on a house.

A conundrum that had nibbled at the edges of Hugh's mind joined the inner dialogue: *Why me?* He could understand that people knew he would be around that day. At his parents' funeral he had mentioned to Dr. DuPont when he would be returning to work. And his office knew. He actually had emailed both not that long ago. But why not get a regular colleague or grad student to run this errand. *Why me?*

Hugh was troubled. His antenna was sky high. But it was a puzzle that would have to be worked out later. Maybe Faccon would volunteer an explanation when he dropped off the package. Maybe the next time he saw Dr. DuPont, she would explain.

Hugh quickly headed into the kitchen, where Faccon said the package would be.

There was no package in the kitchen.

Only a body. On the floor, off to the side where it was not visible from the foyer, in a pool of blood. Hugh was staring at the lifeless body of Dr. Megan DuPont.

This was just the first of three shocks in quick succession. The second shock, almost unnoticed as it was happening, was the nylon-bristled broom falling down and grazing him, smearing his jacket with blood. The third shock, almost simultaneously with the broom, was hearing the siren of a police car coming down the street.

Chapter 4

Suddenly, all of the puzzling observations made sense.

Urgent request. Misleading directions. No package. Dead body.

He was set up to take the fall for a murder. And set up well, like the centermost king pin in a rack of bowling pins. Alone in the house with the victim, whom he knew. Blood on his clothes, no doubt the victim's, spread to him from a broom that had no right to have been upright and bloody. No friends to vouch for him; some acquaintances who probably would claim he was distraught from his parents' deaths— or was an oddball.

And no alibi. Whether it was Faccon or someone pretending to be Faccon, it was clear that the person who called him would deny asking him to go to the victim's house to pick up a nonexistent package. He had to get out of the house, and he had to cover his tracks. Whether they caught him here in the house, over the dead body, or on the run from the house, what difference would it make?

All of this thinking took Hugh less than two seconds.

The next steps took considerably longer.

First was checking for any vital signs in DuPont, in the vain hope that by some miracle she was alive, that looks were deceiving. They weren't. The body was still warm, but she wasn't going to be explaining to anyone, at least not in this world, that he wasn't the attacker. Hugh didn't stay long and was careful to step around the congealing mass of blood, fighting a nausea that threatened to add traces of himself to the scene.

The wiping of the knife handle with paper towels was next, just in case his prints were planted—certainly the attacker's prints wouldn't be on the knife given the care to set him up. Then, quickly he washed his hands in the sink, where he already saw traces of blood. The penultimate series of actions was using the tissues in the living room to wipe the doorknob and buzzer, lock the front door, and secure the gold chain. The ultimate action was using the tissues to lock and close the back door as he exited it—just as he heard the rattling of the front doorknob.

Hugh barely made it to the back of the garage before he saw a policeman move along the side of the house, smash the pane on the back door, open it, and enter. Hugh headed in the opposite direction: tight along a hedge to the sidewalk on the parallel street. And then to his right up the sidewalk.

Hugh's strategy as he moved through the streets had five components.

Four were simple. One, get as far away from the house as possible as quickly as possible. Two, look casual while accomplishing the first goal. Three, keep distance from any potential witnesses. Four, look casual while doing this. Four straightforward, uncomplicated objectives.

The first two were rather obvious strategies. He needed to put space between himself and the DuPont home rapidly and do so without attracting attention.

The problem was Hugh hadn't a clue how to combine these two disparate strategies. It was self-evident that he couldn't run or he would draw attention. And it was clear that he couldn't saunter at a leisurely pace or the police would find him within blocks of the murder.

In the end, Hugh decided to walk at a fairly fast clip while adding casual elements. He swiveled his head as if to look inquisitively at the trees and flowers. He occasionally yawned and stretched his arms. And, probably way too often, he looked at his watch as if in a hurry to get to some unknowable event.

As ridiculous as even he realized he must look, the immediate area did afford some advantages in this regard. In this upscale neighborhood, built on rolling hills, a great diversity of large and impressive trees lined the streets. There were oaks and red maples and elms and evergreens. An even greater diversity dotted the landscaped properties, including gingkoes and Japanese maples and flowering dogwoods. And the property owners obviously put a great deal of care into their flowers. So, Hugh reasoned, it didn't look totally out of character to be glancing at the trees and flowers.

Not that he actually appreciated their beauty. Not really. His head and eyes were turning as if interested, but Hugh's mind was absorbed with the two other simple components of his strategy—and the complex one.

The third and fourth simple objectives were just as obvious as the first two. He needed to keep his distance from any potential witnesses that might cross his path. And he couldn't be evasive in a way that made him stand out. A straightforward plan of action for someone trying to avoid being tied to a murder down the street, where now police and ambulance sirens were converging.

For these latter two strategies, the neighborhood, at least near the DuPont house, was about as good as Hugh could hope for. Most of the properties had well-manicured, tall shrubs. On occasion, Hugh was able to slip detection from the few cars moving through the area by stepping just inside a hedge and stooping to pretend to tie his shoe, the latter in case the property owner saw him. And the rolling hills provided another advantage: When Hugh got to the top of a hill, even with the dusk turning to evening, he could see some distance and plan his route and timing.

But the blocks also were large and once he made a move up a block, the only way to change direction was to turn one hundred and eighty degrees and go back the way he came. Or to be lucky enough to find one of the few side alleys that bisected some blocks.

Four rather simple components—all built around the concept of evasiveness. But it was the fifth component of his strategy, the complex one, that engaged most of Hugh's mind as he moved through the streets. How to get rid of the blood-stained jacket?

It was no longer a favorite possession. It was a jacket with blood traceable to a murder victim. And a jacket that forensic analysis likely could find a link to him, no doubt DNA in some form. In the enveloping gloom, with the sun already below the horizon, it was unlikely one would think of the dark streaks on the dark-blue jacket as blood stains. But with police sirens in the background? That changed the odds. And he certainly couldn't enter a brightly lit bus with a blood-soaked jacket. And if a policeman stopped him?

How to get rid of the jacket became Hugh's obsession.

One expedient fix he repeatedly weighed, rejected, and weighed again was right on the street in front of him, everywhere he walked. Garbage cans. Mostly the thirty-two-gallon-and-up variety. It wasn't as if they were still positioned near the houses. They were lined up on the sidewalks, prepared for tomorrow's pickup. If he could stuff the jacket in one of those, then his problem could be disposed of in the morning by sanitation workers.

But if the police searched the cans? It was risky.

But so was walking down the street smeared with DuPont's blood.

It was in an area with widely spaced properties when Hugh finally stopped and lifted the lid of a garbage can. It was a large, wheeled can, forty-five gallons Hugh guessed, and nestled near a large oak tree in front of a property with a stone wall that rose nearly his height. Hugh saw no one around. Soon he had stripped off his jacket and was on his way.

Hugh's confidence grew as he continued to make progress, block after block, without any noteworthy complications. There were few cars moving through the streets and even fewer people outside their houses. When he did come upon people in their yards or walking on the sidewalk, he mostly was able to keep his distance. Several times he changed his route at intersections. Twice he elected to completely reverse his direction, snapping his fingers and acting like he forgot something and needed to go back. Three times he crossed to the other side of the street. And once he took a side street that bisected a block.

One close encounter that did spook him was when he unwittingly came within twenty feet of a couple getting into their car. But the car was parked in a driveway heavily obscured by hedges, and they were conversing with each other as he walked by. When they left their driveway, they went in the opposite direction as him.

The neighborhood was changing as he walked further from the DuPont neighborhood. There were less hedges, more open properties. But the greater the distance he put between himself and the DuPont residence, the more his optimism grew.

And then the four simple components of Hugh's strategy blew up nine blocks from the DuPont house.

A police car, with a flashing lightbar of red, blue, and some amber, and no siren to warn him, suddenly appeared from a side street to his right. It slowed at the intersection and then veered onto his street. Towards him. Rather rapidly, he thought.

He was caught. He was in an exposed area. He couldn't turn and walk away without attracting attention and looking guilty. He couldn't dart behind a shrub. And he surely wasn't going to be appearing nonchalant by suddenly looking at flowers, trees, and his watch, and stretching and yawning.

The car stopped next to him. Two officers got out. Hugh patiently waited for them, trying on his best face of "This is a surprise! I'm just out for a walk," but probably actually showing an expression of "I almost got away."

They had a lot of questions. Which he answered to the best of his ability.

That is, if one would consider "best of ability" to be limited to the stutter he had used for all but the last three weeks of his life. For, Hugh figured, if people were always getting frustrated and bored talking to him when he stuttered, then maybe these policeman also might become frustrated enough to leave him alone. After all, his answers to simple questions like "What is your name? Where do you live? What are you doing in this area?" could seem to take an awful long time to people in a hurry, as these two officers clearly were.

And the questioning seemed to be going okay. Up until a thought suddenly intruded into Hugh's mind, fully formed, fully shocking: *What did I do with the key to Dr. DuPont's house? Is it in my pocket?*

With that, Hugh lost his focus. He was sure his face transitioned from one of feigned befuddlement to one of real fear. Certainly he was feeling that. Along with a near insatiable desire to touch his pocket, to see if her house key, with his fingerprints, was there, or whether he had left it in her kitchen, or if it was still in the now discarded jacket.

And then, just as suddenly, it was over. The officers were, indeed, in a hurry. This became clear as one groused, "We're wasting time with him. He can't be the one. No British accent."

And with that, they were off.

The wait for the bus seemed interminable. Buses on Sunday evening can be few and far between anyway, but each minute still in the area accentuated Hugh's awareness of that fact.

And now, Hugh sat morosely in a window seat near the back of a bus taking him away from the area. Hoping he didn't have more blood on him that would leave traces on the bus. And questioning the chain of events, questioning his choices. And most of all, as his fingers closed on the key in his pocket, he was reflecting on what a remarkable woman Dr. DuPont had been and wondering why someone would want her dead enough to plan this out.

Chapter 5

Lieutenant Kelly inspired heightened assiduity in his subordinates, who knew that with the slightest misstep or idleness on their part they could be singled out for his steely gaze and then sharp correction. But any antipathy that might arise from such an uncompromising taskmaster was balanced by an equal measure of respect. For once Kelly sunk his teeth in a case, he was a bulldog. Relentless. Fearless. Unyielding. And in his obsessive determination to bring the perpetrator to justice, he was much more successful than not. It was a fact that put the entire Homicide Squad on an elevated plane of esteem among peers in other units.

And given his stern persona, a Kelly guffaw was both rare and a thing of wonder. In this case, the guffaw, coming from Kelly's office at the police station, in the company of two trusted subordinates, signified supreme confidence that he had his sights on the DuPont murderer.

His gut and his intellect now told him clearly who the perpetrator was. At least two Zone 4 cops had somewhat done their job. They had collected the name and address of the lone individual wandering DuPont's neighborhood shortly after the murder who fit the physical descriptions of both the 9-1-1 caller and the old man. Someone who not only lacked a reason to be in the area, but who, it turned out, had contact with the victim. Too many convergences to be a coincidence.

And Kelly had confidence in two unfolding courses of action that would conclusively tie this man to the murder.

One was forensic analysis. But not on evidence gathered at the scene: the fingerprints all seemed to be DuPont's, there was no skin or blood under her nails, and the wiping of the doorknob, and apparently the murder weapon, suggested that the killer might have covered his tracks. The murder scene, Kelly surmised, might not prove all that fruitful.

But he had found something important, nonetheless. Something on the camera recordings from the city buses serving the area. On these video recordings was his suspect, entering the area with a jacket. Leaving the area without a jacket. Somewhere between DuPont's house and where the suspect had boarded the departing bus he had discarded his jacket. And that article of clothing, Kelly conjectured, would no doubt yield blood. And forensic analysis would no doubt conclusively tie that blood to DuPont, and the jacket to his man.

Kelly was feeling smug—justifiably so in his mind—from his quick-witted resourcefulness. Not just getting the surveillance tapes right away. He also had just given instructions that the garbage pickups—refuse, bulk waste, and recycling—were to be suspended in the area. And already he had sent a team searching the dumpsters and canvassing the neighborhood. Finding that jacket was priority.

The second course of action was only in its infancy. Tomorrow would be when Kelly would fully uncoil it. For now, he had only started gathering the information needed. He had talked to the two cops who had stopped the suspect in the area. He had assigned some officers to gather all the background info they could on this fellow. And tomorrow morning, Kelly would himself interview the old man. And, then, after he had gathered the facts he needed, he would unleash his skills of interrogation on this Hugh Holiday.

****

The images kept coming, vivid and binding his senses, fading and replaced by the next, each as graphic as the one before, each sending Hugh spiraling through the emotions he had experienced. The bloody scene in the kitchen hovering in rich but ghastly detail, supplanted by the cop frantically breaking in the back door, displaced by his flight through the neighborhood, succeeded by the two cops questioning him.

The four blocks from the bus stop to Hugh's apartment turned out to be ten blocks on this evening. And all the while the images kept coming, unrelenting, scenes replaying, emotions relived. Hugh was glad that it was now dark since he figured his face, maybe the entirety of his being, couldn't help but show animated expressions of shock and sadness and fear.

His first detour after departing the bus was to look for a place to dump DuPont's key. Two blocks out of his way, he found a quiet residential area where he felt it unlikely he was being observed. He opened the lid of a garbage container placed curbside for pickup, used the key to rip a tear in the securely fastened garbage bag inside, used his shirt to wipe the key of his fingerprints, and slid it into the bag with the garbage.

As he walked away, he realized he now was acting paranoid. It was just a key. He was in a populated area. He could've just thrown it away anywhere, without the unnecessary complexity of the guilty. He chuckled out-loud at his irrational fear. And then ten feet from that thought, he starting worrying that he'd been observed and the curious homeowner would find and retrieve the key and turn it over to the police, or the garbage bag would have a hole in the bottom, which the key would fall through, only to be found and turned over to the police, or …

Paranoia, thy name is Hugh, he said under his breath. He shook his head. He kept going. The trip to his apartment was becoming surreal, like a dream, the unreality heightened by the wisps of fog that had appeared with the dropping temperature. But if it were a dream, it was one with its own dreams, as the images were unremitting. And to the repertoire was added a more vague one of his own creation, that of a homeowner finding DuPont's key.

Chapter 6

A few blocks after ditching his link to DuPont's house, Hugh detoured yet another block to go to a late-night joint specializing in Mexican fast food. He needed to decompress. And he reasoned that, even though he wasn't hungry, he should grab something now considering there was no food of note in his apartment that wasn't spoiled or frozen.

He got a burrito and a taco. Which he tried to eat, but his stomach was tied into too many knots, the incessant images too tormenting, his questions too unsettling. He gave up, dumped the leftovers, and left. He hoped that he hadn't made a memorable impression on the food handlers—a late night stop in which a troubled man throws everything he bought away. He arrived back at his apartment around 11:00pm.

The apartment occupied the second floor of a very narrow, two-story building in a neighborhood of tightly packed two- and three-story residences. Only three feet, brick-paved but uneven and with clumps of weeds, separated the house from its neighbors on either side.

The house was originally a single-family structure. Half a century ago, the owner, living alone on fixed income, had converted the second floor into a separate apartment that he could rent out while he lived below. Cherishing his pocketbook as much as his privacy, he had hastily constructed a wooden stairway to the small balcony in the back of the house, opening a second entrance to the floor—the first having been the inner stairway, which he now closed off with a door. But the closing of the inner route was short-sighted and short-lived. The outside stairway, permitless and flimsy and cheap, worried potential tenants. And, with just cause, given that it gave way in the first heavy snow. The temporary winter-time alternative of re-opening the inner stairway, and adding makeshift walls along stairs that conveniently extended to near the house's front entrance, proved not so temporary. With one door added at the top of the enclosed inner stairway and one at the bottom, this new passageway, since reinforced, now served as the main entrance to both the lower and upper floors. But the outer stairway was gradually nailed back in place and afforded a second access point for Hugh. The owner had since passed on; the bottom floor was occupied now by a childless couple in their fifties.

Hugh's apartment was not impressive by any measure. For one, it was small, about five hundred square feet. The kitchen, into which the back entrance led, had space only for a table and two wooden chairs. Adjourning the kitchen was the living room, where the main entrance was located, and off this was the bedroom. Completing the apartment was a bathroom, accessible from the bedroom. It, too, was small, with a shower, sink, and toilet crammed into a five-foot by five-foot area.

And the apartment was sparsely furnished. Besides the kitchen table, the only other notable pieces of furniture were a bed and dresser in the bedroom, and, in the living room, a comfy chair, two-person sofa, coffee table, bookshelf, and desk and chair—all used, all old, and mostly purchased from Salvation Army stores or picked up at garage sales. Hugh's mother had helped with picking out blue drapes for him to install, which added the only color to the apartment. As far as entertainment, on the desk was a monitor, desktop computer,and compact printer. He was a cord-cutter; there was no TV.

The apartment was in an over one-hundred-year-old house with drafty windows, peeling paint, and creaking floorboards. It was cold in winter and hot in summer. The rent was overly high. But Hugh loved the apartment. It was quiet and allowed pets and was a place he felt comfortable. While the backyard was nothing of note—largely overgrown with weeds and prickly plants—it was someplace Hugh could take Holly at a moment's notice. For this, the back steps were convenient.

When Hugh arrived back at the apartment, the downstairs lights were off, the neighbors asleep. Out of deference to them, he forwent the noisy inner steps and used the outer stairs into the kitchen. Holly had been left in the apartment much longer than he intended; he would take her for a walk in the backyard.

His plans were overly optimistic.

A casual observer or disorganized apartment dweller might not have noticed right away that someone had been there while he was out. But Hugh was not a casual observer. Nor was he disorganized.

In fact, as far as noticing details, Hugh was particularly keen. This likely was a learned, not an innate behavior. He spoke very little, in acquiescence to his condition, and thus spent most of his time observing. Not preparing in his mind what he would say next. Not lamenting the lost opportunity for a witty comeback. Not trying to recall some fact he could interject into a conversation or looking for a pause when he could break in. Never mindlessly rambling on. Just listening, intently. Watching, closely.

Even when alone, when others might be daydreaming about singing on a concert stage or doing something heroic, Hugh eschewed such reveries. For he couldn't sing without stuttering, and at some point a hero would have to speak. Such thoughts were just painful reminders of something not possible for him. Instead, he stayed in the moment, observing everything around him: people, animals, objects.

And as far as being organized, Hugh was meticulous in having everything in its place. He was the nearest thing to someone with an obsessive-compulsive disorder without actually having the condition.

And this was clearly a learned behavior. After finding his family's TV remote once in the refrigerator and his mother's long lost cell phone in the flower garden after the winter snows had departed, Hugh grew to abhor time wasted while searching for lost items. He had read once that an American on average spends fifty-five minutes a day looking for misplaced things—about fourteen full days of the year. He figured his own parents spent about half of that time complaining, "*You* were the one who had it last. What did you do with it?"

Having only a dog as a roommate, of course, allowed Hugh to avoid the time spent on the "you had it last" complaint. He made a point to put things in the same place all the time. The silverware, scissors, fingernail clippers, dishwashing soap, dog shampoo, pots and pans were all consistently returned to their assigned place after use. Drawers were closed, shoes and clothes placed in their respective niches, books neatly placed in the bookshelf.

And thus, as a keen observer who kept a tidy apartment, it took Hugh less than a second upon entering the door to realize that someone had been there that evening while he'd been out.

In some cases, the changes were subtle. It wasn't as if the hand dishwashing soap bottle and hand towels were on the floor, but they were clearly moved. It wasn't as if the contents of the kitchen cabinets and drawers were spilled on the floor. But some drawers were open a crack, including the silverware drawer.

But this was just what he saw in the kitchen. What he saw when he looked in the living room anyone would've noticed. There were unusual novelties in the bookshelf, a book and open journal scattered on the coffee table, and some pictures taped to the living room wall, the latter duplicated in the bedroom and bathroom. The trash near the desk had some printouts sticking out that he clearly had not placed there.

Topping off all this was the behavior of Holly. She was agitated, nervous. And that wasn't the key problem. She was in the bathroom, with the door closed. And Holly hadn't done that to herself, and Hugh certainly hadn't.

When Hugh had returned from his trip earlier that day, he'd had the impression that someone had been in the house during his absence. But he'd given his neighbor a key to keep an eye on things. He had dismissed the little changes as nothing more than that. But one detail was puzzling. It was the absence of one of Hugh's prized possessions: a folding knife. A Kit Carson M16 design, light and streamlined and sharp, it was something he would carry on the streets of Pittsburgh for self-defense. In the haze from his parents' passing, he'd left on his trip without it. When he went to retrieve it before heading off for Faccon's package, it was gone from where he kept it. And that was perplexing.

These new findings weren't puzzling. A quick survey of the room showed that almost everything was part of a pattern.

The extra items now in the room? All related to Dr. DuPont. There were clippings of her speaking at events around Pittsburgh, a copy of a book she published, a journal with one of her published articles, and photos of her in various places. Hugh recognized some items that he had seen in her office: a memento from atop her filing cabinet, some business cards from a holder on her desk, a stapler.

Hugh's desktop computer showed the same disturbing pattern. Hugh noticed right away that his desk chair was turned at an odd angle. A quick check of the computer confirmed his suspicions: There were files that he had not placed there. And all suggested an obsession with Dr. DuPont. There were images of her downloaded from websites, an incomplete poem about her, and a bizarre note on a visit to her office that implied he thought they had a future together. There was a photoshopped image where his head was on another man's body, arm around her waist. The timestamps all revealed different creation dates, and modified dates, and last accessed dates—and all from before his trip.

The movement of the dishwasher soap and towels was something different. Clearly, someone felt the need to wash up in the sink. But why? Was it because Holly had sunk her teeth into the intruder as she was being moved to the bathroom? It was a reasonable conjecture, Hugh thought. Holly can be very protective.

Hugh sunk back in his desk chair, rocking gently back and forth, eyes closed, hands supporting the still hyper and panting Holly curled up on his lap. He was dispirited. Completely. He was being boxed in as the scapegoat for the killing of Dr. DuPont.

Scapegoat. The term hovered in Hugh's mind. He knew the history of the word. He had looked it up in fifth grade. The innocent goat in *Leviticus,* on which head all the sins of the Israelites were placed, and which then was set out alone into the wilderness. The term fit, thought Hugh. He was being set up to take the fall. And he was all alone.

His thoughts drifted back to that fifth grade, back to when he first had occasion to look up the term. He could see it all again. One of the popular kids lifting a test answer key from the teacher's desk while she was out. Everyone gathering to look at it. Everyone except Hugh. The lookout whisper-shouting that the teacher was coming back and running to his desk, everyone scattering to their own desks, the popular kid throwing the answer key haphazardly on the teacher's desk. Soon the teacher sternly demanding to know who had taken it from her drawer. No one answering. Not at first. But, then, when it was clear the teacher wasn't going to let this go, first one finger, than another, pointing at Hugh, and soon the students chanting his name.

He'd never had a chance. The "perfect scapegoat" as he heard a student later describe it. Unable to extricate himself with his words, not believing he could convince his parents of his innocence, he soldiered on, the false accusation, the low grade, and the F in conduct left to stand.

Hugh opened his eyes and lurched forward. He put Holly down and raised himself from his chair. He had an advantage that hadn't been counted on by whoever was framing him. He wasn't in police custody; he had returned to the apartment.

But he needed to move quickly.

Hugh gathered the clippings and photos. He dumped them in a cooking pot on the stove. He turned on the overhead exhaust. He lit a match. He set fire to the clippings.

He set *fire* to the clippings. *In the house.*

The flames shot clear up to the overhead exhaust, which proved totally inadequate to capture the black smoke, which billowed out into the room, which set off the loud smoke alarm in the kitchen.

Hugh next grabbed a dishtowel and moved the pot one handed to the sink and turned on the water, then sprinted to pull the battery on the alarm. The water hitting the burning papers filled the kitchen with even more smoke.

Finally, Hugh stuck a lid on the pot, set it outside on the porch, and opened the windows to air out the room. He tried to ignore the loud cursing from the apartment below.

Plan two. Hugh gathered all the foreign items, including the now half-burned papers, and put them in a garbage bag. He then sat at his desktop computer and began systematically to erase the introduced files he found. He was focused, working quickly.

But soon he realized there was no way he could definitively identify all the foreign files, not with the altered timestamps. So he backed up his key files online and set about nuking the contents of his hard drive. A good computer expert might still recover the files from a reformatted hard drive, but he hoped it would not come to that.

It now reached well past midnight. Hugh made one more check on the apartment to be certain he had not overlooked anything. He then leashed Holly, left some lights on, strapped on his backpack filled with some clothes and his laptop, and grabbed the garbage. Although he had avoided his parent's home since their deaths, preferring to keep his emotions at bay, he would sleep there tonight. But before he left his apartment, he placed one of the dog's toy balls close to the front door. And then, as he exited the back door, he reached around and placed another ball close to that door before closing it. It was his own quickly devised system to see if he had any more unwanted visitors.

It was to be an incredibly long walk for him and Holly. But, he could dump the garbage along the way. And he was unlikely to be able to sleep much anyway. Certainly not in his apartment. Tomorrow, Holly would have the run of the house, and Hugh would try to show up at work as if Sunday had been just another uneventful day.

As he walked, Hugh replayed the day's events. He then re-dialed the number used by the man claiming to be Faccon. As he feared, the phone number led nowhere of value. Or, perhaps it was even worse than of no value: it rang to a suicide hotline. *Great*, he thought. *So much for having that as a defense.* He hung up. Someone at the suicide hotline called back. He hung up again.

His thoughts drifted to Dr. DuPont and how she had been one of the few people who had been nice to him. And now he was being scapegoated for her murder.

And the entire walk, in the cool night air, the images kept returning, becoming clear, fading, replaced by new images, with the apartment scene now added to the repertoire.

Chapter 7

Average. That probably would be the first adjective that came to a co-worker's mind if asked to describe Officer Bill Scott. Average height. Average build. Average looks. Average intelligence. Even his age, thirty-six, was around the national average. He was someone who just didn't stand out. Nor apparently did he seek any promotions or greater responsibilities: ten years on the Pittsburgh police force and he hadn't advanced beyond patrolling the streets.

But for someone thought of as so ordinary, Scott certainly lived well above the mean. He owned a large, modern, five-bedroom house with custom-made, in-ground swimming pool. He boasted a thirty-foot pleasure cruiser that he kept docked in an Allegheny River marina, and he and his wife drove newer model cars. All three of their children were in an exclusive private school.

The area in which he lived—the area he also patrolled—was itself a slice of Pittsburgh that was particularly well-to-do. It was the East End, adjacent to downtown's Golden Triangle and similarly sandwiched between the Monongahela and Allegheny rivers. The East End encompassed wealthy enclaves in Squirrel Hill and Shadyside, was dotted with top museums like Carnegie Museum of Art, and was home to Pitt, Carnegie Mellon, Carlow and Chatham universities. Expansive parks, notably Frick, Mellon, and Schenley, added to the area's allure.

The disparity between Scott's job and his lifestyle—his wife didn't work—was a common topic of interest whenever someone visited his house and marveled at the jacuzzi and three-car garage, the richly tiled floors and gilded faucets. But, as Scott or his wife would explain, Bill received a large inheritance from his parents, who had passed on while still young.

The part about his parents passing while they were still young was true. The part about the inheritance was not. They didn't leave much to young Bill. Rather, Scott had other means that he didn't volunteer. A revenue stream that he couldn't disclose because mostly it involved covering up crimes, looking the other way, providing inside information, and occasionally more forceful, even violent actions.

The DuPont matter was of the latter. And one for which he had been promised a great deal of money. Enough that he could take his wife and kids on that trip to Europe he had been promising. Enough to finalize negotiations on a winter vacation home in the Dominican Republic to escape the harsh Pittsburgh winters. And enough to advance his plan to retire early from the police force and maybe even move his family to that Caribbean home, to escape the expected fall out when he "retired" from that lucrative second job.

But now all of that was placed on the back burner. Things had not gone well.

Not at all.

Scott leaned forward on the sofa in his study, elbows on knees, jaw resting on the thumbs of interlocked hands. The same thought had hounded him the entire night: how could something so simple, so well-planned, have gone so terribly wrong?

The DuPont business had certainly sounded uncomplicated. Dicey, yes. Serious, certainly. But also uncomplicated. He simply had to be the first officer on the scene and kill Holiday.

It had been meticulously planned. Not haphazard or spontaneous as so many other underhanded jobs he was paid to do. It was true that he had only been contacted Saturday night and had been told the operation was to be completed before DuPont was to show up at TMMC Monday morning. But it was clear that every contingency had been taken care of. There were plans and backup plans and alternative scenarios. He just had to play his part.

A day earlier, he had considered it his good fortune that DuPont's home was in his patrol area. Police Zone 4 wasn't perfectly congruent with the East End—it didn't reach all the way north to the Allegheny and it extended south to below the Monongahela. But the two areas largely overlapped. And Scott, as a veteran on the force, had manipulated years earlier where he patrolled. And that was north of the Monongahela, in the area of the wealthy neighborhoods and distinguished universities and top museums and expansive parks. It was a nice slice of Pittsburgh in which to work. And, thanks to his special revenue stream, an even nicer place to live and send his kids to private school.

And, as it turned out, the area where Dr. Megan DuPont had her home, where Scott just had to show up at the right time and kill a man.

Scott knew had DuPont lived somewhere else, it would've been just another Sunday evening for him and somebody else's payday. He was pretty sure the other five police zones had officers doing similar moonlighting jobs. And, likely as well in the bureau headquarters north of the Allegheny. Possibly there were even other officers in Zone 4 on this special payroll. But, the action was to take place on a Sunday, a day he was scheduled to work.

On duty in the right area at the right time. The stars had seemingly aligned.

Except that had been an illusion.

Scott slumped and laid his head against the back of the sofa. He was pulled, ineluctably, like a moth to a flame, into replaying the past day and a half. Reliving the euphoria, the anticipation, the shock, the frustration. The despair.

The euphoria had come Saturday night.

It hadn't started out with euphoria; it had started out with unease, with a tinge of trepidation.

He was in the back seat of a car parked in a remote area outside of Pittsburgh. His gun had been removed, he had been treated roughly when frisked, and, even if it hadn't been a moonless night, he was so far under a tree-covered canopy that there wouldn't have been much light anyway. There was another car parked ten feet away. It had three armed men.

But the men in that car weren't the source of his apprehension. Rather, it was the one man in the car he was in. A big-shouldered, big-headed man seated directly in front of him in the driver's seat, whose features he discerned only by silhouette on those rare occasions when he rotated just enough to look at Scott out of his right eye.

He hadn't been told his name. His usual contact person had only ever referred to him as 'Mr. Z," as in "Mr. Z has a job for you." It was Mr. Z who provided him with all his supplemental income, yet a man whom Scott had never met, never even spoken with. But Scott had a pretty good idea who Mr. Z was. Which was the source of his unease.

Yet, the fact he was would be speaking one-to-one with this big-league figure also meant this upcoming job was a big deal.

How big a deal became apparent within minutes of being placed in the car. He was being offered a lot of money. Not a king's ransom, but maybe for a king's mother-in-law. Enough to set Scott's blood pumping harder than it already was sitting in a dark car on a moonless night with a mob boss and three armed men outside.

But the risk would also be great. Twice before he had been asked to kill "in the line of duty" and had done so. But, this time,

Mr. Z warned, it wasn't going to involve a drug dealer or junkie who had gotten in the way.

"There's gonna be a high-profile person involved. You ready to hear the details?" The voice, gruff and deep and in what Scott assumed was a Philly accent, had an authoritative tone matched by no one he'd ever met.

There ensued an uncomfortable silence as Scott considered what to say next. He wasn't sure he had the option to refuse the offer. In fact, he was pretty sure there was no such option. And he didn't intend to reject it anyway. His mind had already raced on with how to spend his windfall. Still, he had an image to maintain. He needed to let Mr. Z know Scott was a tough guy in his own right, that he makes his own decisions. He needed to mark his territory.

"Before you give me details, could you give me assurances this is well-planned?"

The words no sooner had escaped Scott's mouth when he regretted them. He was a dachshund urinating in the territory of a wolf. Mr. Z swiveled his head slowly, and for half a minute, in complete silence, stared at Scott out of his right eye. In the dark, Scott couldn't read the expression on his face. He sensed it wasn't a pleasant one.

Then Mr. Z began to give the details. And, in so doing, made it clear that it now wasn't a job Scott could refuse. At the same time, Mr. Z disabused him of any concerns about the planning.

It was set up beautifully; intricate, with several steps, but well-planned. As far as DuPont was concerned, Scott wasn't involved. It was to be a professional hit, but made to look like an impromptu, amateur killing. She might have to be restrained for a time, but the actual killing would be when the fall guy was on his way. One of her own kitchen knives would be used to make it look spontaneous. A fake 9-1-1 call would plant Scott in the general vicinity, where he should stay until the 9-1-1 call about an intruder at the DuPont residence. This second call would be placed via an untraceable cell as soon as the intruder retrieved the key planted under the front door mat and started to enter the house.

The more Mr. Z spoke, the more Scott could visualize the plan's success. The more he visualized the plan's success, the more delight he felt, until the feeling transitioned into euphoria. In twenty-four hours, his only hassle involving money would be how to hide it and spend it, no longer how to get it.

Mr. Z scripted out the plan for Scott, with contingencies. The ideal scenario was that Scott would slip through the front door, which the intruder likely would leave unlocked or even open after he entered. Just in case, the back door would be left unlocked. Scott should shoot the guy on sight. Things would be particularly simple if the intruder were in the room with the victim. If he were in another room or even outside the house, then Scott might have to plant a weapon to give Scott a way to claim self-defense. He would be provided one with fingerprints for just that off chance.

"But make sure you get there when the intruder is still *in* the house," warned Mr. Z.

Scott was trying to concentrate on the details, to push out other thoughts that kept intruding, occupying part of his mind. Like planning that trip to Europe. Like that home in the Dominican Republic. Simultaneously, as he listened to Mr. Z laying out the plan, he was figuring the best time to take the family trip and when he could travel to the Dominican Republic to look at properties.

There was one detail that brought Scott fully back. Mr. Z made sure Scott understood that it was his own creative idea, his own strategy to make sure blood ended up on the fall guy. Mr. Z chuckled at his ingenuity; Scott restrained himself from laughing as it was unveiled. It involved a thin thread, a bloody broom. This way, Mr. Z explained, if things did get fouled up, if the fall guy got out of the kitchen before Scott arrived, he wouldn't leave unscathed. Scott was to remove this thread and make sure the broom made it into the pool of blood.

And it would be a very bloody killing. But if the intruder wasn't bloody, Scott was to transfer some of the victim's blood. Not a daunting task at all, said Mr. Z. Just lean over DuPont to check for vitals and then lean over the dead intruder to check on him.

"And don't worry, the coroner's report will back you up whatever happens."

There was one important variable in this well-crafted plan: The "supporting actor" role hadn't been conclusively cast—the role of the person Scott had to kill. But it was a variable in a narrowly defined set. Mr. Z said they had it down to a few candidates who could be induced to show up at the right time.

But one was everybody's first choice, a young man named Holiday.

Given the description, Scott hoped it would be this Holiday guy. He sounded perfect: a loner, not very bright, some kind of societal defect. A person who would have trouble explaining himself. Someone so challenged that if Scott got there late, this person wouldn't even be able to call 9-1-1 and make any coherent sense. Just dig himself a deeper hole.

Mr. Z handed a satchel to Scott with three plastic bags inside. One contained a switchblade from Holiday's apartment. The other two contained handguns from the other candidates. Three possible objects to plant from three possible patsies to justify Scoot's lethal force. Professionally planned. Every contingency.

There was one aspect of the planning with which Mr. Z didn't express comfort, didn't feel he controlled. "From what I'm told, you're scheduled to have a partner tomorrow. Should we handle him? Make some arrangement so he doesn't show up to work tomorrow?"

Scott laughed. If it was a nervous laugh, he masked it well. "Taylor isn't worth a second of concern. I've worked with him a lot. He's the perfect chump. He …"

"Are you sure," Mr. Z interjected.

"I'm sure. The guy's not a leader. He's a follower. I can manipulate him at will."

"We can make sure you're alone tomorrow."

Scott began to worry Taylor would end up on a slab of his own, toe tag in place. He knew Taylor's wife and family. It was a bridge he didn't want to cross. "He'll be a plus," Scott asserted. "He'll back me up on everything."

Mr. Z handed him a cell phone. "From now on, you only deal with me directly. No one else. Keep this on you."

And with that, the euphoria of the meeting ended. And the excitement of anticipation began.

The plan unfolded splendidly. After Scott received confirmation of the fall guy, he ditched the two pistols and kept only Holiday's folding knife. The first 9-1-1 call expertly placed Scott and Taylor five blocks away from DuPont's house. And Taylor proved as easy to manipulate as Scott had boasted. They remained patiently in the area, even after the first 9-1-1 call was determined to be bogus. And thus, for the second emergency call, their patrol car was by far the closest to DuPont's house, and the one that responded.

This second call was also masterfully done. The report of a man forcing his way into a home and a woman's loud yelling was just enough to bring a response, not enough to bring the whole force down on the area. And there was just enough of a rough description of the intruder to be able to later mark Holiday as the perpetrator and close the case down as soon as he was killed. A well-planned operation.

The presence of an old man near the house was a bonus. Serendipitous. Scott pointed the old man out to Taylor. Taylor approached him. Scott got clear first access to the house.

He was feeling pretty shrewd. And pretty giddy with anticipation. Everything had gone according to plan.

But then everything went to hell. And the second emotional swing, from euphoria to anticipation, now transitioned to the third: shock.

Chapter 8

It was totally incongruous with everything Scott had been told. A hand reaching out and wiping the doorknob and doorbell? This was supposed to be a guy who was mentally challenged. He had been described as the perfect patsy, a lamb easily led to the slaughter. *He wiped his prints?*

The initial shock didn't last long. *Holiday is still in the house*, Scott considered. *This'll just make him seem guiltier.*

And again, his partner conformed to Scott's conviction; Taylor patiently waited at the front door, giving Scott the chance to be the first one into the house via the backdoor.

But then Scott found the backdoor locked. *Not the plan*, he thought.

He started to pull the combo windowpunch/handcuff key out of his duty belt before using the butt of his gun to strike the glass pane near the door handle three times in quick succession. Three loud crashes, which he knew would alert Taylor outside and Holiday inside. He reached in the cleared opening with a gloved hand and unlocked the door. He had to move quickly.

But then another shock. The Holiday guy wasn't even in the house. What kind of supposed idiot would have gotten out of the house so soon, locked the front and back doors—*wiped his prints*?

Somebody that was not as described.

Now shock gave way to frustration. This new emotion set in as Scott was moving through the streets looking for Holiday. He couldn't find him anywhere. Scott expected to see him around every corner. Around every corner he found empty streets or streets with neighbors who had not see anyone fitting Holiday's description. The guy seemed lucky. Or maybe Scott wasn't lucky.

The despair set in when Scott's cell phone rang. The one given to him by Mr. Z. He looked at it. He hesitated. He answered.

Reflexively, he knew what Mr. Z wanted. Scott had been looking for Holiday for only a half-hour. Yet, as he intuited, Mr. Z already had knowledge that things had gone terribly wrong. What Mr. Z wanted to know was how Scott had FUBARed so badly, given that everything else had gone according to plan. The question wasn't exactly presented pleasantly.

Scott had a lot of excuses ready. He had been thinking of excuses for Mr. Z ever since he found Holiday wasn't in the house. He could point fingers at the incompetent horse's ass who compiled the god-awful description of Holiday. There was a flaw in the planning. He should have been planted closer to the scene. He'd have done things differently.

Lots of excuses.

He said nothing.

He knew Mr. Z wasn't in a mood for someone deflecting blame. Still, that wasn't the main reason Scott didn't go down the path of pointing fingers. It was where those fingers would end up pointing. Scott knew the exact point where this finely-tuned plot had fallen apart. And it wasn't someone else's error. It'd been his own. It was he who was the horse's ass.

But of that Mr. Z was unaware. And Scott intended to keep it that way.

Actually, the minute Scott saw the hand wiping the doorknob he instantly knew he had messed up: he had allowed the blaring of the siren as he and Taylor sped down the street. It hadn't been a code 3, policeman down; it had been a vague 9-1-1 call with the option of just flashing lights, or maybe nothing at all. But Taylor had used both lights and siren to get through a red light and Scott had agreed with that; he had been in more of a rush than Taylor. Then Taylor had insisted on leaving the siren and lights on. Some overblown, ultimately untimely concern about having lost two buddies on the force who had responded to a domestic violence call. Something about how he believed a big show would help get things in order before they got there, maybe even stop someone in the process of doing violence.

And Scott had let it go. He'd made a judgment call. It'd been a bad one.

He had reasoned that he didn't want any ripples in the relationship with Taylor, not at that time, not given what was about to transpire. He had assumed that it wouldn't matter anyway; the fall guy was an idiot.

Except he wasn't.

It was Scott who'd been the idiot. A silent approach and he was sure he would have surprised Holiday alone inside and everything would be wrapped up. And he'd be planning his trip to Europe. The figurative thread he was hanging onto in his conversation with Mr. Z was at the same time a literal thread: he had removed it and dropped the broom into the pool of blood when he first entered the house. Nothing else had gone right on his end.

Still, all was not lost. There was a contingency plan.

"There's always a Plan B," Mr. Z said to Scott on the phone call. "Do you think I got to where I am without a Plan B?"

Scott had known only what he needed for his job: that a high profile target had to be eliminated within a short time frame and, to deflect attention, a fall guy was needed. Once Scott took care of this fall guy, there would be no cause for the police, the media, the public to look further. Especially, in the case of Holiday, a friendless person if there was one, with no one to care one way or the other that he was no longer on the face of the Earth. And Mr. Z had said there would be plenty of people who would come out of the woodwork to call him unstable, a troubled young man, a loner, and obsessed with DuPont.

This plan hadn't totally failed—the high profile person had been eliminated—and this fact had mollified Mr. Z to some extent. It was just that the scapegoat had disappeared and the police, the media, the public would be looking further.

Plan B was really just a tweak on Plan A: frame Holiday, find Holiday, and eliminate Holiday. Just it would now be done by "suicide." Suicide because of Holiday's remorse or his shame or because he felt the walls of justice closing in on him. There was nowhere that was safe for him. It could happen in his apartment, his car, in a river or the woods, even in a jail cell or "suicide by police officer"—everything could be arranged now that he had run from the scene of the crime. The one thing that was clear: this would never get to the court system. Scott could still be of assistance.

And so Scott had stayed up that night, spending most of his time in the study, listening to the police scanner. Although now off-duty, he could still show up at the scene of Holiday's apartment if needed. After all, Holiday himself lived in Police Zone 4, although below the Monongahela, in a less-than-prosperous neighborhood.

And Scott already had done some good in moving the contingency along. Three major ways, actually. Each designed to tie Holiday definitively to the crime. Each spurred by directions from Mr. Z, but the second and third with Scott's own creative input.

All three involved Lieutenant J. P. Kelly.

The first required inspecting footage from the bus cameras. Mr. Z knew Holiday has come via bus; he even knew the exact route. And as soon as Scott got Kelly's ear, the "bus camera initiative" was set in motion.

The second necessitated going through the garbage containers on the streets. Scott had noticed them when he had been looking for Holiday. And, it was clear that Holiday had blood on him transferred from the broom. Scott hadn't needed Mr. Z's reminder. Either Holiday left the area on a bus with bloodied clothing, which would show up on a camera video, or Holiday would've gotten rid of the incriminating clothing before boarding a bus. And so the "garbage can initiative" made its way to Kelly's ears.

The third was by far the most important: identifying Holiday and connecting him to DuPont. And in this, they got a break. They wouldn't have to wait for the bus footage or finding bloodied clothing or a week of media hysteria until his suicide was discovered and he was tied to DuPont. Holiday had actually been stopped by the police. It was just a matter of pointing out to Kelly that the man identified by the police in the area also had a connection to DuPont.

In all three cases, Kelly had accepted the information from Scott in a matter-of-fact manner. If there was one thing that every Pittsburgh officer knew about Kelly it was his attitude that the job of underlings was to report to the boss and make the boss look good; the boss was burdened with getting the glory. "For the good of the department, of course," or however Kelly rationalized his actions.

Scott couldn't care less if Kelly was a glory hound. In fact, it was to his advantage for Kelly to get the credit and Scott stay low in profile. Scott's only concern was about Mr. Z, and he would be very pleased that these three points had been conveyed to Kelly. It would make the contingency plan go so much smoother.

Scott had crafted the police report so there was no mention of any siren. Taylor had backed him in this detail. Maybe Mr. Z would never know.

The dawn was breaking and Scott got off the sofa to make himself another cup of coffee. No news yet about Holiday.

But Scott felt confident there would be no need for a Plan C. Holiday may not be as dumb as Scott once thought, but the forces lined up against him were formidable. If Holiday hadn't already, it was a matter of time until he ended his own life—with persuasion, of course. And as long as the Holiday incident was resolved satisfactorily, then Scott's job security, the second one, the one with the lucrative revenue stream, wouldn't be endangered.

Chapter 9

Hugh's office occupied one wing of one floor of a ten-story building. Its entrance from the hallway displayed a title more fitting for a much larger space: Pittsburgh Bioscience Center for DNA Diagnostics. Despite its name, only two of the seven employees had degrees in the sciences, Hugh and the founder, Taj Bridgewater.

A graduate of Stanford University, Pittsburgh-native Bridgewater was young and innovative and with big dreams. Standing about six feet five inches in height, on a solid but somewhat thin frame, his size alone drew attention when he entered a room. However, his most memorable physical feature was his infectious and warm smile. And this feature was backed by a casual presence and a caring nature, the latter an attribute so genuine that people liked to do business with him. If they were going to depart with their hard-earned cash, they would rather it be in his hands than someone else.

Bridgewater wasn't the first in his family to go to college—his mother was a nurse and his father a civil engineer—but he was the first in his family to go to such a prestigious university. Even he suffered from a misperception that he got into Stanford on some admissions preference because he was black. Fact was: Bridgewater had a brilliant mind. Valedictorian of his high school, he was an honors graduate of Stanford, completing a B.S. degree in Chemistry with a specialization in Biological Chemistry, while at the same time fulfilling the requirements for a degree in Biology with specialization in Biochemistry and Biophysics.

Combined with his research endeavors while at Stanford, a look at Bridgewater's record of academic and entrepreneurial achievements for a yet 28-year-old would create the impression of someone driven to succeed. That could be misleading. Bridgewater was a rare combination of hard-working and yet gifted with easy-going mannerisms, a person wanting to build a major enterprise and yet supportive of staff members' personal goals even when at the expense of that ambition.

Right now, Bridgewater was only in the initial phase of building that major enterprise. He was paying the bills largely with clients who wanted to check on a possible paternal link. Most of these wanted to prove such a linkage, including tricky cases where the suspected father wasn't willing to be tested. Some of his more wealthy clients were out to counter paternity claims, either because they were the ones accused of being the biological father, or because they were family members of the accused trying to protect their estate from inheritance claims.

There was more. Some clients visited the Center to understand their ancestry, with Bridgewater promising to track their genealogical relationships and geographical roots back thousands of years. Maternity tests, testing for genetic diseases and predispositions: the Center offered it all. Some well-to-do clients had no immediate concerns; they wanted a genetic fingerprint in case of later inheritance claims—or a lost child.

Through hard work, well-nurtured contacts, and endless promotion, Bridgewater already had cornered a substantial market in the Greater Pittsburgh area. Wealthy scions, athletes, and middle-class patrons regularly offered their buccal swabs and blood for DNA analysis. Bridgewater's planned next step was expanding the Center's clientele throughout the US and internationally: doing DNA testing for immigration purposes, international adoptions, native tribe membership, forensics, and whatever other opportunity presented itself.

But, the Bioscience Center didn't yet have even its own laboratory equipment. The DNA analysis—purification, preparation, and testing—was wisely farmed off to The MacArthur Medical Center, where Dr. Megan DuPont oversaw the contracted work.

For TMMC, the process of lysing cells, removing cellular components, adding reagents to the DNA, and printing out results was all part of an automated system that cost TMMC little. But the arrangement saved the Bioscience Center greatly in costs. Until the Bioscience Center had its own lab—another future objective—this relationship with TMMC was a financial lifesaver.

When Hugh first showed up for a job interview a year ago, Bridgewater was more than a little taken aback. Nothing in Hugh's resume prepared Bridgewater for that interview. He soon realized that Hugh wasn't just nervous; this was a serious problem that wasn't going to go away.

But Bridgewater saw something he liked, something that moved his heart, and he creatively readjusted the open position so that it fit Hugh. Of course, Bridgewater wasn't without benefit: he got a talented biochemist for less than the going rate.

Upon his hiring, Hugh became responsible for the freshly-created "non-client-contact middle zone" that bridged the collection of cheek and blood samples performed by technicians and the reporting of the results to the client by Bridgewater. Hugh was the Bioscience Analyst, charged with taking the collected samples to DuPont, receiving the raw data from her, conducting the data analysis, and preparing the preliminary report—with DuPont often serving as his consultant in the analysis. The job fit him well: Hugh was an expert at deciphering DNA data and crafting well-written reports. And his work never had to cross into the two bookends of the process where there was personal contact with clients.

On this Monday morning, Hugh arrived at the office early, much earlier than he originally planned.

One reason was that it had been a fitful night in his childhood home. While he'd finally fallen asleep, he also had woken up very early, his mind racing, reliving yesterday's events and sifting options. Finding it impossible to get back to sleep, Hugh had prepared for his day.

The preparation wasn't ideal. He had brought the clothes he needed from his apartment, but had forgotten many essentials. In his parents' bathroom were a toothbrush and an old razor, the latter only serving to nick him in two spots. He'd been fortunate to find a pair of his old dress shoes in the house, having decided to toss the shoes he was wearing. They weren't only improper for the office: there was no way he could be certain they didn't have traces of blood.

Waking up at an early hour wasn't the only reason Hugh arrived ahead of schedule; the primary reason was driving his parents' "local car." At one time it had been his to use, until he had moved to an apartment and decided the cost of insurance just wasn't worth it. Not when he could take a bus anywhere he needed to go in Pittsburgh.

And it wasn't that reliable anyway. It was a banged up, 14-year-old Ford Taurus, with bald tires and an engine light that stayed on, perhaps linked to the fact that the gas gauge didn't work at all. It rattled badly when one reached sixty miles per hour, and the engine noise threatened to drown out the radio. It had an old car smell and dents and scratches and one zigzagging crack that went up the right side of the windshield.

But the car was drivable. And now it provided him some needed freedom of movement.

Given the early hour he had left for work, the car had gotten him quickly through the streets and into the company's parking lot. There he waited almost an hour until the office opened up, and he was able to greet his boss and co-workers and make his way back to his cubicle.

At first, Hugh welcomed the diverting routineness of being back at work after Sunday's traumatic events. Getting caught up on clients and reviewing lab results seemed to provide some distraction from what was really weighing on his mind. He even felt some of the tension and anxiety leave his body.

But the therapeutic value proved ephemeral. As the morning wore on, his mind continuously revisited the haunting images of the previous evening and night, making it progressively harder for him to focus on the task at hand. It began to feel as if he were in a unreal dream state. Except it had been real.

His day would only get significantly worse in the afternoon.

Chapter 10

Hugh watched from his cubicle as two men entered the office. Two men who attracted the attention of everyone, all of whom, whether seated or standing, stopped what they were doing to stare.

The first man through the door was of medium build, with short, jet-black hair and wire-rimmed glasses. He sported a navy blue uniform, with the shirt, pants, and undershirt so dark it seemed as if he were wearing black. From his thick belt, which actually was black, hung numerous pouches, also black, as well as a quite visible service revolver, taser, set of handcuffs, and radio.

The uniform and duty belt made it obvious he was a policeman. The shoulder patches and chest badge, and the service cap he donned, made it clear he was with the Pittsburgh Police Force. The shoulder patches were of a unique design, the crest taken from the Coat-of-Arms of the 18th century Englishman for whom Pittsburgh was named, William Pitt the Elder. The badge on the officer's left chest displayed the same crest but had additional designs traced to England: the surrounding garter came from an order founded by King Edward III, while the circular shield traced through England to Greek foot shoulders.

But it was the eight-pointed service cap that was so distinctive and wouldn't be missed even a block away. It stood out because of the double-rowed, checkerboard-like band of yellow and black—the Sillitoe Tartan.

From where Hugh watched, the man's nametag over the right chest was unreadable. He could barely make out that it sported blue letters on yellow. Nor could Hugh make out the insignia to ascertain the man's rank. The policeman carried a manila folder in his left hand.

This man stopped just inside the doorway and waited for the second man to enter.

If this first man was impressive, it was this second arrival who had the aura of authority. He was a large man—very big, indeed—and everything about him, from his gait to his slow gaze over the office, indicated he was a man in charge. His white uniform shirt over a white undershirt, which stood out against the navy blue of the pants, made clear he was a major officer. Perhaps a lieutenant or maybe even a commander, thought Hugh. He carried his cap under his left arm.

Hugh watched as the first man spoke with the receptionist, while the big man surveyed the office.

And then his eyes settled on Hugh. And stopped there. Unmoving.

Perhaps for thirty seconds, he stared. Perhaps much more. It would be impossible for Hugh to say how long; he hadn't even realized at first what was happening so intently had he been watching the conversation with the receptionist. When Hugh became aware, when he looked up at the big man and their eyes locked, Hugh also stared transfixed, immobile. As if a deer at night frozen in the lights of an oncoming semi.

Hugh finally swiveled away, eyes back at his desk, pretending to shuffle papers that no longer held any interest for him. When he peered back up, he could see the receptionist guiding the two men into Bridgewater's office, his boss standing at the door to greet them. The receptionist closed the door.

Hugh's boss clearly was caught off guard by the visit. His occasional glances at Hugh through the office's glass wall made it painfully obvious who the conversation was about. And

Bridgewater was seemingly uncomfortable and doing most of the talking. Whoever it was questioning him, they were being thorough. Thirty minutes thorough as it turned out.

Hugh hoped they would leave the office after meeting with Bridgewater. They didn't. Hugh watched as the two men next met with another co-worker, the bookkeeper, who had her own private room to maintain the financial records. She too glanced up at Hugh as she spoke. This conversation was a brief ten minutes in real time, ten minutes short of eternity in Hugh's internal clock.

And then the bookkeeper left the two men in her room and came toward Hugh's cubicle. He watched her walk across the office, hoping she would divert her direction. She didn't. He hoped she would just ask him some mundane question. She didn't. She stood with her arms at her side and said, "There're two officers that want to speak to you, Hugh. They'll meet you in the conference room."

Hugh's heart sank.

He frowned and rose slowly out of his desk chair. His body felt leaden, yet he had a reeling sensation of light-headedness. The walk to the conference room stretched on and on, his shoes seeming to sink into the carpet, impeding his progress, while his wobbly legs and feeling of disorientation created an illusion of walking on a floor of a tall building swaying from an earthquake.

Hugh was conscious of his boss and co-workers looking at him, but his field of sight had narrowed to one of tunnel vision fixated on the conference room. And the closer that he got to that room, the more he was aware of his heart pounding in his chest and a fear that he was going to have a major anxiety attack. He wanted to be anywhere but where he was going. His mind stuck on one thought: *What am I walking into? What am I walking into?*

The conference room was empty. Hugh sat down on one of the side chairs near the middle of the rectangular conference table. He awaited the two men.

His mind was now blank, as if unwilling to consider what was going to happen. He was reduced to sensation, and the sensation was one of his chest being in a vice. A vice that was so tight he felt a constant sharp pain, every breath a labored one.

Hugh sat for what seemed an endless time. And then the two men entered and shut the door behind them.

The big man immediately took up the chair at the head of the conference table, near the door. His name was embroidered into his white shirt and said simply "Kelly." The other man, now clearly seen by his insignia to be a sergeant, sat directly across from Hugh, but slid his chair back from the table as if to watch what was going to be the big man's show. His name tag was metal and said "Cesar." *Unusual to see that as a last name*, thought Hugh.

Hugh was captivated by Cesar's duty belt. It was much more impressive than that sported by the man known as Kelly. It seemed to have so many pouches, with the revolver on the man's right and an evident taser in a pouch on the left, along with a set of handcuffs. But there were so many more pouches. Even when he walked in, Hugh could see a pouch on the back of his belt, near his spine. He had a small flashlight in the center of his belt and a large radio on his left side. Hugh could only guess what the other pouches contained.

The big man had relatively few—mainly the service revolver on his right and pouches of what Hugh deduced were bullets on his left. Maybe his days of being first on the scene were over?

Hugh had time to contemplate all this because neither man spoke. No greeting. They just took their seats and looked at Hugh.

After what seemed an interminable pause, the big man finally spoke, in a voice so deep and strong and well-measured that it left no doubt in Hugh's mind who was in charge.

"I am Lieutenant Kelly. I am here about the murder."

Chapter 11

Here about the murder.

The words reverberated in Hugh's mind. He had expected as much. Still, these were the last words he wanted to hear. What he was hoping to hear was: "Do you know you're driving a car with an expired inspection sticker?" Or, "we believe some vagrant was sleeping at your parents' house last night and left a dog there." Even, "there was a report of a fire in your apartment last night." Pretty much anything other than "I am here about the murder."

Kelly let the words sink in without further comment, ushering in another uncomfortable silence. Hugh was stumped as for his opening move. *What am I supposed to say?* Hugh selected an affirmative nod.

"You *know* what murder I am talking about." A statement, not a question. Yet, one for which Kelly clearly expected a response, not a nod.

Kelly had used eight words, spoken with clarity and unwavering authority. But it was another eight words that preoccupied Hugh's mind, as they had for hours now. He had replayed those earlier words, spoken by another officer, over and over and over: "He can't be the one. No British accent." Just eight words. Words not even meant for him. But words that had put Hugh on an emotional rollercoaster. The first five had sent him soaring with immediate relief, the exhilarating feeling of being in the clear. "He can't be the one." The last three words had plunged him back into the depths of angst. But the last three words also had provided him a way out.

Hugh paused to gather himself and then stammered "Y-y-y-yes."

Hugh had identified rather quickly the import of those last three words, "no British accent." And so that morning, starting with Holly, no longer did Hugh speak with the lowered voice and with the affected accent and mannerisms of a loyal "subject of the Queen." Back was his usual higher tone, the normal American accent—and the relentless stuttering. The last condition had plagued him every day for two decades. It now offered him an avenue of escape. Something far from the description he knew must have been given to the police by the old man outside DuPont's house.

Kelly stared at Hugh for a good thirty seconds. Not moving. Not even blinking. He then continued, "And you know *who* was murdered because…?"

No British accent. Still, the British accent had become second nature for the past couple of weeks. And that concerned Hugh.

"I-I-I……..read online."

The last two words exploded out with a rising pitch. They followed an awkward moment when Hugh's lips had pursed, but no sound had escaped. All to Hugh's relief.

Kelly paused, his eyes unwavering, undecipherable. He finally continued the line of questioning: "When did you read about the murder?"

"Th-th-this, well, morning."

"Where? Computer at home? Computer here in office?"

"N-n-no. Ph-ph-phone."

No British accent. Three words that offered a way out. Something at odds with what the police were looking for. And yet, Hugh had no guarantee, no certainty that he wouldn't spontaneously break out in the now-familiar British accent.

"Your cell phone?"

"Y-y-yes."

No guarantee. And yet, Hugh was very aware of one constant during his life: as far as his stuttering, he always was at his worse under stress. He had spent years trying to avoid stressful situations. And none compared to this.

"You read about the murder before you came to work?"

"Y-y-yes."

No British accent. But the nagging thought kept growing in Hugh's mind. W*hat if I mess up? What if I suddenly use the word* garage *or* privacy *or* schedule *or* accusatory *and the British accent flows?* Even as Hugh said those words in his mind, he could hear the British pronunciation.

"You have a smart phone?"

Hugh nodded.

A way out. *But what if … No, I don't have the luxury for doubt. I'm not going to mess up. I've been stuttering for twenty years. And that's what they're going to get.*

What kind of phone?"

"S-S-S-S-Samsung, um, uh, Note," Overly loud. With the annoying rising pitch.

"Which newspaper online?"

"Uh?"

"Which newspaper online did you read about the DuPont murder?"

"D-d-don't, uh, uh, re-re-re-remem…," Hugh let his voice trail off, the sentence unfinished.

Hugh could see the online world wasn't Kelly's strong suit. He probably liked to deal with people, not things. Hugh liked to deal with things. And if Kelly was hoping for a simple answer of *Post-Gazette* or *Tribune-Review* in order to trap Hugh into revealing details not found in those accounts, then he was sorely out of luck. The web was a world where facts and fictions and speculations were so intermingled that a suitable cover might be found for any slip Hugh might make.

"You don't remember?" Kelly persisted.

"N-n-no. D-d-don't re-re...."

"Really?" Kelly interrupted. "You don't remember which newspaper you read just this morning?"

Hugh shook his head no. Kelly just stared at him.

No British accent. First words in a sentence had been a problem for years for Hugh. It had gotten progressively worse as he obsessed more and more over starting a sentence. But he had found a workaround. He would either just say the first word in his mind and silently mouth it and move onto the second word, or, he would start with one of his filler words, "uh" or "um," sometimes repeated two or three times until he was comfortable to begin. Even when he started using the British accent he at first began sentences with an odd, artificially low "aye" sound that he imagined to be that of a British sailor. Or a pirate.

But not now. Now he wanted every first word, even if it meant he had to shorten his sentences. He wanted ever first word and every problem word like "remember." It would be what would set him far apart from the fluent British man at DuPont's house.

Hugh watched as Kelly slowly raised himself from the chair, never taking his eyes off of his target. He stood at the edge of the table, towering over Hugh, who sat leaning slightly forward, his arms in his lap.

"Why are you so nervous?" Kelly finally said. He was not being sympathetic.

Hugh's voice was again blocked from forming the first syllable. Nothing came out. It was caught in his throat, his jaw muscles and gut tensing. This was not unusual when he was nervous and starting a sentence. Or anticipating a problem word. Sometimes even in the middle of a problem word.

Finally, he interjected: "I-I-I ….s-s-s-stut-stutter."

Stutter. In a cruel twist, one of his problem words. A word that normally Hugh would avoid, either outright by leaving a pause in place of the word and letting the listener mentally fill it in, or substituting something that caused less difficulty. Like "speech, well, problem" or "speech, well, issue."

Hugh was always thinking ahead while speaking in order to figure out what words he might get stuck on so he could dance around them. But not here. Not now. Now he was thinking ahead to seek out words that he could get stuck on. *He can't be the one. No British accent.*

Kelly paused for effect, looking straight at Hugh. And oblivious to the fact that Hugh was finding Kelly's frequent pauses to be mildly amusing, given that Hugh was used to being the one who paused before speaking. No doubt very different motivations—one trying to make his target uncomfortable and foster a communication mistake; the other historically pausing to avoid a communication mistake and to make his conversational partner comfortable.

In strong, and measured, and authoritative tones, Kelly moved in. The preliminary jabs were over.

"Not always, Hugh. Not always do you stutter. Outside Dr. Megan DuPont's house you spoke fluently."

Panic coursed through Hugh's body like an electric shock, leaving his torso tense, his mind muddled. *They know for sure that I was there.*

Hugh's mind feverishly formed an answer, "No. That wasn't me. He had a British accent. I stammer."

But his usual pause before speaking saved him as he caught the folly of what he was about to blurt out. Although trembling, his left foot shaking below the table, Hugh gathered himself.

"N-n-n-no no. I-I-I……s-s-s-stut-stutter."

Hugh's nervousness was making his stammering worse. His was a severe case, but he usually had some fluency: not every word was mangled. But he also wasn't trying hard. He wasn't employing his usual fillers—the "um" and "uh" and "well" and "you know." The interjections that helped make the sentence sound less broken. The interjections that sometimes aided him in pronouncing the next word. It was taking conscious effort not to use them.

Kelly leaned closer to Hugh and placed both hands on the conference table near Hugh. "Son, not always." He said it strongly, commandingly. "You spoke well when you were outside DuPont's house."

"N-n-no. A-a-always."

Kelly sat back down. He looked over at Sergeant Cesar, who was intently watching the exchange. Then Kelly looked back at Hugh.

"You know, son, I checked with an authority on stuttering today. He told me a couple of interesting things. Would you like to hear what I learned?"

Hugh didn't want to hear. Not at all. Hugh nodded yes. Incuriously. He doubted Kelly cared about his response one way or the other.

"Well, one thing he told me was that there was no difference between the terms "stutter" and "stammer." That surprised me. Two different words in the English language. Why wouldn't they have different meanings? In fact, some of my officers insisted there was a difference. They gave me all kinds of distinctions, some of which quite frankly conflicted with others. So, I asked this authority. And he said the two words had identical meanings. Have you heard that?"

Hugh nodded yes. *Where was Kelly going?*

"He actually said the big difference is where the terms are used. Americans historically used stammer more, but now they mostly use stutter. You know which nation uses the term stammer more?"

Hugh nodded yes.

Kelly cocked his head and motioned with an upturned palm for Hugh's answer.

"B-B-British."

"Yeah, British English. That's interesting, isn't it?"

Hugh nodded. He now had a bad sense where this conversation was going.

"This authority told me something else interesting." Kelly paused to gain Hugh's undivided attention. "He said it's not unusual at all for someone with a stutter to not have a problem when singing, or acting.... or... *using an accent*. Like say a *British accent.*"

Kelly looked at Hugh.

Hugh stayed silent. Until he realized Kelly was going to wait for Hugh to respond.

"N-n-not not, uh, uh, me." Hugh was nothing if not succinct.

Kelly looked straight at Hugh, calmly, collected. Hugh kept his eyes diverted, looking down at his own hands, which were now on the table in front of him. His thoughts were racing, wild, uncontrolled. And mostly some repetition of: *I never should've run. This is going badly.*

Kelly rose again from his seat and leaned over towards Hugh.

"Come on, son. We know you were in the house. We're not accusing you of the murder. We just want to know what you saw when you were inside."

The vice on Hugh's chest, which had never loosened since he entered the conference room, now tightened another turn of the screw. *What do I say now? What does he know? Did I leave some evidence behind? Should I go ahead and tell him about the professor's call? Maybe come clean? If I come clean, will he let me alone?*

Hugh tried to take in a slow and strong breath in hopes it would relax him and break the grip of the vice. It didn't.

He shook his head.

Kelly didn't wait this time. "No? Meaning you don't want to tell us what happened inside?"

No, meaning I'm not going down this road. The break-in at the apartment, the clear set-up: I'll never get myself out of this if they place me at the house. And if I give a true story, there's always the blood on the jacket. Too risky for me to admit being there.

And if what he's saying is certain, wouldn't I already be in police custody? He must be bluffing.

But why send a lieutenant for God's sake? And a sergeant too? Is this normal?

"Holiday?"

"N-n-not… um…there." The ever-present vice tightened a notch.

"Son, we have two witnesses that place you in the house. You're not in trouble." Kelly shrugged his shoulders and took a gentle, inquisitive tone. "Just tell us why you were in DuPont's house?"

Two witnesses? Does that mean he doesn't have forensic evidence? Who are the witnesses? The old man would be one. Who's the other? The 9-1-1 caller mentioned online? Anyway, isn't eyewitness testimony often unreliable? What Kelly probably has is the fact that a policeman took my name and address. But I'm here, not in custody. He must not have much of anything.

Hugh shook his head and repeated himself: "N-n-not not, um, uh, there."

Kelly showed visible frustration with Hugh's delayed, and brief, and vague, and pointless responses. He sat back down, but leaned in, with his head close to Hugh's.

And a new concern began to worm its way into Hugh's mind. *What do I do with my eyes? Should I look Kelly in the eyes? I remember a body language expert saying that people lying either avert their eyes or look too much in the eyes. How much eye contact is too little?*

"Where did you get the cuts on your face?"

"Sh-sh-shaving."

"Not a cut from DuPont?"

"N-n-no."

Then again, I spent years learning to not avert my eyes. It's normal for a stutterer to look away. Maybe looking away is good.

"You know we have testimony that DuPont was scared of you. That she told a colleague that you were obsessed with her, even stalking her. That she said you'd show up out of the blue to places that she went."

This keeps getting better and better. Someone has really been thorough in setting me up. Hugh shook his head from side to side.

Then he decided to take the offensive.

"Caaaaaaaaaaan I ask some.......thing?"

Can: as the first word in a sentence, almost always a problem. A prolongation where the sound continued but his lips and tongue stopped moving. The block in "something"—that was a bonus. The airflow stopped in his throat, his lips parted but just no sound.

Kelly recoiled somewhat with Hugh's "can." He recovered quickly.

"Go on."

"W-w-was it it...um, well...D-Doctor, um, F-F-Faccon?

Kelly said nothing. He just stared.

It was a pause during which Hugh's mind continued to be caught in a web of its own making. *Maybe if I look back and forth between Kelly and this sergeant, I can balance my eye contact. And I have to be careful to not cover my mouth. I remember that as a sign of someone that is guilty. Although I'm sure I already look guilty.*

Finally, Kelly spoke. "Maybe it was. Maybe it wasn't. Why?"

Hugh looked at Kelly's face. He couldn't hold his gaze with Kelly looking straight back at him. He shifted his look to the sergeant, who was also staring at him. Hugh averted his eyes again and looked at his own hands on the table.

"M-m-may-maybe he …um, uh… k-k-killed D-Doctor, well, you know, DuPont."

Kelly regarded Hugh, this time with obvious disdain. The impatience showed in his voice. His tone was angry.

"You trying to deflect attention from yourself, Holiday? If so, you picked a poor target. We spoke with the co-workers already. Professor Faccon? In his lab all evening. Anyway, we've an email from DuPont to the professor from Sunday morning saying she feared you. Wanted to cut off all relations with your office when you got back. It was sent from her own email account. Do you…"

Kelly stopped abruptly. He shouted wordlessly at himself, *What the hell are you doing? Shut the hell up.* He switched subjects.

"Let's go back to Sunday night, son." Any effort on Kelly's part to create a sympathetic sounding tone was long gone. "It was chilly, as you know, that night. Yet, you went to that area without a sweater?"

Hugh shook his head. *Not verbally answering questions just doesn't seem so odd when you have a stutter*, he thought.

Kelly would have none of it. "You did *not* have a sweater with you?"

"N-n-no."

"How about a jacket? Did you take a jacket to the area?"

Hugh shook his head.

"Hugh, did you take a *jacket* to the area on Sunday night?"

"N-n-no."

"No jacket?"

"N-n-no."

Hugh saw a small smile creep across Kelly's face. Not a friendly smile. A "now-I've-got-you" smile.

"You made a mistake, Holiday. You want to know what it was?" Kelly waited. Another interminable pause.

"Sh-sh-should, uh, have used sh-shav-shaving, um, cream?"

Kelly regarded Holiday with a look of confusion. Then contempt. The look of a high-ranking police officer who is dealing face-to-face with a cold-blooded killer making a joke.

"Trying to be a funny guy? … No. It was your jacket."

Chapter 12

Kelly reached out and took the folder from Sergeant Cesar. He momentarily reached into the folder but then withdrew his hand and looked at Hugh.

"Why did you lie to me, son?"

"L-l-lie?"

"Yes. About the jacket."

Kelly waited for a response. None came. Hugh looked at Kelly. Then the sergeant. Then back at his hands on the table.

Kelly took out two items from the folder. Photos. 8x10s. He put one face down on the table. He took the other photo and placed it face up in front of Hugh. Hugh looked at it. The vice on his chest tightened another turn of the screw.

"We checked the bus cameras, son. This was taken on a bus going *to* the area where DuPont lived. As you can see, you're wearing a jacket."

Kelly flipped the second photo face up in front of Hugh.

"In this still, you're no longer wearing a jacket. Nor carrying one. This was on the bus you used when you left *from* the area. The two officers who talked to you in the neighborhood also said you didn't have a jacket."

Kelly looked at Hugh.

Hugh said . . . nothing. He sat silently, looking at the photos, almost too frozen to think. The two thoughts that he did have were: *What will come out of the folder next? Did they find the jacket?*

For an interminable long time, Kelly studied him. Hugh felt his graze and again tried looking at Kelly. Then averted his eyes toward the sergeant. Then down at his hands. *This isn't working. I don't suppose I could look guiltier.*

"Well?"

"T-t-took it it off. H-h-hot. Loooooooooooost." *Lost.* Another major problem word when starting a sentence. Thrown in for good measure. But the whole charade seemed pointless now.

"Where did you take it off, son? And when?"

"Wh-when got, um, uh, off b-bus. Sssssssat on, um, um, well, b-bench. L-l-left a-a-accid-accident…" Hugh's voice trailed off.

"You jacket had blood on it. Do you want to explain how DuPont's blood got on your jacket?"

The vice on Hugh's chest tightened yet another turn of the screw.

But then the vice loosened a notch.

Then it loosened one more.

Hugh considered the line of questioning. *They couldn't have found the jacket. For sure, I'd be in custody now. They would've read me my rights. They would've taken samples of my DNA. This has to be some kind of bluff.*

Hugh slowly shook his head from side to side, feigning puzzlement. Kelly waited. Hugh just sat there. Kelly waited some more. Hugh sat quietly.

"Listen, son. You might've thought you could just get rid of it. But we stopped all the garbage pickups last night and right away started a search for the jacket. You never had a chance of getting rid of it."

Kelly paused for a response.

Hugh just sat there. He noted that nothing new seemed to be coming out of the folder. The screw loosened another notch.

****

Kelly thought that he had been prepared for this interrogation. True, he might've taken the target too lightly. Understandably so, of course. He was just a kid after all. Kelly had dealt with hardened criminals, corrupt CEOs, athletes with high powered attorneys, drug kingpins. He had bested them all. But, if he underestimated Holiday, he'd done his due diligence nonetheless.

And that preparation had involved spending part of the morning with a speech pathologist trying to understand what this expert had labeled a "speech disfluency." Kelly had learned about mild, moderate, and severe cases, and how a stutterer might reach very different levels of speech disruption under various stresses. He had heard that stuttering sometimes appears spontaneously, and some recover spontaneously.

It had been an enlightening conversation. The pathologist had gone into detail about core behaviors—repetitions of letters, syllables and words; prolongations; blocks. And Kelly had learned that everyone has disfluencies to some extent, such as using "uh" or "er"—but stuttering takes this to a new level. Particularly in severe cases, where someone may struggle in nearly every phrase and where prolongations may be common.

None of this prepared Kelly for the extent of Holiday's stuttering. Not even the descriptions from Holiday's boss or the policemen who had talked to him on Sunday. Kelly had never heard anyone with such difficulty speaking, not even that special ed kid he had interviewed about a high school shooting. This Holiday kid seemed really messed up. . . . If he wasn't faking it.

Kelly's frustration had grown with every minute, every answer. If the kid thought he would get some sympathy from the lieutenant, he was wrong. Holiday had killed DuPont; of that much Kelly was certain.

And no longer was it just the circumstantial evidence—evidence that put Holiday at the murder scene and with motive: his being in the area, without a reason, at the time of the murder; his knowing the victim, who was concerned he might be stalking her; the ditching of the jacket; the clear identification by the now-elusive 9-1-1 caller; and the old man's physical description as well.

No, this interview, as much as anything, convinced Kelly that he had the right man. His gut told him. Holiday's evasiveness told him. The way the kid couldn't look him in the eyes told him. The kid had guilt written over every fiber of his being.

But Kelly also felt like he was running into a brick wall, one which he could see, but couldn't figure a way around or through. Usually his suspects, especially those as guilty as Holiday, have blurted out something by now that Kelly could use. Yes, this was an informal interrogation. He didn't have enough hard evidence to charge him or hold him. And he didn't want a custodial interrogation where the reading of Miranda rights might have sparked Holiday asking for a lawyer. But Kelly had been sure that something would come out of this face-to-face that would provide just what he would need to box Holiday in.

But this Holiday kid hardly spoke. He wasn't blundering. Not really. Not in a way that couldn't be attributed to a "communications problem."

And his stammering was throwing Kelly off his game. And nothing threw Kelly off his game. But there was no flow to the interrogation. To Kelly, it was all stops and starts and disjointed pauses and high pitches and loud sounds. And it was annoying, almost irrationally annoying. The speech therapist said stuttering was in the ears of the listener. But it wasn't. Kelly found it was frustrating speaking to this Holiday kid. And he was sure it must be that way for everyone.

Kelly stood up and grabbed a bottled water from a credenza in the room. He opened it and poured some in a plastic cup. He sat back down and took a sip. He would try a new approach. He would set it up slowly.

"Son, why don't you tell me why you were in DuPont's neighborhood, so far from your home."

"N-n-needed to, well, walk. P-p-parents' d-deaths."

"Not believable, son."

"T-t-true."

"It's far from your home. You needed two buses to get there."

"N-n-needed to…um….walk."

"We have motive, son. We have you at the scene."

Hugh sat there. He said nothing. He looked at his hands.

Kelly sprang. "One more thing. Say something with a British accent."

"Huh?"

"Say something with a British accent."

"I-I-I c-c-can't."

"Humor me. Say… 'I say good chap. Bloody nonsense, mate. Cheerio.'" Kelly gave his best British impersonation. It was a serious attempt. It would have set half the British Isles laughing had it been captured on video.

"I-I-I s-s-s-say…uh,um… g-good… um… chap. Blooooooooooooody…," Hugh broke off, looking flustered and embarrassed. Like a stutterer forced to say a problem word.

Kelly was jarred by Hugh's explosive "bloody." Loud, prolongated, high pitched; it sounded surreal to him. Nonetheless, he wasn't about give up on this line of attack.

Hugh was the guy. The guy at DuPont's. The guy with the British accent.

"Say "Cheerio, mate.""

"Ch-ch-cherrio. Mmmmm." Hugh broke off, looking down. Like a poor stutterer, being subjected to an abusive and mocking request.

Kelly found himself barely keeping his composure. A brick wall. He had the man. Of that, there was no doubt. But this interrogation was proving to be a big dead end. He couldn't decide if this Holiday guy was just that clever or whether his annoying stuttering had thrown Kelly off his game too much. Maybe both.

He would try a new tack. He rose again, standing straight and close to Hugh, towering over him.

"Where did you go during your three weeks off from work? Your boss says you never called in to report anything. Just a couple of emails when you'd be returning."

"Uh?"

"I want to know the cities, the hotels, the places."

Kelly's face showed disdain as Hugh pursed his lips, and again no sound came out. Hugh didn't miss the look Kelly shot him. He had seen it before. In his own parents.

Finally, Hugh said, simply, "Wh-why?"

"That's our business. If you try to make it difficult, if you don't cooperate, if you continue to lie to us, then we will track it down without you. But it will go far better for you if you just tell us."

"D-d-don't, uh, uh, re-re-re-remem…,"

"Yeah. Got it." Kelly interrupted. "Don't damn remember."

Disgusted, he stood up. "Name one city. Right now."

"Sin-sin-sin…"

"Sin?" he interjected. "What the hell are you trying to say? Sin City?"

Hugh shook his head.

"Cincinnati?" said Cesar. It was the first time he had spoken.

Hugh nodded.

"Where in Cincinnati? What hotel did you stay at?"

"D-d-don't re-re...,"

Kelly cut him off. "Write down a list. Now." Kelly got a paper and pen from Cesar. He placed it in front of Hugh.

Hugh wrote a few names. Cincinnati. Louisville. Columbus. Indianapolis. Then he stopped and looked at the paper. Wrinkling his brow like he was deep in thought. Like he was pretending to remember. An act that was quite obvious to all. And exhausting what little was left of Kelly's patience.

Kelly walked behind Hugh and leaned in on one side, his lips near Hugh's ear. He spoke quietly, almost a whisper, but the voice was gruff, the manner intimidating.

"I know you're a smart guy, Holiday. Good grades in college and high school. Applied to medical school. There's no way you don't remember." He paused glaring at Hugh in his agitation. *Write down some specifics*."

"D-d-don't, uh, uh, re-re-re-remember now. Y-y-you-you're making me n-nervous."

Kelly stepped back. He was appalled at the pitiful sham he was witnessing. But Holiday's pretense would be an effective defense should this interrogation ever come up at trial. The abusive cop and the poor stutterer.

Unless he could show that the kid was a liar. And a fake. And a murderer.

Kelly took a breath to compose himself. He sat back down. He leaned sympathetically toward Hugh. He didn't feel sympathetic. It was now his turn to put on a show.

"I know you're a smart guy, son. But you're being dumb here. Very dumb. I'm going to give you one last chance to come clean. I know that you want to get this off your chest. Tell us what happened in DuPont's house. It's for your own good."

"N-n-not, uh, um, there."

Kelly's brief attempt at composing himself bit the dust. He lashed back, face flushed.

"You should've come clean. We know you were in the DuPont house. You'll be going down for this murder." It was spoken more out of frustration than anything, and Kelly made no attempt to disguise his anger. He said it loud enough that others in the office could hear. He wanted it to resonate, to stick in Hugh's brain. To let him know that he had no refuge in which to hide.

Kelly had no interest in continuing. He couldn't stand having to listen to this stutter any more. And it was clear that the kid was using it an excuse not to say anything worthwhile while pretending to cooperate. As if his words didn't mean anything anyway, because he was unable to express himself. And the kid's faking dumbness also was annoying, as if he were playing to a sympathetic audience, and Kelly was a bully. Kelly would get him another way.

Kelly said nothing more. He abruptly got up and walked out of the conference room and out of the office, with Sergeant Cesar following closely behind.

Only when they were outside the office did Kelly address Cesar. "I want you to find out everywhere he was during the past three weeks. Check his credit card records, phone records, check with hotel clerks whether they spoke to him. We know he took his dog with him, so focus on hotels and motels that accept dogs. He thinks he's smart. But as soon as we find someone who heard him using the British accent, we have him nailed. And follow-up on where we are with finding his jacket and that 9-1-1 caller."

Chapter 13

Hugh stayed seated in the conference room. He was shaken from the grilling. He was the suspect in a notorious murder. That had sunken in pretty heavily. The police even had a motive. And seeing the photos of him on the buses, with and without the jacket, was disarming, to put it mildly.

Yet, as he decompressed from the encounter, he also felt a certain relief and, despite the seriousness of the situation, couldn't restrain a pixieish smile from creeping up on his lips. It was evident to him that much of the time Kelly was bluffing with a hand weaker than he was letting on. And this, too, had been conveyed in the exchange about the jacket.

Hugh got up and started the long trek back to his cubicle. It felt like a perp walk. He could sense the eyes of his co-workers on him, none of whom came to reassure him or ask any questions. He had a hunch what they were thinking: "How well do we know him anyway? He's kind of a loner."

Hugh couldn't let go of the conversation about the jacket, the "you-made-a-mistake-Holiday" gotcha moment and the thrusting of camera stills in front of him. But he also replayed the moment when he realized the police didn't have the jacket; they were still looking for it. They were right that if found, it would be smeared with DuPont's blood. That would be damning. But the police actually had no idea where it was. For the one place they wouldn't find it was in a garbage can.

For sure, the garbage containers, all neatly aligned on the streets for Monday morning pickup, had been appealing. But like most Pittsburgh residents who were in the city the winter of 2014, Hugh had been caught up in the drama of the murders of the Wolfe sisters in the city's East Liberty neighborhood—headline news itself—and thus he knew the police likely would search garbage cans. In the Wolfe sisters' case, news reports highlighted finding DNA evidence on bloody sweatpants that the killer had discarded in a dumpster. This offered reason enough for Hugh to relegate the garbage bin option to one of last resort.

He had opened a garbage can—but only to retrieve a plastic shopping bag. Finding an opaque one of suitable size, but filled with discarded wrapping paper, chicken bones, and miscellaneous other food items, Hugh had dumped out the contents, kept the bag, and closed the lid on the can. Placing his jacket in the bag, he could dodge suspicion as he walked down the street and, hopefully, forestall a trail of blood.

His dark-blue jacket. He had searched everywhere online for just the right jacket. It'd been perfect: lightweight, high-quality, fleece lining, medium-spread collar, zipper, front pockets, not too expensive. Then he had to search everywhere for a place to discard it.

Sitting at his desk, his pulse began to race as he relived the experience.

Carrying the jacket in a bag did relieve some of his dread. But very little. He could hear the sirens in the background, and it was obvious that a manhunt would be underway soon, if not already. He was carrying a bloody jacket. Where to ditch it?

A boat in the driveway of an unlit house caught his attention. He took a step in that direction, then quickly reversed. Would the police really overlook it given that someone's backyard-parked boat was the scene of one of America's most famous fugitive finds? For that was where one of the Boston marathon bombers had eluded SWAT teams. That is, until the homeowner searched the boat after the shelter-in-place was lifted, just before the police riddled it with bullets.

In another yard, a freshly planted sapling, with the shovel left alongside, set off a flight of fancy whereby he would unearth the tree, bury the bag, and replant the tree. Hugh recognized it for what it was: innovative, unworkable. Did he really think he could start digging in someone's front yard and not attract attention?

A more intriguing possibility showed itself in the form of a large RV parked in a driveway. It was covered totally by a tarp, not to mention individual wheel coverings. Given the care exerted to thoroughly protect it, it was unlikely to be in use soon. Even to prepare the RV for a trip, one would have to first take off the tarp.

Hugh got halfway to the RV, intent on jamming the plastic bag and jacket inside one of the wheel coverings, when he spotted the dog dish. It gave him pause. It didn't feel right. He reasoned that maybe the homeowner wouldn't notice anything amiss, such as a lump in a wheel covering. Maybe the police, searching for a murderer, not a bloody jacket, would only give the RV a momentary once-over. But was that dog going to ignore the smell of blood—or the lingering scent of chicken bones? Did he want to get tripped up by a dog?

Hugh trudged ahead, slowing his pace, wrestling for a block whether the RV was the best shot he would get. He was about to start back when fortune shined on him. And this time, it did feel right.

Throughout his measured flight from the DuPont residence, Hugh had been noticing something about the area houses. Almost all had their rain gutters lead to downspouts that, rather than open up on the ground near the base of the house, discharged into larger drainage pipes. It was a resourceful solution to the problem of rainwater or snowmelt seeping into the basement or weakening the foundation—a problem for homes in most areas, but particularly a concern in the rainy Pittsburgh area. Hugh had once read that Pittsburgh ranked fifth among large U.S. cities in terms of the most days with precipitation; over one hundred and fifty days out of the year it was either raining or snowing.

The larger drainage pipes offered some potential as a place to stuff the jacket until he could come back later and retrieve it and properly dispose of it. Hugh felt sure it was a unique solution, so unusual he was confident the police would overlook it.

Except neither of the two designs he was finding were ideal. In the first, the downspouts led to wide, flexible drainage tubes that lay on top of the ground, simply directing the water onto the lawn or driveway and away from the house. Such drainage pipes offered a three- or four-inch-diameter opening where he could stuff the jacket. This is, in some Pittsburgh communities where he had seen this system, including his parents'. But not here. Here the ends of the exit spouts tapered into an opening so narrow, so constricted, that it would be a challenge to shove a jacket in, sort of like squeezing a water balloon into a ketchup bottle. He would have an audience of neighbors before he finished.

The second style seemed promising only from the distance. Here the downspouts lead to a four-inch PVC tube that disappeared into the ground. However, as soon as Hugh got close, he could see that the space between the downspout and the drainage pipe was even narrower.

All this changed a block down from the property with the RV. Here, while the four-inch PVC again disappeared into the ground, Hugh could guess where it came out. On the left side of the property, near a privacy hedge of closely placed evergreen trees, lay a long, deep trench, filled with rocks. Hugh walked near and looked closely: the drainage pipe exited into the trench, the open end of the four-inch PVC pipe partially hidden by weeds.

It felt … right. A place that Hugh could stuff his jacket, out of the way, further hidden by the trees and the trench and tufts of weeds. And far enough from the house, and near enough the trees, that he could come back at a later time and retrieve it without detection. He already knew the weather forecast. After three days of steady rain, it now called for no rain for at least the next three days. And, with no lights on the house, the opportunity was too good to pass up. Hugh stuffed the jacket, still in the open bag, into the drainage pipe, pushing it far back in with his arm.

And now Hugh sat at his desk, and for the first time that morning, grinned.

When the lieutenant had brought up the jacket in the conference room, and the fact that they were looking in garbage cans and canvassing the area, Hugh had felt sure they were on the wrong track. Now, having reflected again on where he hid the jacket, he felt confident.

Hugh kept his eyes on his computer screen, hands on the keyboard, but it was a ruse for his co-workers: he was unable to focus on any work. Every word in the conference room, every gesture, was replaying. Mostly cringe-worthy. The oddest part had been Kelly badgering him to speak in a British accent. Now, this too brought some comfort. He couldn't imagine a scenario where they would find someone to verify that a Hugh Holiday could speak with such an accent. It was a new phenomenon, used only once in the Pittsburgh area. True, he used it on his trip, but witnesses to those brief encounters would be hard to track down. Like looking for a particular smallmouth bass in one of the Great Lakes.

The thought of his British accent now triggered a new concern. While in the conference room, his defense had been his stuttering, but he didn't want to lose the breakthrough that he'd had. The ease with which he went back to stuttering had been welcome; now it was discomforting. *What if I lost this ability to speak fluently?*

He tensed up with the thought. He wanted to say some words in the British accent, just to reassure himself. Even just to whisper them. But even a whisper might be overhead, especially now that everyone was hypersensitized to his presence.

In his head he could hear himself speaking with the accent, flawlessly. Of course, in his head he didn't even have any problems with the American accent. Even in his dreams he was fluent. What he needed to do was speak out loud. Which was exactly what he couldn't do now. He would have to wait until he got into his car.

I'll get it back, he told himself. *I have Holly to help me*.

Holly. The thought relaxed him. Yes, she would help him. She wouldn't be like his parents, who, since he was young, would correct him endlessly, demanding he stop and start over with every single verbal mistake. Correct him until he was messing up every word. Until finally his father, frustrated and disappointed, would lash out with some version of "Christ! What the hell is wrong with you? Can't you even speak!" His parents, determined to fix his every error, had him so focused on his speaking that he would freeze up at even the thought of talking. But now he would be fine. This time he had Holly.

Hugh was just starting to come out of his self-refection when things took another decided downturn. Bridgewater came to his cubicle, pulled up a chair, and politely asked Hugh how he was doing. Not getting much of a response, Bridgewater awkwardly broached his real purpose for approaching Hugh. The news that Faccon had called him. The news that the Bioscience Center wouldn't be able to use the medical college's services anymore. The odd request that Hugh wasn't to go there anymore.

Bridgewater said it almost apologetically. He tried to be upbeat, that he would find another facility until they could straighten this out.

But, as Bridgewater got up to leave, he turned and with wrinkled brow asked, "Hugh, do you ever speak with a British accent?"

Hugh had no trouble looking surprised as he shook his head.

Things did not get better after work when Hugh stopped on the way back to his parents' house to check on his apartment.

Chapter 14

The main and really only building of The MacArthur Medical College was an impressive structure. Situated in a largely residential area, its glass and steel and glazed, architectural terra-cotta construction soared above the nearby single-family homes. It was surrounded by spacious patches of grass, and tree-lined walkways, and a sizeable parking lot. While not as large as the major medical colleges, great care had been put into making this an aesthetically pleasing and functional structure. And adding to the building's unique appearance was the fact that it was composed of two interconnected but very different structures.

The East Wing was the older of the two edifices and the one that employed the glazed terra-cotta. It rose three floors above the ground and had a T-shaped design, with the top of the T farthest from the West Wing and paralleling a narrow side street, and the stem of the T connecting to the West Wing and paralleling a busier and wider, yet still two-lane street. It was in the East Wing, on the second and third floors, where most of the faculty had their offices. The administrative center of TMMC sat below, on the ground floor.

The architectural focal point of the East Wing was near its junction with the West Wing. Here a two-story, convex semicircle protruded from the bottom floors on the street side, taking up about one-third of the length of the T's main stem. Complete with an outside-pillared entranceway, this newer addition served as the primary entrance for the medical college.

To enter the East Wing, a visitor approaching from the street would use a walkway that, halfway to the building, circled a large fountain and gardens, before reaching the pillared entranceway and main doors. Once inside the building, within the semicircle made impressive by its high ceiling, the visitor would arrive to the welcoming desk and the security station.

However, it was West Wing that was by far TMMC's most architecturally attractive structure, a massive, brand new, steel and glass circular building known as the De Angelis Complex. This wing not only dwarfed the East Wing in square footage per floor but also ascended six floors above the ground and had a fully-functional basement level.

It was this De Angelis Complex—located to the left of the East Wing as viewed from the main street—that housed the principal areas for teaching and research. The very generous use of glass in the circular above-ground portion allowed one from the street level to see into the stacks of books and journals in the library on the second floor, the student lounge and cafeteria on the first floor, and several of the classrooms and small group rooms. The De Angelis Complex also included the college's research facilities, operating theatres, patient examination rooms, and large auditorium. The hallways that circled around the first three floors of the De Angelis Complex were connected by walkways to the three-floored academic and administrative offices of the East Wing.

TMMC's property took up an entire block, but most of that was its large, back parking lot. It was off this lot that was located the second main entrance into the medical college. Unlike the pillared public entranceway of the East Wing, this entrance was much less impressive: a private, key-card controlled entrance into the back of the De Angelis Complex and used by faculty, researchers, staff, and students who parked in the lot.

TMMC was brand new—the newest of the nine colleges of medicine in Pennsylvania. Like most medical colleges, TMMC had an accredited program leading to the Doctor of Medicine degree, the M.D., in contrast with osteopathic medical schools that awarded Doctor of Osteopathic Medicine degrees, the D.O. TMMC's own focus was on research and primary care.

If placed side-by-side with its nearest competitor, the University of Pittsburgh School of Medicine, TMMC would be like a four-year-old sapling next to a fully-grown giant sequoia. After all, Pitt Med enjoyed a reputation as one of the most prestigious medical colleges in the United States, with a history that traced to 1883. TMMC was so new that it was not even listed among the *US News & World Report*'s rankings of medical colleges.

But TMMC's founders, trustees, and financial backers were an optimistic bunch. They had watched the course of Geisinger Commonwealth School of Medicine, in Scranton, which had quickly gained in prestige after its founding in 2008. In their view, this TMMC sapling was destined to grow. And even now it was off to a great start, attracting top faculty and researchers, establishing key relationships with neighboring hospitals, and securing good residences for its graduates.

And like all allopathic medical colleges, getting into TMMC was already a difficult task: of about four thousand applicants, less than ten percent would get an interview and fewer than two percent would get accepted. Its new incoming class of about one hundred students—not an atypical first-year class size for schools in its size bracket—was considered to be its best yet.

That TMMC was on a path of quick growth was a fact attributed in no small part to one particular benefactor: Tony de Angelis.

It was for him that the De Angelis Complex was named, and when de Angelis put his name on something, he made sure it was top of the line. De Angelis controlled hundreds of businesses in various parts of western Pennsylvania, eastern

Ohio, and West Virginia. Some were small to medium-sized operations: used car lots, car parts stores, funeral homes, construction companies, recycling businesses, stone quarries, small motels, bars and restaurants. But he also owned large hotels, casinos, and racetracks.

There were open rumors for years that he ran less legitimate operations—that, with the support of the Bruno crime family in Philadelphia and the Five Families in New York City, he had reinvigorated the once all-but-vanquished Pittsburgh Crime Family, the western Pennsylvania faction of La Costa Nostra. But he'd never been charged with a crime, and if the rumors were true, then his operation was carefully run. Certainly, the rumors didn't prevent him from serving on many nonprofit boards and being a key financial mover to take this medical college from dream to reality.

Many of TMMC's faculty and researchers had also benefited in no small measure from de Angelis' generosity.

One of these was Dr. Michael Faccon.

Faccon grew up in Pittsburgh, and as such it would have been unusual had his life not in some way intersected that of de Angelis, simply given the breadth of the de Angelis empire. The first convergence had been Faccon's receiving a De Angelis Scholarship to help pay his way to New York University for his undergraduate studies. This was followed by a De Angelis Scholarship to assist with his medical school expenses at Yale. Some of his subsequent medical research at Temple University School of Medicine had been supported by foundations headed by de Angelis.

And now, having established an international reputation in research, teaching, and surgery, Faccon was considered a big get for TMMC, enticed there by de Angelis himself.

To describe Faccon as a handsome man would be an understatement. And he knew it. The grandson of immigrants from the Lombardy region of northern Italy, who had dropped the "i" at the end of the name on entering the United States, Faccon had heard himself referred to as tall, dark, and handsome. To this description, he would've added rich and brilliant; he wasn't unassuming by a long shot. His deep tan may have been attributed to the time he spent on the beach or on a yacht, but he had it all winter and it mostly was the product of the tanning bed he kept in his home. His hair wasn't as dark as his younger years, but he maintained just the right amount of gray to give himself a distinguished look, which he enhanced by his expensive, well-tailored clothes and the way he carried himself.

His full name was actually Michelangelo Prospero Faccon. And he liked the name. Still, he often introduced himself professionally to new people as Michael, downplaying his Italian heritage. For his scholarly publications, he typically just used initials for the first two names, and thus his full name was generally only known among close associates and those at TMMC. But it was clear that he relished the name "Michelangelo Prospero" being "discovered" by girlfriends, and students, and colleagues. Which was inevitably the case given that it was prominently displayed on manifold diplomas and awards, both in his office and home.

Unlike the majority of faculty, Faccon's own office wasn't located in the East Wing. Instead, it was on the ground floor of the De Angelis Complex, adjoining his private laboratory. The office and lab were on the outer rim of the complex, overlooking a rock garden and the back parking lot. Across the corridor, on the complex's inner rim, were additional laboratories, although not for Faccon's exclusive use.

Faccon's office was pretty much the furthest first-floor space from the East Wing. Immediately counterclockwise from his office, beyond some meeting rooms and small classrooms, the corridor rounded a gently curving bend, near the beginning of which was access to the loading dock, service elevator, and some janitorial and equipment spaces. It was on the outer rim of this bend that was located the Southwest Stairway, one of four sets of wide stairs in the De Angelis Complex. Each of the stairs provided foot access to the upper floors, where the second-floor library was the most popular feature, and to the basement, where the cadaver laboratory was the most notorious but least beloved feature.

Clockwise from Faccon's laboratory, the sights became progressively more interesting and well-traveled. There were classrooms and laboratories and small group rooms and another gently curving bend with the back entrance from the parking lot and a second set of stairs, the Northwest Stairway. Continuing clockwise from this bend, the corridor passed through an extensive lounge and cafeteria area, where faculty and students could pick up their morning coffee, check their mailboxes, watch some TV in one of the many comfortable chairs and sofas, or sit in one of the booths, chatting or reading. From the lounge, one could continue along the corridor until, just after the Northeast Stairway, one arrived at the corridor to the East Wing.

The fact that Faccon's office was located in the De Angelis Complex, rather than in an East Wing corridor, was part of his negotiations to join the faculty at TMMC: he wanted to be near where he taught and where the research facilities were located. And he wanted an easy walk from the back parking lot. The remoteness of his office and laboratory from Dr. DuPont's office was one of the reasons that Hugh had never encountered Faccon.

On this particular Monday, Faccon was in his office, not the laboratory. He was pacing. And irritated. Very much so.

Worried? Not in the least, because he had powerful connections that made worrying unnecessary. And because he trusted in his own brilliance. But he was annoyed by the incompetence he was finding from others he was forced to depend upon.

He'd been assured things would go smoothly. But they hadn't gone smoothly. And because his advice to get Holiday's DNA and spray it onto the crime scene had gone unheeded, rejected as overkill, this loose end continued to roam free.

That the murder of DuPont had to take place and quickly was obvious. She'd stumbled upon too much. Things that she didn't understand, but that she threatened to report to the authorities. When she had posed her concerns to Faccon on Saturday, his assurances that he would look into the matter and get it resolved only bought time until Monday morning.

There really was no resolution—beyond her not making it to Monday.

DuPont was too much of a public figure, too well known, too liked, and quite frankly too photogenic to just slip out of the public's notice quietly. The options were limited. There wasn't enough time to set up an out-of-town incident that would draw little attention, like a brake failure in her car, or a truck-car accident, or a botched robbery, because she wasn't traveling anywhere. No one would buy a drug overdose or heart attack in her case, so those were ruled out as implausible deaths that would attract scrutiny.

The quickest solution all agreed was a simple murder involving an appropriate and soon dead scapegoat, whereby the case could be tied up expeditiously. An easy endeavor with the help of those placed within the police department, the DA's office, the coroner himself. The public would buy it, the police would accept it as commonplace, the staff of TMMC wouldn't think twice.

And Faccon had some good candidates in mind. Particularly this oddball, this loner Holiday. Someone Faccon's network confirmed was due back in time.

But now it was obvious to Faccon that, in his concern to make the plan work, he'd put himself out too openly. Not just the phone call to Holiday and getting him to go to DuPont's home unwittingly. But also showing up when the police were in DuPont's office to promote a motive for Holiday. And then there was the planting of the message on DuPont's email account and lifting items from her office to plant in Holiday's apartment.

He had played his role excellently. It was the other guys that had to do their job and kill this Holiday guy. Until then, Faccon was exposed. The calling of Holiday's employer to stop him from coming around was but a stopgap.

Of course, if Holiday showed up at Faccon's house, looking for answers, that was another matter. Faccon would be pleased to take care of the "unbalanced intruder" himself.

Chapter 15

Hugh didn't try the British accent when he first got in his car in the office-building parking lot. He was too nervous he might be overheard. And he wanted the distraction of driving, to duplicate some of the experience from when he first acquired the accent.

He waited until he was almost halfway to his apartment. He'd considered forestalling until back at his parent's house, where Holly could be a comforting presence. But his anxiety grew and grew and finally got the better of him; he could wait no longer.

Consciously deepening his voice, he placed himself in character, smiling and tilting his head and imagining he was speaking to Holly outside of the British Parliament. Trying to talk himself into being confident, still he started tentatively, with the preceding "aye" sound he'd once employed. He followed this with, "Holly, have you had your vitamins."

Flawless. Relief flowed over him. He continued with, "You need your privacy? Then go to the garage." No problem. He hadn't lost his touch. He smiled.

Hugh arrived at the apartment in great spirits. He'd walked out of the interrogation with the lieutenant unscathed. He still had the promise of a fluent future.

Cautiously, and as quietly as the creaking floorboards allowed, he tiptoed up the front stairway. He slowly opened the door—only wide enough to allow him to stick his head through the crack. His makeshift warning, the small ball, a plaything for Holly, remained in place. He relaxed and entered.

Then he saw the other ball. The one placed at the back door. It was halfway across the room.

Clearly, someone had been in the apartment. Or was.

Frozen in place, Hugh listened. He couldn't hear anything. And from his limited vantage point, he couldn't see much amiss.

With two exceptions.

One was the kitchen light. It had most definitely been off before Hugh had departed the previous night. It was now on. The second was the doorway to his bedroom. Hugh was just as certain it had only been slightly ajar when he left. It was part of his security habit whenever he went out: He'd leave the living room lamp on and allow its illumination to show just slightly through the curtained bedroom window. The living room light was on. But the bedroom door was almost fully open.

He knew these two things were amiss just as surely as a beaver knows water is escaping through its dam, a vulture knows an animal is no longer alive. They were part of Hugh's timesaving ritual. Rather than distractedly leaving the apartment, and then reverse himself halfway down the stairs or on the street to check that the door is locked—and that the stove is off, the faucet is shut, the other door is locked, the lights are off—he had created a mental checklist. Each item would be checked once, in order, before he left the apartment. Point 7: bedroom door slightly ajar. Check. Point 8: all lights off except the living room light. Check.

The question for Hugh now wasn't whether someone had been in the apartment. Someone had been in the apartment. That much was clear. The question was whether someone was still here.

For five minutes Hugh stood immobile in the doorway. Listening. Watching.

He heard nothing. He saw nothing. He stayed fixed in place, listening for the tiniest sound. None came.

Slowly he inched forward toward the bedroom, his eyes fixed on the opening. Halfway across he suddenly bolted, forward not backward, toward the bedroom, slamming the door with his shoulder so hard it smacked against the wall, muscles tense and fists already swinging as he entered, intent on surprising the intruder with his speed, pummeling anyone there.

No one was there. The bedroom was empty. The bathroom as well.

Heart pumping, but with his worst fears allayed, Hugh went back to the living room and locked the door. He looked for anything out of order. He found nothing else.

Save for some footprints in the flour.

The flour had carefully and lightly been sprinkled on the kitchen floor by Hugh before he left the apartment. To a casual observer, nothing more than a normal kitchen spill. To a careful observer, remarkably devoid of any disturbance. Until now. Now it had vestiges of footprints. Large footprints. Two different-sized shoes, thought Hugh.

The implications of the break-in were intelligible enough. Whoever had been here didn't come this time to leave incriminating evidence. They were hunting for him, the loose end in their carefully executed plot. The missing puzzle piece. Perhaps held in as little regard as the horseshoe nail in the proverbial rhyme, "for want of a nail the shoe was lost." But they didn't want to get to the line "the kingdom was lost and all for the want of a horseshoe nail," with echoes of King Richard shouting "A horse! A horse! My kingdom for a horse."

Hugh double-checked the apartment and then he stepped out the back door. He grasped the wood railing. He lifted his foot. He smashed the windowpane above the doorknob. He then called 9-1-1 and reported a break-in.

He waited less than an hour for the police. Which was very surprising. He had expected a much longer wait. Hugh figured breaking and entering an empty apartment in Pittsburgh was as high on the priority list as having a car window broken and the GPS stolen—not very high. No policeman had even showed when his parents got their car broken into while parked on the street; they had to give their report by phone.

But, apparently, burglary was somewhat higher a priority than he imagined. Or it was a slow night. Because, to Hugh's relief, the police did show up. And even more promising, it was two that arrived, officers Eric Vasquez and Samantha Ward.

Hugh pointed out the broken glass, the footprints, his "rolling ball" warning system. The last drew only stares, while the "flour footprints" yielded only disinterest. Hugh acknowledged he wasn't sure what was taken, but the burglars must have taken some things he insisted. He asked the officers if they could take photos of the rooms, dust the doorknob for fingerprints, help him as he looked to see if any other things were missing.

The officers were willing to walk around the house with Hugh. The other things, not so much. Ward offhandedly remarked that there were some nine thousand burglaries and thefts a year in Pittsburgh, about twenty-five a day. Twenty-five a day. The implication of that statement wasn't lost on Hugh: Pittsburgh police had higher priorities than a burglary where nothing of note was taken.

Not what he had hoped for. His optimism at getting detailed notes on what was in his apartment—in case incriminating evidence later was planted—was being derailed before it even got underway. It was falling victim to the officers' indifference. They seemed willing to do little more than talk.

All that changed precisely a half-hour after Vasquez and Ward arrived.

It was at that time that another police officer made his entrance into the apartment, striding in with an "I-am-in-charge" attitude. Lieutenant J. P. Kelly.

Neither Vasquez nor Ward seemed surprised. Hugh was astonished.

The big man didn't say a single word to Hugh. Not even a nodded acknowledgement of his presence. He got a report from the two officers and then instructed them to go through the apartment thoroughly and take the requested photos. Vasquez took gloves out of a pouch on the back of his duty belt; Ward did the same but also removed a small camera from a side pouch. Kelly, still not acknowledging Hugh's presence, took a look at the broken glass in the kitchen and the flour footprints, and then ambled through the living room, stopping to familiarize himself with the books on the bookshelf, which were mostly small, paperback, sci-fi books and large softcover and hardcover college textbooks. He seemed immersed in thought.

He was, indeed, immersed in thought. Kelly knew the police were being played. He had suspected as much when he was alerted to the break-in at Holiday's and ordered Vasquez and Ward on the scene until he could get there. His onsite inspection reinforced his suspicion. The breaking of the glass pane looked amateurish; something Holiday probably did himself. The possible traces of footprints were so vague and diffused as to be worthless; probably Holiday's as well. There was even a piece of glass on top of a footprint. Nothing major known to be missing, despite the "burglary" not being interrupted. Nonsensical.

What is Holiday's endgame? he wondered. He can't be trying to protect himself in case one of his possessions shows up in the DuPont case, because this "break-in" is a day later. Is he trying to lay a foundation for saying evidence was planted, perhaps by the police, should something incriminating be found? Is this related to something new he has planned? Or, and this thought intrigued Kelly the minute it occurred to him, is Holiday being particularly clever: trying to undermine Kelly's case for a search warrant? A warrant that would have allowed the police to really turn the place inside out and seize his computer as well.

Kelly looked over at Holiday guiding Ward in the taking of photos of his apartment. Here was a golden opportunity to blindside the kid.

"Holiday. Did you get together that list of hotels you stayed at and places you visited?"

"N-n-no. N-no t-t..."

Kelly interrupted, "I need a specific list. Hotels, cities, parks, wherever you went."

Hugh shrugged.

"You must have some receipts here. Let's look in the drawers. We'll find some receipts."

Kelly directed Ward to search for receipts in the bedroom and sent Vasquez to the kitchen for the same purpose. He himself looked on the bookshelf and the coffee table, around the computer desk, in the waste basket.

Hugh was unruffled. He was as meticulous in getting rid of unneeded receipts as he was in keeping other things in order.

Kelly wasn't unruffled. The longer the three went without finding any receipts, the more he became red in the face.

He turned to Hugh. "Well, how about in your computer? Maybe we can find some records there. Or maybe your browser shows some hotels you searched. That should jog your memory."

None of it was a question, and Kelly didn't wait for a response. He parked himself in the seat in front of the computer.

It was already on. It had been on since the night before when Hugh had reformatted the hard drive, wiping its contents. Hugh had kept it on while waiting for the police in order to reinstall those programs and files that he didn't access directly from the cloud.

He had not reinstalled much.

For a few minutes, Kelly looked at the monitor, his brow furrowed, growing increasing nonplused by what he was finding. Or rather not finding. He called over Vasquez. Soon Vasquez was in the seat, and Kelly was looking over his shoulder. Now, they were both looking dumbfounded, whispering and shaking their heads.

"Holiday, what the hell is this? There's nothing here. No photos. No word documents. Barely anything. And all what is here has today's date. Did you get rid of everything?"

"I-I-I re-re-reformatted."

Kelly cocked his head and then slowly moved it side to side. He let out a slow breath.

Finally, with eyes the intensity of an owl spotting a field mouse, he looked at Hugh, and with a forceful tone dripping with exasperation, he said one word: "Why?"

"V-virus."

Kelly paused for a half minute. He looked at Hugh. Hugh looked at him. Vasquez looked at both.

Finally, with as much fake cheer and head bobbing as he could muster, now without any eye contact whatsoever, Kelly said: "Alright. I'll tell you what we'll do. We'll take this down to the station and our IT people can recover all your old files, and photos, and programs, and make sure there's no virus. It'll help you out and maybe we also can find something on that list that I need for my DuPont report." As he spoke, he was in the process of unplugging the computer.

"N-n-no," Hugh replied. With unexpected firmness.

"But you need your files. We'll help you recover them. Those IT guys can do miracles." Kelly motioned for Vasquez to continue the unplugging.

"N-n-no. I-I-I'm ok."

"Its alright. We don't mind helping you." Kelly motioned again to Vasquez, who had stopped to look at Hugh.

"Y-y-you c-c-can't can't ...um... take! N-n-no!" Hugh spoke forcefully, loudly, with an increasingly high pitch punctuating the air, drawing the attention of even Ward in the bedroom. Hugh moved over to the computer and started to re-plug everything, as Vasquez looked on.

Kelly's eyes flared. *Who did this jackass think he was talking to? He's just an idiot. Can't even talk right. And he thinks he can give me orders?*

But Kelly also knew he could go no further. If he took the computer without permission, anything turned up from now on would get thrown out of court. Holiday had played him. Effectively. The only thing Kelly had gotten from this encounter was more conviction that Hugh was guilty.

When Kelly finally responded, he didn't repress his choler.

"Listen, son. You can play this game about the stuttering. But, eventually we'll find someone who's heard you speak in a British accent. We'll find evidence of that. There are already a lot of nails in your coffin. That will be the last one, the one that nails the coffin shut."

At first, the look of Hugh's shocked face confused Kelly. He didn't expect that strong of a reaction. Soon it dawned that talking about a coffin might seem insensitive to someone so recently parentless. Not that Kelly felt any blame on his part; no, it was the kid's incessant stammering. But he realized the need to smooth his remarks with different imagery, not for Hugh's sake, but for that of Ward and Vasquez.

"Look, Holiday. I gave you a chance to come clean. You didn't take it. I recommend that you do come clean. You're slipping between the raindrops right now, thinking you're escaping getting wet. But a thunderstorm is coming and you're not going to stay dry. It is just a matter of time."

Kelly then called Vasquez and Ward, and they all left together.

Hugh didn't stay much longer himself. He packed up some belongings and drove back to his parents' home. There he was greeted by Holly, who, despite the daylong wait, was as cheerful and enthusiastic as always, either unaware of her master's darkly reflective mood or playing her role of comforting presence. Hugh fed Holly in the backyard and sat on the bench in the gathering darkness of early evening.

For a while, Hugh felt despair starting to envelop him. It nibbled at the edges of his mind, his thoughts growing more and more pessimistic. The dispiritedness didn't last long. An image of Dr. DuPont's prone body brought up a new emotion: anger. Anger about being considered such a patsy that he was set up to take a murder rap. Anger about the bullying from Kelly. Anger that no one was going to solve the murder of Dr. DuPont as long as they were focused on him.

And as the anger grew stronger, he refocused. His next step crystalized.

Hugh went back into the house and filled a box with more supplies, put them in the trunk of his car, and headed out with Holly. It was already 8:30pm. He made a few stops at stores on the outskirts of the city before stopping at a hotel.

He hadn't called ahead, nor even scoured the Internet for a hotel. Actually, he never called ahead and rarely browsed online for a hotel. His strategy was always to just drive until finding one that felt right. One that fit his particular needs.

As usual, Hugh's checking into the hotel involved agreeing to pay for the room in cash, with extra handed over as an advance for incidentals.

Never his debit card—he had seen enough warnings about using a debit card in a hotel, because the money was taken out right away, sometimes way too much, and it could take weeks before the money for incidentals was reversed. Not good for someone living paycheck to paycheck. Not to mention the risk of someone stealing his number and emptying his bank account.

And only rarely would his sole credit card leave his wallet. Hugh was new to the credit card business, having been denied throughout his college years. But he also didn't appreciate the system of late fees and the temptation to create debt. He used his credit card only when absolutely necessary. Like the hotel he stayed at once that wanted a hundred and fifty dollars just as the deposit for incidentals, and he hadn't been to an ATM in a while. But even when he used his credit card as an imprint for the room or for incidentals, the card wouldn't be charged; Hugh would pay everything with cash.

The poor man's tax. That's what Hugh termed the overdraft charges a bank would impose on bounced checks and overdrafted debit cards—and the interest people would pay on credit card charges they always expected to pay "next month" but never could. Rich people didn't have these problems. Their money multiplied in banks. People like him just ended up just paying fees and overdrafts to support credit card companies and banks. And so, other than the rental car, and a few automatic withdrawals, he was a pay-as-you-go, cash kind of guy. Gas, hotels, restaurants.

Good luck to those who stole credit card and debit card numbers. And good luck to Kelly in finding where he had stayed during his trip.

After checking in, Hugh went back to the car and took out his special, bowling-ball-type bag with air holes. Holly knew right away what to do: go into the bag and be absolutely quiet. No barking allowed in the bag. Do not move or give away your presence when in the bag. This is the training that Hugh initially did so he could take Holly on the bus to the park. But it also worked well for staying at hotels that didn't allow dogs.

****

It was past 10:30pm when Hugh left the hotel. The drive back into the city took Hugh about twenty minutes. Although Pittsburgh lacked a beltway, it had a pretty good and extensive system of highways, and nighttime was a particularly good time to travel. At least in the springtime before the summer construction got underway.

Still, for Hugh it could have gone quicker. Not because he was worried about arriving late. Because it gave him too much time to think. He didn't need time to think. Not about what was coming next—that he was going to have to play by ear; there were too many variables. So instead, he started down the path of thinking about how badly things had gone in just the past twenty-four hours. And from that starting point, he somehow drifted back to much more distant memories. More than half a lifetime ago.

Back to fourth grade, sitting in his combo chair-desk, school book on the laminate top. Isolated from all the other kids in the schoolroom. And not just emotionally. Physically. They were all gathered in a circle in the middle of the classroom, each taking time in turn to read. Hugh sat detached, secluded outside the circle, alone and near the window.

The teacher said it was because he was continually bothering the other kids: touching their pencils, bumping into their arms, making annoying sounds. Perhaps he was. He was a pretty active kid. But no more so than the other boys in the class. And yet, he was the one the other kids openly complained about. To each other. To their teachers. To their parents. Until finally the teacher said if he couldn't control himself, he would just have to sit by himself.

It went on for one week, then another, then another. Every morning he came to the classroom to find his chair separated from the others.

And this was his good part of the school day. At least relative to the lunchroom, where he would eat alone, or the playground, where he would spend recess alone. When the boys selected teams for dodgeball, or kickball, or whiffle ball, Hugh would stand around apprehensively until he didn't get selected, and then go off to play on his own.

He was fortunate that his dad taught him the game of marbles, so he could have some way of looking engaged in something interesting. Of course, if his dad had been observant, or patient enough to talk to Hugh, he would have discovered that Hugh would never come home with new marbles. Sometimes with less marbles, as they were taken, but no one was playing with him. By fourth grade, he already knew not to get in a fight to keep his marbles: the other boys would always make up stories about him to the teacher. With his big size he could win a fight now and then, and if the teachers let things run their course, he might have gained some grudging respect. But the teachers never stayed out, and he never won those arguments.

It was by playing marbles, however, that he almost made a friend. A girl in his class, Ellen, came up to him one day to ask Hugh what he was doing. She played marbles with him all recess. Perhaps she was fighting with the other girls. Perhaps she just felt sorry for him. But it was one of the happiest days of his elementary school years.

There was one other day that almost qualified. It was Valentine's Day, a day that Hugh had learned to loathe, given how rarely the cards and candy came his way. But on this particular day, Ellen shyly came to his desk when no one was looking and put a Valentine's Day heart candy on his desk that had written on it "LOL." Lot of love or laugh out loud, it didn't' matter. Hugh was in heaven all day.

Then, at the end of the day, Ellen sheepishly approached him, as other girls looked on, and said, "I hope you didn't take that candy seriously. My mom said that I had to do it."

Hug shook off his self-pitying foray down memories' backroads. *I need to be upbeat, focused. I still have one major thing to get done tonight.*

Chapter 16

Hugh studied the three medical school students from across the room. He had anticipated he might find some students in this particular bar. After all, it catered to a younger crowd and was near the TMMC campus close to where most students resided. And students would be seeking some way to deal with the shocking murder of one of their professors. Still, it was a Monday night and late, already 11pm, and med students had notoriously tough schedules. So it was with relief that he saw the three students sitting together. And given what he was about to do, he was equally buoyed that they seemed buzzed.

His actual hope had been to find one student alone: it'd be less intimidating. But the three clung together, one petite woman and two guys. From catching bits of their conversation, he began to form an opinion of them. All three appeared to be Americans. The woman, thin and perhaps five feet three inches tall, sported somewhat of a Boston accent. She was probably a first-year student, since she on the table in front of her was a textbook on anatomy, a typical first-year subject in med school. She also seemed to have some anxiety about her courses, as she maneuvered most conversations back to her studies, characteristically touching her short-cropped brown hair when she interjected herself.

The young man seated on her right, who wore glasses and was thin and quite tall—at least six feet three inches—seemed to have a South Jersey or Philadelphia accent, as best Hugh could tell. It was similar to what he'd hear when his family would vacation on the Jersey shore or visit Philly. He seemed the most reserved of the three in the conversation, but emanating quiet confidence.

The other man was seated on the girl's left. He was by far the most loquacious of the lot, but in an entertaining and carefree manner. Nearly equal in height to his bespectacled colleague, he differed in body shape. He was rotund and with an unathletic build; his peer was rangy and looked like he could be a tennis player. Despite dominating the conversation, and the source of the diversions that led the girl continually to redirect, the accent of the more rotund fellow was hard to place. The best Hugh could do was figure out where his accent was not from: it was not that of a Yinzer or native of the Pittsburgh area; and it was not from the south; and it lacked strong accents that he would hear of native New Yorkers or Bostonians.

For Hugh, the two details he had sought he had ascertained: Americans and TMMC students. Well, maybe a third: they had been drinking for some time.

Now that the opportunity was there for Hugh, he felt some inertia in putting his plan into place. His apprehension wasn't because they would later identify him as Hugh Holiday with the fake British accent. Hugh had taken effort to disguise his appearance with items procured from his parents' home and a stop at Walmart on the way to the hotel: his dad's tinted wire-rim glasses, of low enough magnification for him to see; a subtle and temporary tattoo showing through the top of his shirt and another on his forearm near his wrist; and a fake but pretty authentic looking mustache he had spent quite a bit of money on as a teenager to prepare for a Halloween party he never attended. He wore his father's steel gray fedora. He felt suitably unrecognizable.

No, Hugh's unease traced to the fact that these were medical students. And thus, unquestionably bright. One didn't get into medical school without passing through a rigorous selection process; only a few made the grade, as he well knew. If there had been just one student, he stood a better chance. Three? He might well be embarrassingly exposed as a fraud.

And thus the one advantage he was counting on. The third detail. That they had been drinking for some time. How much they had imbibed, how dulled their senses were, Hugh could only guess. Clearly they were nowhere near the "three sheets to the wind" level. This colorful expression Hugh knew to be nautically derived: It traced to having three of the sheet ropes that control a ship's sail be loose and fluttering in the wind, and the ship thus floundering uncontrolled. None of the three fit that definition. In fact, it was pretty clear to Hugh that they weren't even two sheets to the wind.

But probably at least one sheet to the wind. And, if this advantage proved illusionary, if they alertly exposed him as a fraud, with a fake accent and fake tattoos and fake mustache, then he would have to laugh it off as someone just having fun in a bar. Hopefully, if that were the case, they weren't unfamiliar with the common pastime of men in bars: inflating themselves and pretending to be something they weren't.

Hugh told himself one more time that he had to go all out. Nothing to lose. Back against the wall. You only live once. Enough is enough. All the reinforcing phrases he could think to psych himself up. And finally, it was "time for the show to begin." And with that, he broke through the inertia and actually got up. Heart pounding, but moving forward. Showtime.

Hugh wandered slowly by the table with the three students until he heard a distinct reference to their medical studies.

"Blimey. Fellow medical students?" Hugh intoned. Strongly accented. Silky smooth. Slow and measured. Deep voice. Flawless.

"You a medical student too?" said the cheery, more rotund man. He pushed out a chair to Hugh, with a welcoming have-a-seat gesture.

"Well, not in the States," said Hugh, taking the seat and putting his beer on the table. "I go to King's College London School of Medicine. You know, across the pond."

"Really? What are you doing here in Pittsburgh?" asked the woman.

"Came with a professor who is presenting research results to some blokes at the University of Pittsburgh. How about you? Do you go to Pittsburgh Medical School?"

"No," the woman replied. "TMMC. You know, MacArthur. The MacArthur Medical College."

"Oh, of course. I was reading about one of your professors who died on the weekend. A French name…. DuPont?"

The woman winced. "We were just talking about her. She was so wonderful. It's really shocking."

There was a moment of silence. Hugh stayed quiet to see where it would lead. It didn't lead anywhere. Soon, the rotund student changed the topic. Unfortunately, Hugh thought, back to him.

"What year are you in King's College?"

"Second. Just my second."

"Ah, like the two of us," said the rotund fellow, gesturing toward the other man.

"Yeah, but we do things quite a bit different than you here in the States. We enter med school right after secondary school, not from university. Still a long ways to go." Everything Hugh knew he learned surfing on the Internet. He had never even been to England.

"And already you're doing research? Just in your second year? That seems a bit unusual," said the lanky student. Rather sharply, Hugh thought. Maybe not even one sheet to the wind for that one.

"True. Normally students might not get a chance to do serious research until their elective period. You know, during the clinical time near the end of their fourth or fifth year." Hugh was straining to remember what he knew about the British system. Which wasn't much. "I just got the opportunity to do research last summer, during our break, and then a little during the year to assist the professor."

"And you got to come here with the professor," the lanky student pressed.

"Well, I paid my own way! We're on a break this week." Hugh was feeling uncomfortable now. If he didn't know all that much about the British system, he knew next to nothing about **King's College London School of Medicine.** Did the lanky fellow suspect?

"Bejesus! This chair is a bit wonky," Hugh suddenly added, looking down at his not-so-wobbly chair, and then exchanging it for one at the near table.

The cheery fellow broke the seriousness with a big smile. "I'm Peter, by the way. This is Josh. And this is Emily."

Hugh took a stab with an opening line he had used with sporadic success during his trip. "Nice to meet you. My name is Bond, James Bond."

The students laughed. Even the lanky one. Maybe they were all at least one sheet to the wind.

"Well, then I am changing my name to Ms. Moneypenny," giggled Emily. "Although I won't have a penny left after all these med school loans."

"Well, I for one am doubting you're 007," Peter with a mock serious squint. "After all, you showed up with a beer, instead of a martini, shaken not stirred." All three students laughed. Yes, at least one sheet to the wind.

"Well, it actually Philip Shuttlesworth." He gestured to the girl. "Are you also a second-year student?"

"Just Peter and Josh," Emily offered. "I'm first-year. But we should all be studying, of course," she added with a reserved laugh.

"By the way," said Hugh. "There is one professor at your college who was the main author on a research paper I came across. A Michael Faccon. Do any of you work with him?"

"Ah yes, Michelangelo," chortled Peter, as Emily and Josh laughed at his pretentious sounding pronunciation.

"No. Not working with him. And thankfully so," said Josh, as the others nodded. "But every student has him the first year. He's head instructor and a professor of surgery—head of the department, actually. And so we all had him for anatomy class. Right, Em?" he added with a twinkle and nod toward Emily.

"Yes, he introduced me to Billy Bob," she said, as the two men laughed loudly, more so than Hugh had heard them previously. It was obviously some kind of inside joke.

"Billy Bob?" Hugh looked intrigued.

"Yes, Billy Bob. That was the name I gave my cadaver. I don't know what you do in England, but here in our first year…"

"At TMMC, the very first *day* of instruction!" interjected Peter.

"Yes," continued Emily, opening her eyes wide for effect, "our first day, they introduce us in anatomy class to our very own cadaver, who we are to dissect throughout the year. They didn't tell us much, just the cause of death and age. So I gave a name to my fellow: 'Billy Bob.' We didn't get to see the faces until much later in the course…"

"They keep them covered in a white knit sock," added Peter.

"Yes. At any rate, when I finally got to see the face, I was shocked how much he actually ended up looking like Billy Bob Thorton. I thought I was dissecting a movie star." The students laughed again, joined this time by Hugh.

"Actually," continued Emily, "I couldn't sleep the whole night after getting my cadaver. First day and we already had to make our first cuts. Between the smell and peeling back the skin, I nearly retched." She seemed to recoil as if relieving the experience. "I couldn't eat for two days. I called it the Billy Bob Diet."

She paused. "I still get a gag reflex. I'm worried that I will be 'that girl.' You know, the one everyone is pointing at throughout medical school and saying, 'That's her! She's the one who vomited in the body of her cadaver!'"

"You're already doing better than some," added Josh with a comforting smile. "In our class, one student left the room the first day and we never saw him again." He looked at Hugh. "This is a rite of passage in the United States."

Hugh nodded knowingly. He had absolutely no idea what they did in England.

Peter saved him from trying to explain what they did in England. "I was told about a case at another school where an instructor had willed his body to the medical school. The students got him for dissection."

Awkward pause. Hugh felt like any minute they would direct the conversation to what he did. When would a British med student get their cadaver? They start as an undergraduate not as a graduate. It seemed like a pretty basic point for him not to know.

Peter broke the silence. "You know, they didn't like us naming the cadavers. You were supposed to be 'more respectful.' Heard of one kid who got booted out for taking a goofy selfie with his cadaver." The students exchanged knowing nods. "But, if I had named mine, it would have been Ernest Hemingway. He seemed to have lived a very full life. He had everything. Cirrhosis of the liver, no doubt from drinking. Emphysema, probably from smoking. Quite a bit of fat, so if he wasn't rich, his food probably was. He had a tattoo. He had some scars that looked like from knife wounds or shrapnel. He had a wound that looked like he had been shot. He also had quite a chiseled face and pretty strong looking arms; quite tanned also. Probably attracted women like Hemingway. At any rate, in the end he died from congestive heart failure, not the way Hemingway went out."

Josh nodded and added, looking at Hugh, "A lot of schools in the U.S. are moving toward professionally pre-cut body parts and virtual cadavers. You know, with 3-D imaging technology."

"Yeah, but not TMMC," added Josh.

"And so this dreaded *rite of passage* continues here in Surgery 203," chimed in Emily, with a shake of her head.

There was a lull in the conversation. A lull where Hugh knew he was expected to now tell his experience in England. His training with a cadaver. Whether England was moving toward computer simulations.

But he couldn't tell them anything about the situation in England. Nor Australia. Nor even Canada. They probably knew more than he knew. He moved the topic to his real interest.

"What's this Mr. Faccon like?" Hugh had read that surgeons in England were referred to as Mr., not Dr. He had no idea if what he read was accurate.

"Dr. Faccon is brilliant," said Emily, gently correcting Hugh's use of Mr. "Great lecturer. A reputation as a top surgeon."

She paused. Then spoke in hushed tones. "He sometimes isn't terribly dependable. He expects you to show up on time. Blasted me one time for walking in five minutes late, and I had an emergency. But he can be late or even cancel classes at the last minute or not even show up to the lab." Some bitterness showed in her tone.

"What his problem? Have ankle-bitters that he has to get home to."

Emily laughed, although she had no idea why. The other two looked at him in puzzlement.

"You know. Children."

"No, no children," said Josh. "Just ex-wives. He's a real playboy. Quite a reputation."

"But those women probably don't see the side of him that we do," added Emily. "He can be really arrogant, even toward the other instructors when we're doing surgery on the cadavers. And these are people who also have a M.D. just like him."

"Sounds like a real arse. A shirty kind of guy" added Hugh, trying to find some appropriate British slang.

"Fact is, he is an arrogant SOB," said Josh. He looked around. Apparently satisfied that he didn't see any other professors, or heaven forbid, Faccon himself, he continued. And with some disdain, as if he had a personal bad experience. "He thinks he's the smartest man on earth in every single area. Histology—the expert on human cells. Disease diagnosis—number one in the world. OB/GYN—knows women's bodies better than even a woman doctor. Pharmacology—he's the world's expert on drugs."

"Doesn't hurt that he's a consultant to big drug companies," added Peter, his jovial nature not coming through in the discussion of Faccon.

"How so?" said Hugh.

"He's a consultant to Big Pharma," replied Josh. "Gives speeches at their events. Serves on some boards. That is why I think he is gone so much—he is traveling to meet with drug company execs. Travels to New York and Boston. Last week Em had a class cancelled because Dr. Faccon traveled to New Jersey, where a lot of the big pharmaceutical companies are based."

"He does bring in a lot of pharmaceutical industry money to TMMC," added Peter.

"Anyway. He may actually be an expert on drugs and their impact on the human body," added Josh. "But I never heard him brag about biochemistry. That was Dr. DuPont's area, and I think he knew he didn't hold a candle to her."

With the mention of Dr. DuPont, the students became quiet. They stared down at their drinks. Josh slowly drank his beer.

Emily broke the silence.

"I heard from some of the doctoral students who work with Dr. Faccon that he's a real bear to work with. Hot temper. Gets angry if they touch anything of his or, heaven forbid, show up late at night to the lab unannounced. Sends them right out. Some are very bitter that they ended up working with him."

"Well, let's put it this way," said Peter, who started to smile broadly, and then spoke perhaps louder than he intended. "If he died and willed his body to the medical college, I wouldn't want to cut into him." He paused for effect. "But that's only because I sure as *hell* don't like waiting in *real ... long ... lines.*"

The three students laughed. But it seemed bittersweet. Hugh thought he could detect a cloud of memory of a different professor passing over Josh and Emily's faces.

Hugh decided to press onward.

"Why doesn't he let students work in the laboratory late at night?" Hugh started to say "lab," but then substituted the full version. He found the British "laboratory," pronounced so differently from American English, had a wonderfully exotic feel to it given how the term sometimes stuck out in science fiction movies.

"I guess he's a control freak. Certainly is with respect to his own research," said Josh. "A lot of it he doesn't even share with the students. He has one lab that is attached to his office and where only he works. It's possible, I guess, that he is afraid someone will steal his ideas. Research can be very competitive, and I guess he's quite innovative. At any rate, he's certainly protective of his research. Every time I walk pass his lab, the shade is down. I pity the poor guys that have to walk on egg shells around him."

"You know something else?" added Emily, looking around as she spoke. Satisfied, she continued, "He's quite the sexist." Her voice seemed to rise, tinged with indignity. And genuine,

Hugh thought. "Tells the women they shouldn't go into surgery, just be pediatricians, or anesthesiologists or some other profession where having a baby won't interfere."

"Wow. I am godsmacked. The guy sounds to me like he's all mouth and no trousers."

This time, not even Emily laughed. He caught the looks of confusion on their faces. "You know, boastful." Hugh knew it wasn't quite a segue from Emily's remarks. The slang had occurred to him a topic or two late.

"To be honest, he walks the talk," replied Peter. "The guy is justifiably brilliant. Lots of publications. Great lecturer. His surgery instruction is top notch."

"Does he also do surgery in area hospitals?" probed Hugh.

"Rarely," replied Peter. "At least according to the third and fourth year students I've talked to."

"And he doesn't always even show the surgery for my anatomy class," chimed in Emily.

"Yeah, for us it was the same," said Josh. "He often would have professors at another medical school, some experts in the technique, show us a spinal surgery or brain surgery that they were doing for their classes. They would use a wearable computer with camera and monitor and simply do a real time broadcast to us."

"Interesting" said Hugh.

Peter added, "When Dr. Faccon did his own classroom surgeries he often used Google Glass, so that we could all watch even if not looking over his shoulder. We could review it over and over before we would do our own surgeries on the cadaver."

"Add *tech* to the areas he considers himself the world's expert," intoned Josh with a shake of his head.

"*Michelangelo*," Emily laughed, "spent some time in going over with me about how to use a wearable computer. I thought he might be hitting on me." She laughed again. "At any rate, it is pretty neat. He showed me how to pull up patient information, get medical info or a consult, everything while doing the surgery. All hands free, just on voice commands. Of course, we don't have that for our cadavers, since we don't have any patient information."

"It might come in handy in our third and fourth year. You know, when we are getting experience in hospitals," noted Peter.

"Glass?" said Hugh. "Aren't there privacy issues? Confidential patient data and the like? You know, uploaded to the Cloud?" He no sooner said it then he worried that he had stepped too far from his assumed role as a medical student. Shouldn't he know all this? But the others didn't seem to notice.

"Nah. There is special software so no privacy stuff about the patient gets out."

"Do you have something online from your anatomy class? Could I see something? We don't use that in my anatomy class." Another misstep, Hugh realized. Should he be taking anatomy? Would he then have a cadaver? No one seemed to pick up on it.

"Sure," said Emily. "Let me pull up a snippet from last week's surgery." She took out her iPad and started to hold it out across the table for Hugh to see. He instead got up and moved around behind her, so he could not only see, but also use her earphones to hear.

Hugh looked at the surgery, but didn't really see it. He was concentrating on the voice. He asked for it to be made a little louder.

It was very clear. It was the same voice that he'd heard on the phone on Sunday. He put down the earphone and nodded thanks. There was a moment of silence.

"You want another drink? I'll treat." said Peter.

Time to go, thought Hugh. Before they probe into his nonexistent experience in medical school. Hell, his nonexistent knowledge of England.

"No. I don't want to get legless. I'm off to see a man about a dog." He paused and translated again, "You know, I'm excusing myself. Nice having a chin wag with you. Goin' to head out, mates."

Chapter 17

After another fitful night, this one in a hotel room, Hugh drove with Holly to his apartment, arriving just as the sun was breaking the horizon. He wasn't surprised with what he found: someone had been there the night before. This time, he wasn't as troubled by the incursion. In fact, he was counting on it happening at least one more time.

Hugh let Holly roam freely. She was excited, running into and out of the rooms. Perhaps it was being back in familiar surroundings. But Hugh suspected something else: that she was picking up new smells from the trek of policemen and intruders over the past two days. Or maybe old smells, if last night's visitors had been the same as the ones who had locked Holly in the bathroom two nights ago.

It often slipped his mind, yet he knew the dog had a remarkable sense of smell. Probably all dogs, he guessed. How much more acute than humans? One thousand times? Ten thousand times? One hundred thousand times? Hugh had heard all kinds of estimates for the top breeds. That if it were vision, it would be comparable to his seeing something a football field away that a dog could see just as clearly from New York City to Miami.

Holly's own ability had been indelibly displayed to Hugh just the previous summer, during a weekend stay at a cabin. When Hugh disposed of some leftover chicken bones in the woods, he had walked a somewhat circuitous path before finding the right spot. When he later walked out of the cabin with Holly, Hugh watched with amazement as Holly followed the exact same route Hugh had taken.

Hugh was grateful that either the police hadn't tried to use tracking dogs to follow his trail and find his jacket or that the attempt failed. Probably it just wasn't possible given all the variables: The confusing scent from policemen running around looking for him with crime scene blood on their clothes; the fact that the police didn't know right away who they were looking for and thus no timely sample of clothing; the city environment with its myriad of smells; the trail-masking oily mess of chicken bones and other food that had been in the plastic bag he used to stuff his jacket.

And not one of these was even the most glaring complication. The most glaring complication was the fact that he wasn't the actual perpetrator. Someone else or somebodies else left the bloody crime scene before he got there. And they probably went to a car. Good luck with using a tracking dog with that murder.

At any rate, the police clearly hadn't found his jacket. That was evident by the very fact that he was still a free man.

Hugh called Holly and she came right away. He scratched her for a minute, trying to calm her down. Which failed, but he had to move on to the task he'd come to do: installing a Cloud-based recording system using the webcam connected to his desktop computer. Equipped with a motion sensor, this would give him continuous live video once someone started moving around his apartment. Since it would record to the Cloud as well, he could view it at his convenience. And he could activate the system to get a live feed at any time, regardless of motion. From now on, his laptop, his phone, his tablet would be all the tools he would need to find out who was entering his apartment and ideally pick up any conversation as well.

Hugh's next stop was his neighbor's house to drop Holly off. The neighbor was friendly, as always. But curious.

"Where've you been staying, Hugh? I'd been looking for you. I brought you some dessert, but you didn't seem to be around."

The question caught Hugh off-guard, but he smiled broadly and asked what kind of dessert. "Well, it's gone now," said the neighbor. Hugh explained where he had been. Staying at his parents' house. Doing some work on the property.

And then he drove to his parents' place to do some work. And here, too, Hugh could see signs of an intruder. Again, he had anticipated as much. He'd even parked some distance away and watched the house before entering.

Still, the invasion was disconcerting. His apartment, his parent's home—now his home—they were supposed to be safe places, refuges from the outside world. Now he had less anxiety outside. He would do what he came to do as fast as he could. He wouldn't spend an extra minute in the house.

It took him about twenty minutes. He set about installing a wireless security system similar to that at his apartment, although this time using a complete bundle purchased late the previous night from Walmart. Like the webcam system, the wireless camera was motion activated and could be remotely triggered at any time for viewing. The system would do live video streaming and offered automatic recording. No sound, but maybe he could see what his hunters looked like so he wouldn't be caught unaware walking outside one day.

And then it was off to work. Uneventful, try-to-make-oneself-look-busy work. Because there was still no replacement lab to analyze the samples, Hugh spent most of the time reorganizing his files and familiarizing himself with the reports prepared in his absence. The rest of the time he spent checking on the monitors in the apartment and house. As yet, nothing to see.

Hugh stayed in the office until he was the last staff member left. Even after Bridgewater left, he stayed. Hugh remained because of a growing fear of losing his job. Three weeks of missing work. Followed by the police interrogating him in the office. Followed by Faccon canceling TMMC's agreement with the Bioscience Center. Hugh wanted to make himself look busy. Indispensable.

But he wasn't either of those. Especially indispensable. The reports done when he was gone were crafted by Bridgewater himself. And they were competent. Probably a strain on Bridgewater's time, and the shortcuts and haste showed through. But they were good enough.

For the Bioscience Center, Hugh was replaceable. For Hugh, the job wasn't replaceable. He couldn't afford to lose it. It had been hard enough finding this one.

Twenty minutes after he finally left, Hugh's concern was no longer about being replaced. It was about being placed—six feet under.

Chapter 18

By the time Hugh left the office, the parking lot was largely empty. Even before he pulled out, his thoughts were locked on his next stratagem: to find out where Faccon lived and his schedule. Then perhaps Hugh would be able to find a way into Faccon's house and maybe, just maybe, he would be lucky enough to find something that let him know what was going on.

But he hadn't been able to find out where Faccon lived. His address wasn't listed anywhere he could see. It would be the height of folly to call TMMC to inquire about a home address given his two options: a stuttering American accent tied to a murder suspect, a British accent tied to a murder suspect. And breaking into the secure TMMC computer system—well, that just wasn't part of his repertoire, no matter how simple it might be for an experienced hacker. And so, he decided on the next best thing for a man with plenty of time: he'd wait for Faccon to leave the office and follow him to his home. That is, after picking up Holly.

Hugh was still lost in thought when a GetGo gas station on his right entered his consciousness, triggering two other nearly simultaneous thoughts: the non-functioning gas gauge; a decision to pull in for gas. The latter of which wasn't easy. He was in the left of the two westbound lanes; the gas station entrance was almost on top of him. But he solved the dilemma by abruptly veering from the left to the right lane, and then breaking to turn into the gas station entrance. All remarkably accomplished without the use of a turn signal ever entering his consciousness.

Which had a number of consequences beyond his simply getting gas. For one, a car already in the right lane, and nearly in the space Hugh intended to occupy, had to brake suddenly to avoid a collision. And the car behind Hugh decided to brake from the suddenness of the maneuver. And then the slowing of those two cars, and their lit brake lights, set off a chain reaction of slowing cars and lit brake lights. All followed by a cacophony of blowing horns.

Hugh was immediately aware of what he had done. He glanced in the rearview mirror. He could see some cars still stopped from the chair reaction, some turned at odd angles, and one car, a midnight-blue sedan five cars back, had, judging from its forty-five degree angle to traffic, elected to swerve all the way from its original lane, to the right lane, to near the curb, where by good fortune there weren't any parked cars at the time, but where it still managed to block the right lane.

Hugh quickly raised his right hand to indicate he was sorry to the inconvenienced drivers. The gesture wasn't interpreted as such. More blowing horns.

Pulling safely into the gas station, Hugh was chastised, but relieved. Chastised by the other drivers, relieved that he didn't seem to have caused any actual accidents. He probably added to someone's repertoire of conversations about bad drivers, but at least not to the repertoire of police reports about bad drivers. A bonus given that he wasn't even sure his parents had maintained the registration and insurance on this car.

Hugh filled up and clicked the trip odometer to record his mileage. With the nonfunctioning gas gauge, it was the only way he had to track when he needed gas. The car had a large, eighteen-gallon tank and got twenty-five miles per gallon in highway driving, eighteen in city driving. That meant he could get anywhere from three hundred and twenty miles to four hundred and fifty miles on a full tank. But it was an imprecise science. What if he sat in rush hour traffic, or was hitting every red light? So, Hugh always tried to fill it up before it got to three hundred miles.

Which would have been fine. Except the last time he got gas, when he left his parents' house the morning after the DuPont murder, he was short on cash and only put in seven dollars' worth. And thus the sudden realization, the absent-minded maneuver.

Inside the GetGo, Hugh grabbed a quick chicken sub and was soon on his way. Exiting the station, he was much more careful in looking at traffic than when he entered. As if to signal to any who had witnessed his earlier maneuver, "See, I am a careful driver."

Surprisingly, there was at least one witness. As he nosed out into the right lane, Hugh saw the same midnight-blue sedan, the one that had swerved so dramatically. Now parked at the curb, only at this moment was it preparing to ease back into traffic. Hugh wondered just how shaken up the driver had been. Or whether Hugh had so irritated the two drivers in the front seat that they were planning to do some road rage thing with him. Which didn't make sense. Not really. He had been at the gas station. They could have just driven into the station and given him a piece of their minds. Apparently, a coincidence of timing.

For the next block and the one after that, Hugh combined taking bites out of the chicken sandwich with glances in his rearview mirror. The midnight-blue sedan was still there, staying several cars behind. He made a left and took Forbes Avenue, now going north. The midnight-blue sedan turned as well. He turned onto Schenley Drive, drove through Schenley Park, and then re-entered Forbes Avenue. A scenic detour. Not a popular route, and not exactly a shortcut, but not completely unusual. The midnight-blue sedan followed.

Hugh turned onto a cobblestone road. This was an unusual route. This wasn't one of downtown's smooth cobblestones. This was one of the East End's cobblestones. And nobody goes down one of these unless necessary or they lived along one. Certainly not as a minor shortcut. Too jarring on the passengers, too jarring on the car. At fifteen miles per hour one felt like the car's muffler would come off. At thirty miles per hour, one figured the muffler was now off and one's dental fillings were in the process of joining it.

The midnight-blue sedan continued to shadow him down the cobblestone road. It did not stop at a house.

The sedan kept its distance. But there were no cars now separating it from Hugh's and even with the distance, even with the sedan's tinted front window, Hugh thought he could discern something of the men's faces. A hard look. A serious look. An unnerving look. As if they were intending this to be his last day on the sunny side of the ground.

The cobblestone road ended and Hugh reached a main street, a four-lane road, with two southbound lanes and two northbound lanes. Hugh turned right, in the southbound direction. The midnight-blue sedan made the same right. It stayed well back.

Hugh wiped his brow and became conscious that he was sweating. And more. The chicken sandwich picked this time to decide it didn't like being in the acidic pond into which it had found itself and tried to leap out, upsetting his stomach and burning his throat as if, in a panic, it were scratching its way out with acid-tinged claws. He felt sympathy for its plight but wished it would just crawl back into its watery grave.

And then Hugh's right leg began to feel weak and started shaking. This later effect was by far the more troubling of his reactions: it made it hard to control the car pedals. The leg started shaking so much that Hugh used his left leg momentarily on the brake when he had caught himself drifting into the lane with oncoming traffic as he fixated on looking in the rearview mirror.

That he might be giving himself away with his glances in the mirror, and the cobblestone road detour, and the circuitous route, and now the erratic driving, was not lost on Hugh. Yet, the two men kept their distance. He felt he understood their objective. To find out where he was headed. Where he stayed at night. Quite possibly to pick him up if he stopped.

So Hugh didn't stop. He remained on the four-lane, with plenty of traffic, plenty of potential witnesses, but driving aimlessly, trying to figure out what to do. Which was an accomplishment in its own right, since a feeling of lightheadedness had joined his other symptoms. Twice he felt completely disoriented and as if there were a fan running near his ears. The chest-clamping vice was in full return. His body seemed to sink into the car seat.

Hugh took a deep breath to calm himself. Then another. Then a third. He couldn't drive forever. He hadn't made any totally illogical driving moves as yet. His route could be seen as a way to drive around congested city traffic. Even the cobblestone road could be seen as a shortcut. Maybe just direction from the disembodied voice of his phone.

But if he kept going the way he was, he was going to run out of populated real estate soon, and then he'd be vulnerable. And at some point there would be no doubt in these men's minds that they had been made and then they'd lose patience. They would get tired of the cat and mouse game and move onto the next stage. Maybe even a staged accident to get him stopped.

Hugh continued on the four-lane road, in the right of the two southbound lanes. Only one car separated Hugh from the midnight-blue sedan. But its driver had a tendency to weave back and forth. Distracted? Maybe impatient? The motive for the driver was the farthest thing from Hugh's mind. But his actions did allow Hugh occasional side-mirror glimpses of the two men in the midnight-blue sedan. Both were large men, with rough features. Hugh wondered if they were the men who had been in his apartment.

Hugh neared an intersection with a two-lane, two-way street and slowed as the traffic light turned yellow. He put on his right turn signal. And abruptly turned from the right lane into the left, cutting off an SUV in the left lane that was slowing for the red light. Hugh was partly stuck out in the intersection, but not enough to block traffic. His second "bad driver" maneuver since he left the office, this one intentional. The driver of the midnight-blue sedan squeezed behind the SUV into the left lane as well.

The light had no dedicated left-turn signal. Drivers in the left lane, like in any city, had two choices: either go straight or, if they wanted to turn left, wait for oncoming traffic to clear. And with the line of oncoming cars, the wait would be a while before traffic cleared enough to turn. And then Hugh would go through the intersection and the midnight-blue sedan would go through the intersection and they would be back where they started.

Except this wasn't any city. This was Pittsburgh.

Shortly before the light turned green, Hugh put on his left-turn signal and flashed his lights. The front drivers in the opposing traffic flashed their lights in return. And, as the red light turned to green, Hugh made what is known as the "Pittsburgh Left."

Technically illegal. Sometimes a confusing annoyance or even unanticipated danger to out-of-town pedestrians crossing the street. But practical in that it helped the overall flow of traffic through an intersection. Hugh turned left and proceeded just ahead of the now slowly advancing opposing traffic that, with Pittsburgh courtesy, let Hugh through.

But the Pittsburgh Left involved politeness to a point. Only the first car got this special privilege. Only Hugh's. Not the midnight-blue sedan. With the SUV proceeding slowly through the intersection, and the heavy traffic closing quickly behind Hugh's car, the midnight-blue sedan had to wait for the intersection to clear. And it was a long wait.

Hugh didn't see his pursuers the rest of the drive. He took side streets, drove through a couple of red lights, and made a right turn on red where a right turn on red was prohibited. All in all, plenty of bad driver maneuvers. But he reached his destination, which was two blocks from his apartment, on a parallel street. He then walked through the backyard of a house on that street to get to where Holly was.

Hugh was apologetic for not being able to spend much time with the neighbor. Who, in turn, was surprised to see Hugh head out through his backyard, as opposed to going to the apartment or directly to the street.

Hugh then drove to the airport and picked up a rental car.

His final shopping stop that evening was to find a place that sold plastic shade devices for car windows.

Chapter 19

Two quiet streets bordered the far side of the TMMC parking lot. One was a narrow, two-way street that traveled east-west, paralleling the back of the medical college. The other was a narrow, one-way, southbound street nearest the De Angelis Complex. Characteristic of the neighborhood, opposite the streets were mostly single-family homes, generally two-story, many now converted into apartments rented by med students. Some had been purchased by rich parents for their son or daughter to use while attending med school and to be rented out afterwards or sold to the next set of rich parents.

It was near the intersection of these two quiet streets, on the left side of the one-way going south, that Hugh parked. With the TMMC parking lot an open one, surrounded only by a border of grass and small shrubs and an occasional slender tree or well-placed boulder, this proved a convenient setting for Hugh to see most of the lot and the entrance to the De Angelis Complex.

Hugh was in his new rental car. A compact, two-door Ford Focus. Great on gas mileage, not a car that would stand out from other cars. And that latter feature meant that the car wouldn't draw attention from those in the nearby houses and apartments. Nor those driving by. Nor, especially, those who might look out of a window from the Complex.

But if curious eyes wandered in his direction, they likely wouldn't find much anyway to attract interest. For one, it was now dark outside, and the Focus was dark blue. And it was parked in a long line of cars, most more interesting than a compact, two-door, dark-blue, Ford Focus. To this, one could add the fact that the car's side windows were now obscured by the newly purchased, suction-cup-affixed shade devices.

There was still the matter of Hugh's stocky, six-foot two-inch frame. But he slouched down in the driver's seat as best as possible and had the foresight to wear dark clothing. He was mainly at risk of inviting attention when sitting upright to look carefully at activity in the parking lot. Especially when he held up the binoculars he had brought. But, they too were dark. And palm-sized. And used sparingly.

There was one main obstacle to his desire for invisibility. Holly. Eyes are naturally drawn to the sight of a dog in the passenger seat of a car, especially a cute dog, and Holly was both cute and visible through the front window. The only other occupant that might have attracted more attention would have been a statuesque blonde in the passenger seat. People who might normally have immediately diverted their eyes should they come across a man generally feel no such compulsion to do so should it be a pretty girl.

But Holly was able to do something that a statuesque blonde couldn't do, and that was curl up peacefully on a blanket on the seat. And this Holly did, satisfied by the occasional scratching behind her head that Hugh offered. As it turned out, few people walked down the street. None seemed to pay any attention to the car and its two occupants.

When Hugh had first arrived at 8pm, he had been sure he was too late: There were less than twenty cars still in the parking lot, and some of those likely belonged to security and maintenance staff or maybe a medical student studying in the library. But one car stood out from all the others. The sight of it filled Hugh with optimism: it looked like a car Faccon would own. A Jaguar XKR-S **coupé.** A sleek luxury model with seating for two, an eye-arresting French racing blue color. Parked under one of the lot's pole lights, it stood out like a powerful horse alone on a wind-blown, ocean beach. Or maybe like the big cat itself, up close and personal. Hair raising, pulse quickening. It probably carried a sticker price of over one hundred and thirty thousand dollars. Not exactly what one would expect for security, or maintenance staff, or a medical student.

Hugh watched as people left the building, got in their cars, and drove out of the parking lot. None were Faccon. The Jaguar remained.

Hugh glanced at Holly, envious of the dog for its carefree existence, wishful that he could join Holly in sleeping without a concern in the world.

But Hugh stayed watchful. And he figured he wouldn't have slept regardless. It wasn't how he was wired. His mind dwelled on an Irish proverb he had run across when he briefly toyed with the idea of using an Irish accent: "By nature five hours, by custom seven, by laziness nine, and by wickedness eleven." It suited his lifestyle. From his late teenage years he had realized he just didn't need as much sleep as most others. If he slept four or five hours, he was fine. Great, really. More sleep didn't make any difference; if anything, he felt groggy and less alive.

What it meant, he wasn't sure. Hugh knew that some geniuses slept a lot, claiming it helped their creativity. Einstein, for one, liked to sleep ten hours a night, and even eleven if working on a difficult new concept. And then there were those studies that reported correlations between sleeping seven or eight hours a night and good health.

On the other hand, there were the habits of Thomas Edison and his rival in inventions, the "mad scientist" Nikola Tesla. Edison would boast that he slept no more than four hours a night— fitting for the man whose invention, the light bulb, kept people up at night. Tesla, ever the competitor, claimed an even greater feat, that he slept only two hours a night; although, like Edison, he conceded to taking naps. Edison and Tesla weren't only widely productive but both also lived long lives into their mid-eighties.

Hugh had eventually turned to bioscience for the possible explanation. He guessed that he probably was in that small proportion—one percent? three percent? —who had a genetic mutation where they were truly short sleepers and could do fine on less than five hours of sleep. Maybe science in the future would identify the DNA sequence and then some biotech firm would market it and future "designer kids" would all be going on a few hours of sleep. Whatever the reason, it was coming in handy this week.

Hugh watched as a car drove into the lot and parked. Three students emerged. They walked up to the back entrance leading into the De Angelis Complex. One swiped his ID card in front of the scanner installed in the vestibule between the outside set of glass doors and the inner set. The three entered.

Hugh longed to be one of those students, studying to be a doctor. Perhaps they were headed to the library or maybe visiting the student lounge for a break.

The students had no sooner entered when Hugh saw Faccon leave the Complex through the same back entrance. He moved at a brisk pace across the parking lot and got into the Jaguar. Within seconds, the Jaguar was moving.

An easy car to follow, thought Hugh. Even at a distance, its characteristic form stood out. And at night its distinctive and bright headlights, some form of high-intensity discharge lamps, set it apart from most other cars.

It wasn't an easy car to follow. Its distinctive shape and headlights did help it to stand out. And had it stayed in the city, it might have been easy to keep in sight. That certainly was the case for the first ten minutes. But Hugh had assumed that Faccon would live in one of the better neighborhoods in the East End, rather than in one of the enclaves outside of the city. To his surprise, the Jaguar was soon turning onto the approach ramp to Interstate 376.

And this was the problem with keeping it in sight. The Jaguar was ridiculously fast. This feature wasn't unexpected. While waiting for Faccon, Hugh had used his phone to access data on the model. A 550 horsepower engine with supercharged, 5 liter V8 engine. Top speed of one hundred and eighty-six miles per hour. From zero to sixty in just 4.2 seconds.

And apparently Faccon wasn't afraid to use that engine, traveling well above a hundred miles per hour on the interstate. Faccon seemed to have no trepidation about being pulled over for speeding despite his prominent position in society. Like a politician or Steelers football player, he would make the papers being ticketed at such a speed. Something gave Faccon confidence there were no radar traps on his route, or that he wouldn't be stopped if there were.

Hugh had no such confidence. *It would be just my luck*, he thought. *If Faccon is pulled over, he'd probably tell them he's off to a medical emergency and they'd let him go. Me? I would probably find Kelly joining the police who pulled me over.*

Hugh was grateful he wasn't following the Jaguar in his fourteen-year-old Taurus. It would have been like a puppy chasing a horse. But even following in this rental car seemed hopeless. He actually had no idea how fast the Jaguar was traveling, it was so rapidly putting distance between itself and Hugh's Focus. Only once was it impeded in its progress, when blocked by slower moving cars occupying all three lanes. As it rode close on the tail of the leftmost car and then the one in the center lane and then back to the leftmost car, Hugh closed the gap considerably. But, finally the leftmost car moved far enough ahead that Faccon squeezed through. Soon, the Jaguar was so far ahead that only the bright headlamps were giving it away.

Then those headlights veered to the right and disappeared from sight.

And with that Hugh's plan for the evening was undone.

Hugh hadn't driven a whole lot in his life. That hadn't stopped him from forming a theory about driving in the Pittsburgh area, a theory that he figured it held true about ninety-nine percent of the time. He had just needed tonight to fall into that ninety-nine percentile. It hadn't.

His theory—ill-formed at best, fallacious at worse— was that speeding drivers on the highway rarely gained much advantage from their speed. Maybe at times they shaved off enough precious seconds to arrive in time to witness a childbirth or get to the bank before it closed. But most times he figured speeding was "much ado about nothing." He had watched speeding cars weave in and out of traffic or fly through a red light only to end up gaining but seconds or even end up stopped at the next intersection. Sometimes they squeezed into a lane that ended up moving slower.

One time during his trip, he had been passed on a straight stretch of highway by a red SUV that seemed in no small amount of hurry. It had blasted by him on the left but then alternatively moved from left lane to right to left in the heavy traffic, riding on the bumper of any car going too slow for its comfort and at one point forcing its way into the front of a tight line of cars passing a truck. And all this despite the fact that the traffic, even crowded, had been moving near the speed limit. About ten minutes later, as Hugh reached the top of a hill, he spotted the red SUV again far in the distance, climbing the next hill, still weaving in and out. Hugh had counted the seconds to the top of that hill. Thirty seconds. The driver had gained thirty seconds to that point. Maybe thirty seconds was a big deal if being pursued by a saber-toothed tiger or trying to spear prey for food. But to get to a zoo or restaurant thirty seconds early? It seemed hardly worth it given the time probably lost somewhere else during the trip—at a rest stop or gas station—or paid for in annoyance with every obstructing car in the left lane that slowed one down.

But the one time Hugh needed this theory to bear fruit, it had failed. Speeding had paid off for Faccon, He was out of sight.

Hugh reached the exit almost a minute later—seemingly an eternity for a Focus following a Jaguar XKR-S coupé. While he hadn't much hope of picking up the scent of the Jaguar, he would see where the road led and then head back to his hotel.

The Jaguar was dead ahead. At the end of the long, slightly curved exit ramp, one hundred yards away, at a stop sign. It was just now making a right onto a four-lane road.

Perhaps delayed by a car in front of it that had only hesitantly merged into traffic? Possibly waiting itself for traffic to clear on the four-lane? Must be the former, Hugh deduced. Zero to sixty in 4.2 seconds. A supercharged, 5 liter, V8, 550 horsepower engine. Top speed of one hundred and eighty-six miles per hour. Merging was not a problem. And yet, all that, and still not out of sight. Only one hundred yards.

Hugh reached the end of the exit road and looked to his right. And again, there sat the Jaguar, turning left at an intersection, its four tailpipes adding to its iconic look. Zero to sixty in 4.2 seconds, but even Faccon had to wait for oncoming traffic to clear.

Although the four-lane was busy, with several cars moving through the intersection, both sides of this section of highway appeared uninhabited. There were no streetlights or houses visible for as far as Hugh could see. The left side was completely dark, a solid wall of trees, illuminated here and there by the headlights of passing cars. The right side had more open area, less trees, but still only one building. This was situated right at the intersection, where one might have expected a road to be placed had it been a four-way intersection. But it was a three-way, not a four-way. The only secondary road was to the left, opposite the building. It was the road Faccon had gone down.

Hugh waited for a break in traffic and pulled into the four-lane. As he approached the intersection, he found that the building on the right was an auto body shop. No lights were on; it was closed for the night. In fact, the only illumination, save the headlights of passing cars, was the signal light, which remained a steady green. Hugh speculated from the many cars traveling this section that there would be housing developments ahead and shops behind. Or vice versa. But this immediate area was dark and desolate.

When Hugh reached the intersection, he realized both why the signal light remained green on the four-lane and why the left side was so dark. The road to the left lead into a park, and there was a sign that announced: Park closes at dusk. Faccon had driven into a closed park.

Hugh sat at the intersection in the left turning lane, where the Jaguar had been minutes before. Not just waiting for cars to clear, but figuring out his next step. If this is the only road leading in and out of the park, he couldn't follow unnoticed. And another thought bothered him: *Did Faccon know he was being followed? Did he see me while I was sitting outside TMMC? Did he deliberately lead me to this closed park?*

Hugh swung to the left, but only to make a U-turn past the park entrance, continuing on the four-lane, now in the opposite direction. It was a long stretch before he had the opportunity to do another U-turn and double back. He had been right about one thing: there was a strip mall ahead, including a busy restaurant and an open pharmacy.

On his return trip, he pulled into the auto body shop, parking next to some cars left for repair. He turned off his lights, gave Holly a gentle scratch and reassuring words, and then checked Google maps on his phone. He soon found what he was looking for. Across the intersection was indeed the park's sole entrance and exit. Which left him in a quandary regarding his next move. Proceed cautiously on foot into the park? Wait for Faccon to exit?

As he sat and watched the cars, Hugh noticed a white Ford Taurus move into the intersection. The light bar on top indicated it was a police car; the black and gold stripe and the words "City of Pittsburgh" trumpeted that it was with the Pittsburgh police force. Which ... was odd. For sure they were outside the Pittsburgh jurisdiction.

Even more unusual was to see the police car make a left into the park.

Hugh waited a few more minutes. Then he poured some water from a bottle into Holly's bowl, turned off his phone, and quietly left the car. The night had a bit of chill and slight breeze. But it was silent. Other than the traffic speeding by, the only noise was the sound of car locks engaging as he used the remote. He would go into the park by foot.

He had nearly moved beyond the cover of the cars in the lot when another vehicle pulled into the left turning lane at the intersection and then made the left into the park. It was a red Bentley Continental GT.

Hugh was astonished. *A Bentley and a Jaguar? What is going on in the park, a surgeon's convention?*

Chapter 20

The park road was narrow, but paved. Hugh dashed through the intersection to this road as soon as he saw a break in the cars on the four-lane and none coming off the interstate exit ramp. He continued to jog until he was out of sight from the highway. Then he stopped.

He was enveloped in darkness. It was nearly pitch black. While the sky was mostly clear of clouds, and the stars were out, the moon was but a crescent, three days past the new moon. And this sliver of Earth's satellite was setting in the western sky, barely above the tree line. Where Hugh stood, there were no streetlights, no lights from car headlamps, no artificial illumination of any kind. Just stars, and the moon, and a covering of woods.

And it was quiet. Behind him, the sound of cars on the highway provided a reminder that he wasn't in a rural area. But otherwise the night was still, with the sound of every step, every chirping cricket, every occasional breeze through the leaves magnified.

Hugh hugged the right side of the park road as he walked, placing himself in position to be able to quickly enter the woods should yet another car join the procession. But he also stayed clear of the road's shoulder, because it was near impossible to see what lay ahead of him. The last thing he wanted was to step on a branch or stumble over a rock, announcing his presence. As it was, he was able to quietly and somewhat quickly advance, concerned only that his footsteps, light though they were, clashed with the night sounds. He was comforted by the fact that the darkness and stillness of the night would provide him ample warning when he got close to whatever was happening.

Hugh's swift progress ended little more than seventy-five yards from the highway, just around a bend in the road. He didn't see it until he was nearly on top of it. The darkness and stillness had not provided ample warning because there had been no light, no sound ahead. Just a car. A car with its engine and lights off.

Hugh sucked in his breath and froze. From the outline of a light-bar on top, it was evident he had stumbled upon the police car. It was blocking the road.

He listened. Not daring to turn his head, his eyes combed the darkness. Unable to clearly discern much of anything beyond vague forms, his imagination worked its own magic. Like a child alone in a bedroom at night seeing a monster in discarded clothes on a chair, Hugh conjured up an image of a policeman sitting in the driver's seat and of one resting on the back bumper.

He waited silently for a warning voice to break the quiet. None came.

As his mind calmed, he realized he couldn't detect anyone in or near the car. It appeared that the car was unoccupied, a simple tool to block the entrance to the park. Although out of its jurisdiction, no one planning to use the park as a lovers' lane, or drug drop-off point, would stop to question the presence of a Pittsburgh police car in their way.

Hugh moved cautiously past the vehicle. He could now hear faint voices further up the road. He picked up his pace, the sound of tennis shoes meeting pavement not drowned out in the quiet night, but the voices sounding quite far ahead.

But they weren't that far. As he rounded a right bend in the road, he could see lights through the trees ahead. He slowed. Another fifty feet further and the scene became clear.

Two cars and three figures were in a parking lot ahead on his left, separated from the road by some sparse woods around which the road apparently circled to reach the lot. The car engines were off, or at least remarkably quiet. But the cars' parking lights were on, providing the only illumination, save for the starlight and waxing moon, which now was nearly hidden behind towering trees.

Two of the men stood. The third was seated on the hood of the Bentley. One of the standing men was in a police uniform and held an oblong object. Hugh deduced it was a switched-off flashlight. The other standing man was Faccon, evident from his posture, although he was so far away, and in relative darkness, that Hugh couldn't clearly discern the features of his face. The third man seemed to be of shorter stature, any other distinguishing feature obscured by the night. Hugh silently cursed himself for having left his binoculars in the Focus.

He crouched down. He was going to have to get closer. Not for the visuals. For the conversation. It was animated, but not loud enough for him to make out what was being said, other than an occasional word spoken loudly for emphasis or in apparent anger.

Still crouching, Hugh placed his left hand on the ground for balance and twisted his upper body so he could look behind, in the opposite direction from the parked cars. Near the forest floor was a solid wall of trees and shrubs. He couldn't see into the forest more than a few feet. Only higher up, where the stars twinkled through openings in the canopy, could he delineate any outlines. With the woods as his background, he reasoned that the three men couldn't see him even if they looked directly at him. There could be a four-hundred-pound black bear standing ten feet away and he wouldn't see it. Or a hundred-and-fifty-pound white-tailed deer twenty feet away even if moving. Sound was his only drawback.

Hugh rose and crept down the road, with slow and measured steps. He wouldn't see a tree branch until he stepped on one, but so far the paved road had been devoid of anything noisy. He just had to keep from stepping off the pavement, where surely there would be twigs and branches. But such total darkness meant that he had no guarantee he wouldn't wander off the park road.

While behind him the woods were impenetrable to the eye, there were two areas where he had some visibility. One was the light forest directly between himself and the three men, where the cars' parking lights filtered through the woods. Perhaps no more so than a campfire would provide, but enough that Hugh could see that the trees and brushes between the three men and himself were sparse. He could make out the three men even if they couldn't see him.

The other area was the space created by the road itself. While the trees hugged the road on either side, their canopy didn't cover the road. As a result, the area cleared for the road was evident from looking up at the stars. Hugh could deduce that the road angled tantalizing close to the three men before continuing on past them, and probably then, he surmised, jutting sharply to the left and into the parking lot. If he could get another hundred feet up the road, he might well be close enough to make out at least some of the conversation.

Hugh kept his eyes down, peering at the road as he crept ahead, concerned about some noisy obstacle in his path. He strained his ears to hear, trying to piece together the rare bits of conversation he could make out. Words like "retarded," "jackass," and "fix it!" Occasionally more choice words broke the silence. At one point, he swore he heard his name, "Holiday," and he glanced to his left.

Something was wrong. He sensed it before he could figure out what it was. He could only see two men, both standing. But neither was the policeman. He couldn't see the policeman. He looked at the cars. No third man. He moved a little farther up the road, in case trees were blocking his line of sight to the third man. No third man. He closed his eyes, gentle massaged them and then opened them and tried again. He squinted. Only two men.

A light went on to his right. The policeman had switched his flashlight on. He was headed out of the parking lot. Headed toward the bend in the road ahead that would lead straight to Hugh.

Hugh instinctively moved to his left to find cover among the trees and brushes off the side of the road. Five steps towards the woods, he realized his mistake. If the two men in the parking lot looked toward the departing policemen, Hugh would be silhouetted by the policeman with the flashlight. Likewise if the policeman glanced back at the two men with their parking lights.

Hugh now quickly moved to his right, feeling with his feet for the side of the pavement. When he found the edge, he looked up. The policeman had already rounded the bend and was moving directly towards him. Still two hundred feet away, but the flashlight beam was directed a good thirty or forty feet ahead of him. He was moving at a quick pace.

Hugh inched off the road cautiously, each step barely in front of its predecessor. The voices of the two men had seemed to lower and the night was again very quiet. Hugh needed to make it to the trees or a bush on the side of the road. But he sensed the danger of his breaking twigs, or branches, or crunching dry leaves. Still, he had to get in farther.

The ground on the side of the road sloped down at a strong angle. Hugh stumbled but caught himself. It was a drainage ditch prepared for storm water runoff. Hugh got down on his hands and knees and crawled into the trench, relieved that he didn't trample any noisy twigs, or branches, or dry leaves. He laid face down and lifted the collar of his dark blue polo shirt over his neck. His pants were dark, his socks dark. He would have to risk that the policeman wouldn't notice him.

Hugh closed his eyes and tried to focus on slowing his breathing— not an easy task given that he was in a near state of panic. He told himself, "you're invisible, you're invisible, you're invisible," not believing a word of it.

A new concern took over, that he might sneeze or cough. The thought of it brought an irritation in his throat, a need to cough, to clear his throat. The irritation grew to a nearly overpowering need to cough. He tried not to focus on it, but it began to dominate him. The policeman was now but fifty feet away. Hugh could hear his footsteps and sense the light that must be nearby. The cough was in his throat.

The officer walked by.

Hugh didn't dare to look up at all until it was very quiet save some muted footsteps. When he did, when he twisted his neck to look behind him, he could see the light a hundred and fifty feet past him. He stayed in the trench until the light was gone and more.

Then Hugh coughed. Twice. Softly but deliberately, seeking release for the thought that had preoccupied him.

Hugh was already out of the ditch when he heard behind him the distant closing of a car door and the turning on of a car engine. He renewed his aim for the place where the road seemed to come close to the two remaining men. He picked up his pace considerably. If he saw lights from a car, or heard a wailing engine, he would get well off the road this time. But for now, he needed to hear the conversation.

And soon he could, as the men began speaking louder and more passionate.

He was familiar with Faccon's voice. He hadn't heard the mystery man's voice. But it was the first one he understood clearly, even before he got to the closest location. It was very deep and the voice of an angry man. Measured tones.

Authoritative. But angry. And loud. Hugh found he could now piece together the conversation, patching words together into intelligent sentences, his mind here and there effortlessly filling in spaces that were inaudible or muffled.

"No, professor. Again. I could *not* disagree more! If Scott picked him up for questioning and then disappeared him, we'd end up with Kelly on our tracks."

"But, if...." interjected Faccon.

"Too many people, *too many*, notice police cars and policemen," continued the deep voice. "And Kelly has his eyes on this Holiday. We have to stick with our plan B. It'll work."

A pause. Then Faccon spoke again. He, too, had gained in volume. "You know... I *really* don't understand how you haven't gotten him in two days now. What are your men doing?" It was an accusation, not a question. That fact wasn't lost on the mystery voice.

"Look. We all underestimated Holiday. You, too. He ain't done nothing like we expected. But listen, professor. Make no doubt about it. We *will* get him. And soon. He may not be staying in his apartment or the house, but he's still showing up for work. Everything's on track."

"Maybe Holiday was underestimated. I'll grant you that." Faccon was speaking fast, each word tumbling rapid fire upon its predecessor. "But I wonder if I'm not *overestimating* you and your crew. I stuck myself out setting everything up for you. Can't you get rid of one small problem? How incompetent ..." Faccon trailed off. Hugh could see him slowly shaking his head. The intent was clear. Even from where Hugh sat, he could hear the judgmental tones in Faccon's words and he knew that "are you" was the unfinished phrase.

There was a pause, where the two men looked at each other.

"You know, professor," the mystery man said with a still-measured tone, "your *arrogance* knows no bounds for a guy we had to bail out. Don't ever forget your own incompetence. For

God's sakes, checking your *email* while doing a surgery? No doubt messaging some smoking hot young thing. If not for us, you'd've lost your license. Don't ever forget that."

Another pause.

The mystery voice continued. "And you also screwed this up in the first place. Don't forget… "

"I didn't' screw it up," Faccon interrupted with the air of absolute defiance. "It was a complete quirk. One overzealous first-year student sticking his nose where he shouldn't have. A one-in-a-million anomaly. With DuPont dead, the problem was taken care of…. That is, if you'd taken care of Holiday."

"Look," the voice was calming now, as if trying to defuse the tension, or show authority through restraint, "I just said, I've a top professional coming in now. This's his expertise. The Holiday problem, it'll be solved soon. Very soon. As for Scott, I don't want him too much in the loop. He just needs to be our eyes and ears on the inside now."

"Well, it *better* get solved right away." Faccon's voice was still tinged with annoyance. "And I'm not anxious for this shipment to come in on Thursday and still have this loose end running around."

"Listen, as I said, except for this, everything's been going great. You got your money. The Five Families are pleased. They got their product. They're being educated. Philly is happy. Boston is happy…"

"Of course! Just make sure Holiday is taken care of. I can do my part."

"No worries, professor. Seriously. No worries. Just be ready Thursday evening…And remember, no phone calls like you did last Saturday. Nothing that people can listen in on or get. If you need to meet me again, use the usual method."

Faccon nodded.

"We okay?" the mystery voice asked.

And with that, Faccon nodded again, gave a brief wave of his hand, and got into the Jaguar.

Almost before Hugh had time to react, he saw that the Jaguar's bright headlights were on and Faccon was barreling out of the parking lot and up the park road. Fast. Very fast. Hugh ran to his right and tumbled down the slope to the ditch, landing on his side, face up toward the road. This time twigs snapped, and he came to rest on a dry branch in the ditch, one that pinched his side and threatened to break with a loud crack. He hoped that the revving of the Jaguar's rapidly accelerating engine would cover the noise.

He needn't have worried. When he next looked up from the ditch, after the sound of the Jaguar was far in the distance, he could see that the Bentley driver was on his phone, his back turned to Hugh. He was pacing as he spoke. Hugh debated his next option. *Do I wait for him to leave? Do I hightail it out of here now?*

He hightailed it out of there. Each time he looked back, the mystery man remained on his phone, oblivious to Hugh's presence in the park.

When Hugh made it to four-lane road, he didn't wait for a break when there were no cars, but ran across the intersection in full sight of some vehicles. Only when he reached the front door of his car did he suddenly corkscrew about, wondering if the police car might still be around. It wasn't.

Holly greeted Hugh with great affection. She obviously expected now to get out for a walk. But that wasn't to be the case. Hugh had her lie on the seat. He started the engine and pulled out to the four-lane. He kept his eyes peeled on the park road. No lights were coming. Then, when there was a break in the traffic, he pulled out to his right and drove a hundred feet up the road and made a U-turn and pulled off to the side.

And he waited for the Bentley.

He had to wait only about ten minutes.

Following the Bentley proved much easier than the Jaguar. The mystery man kept barely above the speed limit. The few cars on I-376 and subsequent streets allowed Hugh to keep his distance without losing the Bentley. And he didn't have to follow far. The driver pulled into the gated driveway of a house on the outskirts of Pittsburgh, some twenty minutes from the park.

Chapter 21

For a person ascertained to have "spatial abilities off the chart," as the psychologist had categorized him as a youth, he certainly was lost. It had seemed like a good idea. It was dark out. It was near midnight on a weeknight, so most people were asleep. Excellent time for Hugh to go back to DuPont's neighborhood and retrieve the jacket.

Except he couldn't find the property where he'd hid the jacket.

Hugh had departed directly from the Bentley driver's house. He had made one stop along the way, a 24-hour Walmart, where he purchased a pair of scissors, a bucket, and a bottle of both Clorox and peroxide. He would shred and destroy the jacket, and any trace of DNA, before dumping it. Everything was in order.

Except finding the jacket. Everything looked so different at night. And when he had fled from the crime scene, he'd been focused on escaping—dodging behind hedges, cutting through alleys, reversing direction. Remembering the route he'd been taking had been the least of his concerns.

And now for fifteen minutes he had been driving around without success. So long that he was beginning to worry that someone might see him as a risk to the neighborhood.

Hugh restarted for the second time at the DuPont residence, intent on retracing his tracks. Again, he couldn't recognize the properties at night.

And he was starting to panic. There might be times a panic is helpful. Running from a charging rhino, maybe. Getting out of a mall at the sound of gunfire, surely. This wasn't one of those times. Hugh was now driving round and round, too nervous to recognize what he'd seen just two evenings ago. Or, when he did, too frantic to remember at what point during his flight it had occurred. He spotted alleys that looked familiar, but wasn't sure. He recognized the house where he almost had been spotted by a couple getting into their car, but couldn't remember if he'd been there before or after he ditched the jacket.

Hugh reconsidered and dismissed again using Google street view. It would help him find the property, of that he was sure. It would show the streets during the daytime and he might even find the trench with the drainage pipe. But it also would provide the police a record of his searches, one of particular interest, no doubt, to Kelly. As it was, he'd left his phone off anyway so there wouldn't be a GPS record of his being back in DuPont's neighborhood.

When he finally stumbled upon the property, it was by blind luck more than reasoning. But there it was. He pulled the car over to the curb. Relief washed over him. But he was still shaking.

He looked around. The area was quiet, with most house lights off, including those of the property he was interested in. Hugh didn't see anyone in the streets or looking out of windows, no police car parked or following him. He got out of the rental and left the driver's door slightly ajar, then reconsidered and pushed it shut. He didn't want Holly to mistake this as an invitation to join him for a walk.

Hugh hugged the hedges next to the trench with the drainage pipe. He walked slowly, not wanting to risk a stumble. Soon he was at the four-inch PVC pipe and able to reach his hand in and retrieve the jacket. Easy. No problem. Relief.

Still, Hugh had a foreboding that when got back to the car with the jacket, the dog would start happily barking while Kelly would walk up and say, "We were waiting for you to retrieve the jacket."

No one walked up. He and Holly drove off.

Hugh parked where he could make his way to the banks of the Monongahela River. There he used the scissors to cut the jacket into pieces and soaked them in the bucket with the Clorox and peroxide. He then dumped the contents into the river. So much for Kelly finding this jacket.

And, finally, Holly could take her long-awaited walk. A "coach dog" notwithstanding, Holly had been confined for hours to the car; she needed to expend some energy. And Hugh, near ecstatic with the evening's accomplishments, needed as well to settle his mind, to calm his charged-up body.

Sometime after one in the morning, Hugh and Holly arrived back at the hotel.

The hotel was inexpensive, small—only two stories high—and with just the basics in guest facilities. There was no swimming pool, or sauna, or business center, or restaurant. But there was a small exercise room with three machines, a couple of vending machines, and the hotel did promote a free continental breakfast.

Hugh's room was on the topmost floor, facing the parking lot. Cramped, with a musty smell, it had a twin bed, and a rickety desk and chair. It had few amenities: a small TV and soap and shampoo and towels. No kitchen facilities, of course. But also no mini bar. No hair dryer. No iron and ironing board.

It did have WiFi.

Hugh set up his laptop and accessed the webcam connected to his apartment's computer. The live image showed everything in order. He minimized the screen and brought up the wireless camera in his parents' house and accessed that as well. Likewise, everything in order. He checked the recordings. There hadn't been any activity in either the apartment or house: nothing had activated the motion detectors. Hugh positioned the images from the webcam and camera side-by-side, and sat on his bed to watch TV.

The TV was on more for a distraction than anything else. Hugh didn't own a TV himself; he hadn't watched TV since living in his parents' home. Everything he wanted to see, everything he wanted to read, everything he wanted to listen to was accessible via his apartment's old desktop computer, his college-bought laptop, his new tablet, and his smart phone. He streamed TV shows and played those online strategy and first-person-shooter games where he didn't have to speak over a headset. Before his breakthrough, speaking on a headset was like his speaking on a phone, disjointed, a phobia carried over since his first time speaking on a phone and being mocked. But he already had tried some games with the British accent during his trip; it'd be a new world for him.

Hugh wanted so much for all this to go away, to speak all the time in a British accent. To impress his peers. To let it all filter back to those kids in his high school that had looked down on him and taunted him. To have his own story like that girl who was mocked in high school as fat and then ended up being a supermodel with an ad running during the Super Bowl.

It was the lunchroom that was always the most painful place for him in high school. In his junior and senior years, he learned to pack his own lunch, and then he would sneak off to an isolated corner of the school to eat by himself. But as a freshman and sophomore, his parents always had him buying the school lunch.

For a while, after being rejected at other tables, he found himself sitting at tables with the kids in special education—those placed there for learning disabilities, not high IQ. As he would walk through the cafeteria with his tray, he would try to avoid passing near the "popular kids" who felt he was even a better mark than the special ed kids—particularly since Hugh had blundered into half-heartedly, and ineffectually it turned out, physically fighting back early in ninth grade.

But it wasn't just the popular kids. To Hugh, it seemed like he had become the unifying force between all the various school tribes. The jocks, the popular girls, the burnouts and stoners, the nerds—they all found him a target for their jokes.

"Holiday can't talk to you right now. This is only a forty-five-minute lunch period."

"I heard Holiday has a new job working at a call center where customers pay per minute. They hired him because he runs the phone charges up so much."

"Does Holiday suffer from mental illness? No, he enjoys it."

"Did yinz hear about when Holiday went parachute jumping? The instructor told everyone to count to ten and then pull the chute, but told Holiday to just count to one."

"Remember when Abraham Lincoln said it is better to remain silent and be thought a fool than to speak out and remove all doubt? He was talking about Holiday."

"Holiday is what's known as a miracle public speaker. If he can speak in public, it's a miracle."

For a while, it seemed like the lunchroom comedians were in a competition to come up with a stuttering joke each day. Some, even he found witty. Others weren't even borderline jokes.

"Holiday is living proof that a human can live without a brain."

"When Holiday's mom was pregnant, I heard she was drinking mercury straight from the thermometer."

"Holiday, did your parents ever ask you to run away from home?"

"I once saw some people like you, Holiday. But it was in a freak show, and I had to pay admission."

Hugh stopped pacing in the hotel room as these memories came back all too clear. He knew that if he didn't shut off this foray into melancholy, he could get himself too depressed to think straight. He didn't have that luxury. He needed to focus on some happy thoughts. He....

Hugh's eyes were drawn to the laptop. His brow furrowed. The split screen was only showing the image from the house. The left side, which should have been showing the apartment, was blank. Hugh restarted the operation to get the live feed again; the webcam image was gone. He reviewed the recording in the cloud. The image had stopped just seven minutes ago.

Odd, he thought, *why did the cam stop working? Did the power in the apartment go out?*

Then, as he was pondering his next step, the image from the apartment cam suddenly returned. Showing an empty apartment as before.

But something wasn't right. Hugh looked at the ball he'd placed near the back door. The dog's plaything was near to where he had placed it, but not exactly. He had placed it precisely to the right of the grout line on the tiles. It had been there every time he had looked. It was now on the grout line, and a little further out. He looked at an earlier recording. Yes, he was right. A small difference, perhaps...

Suddenly, Hugh turned the laptop off, packed his things, grabbed Holly, looked out the window, and not seeing anything in the parking lot to cause alarm, went down the stairs and out the back exit to his car. He apologized to Holly, "Sorry, mate, but better safe than sorry." He drove out of the hotel parking lot.

Hugh stopped nearby, in the lot of an adjacent used car dealership where he could keep an eye on the hotel. *If they were smart enough to hack the webcam image, they probably are smart enough to figure out the IP address, and it might lead them to the hotel.* "Sorry, mate," Hugh said again. "We better stay in the car tonight."

As he looked through the window, he saw a white van arrive and drive into the hotel's parking lot. It was a cargo van, with no side windows save that for the driver and passenger. The window on the back was obscured by a curtain. Only one man was in the van. When he opened the door, no lights went on, leaving the man poorly illuminated. But as the man walked briskly to the front entrance, Hugh could see that he was of ordinary size.

About ten minutes later, Hugh saw the light in his recently vacated hotel room go on. About five minutes later this light went off again, and shortly afterward the man returned to his white van and drove off.

Chapter 22

Karsten figured he couldn't have missed Holiday by much.

He had traced the IP address to this hotel and had arrived but a half-hour after noticing Holiday's activity. No time had been lost with the hotel clerk, the sole person manning the front desk at this late hour. One look at Karsten's ID, signifying he was an investigator with the Bureau of Alcohol, Tobacco, Firearms, and Explosives, and the young man had been cooperative, if not bowled over. The clerk recognized Holiday's photo as that of the person who'd returned to the hotel sometime after 1 am, the person registered as Edward Butler, one of the few hotel guests that night. Then, the clerk had given the senior Justice Department investigator immediate access to Butler's hotel room, dutifully staying at his post as ordered.

One-half hour between noticing Holiday accessing the Internet to arriving at his location. And yet, when Karsten had entered the room, it had been empty. Or nearly empty. Just some spilled dog food on the floor and fast-food wrappers in the wastebasket. But Holiday was gone. By less than one-half hour he had missed the opportunity to kill him.

But, he thought, a wry smile crossing his lips, at least that nice fellow at the front desk wouldn't have an unfortunate demise on the way home from work. Those needle marks were a dead giveaway for someone headed for a not-so-accidental drug overdose. Collateral damage is a bitch.

Which, he realized, on second thought, was an odd phrase in this case. Because the bitch would also be collateral damage.

The hotel hadn't been Karsten's first stop. His first stop after arriving in Pittsburgh three hours earlier had been Holiday's apartment. He had parked his van on the street outside, where he patiently waited, cloaked behind thick curtains pulled shut on the passenger's and driver's side, and a sun reflector placed on the front windshield. With its tinted windows, the thick curtain on the back window, and the specially constructed panel with door separating the front seats from the rear of the van, the vehicle was an ideal cover for surveillance. Just one of the ubiquitous white vans seen on the road, this one lacking even a company name on the door.

But this nondescript van was far more than a cover for surveillance. And it was anything but ordinary. Carefully hidden in the back of the van, behind the panel, was a cornucopia of state-of-the-art surveillance and computer equipment. Equipment to monitor cell phone locations and conversations, ferret out IP addresses, and do GPS tracking on vehicles. Equipment to receive feeds from a city's closed circuit traffic cameras and capture keystrokes from those using wireless keyboards. And this wasn't even counting the myriad of mundane accouterments like lock pick sets and fake IDs.

Karsten was the new age of contract killer.

Physically, he was not imposing at first sight. He stood about five feet ten inches tall, with short, light brown hair, and a moderate frame. Other than his somewhat thick neck, he gave the appearance of someone of ordinary build. But that was deceiving, his muscles typically hidden beneath an attire of loose-fitted clothing. Karsten worked out regularly and intensely. He was iron strong, agile, and quick.

But his physical attributes were not what made his services so coveted. He was tech savvy and with an ability to blend inconspicuously into the surroundings when needed, or to appear as an official of various agencies when those deceptions were required. These traits came in handy with his particularly specialization: finding individuals who didn't want to be found and breaching places with tight security. Mob informants in the witness protection program, sequestered jurors leaning toward guilty verdicts, witnesses to crimes now in safe houses, men or women who owed or stole mob money or held secrets and had run into hiding—terminating these threats were some of the tasks for which Karsten's unique skill set was sought. And for which he was paid handsomely.

Karsten could track down anyone, provided they weren't living off the fat of the land, isolated from civilization. Or were already dead. He located one target hidden in the witness protection program, not through hacking government computers, though that was part of his broad repertoire, but through an algorithm he devised. The algorithm looked for a particular set of Internet browsing habits. Unfortunately for the target, it wasn't aimed at his own browsing habits—he had craftily run everything in his house through the anonymous TOR network using a virtual private network—but it was his daughter's searches on her high school network. Two weeks later, Karsten found another target using facial recognition software, and yet another through listening into phone conversations.

The irresistible drive people had to go online had greased Karsten's work. It was a matter of finding the person online and then Karsten could track him down via the IP address and then the MAC address—the unique "burned in" identifier stored in the hardware connecting each electronic device to a computer network. A hard-coded identifier that Karsten himself carefully masked for his own electronic devices.

Once the individual was located, Karsten was an efficient and ruthless killer. And yet one whose intelligence and renaissance-man knowledge allowed him to make the death look convincing to the police and public. Heart attack, accidental fall, suicide by poisoning, car accident, drowning, accidental electrocution— a few of the modes that were done so effectively that coroners saw no reason for police to look any further than the victim himself or herself.

In this case, Karsten's instruction was clear: Holiday was to meet his demise by suicide. Preferably a hanging. But whatever would work, as long as it was done soon and convincingly. The buttressing details had already been taken care of. A suicide note. Witnesses that he had a dark side. Despondency from the fact that he had taken the life of a medical school professor, a Megan DuPont.

Karsten himself had taken care of the suicide note before he ever drove into Pittsburgh. He had asked for, and been provided, some of Holiday's old penned and penciled notes still in the family residence. With these and computer software, he had produced a reasonable facsimile of a handwritten suicide note, which he then expertly traced on a scrap paper taken from Holiday's apartment. Even the pen used had Holiday's fingerprints.

It was just a matter of finding Holiday and executing the plan. Which had almost turned out to be tonight.

As Karsten sat in his nondescript, not-so-ordinary van in the hotel parking lot, he reviewed his actions. He needed to figure out if he'd made a mistake. He wanted to better understand his quarry. As he so often did when on the hunt, he visually relived key parts of his day to see if he had overlooked anything. And the key part of his day had started at Holiday's apartment.

When Karsten first arrived outside Hugh's apartment, he had no expectation of finding Holiday there. Not based on the information he had gleaned. Still, there was a light on in the apartment, and that was cause for some guarded optimism. Moments later there was cause for serious optimism. He found an active network in the apartment. An open network that, once compromised, he found was connected to a camera.

Which meant he had access to three valuable things. First, he could see whether Holiday was remotely viewing the network, and if so, Karsten had the means to figure out where he was at that very moment. Second, he could gain access to Holiday's computer files. And third, he now had a cam's eye view into the apartment to see if Holiday was there.

But none of these materialized. Not at first.

No one, save Karsten himself, was accessing the network. A dead end. Breaching Holiday's computer via the network showed the machine was virtually devoid of files. A second dead end. And the cam's eye view was too limited. It showed only the living room and kitchen and these were empty. It didn't show the bedroom. Not a complete dead end, but Karsten was hoping for more. He was hoping to know whether or not Holiday was there. Now, he would have to enter the apartment to either eliminate the possibility or to eliminate Holiday.

Other intruders might well have cut the power to the apartment—eliminating the use of any surveillance requiring a power source. But this would have all sorts of repercussions. It would announce the intruder's arrival should Holiday be in the apartment and still awake. The blinking alarm clocks and oven clocks would have to be reset or else would announce the next day that someone had been in the apartment. An error might result in the lower apartment's power being cut as well, altering the couple there. Much simpler to create an interference with the network so that the surveillance signal would be lost.

And this is what Karsten did.

And, upon slipping into the apartment, using the back entrance, he found what he had expected: Holiday wasn't home.

But Karsten hadn't reached the pinnacle of his profession by being stupid. Before he entered, he had studied the cam view intently. Enough to know that one item would be moved by his entering the apartment: a small ball near the back entrance. And so he replaced the ball and exited via the front entrance. No one would ever know he had been there that night. He ended the signal interference as soon as he got back to the van.

The plan for his next step was to repeat this at the Holiday house. But he never made it that far. When he ended the signal interference, he noticed that he wasn't alone on the network. Holiday was remotely accessing it.

Tracking the IP address led to the hotel.

It had all been too perfect. The quarry all alone in the small hours of the night. In a hotel nearly devoid of guests, and none near his room, thanks to Holiday's own request for privacy. And listed under an alias, as if running from the police. Just add a "do not disturb" sign so the maid wouldn't discover the body until the next afternoon, get rid of some of Holiday's identifying information, and disappear the dog, and there might be a delay of a day or more until the body was identified and then the suicide/confession note found. He himself would be long gone.

And with no witnesses to Karsten ever have been there. One lousy hotel clerk. And that guy had agreed to keep quiet and would—at least long enough until his overdose occurred that morning after he left for home. One bump of his car, and he would pull over, and the rest would be easy. With death from accidental drug overdose so common—forty-four thousand cases a year in the United States, and for the clerk's age group more common than deaths from car accidents—his demise wouldn't draw even a first look, let alone a second. Certainly no reason to connect the death of the drug-using front desk clerk in another part of town, at another time, with the suicide of Mr. Edward Butler. And no reason to look further into the suicide. Everything neatly tied up. And with the coroner to back him up if needed. Perfect.

The only problem was that Karsten hadn't expected Holiday to be gone.

Karsten couldn't see where things might have gone wrong. He had cut the signal for probably less than ten minutes. He had even replaced the ball. Perhaps he should have been more careful to hide his own presence on the network, but neighbors are always stealing other's WiFi. No excuse for Holiday to be so jumpy.

Getting his target within three hours of arriving in the city would have been close to a personal best. But Karsten did love a good challenge. It helped him feel alive even if it didn't do the same for his adversary.

Chapter 23

He felt disoriented. Coming from such a deep sleep, and in unfamiliar surroundings, in near darkness, Hugh at first struggled to remember where he was.

Ah, yes. The Walmart parking lot.

Hugh exited the Ford Focus and stretched, trying to loosen the kinks he felt from his awkward sleeping position. Being six foot two, he didn't exactly fit in the back seat of this economy car. Holly had been right at home in the front passenger seat.

Hugh felt the stubble on his face and squinted his eyes as he looked around. The sun had barely risen, but even the reflected glare off the bare pavement irritated his half-opened eyes. People were already going into the Walmart. And coming out. Actually, it had been that way all night. Maybe just busy enough that no one had paid any attention to his car parked on the edge of the lot for hours. If he had to do it again, he would risk the luxury of folding down the split rear seat and stretching his legs into the trunk.

Hugh let Holly out for a couple of minutes to take care of her business and then put her back in the front. He opened the trunk and took from his backpack a razor, toothbrush, and small tube of toothpaste. He put them in his pants pocket, joining the comb he always carried, and headed for the entrance of the Supercenter.

Hugh did his best to clean up in the bathroom, taking off his shirt to wash his upper body with soap from the bathroom dispenser, shaving without shaving cream, brushing his teeth.

He stuck his head partly under the faucet, lathered up with more soap from the dispenser, and washed the soap out. He walked out of the bathroom with wet, but combed hair.

Hugh next bought some yogurt for himself and a packet of baby carrots as a treat for Holly. Most people thought dogs, being descendants of wolves, wouldn't be big on vegetables, but even wolves consume fruits and vegetables when convenient. And Holly liked them all: broccoli, green beans, carrots, asparagus, apple slices, cantaloupes, blueberries. Hugh would toss him some unbuttered popcorn while he watched a movie on his computer. Holly enjoyed it whenever he got any kind of special treatment. Hugh just had to be careful of some foods, like onions or grapes or chocolate or things with caffeine.

When he arrived back at his rental car, Hugh took out a clean shirt from his luggage and changed right on the lot. The wrinkled pants would have to do for today. He then found a nearby neighborhood park where he could eat his yogurt, feed Holly, and take her for a walk.

It was still very early. He had to kill some time before it was a reasonable enough hour to show up at his neighbor's to drop Holly off.

He took a drive to the outskirts of Pittsburgh, to where he had followed the Bentley the previous night. In the daylight, Hugh could see just how well-to-do the neighborhood was, with relatively expansive properties and houses set well-back from the street, most shielded by tall, privacy hedges. Still, it was not as ostentatious as he expected for the home range of a Bentley owner.

Hugh drove slowly past the property he had seen the Bentley driver enter. Situated on the right side of the street, it had a seven-foot stone wall bordering the sidewalk, with sharp stones lining the top. Near the middle of the wall was the access to the property, guarded by a steel gate. It was the only opening through which Hugh could see the house, which, from what he could see, wasn't as impressive as expected. It was three stories, modern in construction, and with a two-car garage connected to the house. The blacktop driveway from the gate went straight for about half the distance, where it then made a circle in front of the home. There was a well-maintained lawn, dotted with some large maple trees.

But still, Hugh had expected an estate. This was the house of someone well-to-do, but not rich. Not Bentley rich. Not one percenter rich. Maybe someone aspiring to be rich. Certainly someone trying to give the impression he was rich by the car he drove.

Hugh was nearly past the property when an eye-catching glint of morning sunlight reflected from one of the trees. He pulled over two houses down and got out and looked back at the trees extending above the wall. Cameras. What the property may have lost in visual impressiveness was seemingly made up for in security.

What he hadn't seen—what he had been hoping to see as he drove by—was a house number or name.

He looked around. He would have to catch the street address for houses on either side and then try his luck on the web. Far too much risk in asking the neighbors or someone walking down the street who lived there. Using his British accent, stumbling through his stuttering—both would be too memorable and might end up being reported to Mr. Bentley Owner.

Another option presented itself.

It arrived in the form of a station wagon and a driver delivering the morning *Trib* to homeowners. Including one to a property with a seven-foot stone wall with sharp stones lining the top and surveillance cameras in the trees.

As soon as the car had moved on, Hugh got out and walked nonchalantly to the postal box. He stayed close the wall, trying to stay out of view of the cameras. He reached the end of the wall at the gate, reached around with his left hand, and removed the paper. He stole a quick glance at the name and address before returning it and walking back, hugging the wall once again. A few minutes later, he was out of the area.

He mulled over the name. It wasn't what he'd been expecting. It was a woman's name: Sophia Zanini. If the woman was not Mr. Bentley Owner's wife, or if the wife had a different last name from his, then tracking down his identify might still not be easy.

Hugh's final stop before going to work was one he wished he didn't have to make. Parking once again on a parallel street and walking through the adjourning property, he trudged into his neighbor's backyard to drop off Holly. To his neighbor's surprise, Hugh requested to leave Holly for a few days while he went out of town. The neighbor's bafflement was complete when Hugh again headed off through the backyard. Hugh didn't look back. He had no explanation he could give that wouldn't sound odd.

Hugh's office colleagues would've found his behavior equally odd if they had seen the route he took to their building. He parked several streets away, north of the office. Then he took a bus to a stop south of the office. From here he walked to the building, but with occasional detours into coffee shops to stare out the window and see if he was being followed. Even so, he sensed that even showing up at the office was risky. Especially after the conversation he overhead in the park: the "still showing up for work" comment from Mr. Bentley Owner. But, he also couldn't afford to lose this job.

Sophia Zanini. The name had occupied the bulk of Hugh's thoughts by the time he begin searching on his office desktop. It didn't take long. There was a likely candidate whose name was prominent in the society pages. There in *The Trib* was a photo of a Sophia Zanini at a charity ball, the same Sophia Zanini attending a fundraiser for a local hospital, the same attending the groundbreaking ceremony of an industrial park.

In each photo, she was with her husband. A man whose profile looked very much like that of the broad-shouldered person Hugh had seen in the park. A man who fit the category of someone well-to-do, aspiring to be rich. Not the owner of any business, but the manager of quite a few. Pizza joints and convenience stores mostly, and one full-service gas station. But also a restaurant and a nightclub. Hugh had a name to attach to Mr. Bentley Owner. Claudio Zanini.

Chapter 24

Claudio Zanini was not a native-born Pittsburgher. He had arrived in his early thirties from Philadelphia and at first found the Pittsburghese dialect jarring. Between the various terms handed down from the early Scotch-Irish immigrants to whatever other influences lead to the dialect of the "yinzers," the phrases and the slurred words and the dropped t's ("Chrissmas," really?) stood out to his ears as unsophisticated. From "n'at" for "and that," to "proximidy" for "proximity," to "haaja" for "how did you," Zanini at first proudly resisted getting drawn into using the dialect. As if phrases like "fer cryin in da sink" weren't annoying enough to him, there was the native penchant for using "yinz" for "you all"— as in "Where yinz going? To da Stillers game?" No, Zanini was resistant to being seen as a yinzer.

But that was a quarter of a century ago. Zanini, now fifty-four, had not only gradually adopted many of the area phrases and traditions, but he had grown to admire how the Burgh residents had transformed their city in the years since he had moved to the region. Before his day, the Steel City had produced half of the country's steel—and much of its soot. But then came the lows of the early 1980s, when the steel era suddenly collapsed and one hundred and fifty thousand area jobs were lost. An extraordinary loss of jobs.

But what happened next was a marvel of ingenuity and tenacity. The residents completely reinvented the city. Zanini had watched as it became a high employment, diversified economy, strong in technology and health care and education and energy and finance. An attractive place that drew in many people from outside the area, including students attending its respected universities.

There was another aspect of the character of Pittsburghers that surprised Zanini. A native of Philly, who also had spent a long time in New York City and northern New Jersey, Zanini was used to a certain aggressiveness in daily life. The Pittsburgh region was a study in contrasts. It seemed to him there was a Midwest vibe to the area.

Nowhere was this more evident to him than in the driving habits. A driver trying to turn around on a busy street to claim an empty parking spot on the opposite side? More often than not, the Pittsburgher driving down the street flashes his lights to say "Take your time, I'll wait while you execute the turn." Need to change lanes to get into the highway exit lane, or trying to squeeze onto a packed secondary road from a highway exit? The Pittsburgher politely makes space. People crossing the street even where there's no crosswalk? The Pittsburgh driver doesn't typically barrel through, horn blaring, as if to say, "Hey, I got two tons of steel here. You want to take your chances?" The Pittsburgher slows and waits.

Quite a contrast with the blowing horns or cutting one off or speeding up to prevent a merge that Zanini was used to. The character of a Burgh resident was charming, thought Zanini, but it went against "the strongest prosper, let the weak be damned" philosophy that he ascribed to. It was a Pittsburgh trait that Zanini made clear he wasn't going to adopt.

If Zanini's acceptance of the yinzer dialect took time, his integration was much quicker and more linear into Pittsburgh's Italian-American community. And this was a big community, one of the nation's largest. In Pittsburgh, only those of German and Irish background exceeded the numbers of those identifying as of Italian descent. And it was a respected community, a culture that on the national level was known for many desired values: low unemployment, hard work, low rates of incarceration, low divorce rates, high proportion of two-parent families—families that took care of their elderly at home, who ate together, who didn't go on welfare.

But it wasn't the Italian-American community at large that Zanini was interested in. It was a very minute subculture within that community. A subculture that made up only about one hundredth of a percent of that community—just one out of ten thousand. A subculture that fell short of the Italian-American reputation for values, and which other Italian-Americans, like Rudy Giuliani and FBI director Louis Freeh, had worked to crush. One that other Italian-Americans had crusaded against. But a subculture that had been attractive to Zanini since his youth and which had provided him with a sense of power. And very real wealth.

Zanini fit in instantly. Indeed, Zanini's initial introduction to this subculture in Pittsburgh had been by a close associate of Uncle Joe Ligambi, the eventual Cosa Nostra boss in Philadelphia. This associate smoothed the rails, making it clear that Zanini was "a friend of ours." Zanini was a made man in the Philly mob. His move to Pittsburgh harbingered a new era of cooperation, with alliances being established among the five families of New York, and groups in Chicago, Boston, and now western Pennsylvania.

Zanini didn't boast Hollywood heartthrob looks. His height would have been fine—five feet seven inches tall, the same as Tom Cruise and Al Pacino—but he was close to two hundred pounds. Still, his very wide upper body with broad shoulders gave more the impression of a muscular weightlifter than someone overweight, and was complemented by a large head with tanned face, strong jaw, and tight-lipped smile. His black hair did show some gray, most notably around the temples. And he did have a tendency to squint in his right eye, above which there was also a scar that he felt added some character to his face. But one's first, and lasting, impression was of a powerful man, someone you didn't want to mess with. And that was after you got past his ever-present gold chain and sunglasses.

Yet, it wasn't Zanini's physical presence that set him apart. It was his calculating intelligence and ambition and matchless self-confidence. He was a man who generally got what he wanted and few were willing to cross.

An associate one told Zanini, to his face and rather obsequiously, that Zanini was the alpha male in any room he was in. And this was generally true. Certainly in the classical, animal kingdom sense of dominance and intimidation and fearlessness. But even in the human sense for many traits: the aforementioned confidence, his calculating and composed nature, the way he talked slowly and walked slowly and was the center of attention. And the fact that he was a winner.

But not in all traits in the human sense. A true alpha male in the human world is generally considered one who doesn't betray others or lie or bully to get ahead, or blame others when things fail. Those were not Zanini traits.

Zanini himself liked to think that he had developed study-worthy leadership skills. Those "skills" relied a lot on fear of retribution should he be crossed. Indeed, Zanini was known to be as ruthless as he was sharp-tempered, and those were as dominant of traits as his self-confidence and ambition. Among his subordinates, it was often whispered that he had personally killed more than twenty people. Whether a rumor to embellish his reputation, or a fact, wasn't known. What was known was that his own hero had been "Lucky" Luciano, the father of organized crime in the United States and perhaps the most powerful mafia boss of all time. Zanini carried a tattoo on his left wrist with the words "Lucky" in tribute to Luciano, along with the image of a clenched fist, indicating Zanini's own conviction that he made his own luck through force.

At one point, it seemed that Zanini was a rising star in the Philly mob. But his breaking off of his engagement with the consigliere's niece to take up with the raven-haired beauty Sophia De Luca was a near fatal mistake. It was a case of heart over head. Sophia, herself raised by "Old World" parents in South Philadelphia, was every bit Zanini's match, but in different qualities: beauty, a disarming and teasing wit, and grace. She was quite a bit taller than he was and with the figure of a curvaceous, swimsuit model, but invariably impeccably dressed in high-end clothes and expensive jewelry.

Before Zanini won Sophia, she was well known and courted by many in the mob, and it was rumored that many of those killed by Zanini were rivals for Sophia's affections. That Zanini was sent out of town with Sophia, rather than be killed for the broken engagement, was the best fate that he could of hoped for. But he was particularly well liked by Ligambi, and his loyalty to the powerful Cosa Nostra figure saved his life.

To say that Zanini was successful in western Pennsylvania would be an understatement. It wasn't his many "managerial" positions, which were really no-show jobs. Only at his office in the nightclub would he make a perfunctory appearance, and in those cases to conduct other business. Zanini's real job, his real success, was as a caporegime. As capo, he headed up a crew of soldiers and was a respected and feared man in the Pittsburgh mob.

Zanini's alpha male status took a back seat to only two people, Tony de Angelis and Joseph Salerno.

Chapter 25

Hugh left work early that Wednesday, citing the need to get ready for the DuPont viewing. Fact is, he had been so preoccupied he wouldn't even have realized the viewing was that night hadn't it been for two co-workers asking him whether he'd be going, half-hearted conversation breakers that did little to defuse the tension that had been in the office since the police had visited two days earlier.

The actual reason Hugh left early had little to do with the viewing. By now, he figured he would be followed; leaving at an odd time might work to his advantage. He waited inside the street-side entrance until he saw quite a few people walking by, then left quickly to join them. He took an oddly haphazard route, winding down streets, cutting through one restaurant completely by passing through the kitchen to the back door, and going into the front and out the back of an office building with dual entrances. He then caught a bus to a location east of his car and continued his convoluted circuit.

It took him about a half hour from office to car. Whether his leaving early worked or not, or whether his contorted path was the key, or whether he was ever being tailed to begin with, he didn't know. At any rate, when he arrived at his car, no one seemed to be paying him any attention.

Hugh spent the late afternoon driving to several establishments he had found linked to Zanini's name. For those businesses where there was an inconspicuous place to park nearby, he sat watching for a time. He did not spot a Bentley at any of the locations, and he saw no sign of Zanini.

Hugh then stopped by a mall store to buy an inexpensive suit, shirt, and tie for the viewing, electing not to return to his apartment for the ones he wore to his parents' funeral. He was pretty sure that he wasn't being paranoid: the invasions of his apartment, the mysterious man who came in the dead of night to his hotel room, the disconcerting conversation in the park—all pointed to a certain peril should he be grabbed out of sight of the public. While in the mall, he got a haircut and then shaved and dressed in the mall restroom.

Hugh's unawareness notwithstanding, the viewing was a big deal in the Pittsburgh area. Not a legendary-coach-of-the-Pittsburgh-Steelers-Chuck-Noll kind of big deal. And maybe not on the level it would be should a congressman or mayor pass on while still in office. But certainly more than that for a former two-term congressman or ex-city official. After all, Megan DuPont was, until three days ago, beautiful, relatively young, with a sweet personality, and at the pinnacle of her profession, a specialty that was highly respected by the public. She was a Pittsburgh native and a member of a powerful American family.

And her murder had riveted the public's attention, perhaps more so with the killer or killers still at large and no motive that allowed the public to place the crime in a neat box and say, ah yes, it was a drug overdose, or domestic violence from an ex-lover, or any of a multitude of other ways in which they could abate their own fears.

The viewing and funeral details made both the *Post-Gazette's* and *Trib's* front pages. Both events would be open to the public. The viewing, in order to accommodate the more than one thousand people expected, would be held at the DeSandis Funeral Home and, after an hour of private viewing for immediate family, would be open to the public from 6pm to 9pm. It would be open casket. No cameras would be allowed.

The funeral would take place at the Episcopal Church the next day, beginning at 10am.

It was at 6:30pm that Hugh arrived within sight of the funeral home. Fully named the DeSandis Funeral Home and Crematory, it was a very large facility and stood alone on a sizeable plot of land. And it was quite elegant. Or, perhaps one might best describe it as eccentric in appearance.

The funeral home looked to be a Victorian-era house with elements of a Queen Anne Style mixed with a Gothic flavor. Largely asymmetrical on the outside, it rose three stories above the ground, although whether it was indeed three stories or four could be a point of debate. For from the third floor's gray, heavily slanted roof ascended a narrow, largely rectangular tower, with windows, that extended from the base of the third floor to well above the third floor's already high roof, creating the concept of an additional space. This tower was centrally placed and had sides that curved inward near the top, while still managing to have a flat roof. And this flat roof, bordered as it was by a decorative, black metal fence of sharp points and crosses, created the impression of a crown on top of the building.

The other elevated spaces on the building were mostly an eclectic amalgam of triangular shapes—pointed arches and spires—and rounded towers. None rose as high as the middle tower, but were nevertheless eye-catching. The sash windows on the second and third floor, and central tower, were mostly small, with decorative gray shutters on either side. The house was covered with a siding of gray fish-scale shingles and altogether was almost entirely white and gray in color.

The one prominent exception to the funeral home's asymmetry was the large wraparound porch that covered the entire front of the bottom floor and apparently, as best Hugh could see, also wrapped completely around the sides as well. It was largely hidden by an equally symmetrical, plain black awning. In the center of the porch, wide stairs descended to the ground, the stairs themselves covered by another awning, this one extending out some fifteen feet from the house and emblazoned at the front by a gold circle with the symbol DeS— the logo of the funeral home.

Hugh could see a large parking lot in the front of the building and a driveway that led down the back as well. But he eschewed driving into the lot. Instead, he parked three blocks away. He sat in the car, engine running, until he felt confident that no one was shadowing him. He then walked quickly up to a parallel street and around the block, reaching the funeral home from the opposite direction as his car.

The line of people was breathtaking. It extended out through the canopied steps, onto the sidewalk, and into the parking lot. And it was growing by the second.

Hugh had just been to a viewing and funeral: his parents. There was no line, just a small number of acquaintances and his own work colleagues. There was only one other close family member there, an aunt on his mother's side. His parents were not young when they had the car accident—they had given birth to Hugh when in their late thirties—and his grandparents had already passed on. Those who attended walked by the cremation urns, bordered by pictures of his parents, and then shook his hand and offered their condolences or, in a few cases, shared some memory of an experience with his parents.

His parents hadn't deigned to prepare for their death and hadn't made their own funeral wishes known. They hadn't made arrangements for a burial plot or expressed interest in a casket. The funeral director, noting that his parents' bodies were too badly marred by the accident to make an open casket prudent, had advised cremation, and Hugh had concurred. The jewelry was removed, the undertaker made sure there were no implanted devices that could damage or explode the crematory, and then the bodies were vaporized and oxidized by temperatures nearly two thousand degrees Fahrenheit. Hugh received the ashes—really, the pulverized dry bone fragments thanks to a type of blender—and located some photo to show at the funeral with their remains.

After the ceremony, Hugh went with Holly to an isolated part of a mountain and scattered the ashes, oblivious as to whether this was legal or not, but at any rate, this ceremony was unattended and unwatched. The entire event, from learning of their death to the writing of their obituaries to the scattering of the ashes, was mostly a blur.

A few more people at this current viewing, thought Hugh. His parents had drawn about forty people tops. Here there were too many to count. Many were already leaving when he arrived, either courteously making space inside for others or perhaps really having very little reason to be there anyway.

Hugh was in a little different category than the latter—the police thought he was the one responsible for this event. But he hadn't been named, as far as he knew, and hopefully the police had the decency not to promote his status to the immediate family members. It would get pretty uncomfortable if he was mistaken about this point.

Hugh joined the end of the line. It took about ten minutes for him to reach the awning with the gold circle and DeS symbol. It took another fifteen minutes before he reached the large, high-ceilinged entrance foyer inside. And here, between two awe-inspiring rows of large bouquets, the line continued to snake towards a larger room ahead.

On either side of the entrance foyer were two rooms, where one could see ornate furnishings: vintage sofas and chairs, Tiffany lamps, antique floor lamps. But few people were in these side rooms, which Hugh surmised were designed for smaller gatherings; everything was centered on the room at the back of the foyer. At the door stood an exquisitely dressed, distinguished, middle-aged man, who was greeting each guest with a handshake and pleasant smile, interrupted only by the occasional need to give directions to staff approaching him with questions.

As Hugh got closer, he overhead this man addressed as Mr. DeSandis. And treated with utmost respect, almost servility. It was easy to guess who this was: the owner of the funeral home. And, this being a family business, quite possibly serving as the funeral director for this viewing as well. Apparently, the event was flowing so well that he felt he could spend some time at the one location where he could naturally meet the many distinguished city leaders who were gathering at his establishment.

And then, something peculiar happened. Something that made Hugh instantly uncomfortable. Something that put in doubt his assumption that his being a suspect was information shared only within the police fraternity. For Mr. DeSandis' eyes, in scanning the line, locked on Hugh's face and a look of surprise broke his otherwise collected demeanor.

The funeral director continued his routine for a few more guests, never again looking at Hugh, but soon was excusing himself and disappearing from sight. His place was taken by another man, a younger fellow. A son, perhaps?

Hugh considered the possibility that he was becoming paranoid. That he was seeing things that weren't there. That maybe the funeral director had simply remembered something that needed to be done, and his eyes were on Hugh's face when that uh-oh moment had occurred.

But no. Hugh was sure of it. The funeral director's flinch was tied to seeing Hugh, not some coincidence of timing.

Hugh continued to flow with the line through the long foyer, between the rows of flowers, ever closer to the main room. He seemed to be sandwiched between a group of five medical students directly ahead, their status evident from the fact that one had neglectfully left his ID tag still clipped to his belt, and a group of medical professionals behind, their status obvious from their conversation. Probably, Hugh thought, many of the young men and women his age at the viewing were medical students. And, likewise, many of the older men and women gathered were likely doctors or professors associated with TMMC or Pitt's Medical School. A single medical college could have hundreds and even thousands of such affiliated professionals, with the students being taught onsite at area hospitals for pretty much their third and fourth years.

Medical school. Physicians. Like a kidney stone one cannot expel, Hugh's thoughts glommed for the millionth time onto the medical profession. Onto yet another reminiscence of how staggeringly difficult it had proved to join that fraternity.

For Hugh, as for most aspirants, the planned destination morphed into an air castle during the application process. GPA, MCAT, recommendations, and interviews: those were the classic four horsemen standing in the way, guarding the entrance. As an undergraduate, Hugh had worried about even getting one mediocre grade, one C, particularly in a science subject, given how admissions committees poured over transcripts. But for many, the dream dissolved not with the grades, but with the Medical College Admissions Test. Or, with finding solid enough recommendations. And those three components were just to get your foot in the door, a chance to pitch yourself at an interview.

And those were just the original four horseman. As admissions became more competitive, a fifth horsemen had joined to guard the entrance. This was experience. The need for students to enhance their resumes with voluminous medically related activities: shadowing doctors, doing research, volunteering at clinics, working in hospices. And, heaven forbid that your background included the wrong kind of experience, some foolish, youthful error in judgment. Every detail would be scrutinized, analyzed, weighed.

And during the entire process one had to face the reality that the acceptance rates for individual medical schools hovered only around one percent to three percent. One to three percent.

Yet, even if you surmounted the five horseman and got into medical school, your journey for the Holy Grail was but underway. Four years in medical school, with a need to pass the Medical Licensing Examination before even getting to years three and four. Then another exam. Then the need to secure one of a limited number of residencies.

If you failed that, if you didn't get a residency—well, you wasted a small lifetime by then. And with hundreds of thousands of dollars in debt as your new starting point. If you got the residency? You still had some three years—seven if you went into surgery—to finally be a full-fledged member of that exclusive fraternity.

Small wonder that doctors were so highly respected. Sure, Hugh had seen people that as an undergraduate had cheated and cut corners. But mostly he was filled with admiration—even for those who, like himself, had strived so hard only to fall short.

Hugh, finally, reached the entrance of the larger room. Near the doorway was an antique table with a guestbook. The new attendant at the door, the one who had replaced DeSandis, motioned to Hugh, and he took up the pen and signed his name: Hugh Holiday. And then he turned the pages and studied the names of the other guests.

There were a lot of DuPonts and duPonts and Du Ponts on the first page. But there, on the first page, was also a line with the names Tony and Violetta de Angelis, just below a Charles Du Pont and just above a line with the names Joseph and Giovanna D'Alfonso. And a few lines further down the first page, the names Claudio and Sophia Zanini.

Hugh didn't recognize any other names on the first page or second, but on the third page, in flowing script, was the name Michelangelo Prospero Faccon.

Chapter 26

He had been forty-five minutes standing in the line so far. But at least he was inside the viewing room. Still the line snaked on.

The chamber in which Hugh now found himself was quite large, some one hundred feet by seventy feet. And with its lack of windows and high twelve-foot ceiling, it had the feel of a conference-room-like space. And this was exactly what Hugh wondered, whether it doubled for seminars and conferences or just catered to the funerals of the rich and famous. Probably the later, he concluded. Who would hold a seminar in a funeral home? Morticians? Grief counselors? Expos on the latest in caskets? How big an audience could those attract?

Despite its size, the viewing space was packed nearly wall to wall with people milling around or sitting in the antique sofas and chairs. Only the innumerable floral bouquets, dominated here by lilacs and lilies and orchids, added color to a milieu of men and women dressed in black and other muted colors, and furniture conveying equally somber tones.

Hugh scoured the room for Faccon and Zanini. He could spot neither. If they were in the room, it was too crowded to find them from where he stood.

There were two entrances into the viewing room. It was the left entrance through which the line passed. It then hugged the left side of the room until it reached the back of the hall. At that point, it made a right turn and continued to the center of the far wall. Here was positioned a skirted stage made with three risers, totaling twelve feet by four feet, set a good foot and a half above the floor.

And there in the middle lay the casket. With stairs bookending the stage, guests would walk, one by one, onto the stage from the left, pass a large portrait of Megan DuPont set on an easel, and arrive at the casket to pay their respects; they would then exit the stage to the right. On this side of the stage, many of the immediate family were standing, dutifully receiving condolences from the assembled guests.

There was one more feature of the process. To the left of the stage, near the stairs, were two large vases filled with white roses. Hugh observed that guests in front of him would pick up a rose from a vase, aided by an attendant, and then enter alone onto the stage, holding their rose while viewing the body in repose, finally placing the flower on a small table to the right of the casket. As Hugh watched, the vases were replenished with roses by attendants; the same attendants occasionally unburdened the small table to the right of the casket of some of the flowers.

As Hugh grew closer to the stage, the details of the portrait clarified. It was oil painting that was both life-sized and rich in color. It appeared to be a very expensive work, perhaps commissioned by her parents some years ago, for in it she was younger, likely in her early twenties. The portrait showed DuPont from the waist up, her raven hair left long and flowing, encircling fair skin—not tanned as he had known her—and falling across the front of her dark pink, perhaps fuscia-colored, blouse.

But two features, captured with such subtlety in the soft silhouette of her face, drew Hugh's attention above all else. One was her eyes, with their captivating, deep, cobalt-blue color, framed in beautiful lashes, which, combined with the other feature, seemed to be twinkling in joy and warmth and intelligence.

And this other feature was her smile. An embracing and, to Hugh, flawless smile. One where the full lips, slightly upturned at the corners, and the gently curving Cupid's bow of the larger upper lip perfectly enveloped the upper teeth to create the most sincerely cheerful and pleasant and attractive smile Hugh could imagine.

This was the person Hugh had known: kindhearted, intelligent, full of life and joy. And beautiful. Had she gone into a different line of work, she could have been a model. But she had gone the academic route and achieved the highest degrees in her field. And now the light of this intelligent, gorgeous, embracing women had been extinguished.

Five people remained between Hugh and the stage. The TMMC students. Hugh watched each of them as they took turns walking on stage. Most seemed visibly shaken, including one with tears streaming down her cheeks. As medical doctors they would deal with death. But this one wasn't just someone young and vibrant who had passed unexpectedly. This was a person who had been side-by-side with them on their journey to be doctors, teaching them, perhaps counseling them personally.

And now it was time for Hugh to walk on stage.

The emotional dam burst.

He had taken but one step onto the stage. He had his white rose in hand and was looking at the portrait as he walked, the casket occupying the periphery of his vision. And then a tsunami of strong emotion suddenly rose and overtook him. He began to sob.

He wasn't even sure why. Certainly, she had been special to him. No question about that. Someone who never once brought up his stuttering. Who treated him with respect and dignity, as if he were someone important, someone to be valued. As if he were someone who was great just the way he was.

But these were the tears, the feelings, of having lost someone very close, not someone whose professional services and advice were used once a week. He hadn't openly sobbed at his own parents' funeral. Perhaps, he considered, it was all the tension from the past few days culminating in this moment, that he was so worn down that his emotions were raw. Or was it that in his world, with so few friends, she had been like a big sister to him? And now he truly felt alone.

Whatever the reason, this was not good. He had to stop. He understood that immediately. He was a suspect in her murder. Probably the sole suspect. And his emotional outburst was just attracting attention to him, making him look guiltier.

Hugh swiped away the tears. He tried to refocus. He had reached the coffin now, and she seemed stunning even in repose. For a full minute, he just stood there. But he spent the time no longer reflecting on her, but steadying himself, hardening his heart. He had the sense that many eyes in the room were on him.

Just a professional colleague. Nothing more. A professional colleague. He almost convinced himself.

Hugh placed his rose on the table to the right of the coffin, and moved to the edge of the stage. But he then paused. He used this vantage point to look out over the crowd at the other guests. Most were engaged in quiet conversation with one another. But quite a few were looking at him. Including a group of several right near the center of the room. One of which was Zanini. Looking right at him.

Hugh averted his eyes. He walked off the stage.

Hugh had no time to process the faces he had seen. He was thrust into the task of greeting the family members. A situation made many times more awkward by a nagging concern that some of them may have been told he was a suspect. Maybe even shown his photo.

None gave any such indication. It seemed he wasn't anything more to them than the other countless guests that they had never seen. It was hard enough that they had to stand there and be greeted by strangers, but in the case of Hugh, he felt that his need to maintain a stuttering persona compelled him to not say anything.

An assistant to the family helped the proceedings by periodically identifying the family members to the guests. "This is Dr. DuPont's parents…This is her sister and her brother-in-law." Hugh passed through the line, nodding sympathetically, shaking hands, saying nothing.

Both of DuPont's parents were alive and had flown in from Boston; this Hugh had read on his phone will waiting in line. The family resemblance was so strong that an introduction really wasn't required. The father maintained a stoic face that broke into a warm smile with every new guest that greeted him. The mother was emotionally distraught but doing her best to comfort and thank those who had attended the viewing. The sister's eyes were red from tears, and she offered Hugh only a limp handshake.

Hugh had reached the last relative, and an attendant, who was making sure that the line didn't slow, guided him toward the main area of the chamber. He walked for some twenty feet, glancing at the assembled guests, searching specifically for an opening where he could see the clique in the center that he had spotted from the stage.

He found the opening.

He had been right: one was Claudio Zanini. Mr. Bentley Owner. The images from the society pages merged with the bearing of the man Hugh had seen in the park. Near him, but towering above him in her high heels, was his striking wife, Sophia. But she was talking to two other ladies, while Zanini was engaged in conversation with two men.

One Hugh also recognized. But not from the society pages as he scoured the web for Zanini. From photos everywhere: on the walls of TMMC, on the walls of businesses in the area, on the front pages of newspapers laying on newsstand shelves. It was Tony de Angelis. The namesake of the De Angelis Complex himself.

The third man Hugh hadn't seen before. Could it be this Joseph D'Alfonso who signed the register after de Angelis?

All of this Hugh gathered in three seconds. The reason he didn't look longer is because the three men also were glancing at Hugh as they talked. As soon as Hugh and Zanini's eyes locked, Hugh switched his gaze to the crowd. Nonchalantly. As if he had never noticed Zanini.

That maneuver was futile. For the next recognizable figure that crossed his field of vision was Dr. Michael Faccon, who was moving across the room toward the triumvirate. Bringing Hugh's eyes right back to the six-person clique.

Faccon wasn't alone. He was accompanied by a statuesque blonde. Although she wore black, she stood out on this somber occasion. Her side-swept hairstyle had her wavy hair cascading over her right shoulder, partially obscuring a diamond necklace and part of her right eye, and no doubt a dangling diamond earring on her right ear judging from the one on her left. Locked arm in arm with Faccon, she looked at least twenty years younger than he. And she looked like she was dressed to impress rather than attend a viewing.

For the next few minutes, Hugh was caught between stealing glances of the four men—and Faccon's dazzling companion—and trying to avoid the gaze of Zanini, who, unlike his original two companions, seemed fixated on him. Indeed, Zanini hardly acknowledged Faccon; all of the conversation was between Faccon and de Angelis. Zanini spent his time watching Hugh.

And then Faccon glanced straight from de Angelis face to Hugh's face, not missing a beat in his conversation. He was, very evidently, aware of Hugh location.

That Hugh had made a major strategic error in coming was crystal clear. *What was I thinking? That I could just waltz in here and pay my respects? That my showing up would make me look innocent to the police or some jury down the road?* Even as Hugh made his way toward the exit at the far end of the room, he saw Zanini working his phone.

Hugh fixated single-mindedly on his next steps. Get out of here as quick as possible. Make my way to the car unnoticed. Drive away. He looked at the crowd and furniture congesting the pathway to the door and set about mapping his quickest exit route.

The mental map dematerialized with a touch on his arm.

"Philip! What a surprise seeing you here!"

Hugh turned. He stared in disbelief.

He wasn't a person who swore much, even internally, but if he had this would've been a good opportunity for an internal invective. Instead, he was too stunned for even that. Before him stood Emily, the medical student he'd met in the bar two nights earlier.

Seeing shock yet recognition in his eyes, Emily leaned in and whispered in mock conspiratorial tones, "Or should I say Bond?" She tossed her head and laughed.

Hugh's mind had trouble comprehending this scenario. *I was in disguise! How?* There were times he didn't even recognize his own professors when he ran into them in an unexpected locale. How could she pierce through his disguise?

Hugh was frozen, unsure of his next step.

"It's me. Emily. You know," she said placing her right hand on her bosom, "the medical student from TMMC."

"Wh-wh-who?" Hugh stammered in reply. "I-I-I n-n-nev-never um, uh, met you."

With his words, a bewildered look passed over Emily's face. "You're Philip Shuttlesworth? Right? We met Monday night? At Gallaghers?"

Hugh felt panic. She even remembered his fake last name! The one he had used at times on his trip when in character.

"N-n-not me. S-s-s-sorry."

Emily seemed like she was going to continue further. But she just offered a mumbled, "I'm sorry. My mistake." She looked quizzically at him for a few seconds more, and just before withdrawing to blend again into the crowd, she added, with a shake of her head and a perplexed smile: "Must be your doppelganger."

Emily turned away. Hugh pivoted back toward the exit, visibly relieved.

It was a reprieve that lasted for about one second. For it was then he saw that the he and Emily were being intensely scrutinized by a large man, not more than thirty feet away. Lieutenant J. P. Kelly.

Hugh rectified his earlier missed opportunity with a suitable internal invective.

Chapter 27

Kelly began to move in the direction of Hugh. Or was it towards the medical student, Emily?

It did look like he was going straight for Emily. A sense of dread washed over Hugh: if Kelly talks to this student, it'll be devastating. And the items used for his disguise two nights ago? Still in the trunk of his rental car. Kelly only needed a reason for a search warrant. That reason was now twenty feet away from the approaching Kelly.

Hugh cut off Kelly's path.

"L-l-lieu-lieutenant. Um, uh, hi."

Kelly stopped and eyed Hugh. He said nothing. His head turned away, his eyes shifting back towards the med student. Hugh's next words brought him back.

"C-could you g-g-give me, uh, uh, ride to my a-a-apart-apartment?"

Kelly stared at Hugh. His brow furrowed. He said nothing.

"O-o-okay?" Hugh looked at him entreatingly.

Kelly stayed silent. Emily began to blend in with the crowd.

Kelly broke the awkward silence, "Okay, son. Let's go."

He had found something more intriguing than the stranger he'd saw talking to Hugh. An odd, incomprehensive request. But maybe the breakthrough he was seeking.

Kelly's large and authoritative presence, complete with full dress uniform, easily cleared a path through the crowd. Before his unwavering, straight-line approach, people parted like a school of fish bisected by a shark. Some, engaged in conversation, their backs to Kelly, were guided out of the way by their conversing partners. None hesitated to make way. Together, Kelly and Hugh walked silently out the viewing room exit, through one of the side rooms, and out of the funeral parlor.

Kelly led Hugh into the parking lot to a police car, where he motioned for Hugh to sit in the front passenger seat. It was apparent to Hugh that Kelly was here on official business. Perhaps as representative of the police department. Perhaps to keep an eye on Hugh himself.

Kelly drove for two blocks, unspeaking, until, with a peremptory tone, still staring straight ahead, he challenged, "What's on your mind, son?"

"Z-Z-Zanini." Hugh had prepared a line of conversation during the nerve-wracking walk from the funeral home.

"Zanini?"

"Uh…um, wh-who is C-Claudio Z-Z-Zanini?"

Kelly took his eyes off the road to look hard at Hugh. He focused back on his driving, pausing a long time before responding. This was not a strategic pause: he was delayed by an inner dialogue that felt a lot like a chess master debating his next move. And he hated chess. In this case, his initial thought to this unexpected question had been to ask Holiday why he wanted to know. To probe that avenue first. But his experience with Holiday so far had been that most of the conversation with him was torturous and a waste of time. Just like the laborious process of maneuvering around and through those pieces protecting the king. Still, as he considered the question, he had a growing sense of where Holiday might be going. He got right to the point.

"Zanini isn't someone you want to cross, son. He's a major leader of the local mob. A *capo,* if you know what that means. And a killer. Before he got to our city, he was accused of a murder in Philly. Probably one of many."

Kelly paused, wondering how much to share. If he was right, he needed to reveal enough to scare Holiday. He continued, with occasional glances at Holiday, who, with a thoughtful expression, was staring at the glove compartment.

"In the Philly case, the key witness died suddenly, and Zanini was acquitted. An informant also died under suspicious circumstances, and he'd been under protective custody. Even some of the jury may have been tampered with. .... Son, I've personally seen some of his work around here. Bodies that looked like they'd been tortured for hours before being dumped into the trunk of a car."

Kelly looked at Hugh. He had seen the bodies. That part was true. The rest were just allegations; rumors, not evidence, tied the deaths to Zanini. But he hoped this might set things in motion. If he were right.

Hugh shifted forward to look out the side mirror as Kelly spoke. Some distance behind he saw what looked like it could be the same white van that had pulled into the hotel lot shortly after Hugh had abandoned his room.

"D-de ...um...A-Angelis?"

"De Angelis? . . . Tony de Angelis?"

Hugh nodded, at the same time pivoting to his left to look out the back of the car to see if he could spot the driver of the white van. It was too far away and the windows were tinted. And no front license to help track the van. Pennsylvania was one of those nineteen states that required only a rear license plate.

Again, Kelly paused before answering, noting Hugh's concern and glancing himself in the rear view mirror.

"Well, off the record, he's head of La Costra Nostra in this area. You know. The mafia. The mob."

"Wh-Why not in, well, j-jail?"

Hugh looked out the side mirror again. It was not the best vantage to see who was following. But the white van was still there, despite their having made a right turn.

"Well, for one, de Angelis runs a tight operation that doesn't leave him exposed. ... And, off the record again, he's actually respected, quite a bit actually, among those who run the city."

"R-r-respected? B-by uh, uh, p-police?"

"Even city hall. Look. He brought us a break from what'd been a mess of endless turf wars and drug wars and senseless killings. He's made life easier in some quarters." Kelly wasn't playing a role. For the police on the street, it did matter.

Kelly continued, "And supposedly he's not into hard narcotics and flooding the area with drugs. Fact is, there's word he's turning the operation more and more legitimate." *Let the kid feel my honesty*, schemed Kelly. *Then when I lower the boom....*

Hugh could see that the white van was staying right with them. Pretty far back, with a lot of cars separating them. But clearly following them.

Kelly glanced at Hugh, who was looking through the side mirror. Time to seize the opportunity.

"Son, I know what's going on."

Hugh turned to Kelly. Hope was written on his face. "Y-y-you do?"

"Zanini. de Angelis. They're after you because you killed Professor DuPont. Right?" Kelly spoke as if with genuine concern, as a parent counseling his son.

Hugh's face dropped. He said nothing. He looked back at the white van. As soon as he got dropped off at his apartment, whoever was in the white van would have him dead to rights. He immediately regretted the concreteness of that last thought

"Son, I know that de Angelis was fond of DuPont. He, Zanini, they were there at the funeral. If they're after you, you won't survive the week." *Blunt*, Kelly thought. *It should get a response.*

It didn't. Hugh stayed silent. Kelly had made another right turn and still the white van was behind them. If he got out at his apartment… He shuddered.

Kelly continued, with the faux I-am-concerned-about-you tone: "Son. If Zanini's on your case for the DuPont murder, it won't be a pleasant death. He likes to send messages…. Your best option is confessing to the police. De Angelis, Zanini and company, they won't bother you as long as they know you aren't getting away with it."

Hugh stayed silent.

Kelly, sensing he was making inroads, continued to elaborate on why it was in Hugh's best interests to tell the police all that he knew. But it was just background chatter. Hugh's attention was on the white van. He had felt some momentary hope when it got stopped at a light. But then it had reappeared in the mirror.

"Son, you keep looking in the mirror. Do they already have someone following you?"

Hugh cringed. *Kelly is right about that, but for all the wrong reasons.*

"M-m-may-maybe Z-Zanini and F-Faccon, um, well, k-killed, well, D-doctor DuPont."

Kelly shot Hugh a look of disappointment, annoyance. He looked back at the road.

"I see." He paused, clenched his jaw, flared his nostrils, and then let out a very audible breath of air through his nose. "Faccon again." He shook his head. "It's just you and me, kid, no audience. Yeah, I saw him at the funeral, too. And with de Angelis. But you'll have to try better than that. He's just a professor. And we both know that you were the one in the house, not Faccon."

Hugh turned in his seat once again to look out the back window. The white van was there. Block after block it was keeping the same distance and turning every time Kelly turned. He had to do something.

"Caaaaaaaaaaan you d-drop me, uh, um, well, at the m-mall? Um, j-just ahead." Hugh pointed to where Kelly would have to turn.

Kelly did turn. Suddenly. Braking abruptly, he pulled off to the side of road. Hugh looked with shock at Kelly's angry face. Kelly was still staring straight ahead. But with eyebrows lowered, lips pulled tight, reddened face. Then Hugh turned and looked over his left shoulder. The white van had vanished. It must have turned off a side street when Kelly braked.

Kelly turned in his seat to face Hugh squarely. "This is a police vehicle, Holiday. This is *not* a taxi service." He paused. "You want to go to the mall, there's a bus stop not far ahead."

Hugh looked up ahead, then shifted forward to glance in the side mirror. The white van had reappeared, sticking its nose out a little on a side street.

"P-p-please." Hugh was imploring now.

"If you're in trouble, you best tell me. You also saw de Angelis and Zanini at the funeral, didn't you? Believe me, there were other mob leaders there as well, including de Angelis' right-hand man, D'Alfonso. If they even *think* you killed DuPont .... Remember that no one gets away from the mob on their own. No one. Only we can protect you. Only the police. Do you understand?"

Police protect me? You don't know how wrong you are. Hugh didn't speak. He just looked out the side mirror again. The white van's nose was still sticking out of the side street. Not easy to see. But no doubt the same white van that had been following.

There was a long pause, as Kelly sifted through various scenarios for advancing the conversation, but all pointed to a waste of time, listening to Holiday stuttering and saying nothing. For his part, Holiday had only one scenario in mind.

Finally, Kelly spoke. "Okay, son. I'll let you off at the mall. I can see you're scared. But there's only one way to be safe. I don't want to be picking your tortured body out of the trunk of a car…. You understand?"

Hugh nodded.

Kelly pulled back into traffic. For the seven-minute drive to the mall, both Kelly and Hugh remained silent. Kelly steaming mad by the waste of his time, but still holding out hope that Hugh would blurt out something useful, motivated by the fear of torture. Hugh hoping that Kelly wouldn't continue to torture him with his all-too-obvious tactic.

Kelly pulled into the parking lot, near the west entrance— not too close to the doors, enough to sit and engage in yet another one-way conversation. A monologue where Kelly reminded Hugh again that only the police could protect him. That he only needed to confess the crime.

Hugh gazed nonchalantly at the parking lot as he got out of the car, half-listening to Kelly and then thanking him sincerely. He didn't see the white van, but he knew its driver was watching from somewhere. Watching, but unaware that Hugh knew this, and Hugh was careful not to scrutinize the lot. His eyes darted here and there, but his head stayed fixed on the west entrance.

The mall was a large one. There were two levels and three main entrances, in addition to those entrances attached to specific department stores. And as soon as Hugh was inside, he moved at a rapid pace, even jogging, to the area of the north exit, where a Sears was located. Hugh quickly bought himself a new pair of pants, a hoodie, tennis shoes, and sunglasses. He changed into the clothes, placing his suit and tie and dress shoes in the empty shopping bag. He then left via the north exit, his hoodie pulled over his head, and assumed a sauntering gate to the mall bus stop, taking the first bus that arrived.

Sitting in a window seat, he saw the white van driving around the parking lot, its occupant oblivious to the fact that its target had left.

Within thirty minutes, Hugh had doubled back to his car near the funeral home and was headed to his next destination. The burn-the-bridge-behind-himself one.

Chapter 28

Kelly's characterization of Tony de Angelis was basically accurate. Anthony Vincenzo de Angelis was indeed head of the Pittsburgh faction of Costa Nostra. And he was well liked among city officials and even members of the police force: the city officials because he was charitable with their campaigns; the police because they credited him with bringing stability where there had been chaos.

De Angelis had gone quickly up the ranks in the Pittsburgh mob. Which wasn't all that hard at the time he made his move. Once Pennsylvania's strongest crime family, with tentacles that extended even into Buffalo and Cleveland, Pittsburgh's mafia was in shambles by the time de Angelis came on the scene. Its principal undoing: drug trafficking. As soon as the Pittsburgh mob got involved with heroin and cocaine, and it was moving drugs into Ohio, New York, and West Virginia, its days were numbered thanks to the renewed federal attention and long prison terms. Only when the FBI had moved onto terrorism would there again be space to operate. But by then the mob had all but ceased to exist in Pittsburgh.

The family was reinvigorated with the help of the New York families and the Philadelphia crime syndicate, who looked askance at the messy succession struggles that had taken place below the public radar and recognized in de Angelis a true, old school man of honor. A man who exemplified the virtues of being a loyal team member, with a reputation for being truthful, obedient, and always available to superiors, not to mention respectful of other men's wives, and passionately devoted to the absolute silence "oath of Omertá."And he was smart, effective, well-liked, strategic.

About the only traditional Costa Nostra virtue de Angelis didn't hold was keeping his distance from the police, a byproduct of placing his own unique stamp on the organization. His John Hancock was a move toward more legitimacy and allowing his reputation to spread into the public arena. The acclaim he gained for his business empire was challenged only by his fame in the nonprofit and educational sectors.

For all appearances, de Angelis, now in his early sixties, was a kindly person, hardworking, philanthropic, a good family man. Six days a week he would rise early and start work before all but his bodyguards. Every Sunday he went to the Catholic Church and, despite various Popes' proclamations that mob members were excommunicated, he was never denied mass. He was renowned for his generosity toward area charities; de Angelis even showed up to police benefits with his wife of over thirty-five years, Violetta. His three sons held leadership positions in legitimate companies under his ownership; his daughter was herself married to the owner of a successful shipbuilding company in Connecticut. Nice family. Nice man. For all appearances.

Which was hardly the full measure of the man.

Certainly, one was well advised not to take de Angelis' generosity and harmless look— he was bespectacled, thin, and about five-foot-ten—for weakness. His nickname "the Angel" may have been linked to him by some for his good works; for his closest associates, it was used in the sense of the archangel Lucifer. De Angelis had paid his dues in the mob, and he wasn't beyond that reputation if it suited him. But generally, he had nurtured the type of leadership skills that he felt earned him sincere loyalty and respect, not an illusion brought on by fear.

De Angelis had watched many crime lords go down. Gino Bruno, shot in the back as he sat in a car on orders from Caponigro, captain of the Philly mob's Newark Branch, who in turn was tortured and murdered. Philip Testa, who lasted just a year before killed by a nail bomb detonated by remote control (an act, de Angelis believed, directed by Testa's own underboss). The narcissistic and ruthless Nicky Scarfo saw his celebrity as Philly crime boss go the way of prison for extortion and murder.

Even in Pittsburgh, the early crime bosses left the scene in dramatic fashion. Founder Stephan Monastero murdered in 1929. His successor, Giuseppe Siragusa, murdered in 1931. And his successor, John Bazzano, Sr., ambushed in 1932, where he was strangled, ice-picked, and dumped in a burlap bag—all on orders of the New York "commission" for his own unsanctioned bloodbath of former business partners.

De Angelis had a way that deviated from the flamboyance and revenge-driven leadership that brought down so many before him. Although he was willing to adjust as deemed necessary, he took as his motto a phrase he'd read as a youth in a science fiction book: "violence is the last refuge of the incompetent." His default position was to solve a problem creatively. He mended fences, made alliances, found outcomes that satisfied those below him. He used his active and fertile mind. He was willing to weigh opposing points of view.

It didn't hurt, of course, that he did all of this with the very real threat of fear in the background should someone step too far out of bounds. If he gave the word, people disappeared. Not blown up by nail bombs or shot in a restaurant in front of horrified onlookers. Not found in the trunk of a car with dollar bills stuffed in their mouth and anus. But, nonetheless, they ceased to be problems.

The New York families liked de Angelis almost from the start and helped him rise to power. And they grew to accept his way of doing business, which was to gradually fade out those parts of the operation that he found personally offensive—such as heroin trafficking and sex slavery—and expand more and more into legitimate enterprise. But he made a calculated, and perhaps unique decision not to dominate in any of the lawful areas. This policy not only helped him stay below the radar, but more importantly, helped ensure that his underlings wouldn't get overly aggressive in trying to remove or discourage competitors using the time-honored methods of the mob—methods that had ended in so many deaths and convictions.

That didn't mean he forsook operations in the not-so-legitimate areas. He kept them, built them, and they were profitable. And in these he didn't allow competitors. De Angelis particularly expanded into what he considered "victimless" businesses like gambling and sports betting, hauling cigarettes into New York State, loan sharking, and prostitution. During the housing bubble, he took advantage of lax oversight by banks by having those owing money to the mob take out home equity loans, repay the mob, and then default on their loans.

But it was the gambling angle that had proven most consistently lucrative. Originally, it relied a lot on running a numbers racket, the "Italian lottery." Bettors would pick three numbers and try to match a random drawing the next day. Most often this was based on the last digit of the dollar amounts of the show, place, and win bets at a local racetrack. Even after the Pennsylvania State Lottery, with its "Daily Number" game, cut into profits, the numbers racket continued to make money. After all, it offered a lot of advantages to a bettor, who could do it on the phone and on credit, and there were better payoffs, no legal-age limit, no taxes.

Then came the legalization of gambling and with it a whole new pile of money for de Angelis' operation, as he soon cornered the market on casinos.

De Angelis' operation also penetrated such staples as extortion, bribery, and racketeering. It was just that these, as with any unsavory activity that was more likely to draw attention or anger people, were kept at a distance from de Angelis. They were run under the somewhat independent auspices of his capos, who were advised to keep a low enough profile that attention wouldn't be brought from federal authorities or the Pennsylvania State Police. The de Angelis operation was fully greased, with proceeds from any illegal activities smoothly moving into the myriad legitimates—the recycling industry, auto stores, used car lots, grocery stores, construction companies.

De Angelis had a loyal underboss in Joseph Salerno, a trusted consigliere in Joseph D'Alfonso, and three ambitious and successful caporegimes who headed the crews of soldiers. Zanini was perhaps the most capable capo. He caught de Angelis' eye when he was sent to the area from the Philly mob, perhaps as a banishment, perhaps as an olive branch, certainly also to keep an eye on de Angelis.

Zanini's only shortcoming, in the mind of de Angelis, was that he wasn't of southern Italian or better still, Sicilian descent. De Angelis own ancestry came straight from the toe of Italy, Calabria, just north of Sicily. Zanini's ancestry, like Faccon's, traced to northern Italy. In days long past, when families didn't relocate so much, this would have been enough for him to not rise in the mob ranks. Even to have been excluded altogether. But this was a new age. One in which even half-Italians like John Gotti could advance to the top. Zanini's effectiveness had resulted in his quick rise from soldier to capo and now to where he could run the bulk of de Angelis' less legitimate operations.

Chapter 29

Hugh parked in a residential neighborhood four blocks north of The MacArthur Medical College.

He had been to the medical college numerous times in the past year, mostly by bus, a few times using his boss's car. Whenever he drove, he would park on the street near the front entrance to the college—the entire side was metered parking—or in the small visitors parking lot just off the street, near the southeast corner of the block. It was near this corner that the bus also stopped. Either way, he would approach from the sidewalk, stroll around one side of the pathway encircling the fountain, and stride into the East Wing's main entrance. There he would sign into the guest book at the greeting/security station and receive a visitor's pass to go to DuPont's office.

But the East Wing was locked at this time of night. Sure, security staff would come to the door if someone appeared there. But visitors didn't come to TMMC at 10pm. And, at any rate, Hugh wasn't coming as a visitor. And didn't want to be greeted by security.

Instead, Hugh trekked four blocks, cut through the nearly empty back parking lot, and arrived at the De Angelis Complex entrance.

He took a deep breath. Then he opened one of the exterior glass doors and sauntered inside. Calm, casual, head slightly bowed. Just as he had rehearsed in his head on the walk from his car.

Another set of glass doors blocked him from entering. And these, Hugh knew, were locked. The safeguard for this entrance was not a manned security station. Rather, on the right side wall of the vestibule was a scanner, which would read the key cards of the students, staff, and professors who wanted to enter the medical college directly from the parking lot.

And tonight, Hugh had a key card. It would read "Thomas Fleming" and state "Med Student" in bright red letters, and have a photo that looked nothing like him. But other than those details, it was authentic. It was just that the photo matched that of the TMMC student who had been standing in front of Hugh on the crowded viewing line, key card dangling from his belt.

It was the viewing that had given Hugh the confidence that he'd be able to move unhindered and unrecognized around TMMC. The number of students and professors at the DeSandis Funeral Home made it apparent that the medical college would largely be empty, save for security and maybe a skeleton staff. And it was clear Faccon wouldn't be there—he evidently had other plans given the date he had shown up with for the viewing and how she was dressed.

Hugh swiped the card and pulled the door open, all as nonchalantly as possible. Externally, he figured he might have pulled off the act; internally, he was a mess of nerves and tense chest muscles and rapid heartbeats. He was well aware of the surveillance camera focused on this entrance—its image was always on the largest, central monitor among the wall of such displays behind the East Wing security station.

Perhaps even now a member of the security staff might be observing him enter. But, if so, security wouldn't see the swaggering, sunglass- and hoodie- and sneaker-wearing kid that had emerged from the mall earlier. Hugh had changed back into the dress jacket and shoes he had carried out in his shopping bag. He now looked every bit the part of a student returning from the viewing to get some studying done in the library or continue with his graduate research. It was likely he would be dismissed as such.

Hugh had entertained the strategy of using a disguise. Some fake glasses and facial hair. Maybe the addition of a hat. Much more likely he wouldn't be recognized by security, either on the monitors or personally in the hallways.

But being caught with a disguise? He figured his goose would be cooked. He hadn't the foggiest idea why anyone would consider his having a cooked goose to be a problem; he clearly saw the problem with being caught wearing a disguise. It wasn't exactly something he could talk himself out of and only increased the odds he'd be seen as a threat. Maybe turned into the Pittsburgh police and Kelly, who would find wide open a new front to nail him with the murder. The thought of wearing a disguise had disappeared the instant the last image had formed in his mind.

Having passed through the inner double doors, Hugh now stood in an open foyer with some couches and chairs. Directly to his left was the access to the Northwest Stairway, nicknamed the Kardashian Stairway by the students, tongue-in-cheek props to the fact Kim Kardashian's daughter with Kayne West was named North. Beyond that was the student lounge and further yet the Northeast Stairway and the East Wing.

But Hugh turned right and proceeded down the wide corridor that wove counterclockwise around the De Angelis Complex and, for the moment, farther from the East Wing and its security station.

Hugh had been in the De Angelis Complex before. Not often. But he wasn't unfamiliar with its layout. Some areas he had wandered through on his own after a meeting with Dr. DuPont. Other parts he'd been shown by Dr. DuPont. He was cognizant with how the corridors in this disk-like building actually only curved at the four "corners," not continuously in alignment with the circular outside. Between these four bends, the corridors were straight.

Hugh was in just such a gradually curving section of the corridor now, passing a number of small group rooms. These were darkened, the ambient light from the hallway filtering through the glass panes on the doors allowing Hugh to vaguely make out conference tables and chairs. These types of rooms, he knew, were a staple of the medical college, scattered on every floor. Here students would sit with their laptops and watch podcasts, or display images on the SMART Boards, or write on the white boards, or just study. But all were vacant this night.

Hugh passed one open space labeled "Virtual Anatomy Lab," which had several computer stations. All empty.

He reached an area with a larger conference room and then three Clinical Skills Rooms. He hadn't seen these three rooms before. Still, he was aware that they were like, yet unalike, the Patient Encounter Rooms located on the same floor, but near the East Wing. In a Patient Encounter Room, first- and second-year students met with "standardized patients": real people carefully coached to imitate actual patients with illnesses. In a Clinical Skills Room, the patients were lifelike mannequins with sophisticated, wireless software that could simulate having a baby or a heart attack, or scream they were hurting. All three rooms were dark this night.

In fact, everything seemed eerily quiet. Hugh had been right about the place being empty. There was no one in the hallways or rooms.

He was in a section of the first floor he hadn't previously been. He had visited the student lounge on the first floor, the library on the second floor, some laboratories and classrooms on the third floor, and the basement with its cadaver labs. Everywhere he had gone the hallways had been full of students and professors and staff, in perpetual motion like red blood cells coursing through arteries and capillaries. But not this area, not tonight.

Hugh wondered how busy this sector would be on a regular weeknight. Maybe not that much, he decided; it really was out of the way.

Still, it was unnerving finding it so devoid of activity. This was what he'd been hoping for; yet, the deserted hallways, the dimmed lighting, the quietness made him uneasy. If he ran into someone he would stand out. He wondered if he could look natural, or if he would look like someone who didn't belong.

Hugh had reached the end of curve and could scan down the straight corridor. It was long. He couldn't see anyone. Empty. Quiet. Dim.

As he walked, two of the rooms just past the bend caught his attention, one on either side of the corridor. Each had two sets of single wooden doors: an outer door with a glass pane, and a solid inner door set four feet further in. Hugh peaked through the glass pane of each. Both times he saw that the inner doors had a sign with a trefoil symbol on top of an inner ring, bearing the words "Biohazard." Neither laboratory was what he was looking for.

Hugh was walking down the straight section now. Still he encountered no one, not even a janitor. He looked at the ceiling and top of the walls. Looking to scope if there were surveillance cameras trained on the hallways. He had seen them before when he walked through TMMC, in the elevator, the foyer, the student lounge. He hadn't seen any in the hallways then, nor did he see any now. He wondered if the professors had resisted placing any as an invasion of privacy, where their every move, every hallway interaction would be observed and recorded.

Hugh plunged on toward his goal: to find and gain access to Faccon's office and laboratory. He had heard they were on the first floor, and so far all the rooms had been labeled in one way or another. He expected Faccon's rooms would likewise be identified.

The longer he was walking, the more the stillness played on his nerves. What would he say if a security guard came down the corridor and asked him where he was headed? With each step, his body tried to pick up its pace, only to be countered by his mind ordering it to act naturally, to not walk so quickly as to seem odd if observed. Meanwhile, his mind itself raced ahead of the body it was slowing down, imagining peril around every bend, and with little else to occupy it, danced with imagined dialogue.

"Where you headed, son?" said the phantasmal security guard.

"Just going to the cadaver room, officer, to check on my cadaver."

"What, are you afraid it's going to walk away?"

"Just kidding. Heading to the library."

"But that's on the second floor. Why didn't you use the stairway near the parking lot entrance."

"Okay. You got me. I was looking for Dr. Faccon's office."

"Why? It's late at night."

"I was going to break into it, because I couldn't find his home to break into."

"Oh, why didn't you say so in the beginning? I can unlock the room for you. His laboratory, too. And I can get you Dr. Faccon's home address. Oh, and one other thing: don't you normally speak with a stutter?"

Hugh's reverie broke as he reached a couple of promising rooms. The one on the left was labeled "Anatomy Lab Four." On the right was Room 118. But neither carried the name Faccon. His antennae said to move on.

He passed a couple more. None were what he was looking for.

Halfway down the corridor, he came to another laboratory on his right, which had a similar double door setup as the ones he had seen with the biohazard signs. Only the sign on this solid inner door stated: "Restricted Area: Authorized Personnel Only." A smaller one below that read: "No entry to cleaning staff." And an even smaller sign next to the door read "Room 112: Innovations Lab."

The name of the lab jogged Hugh's memory. He had seen it before. It was in some of the medical school literature, connected to Faccon's name. Hugh moved to the next room. It read "Room 110: M. Faccon."

He had found Faccon's office. But other than that, he hadn't been lucky. What would have been lucky would have been to find a simple lock, like the one in Hugh's own office. One similar to those in some of the rooms he had just passed in the corridor. Something he knew how to open, where he could use the tools he brought. He had been prepared for that.

But what he saw at Faccon's office wasn't a simple lock: it was two locks and one was a dead bolt. He went back to the Innovations Lab. While the laboratory's outer door had a lock that looked solvable, the inner door had two locks as well, with one probably a dead bolt. He was experienced with opening only a few simple kinds of locks. These weren't among them.

Hugh had found what he had been looking for. But he wasn't going to be able to enter. He had needed some luck and right now he felt like Bad Luck Brian. The one who "stops, drops and rolls—into another fire" or "gets scared half to death—twice. "

Chapter 30

Joey Colombrito, having convincingly assured the Boston client that everything would go seamlessly, that they hadn't a worry in the world, got into the white Chevy cargo van and shut the driver's side door. Salvatore Leone was already in the passenger seat, having secured the client's cargo in the insulated rear compartment.

From external appearances, it was rather ordinary for a full-size van with an extended wheelbase: eighteen feet long, fourteen feet of cargo space, seven feet high. But it was a custom-built refrigerated van. The double-decker cargo system was equipped to allow Salvatore to easily load the cargo by himself, and the Thermo King Refrigeration System had the capability to maintain temperature anywhere between +68°F to -35°F, a somewhat stronger unit than normally seen in the refrigerated vans or box trucks coursing city streets. It allowed a stable environment for their cargo, regardless of weather conditions or, heaven forbid, unforeseen delays, which they'd had a few too many of lately.

Two other pluses: its size meant the drivers didn't need a commercial driver's license, and its Mercedes diesel engine got good mileage for a reefer, nineteen miles per gallon on the highway.

Colombrito drove about half a mile and then eased the Chevy van onto Interstate 93. The ultimate destination for the cargo was Pittsburgh, but for now they were headed for I-95 and New Jersey for one more pickup.

Joey and Salvatore were a study in contrasts. About the only overt appearances they shared were that both were clean-shaven and with short-cropped dark hair and brown eyes. But Joey was short—about five-feet six inches— quite slender of build, and very studious looking with his wire-rimmed glasses. His complexion was light, and he had an infectious smile. Salvatore was a very large, big-boned, big-midsection type of guy. He stood almost a foot taller at six-five, and weighed well over three hundred pounds. His deeply tanned skin was rarely offset by a smile, the later trait giving him an intimidating presence relative to Joey's accommodating and friendly demeanor.

Regardless of their differences, both shared an important commonality: both were soldiers serving under Claudio Zanini in the de Angelis empire.

Wasting time. Hugh knew that's what he was doing. Ostensibly he was mulling whether to leave the building or press forward with a hastily conceived backup plan. A plan of dubious merit, considerable risk. But he would never get an opportunity as good as he had right now. And this glaring fact had ended the debate between fight versus flight five minutes ago. And still he paced outside Faccon's office door. What he really was doing was trying to talk himself out of something he knew he was going to do. Wasting time.

But once started, he moved quickly.

Rather than double back—crossing anew into the path of the entrance security cameras or someone entering or leaving the building—he forged ahead, continuing his counterclockwise movement. He passed small meeting rooms and classrooms, then the access door to the loading dock on his right and a service elevator on his left, both emblazoned with "authorized personnel only" signs. Just beyond those, in the middle of the next bend, the Complex's southwest curve, he reached a broad stairway to his right.

Hugh sprang up the stairs two at a time and exited one flight higher. Here the corridor broke from convention and wound only three-quarters of the way around the floor. This was because of the library: this impressive structure took up the entire space between the corridor and the street-side windows, swallowing up what on every other level was a passageway on the south side.

Hugh was in an unfamiliar sector. He had been to the library many times. But the main entrance was on the complete opposite side, near the passageway to the East Wing. Where he stood, the only entry to the library was by a key-access door, just to the right of the service elevator.

The architects who had designed the De Angelis Complex had masterfully combined function and beauty, and the second floor was no exception. Their principal inspiration on this level was to make the corridor wall bordering the library entirely of clear glass, save a few spots where climbing green plants provided some cover. The merging of this feature with the building's predominantly glass exterior made the library the largest, most visually open structure in the building. Passersby on the main street, others walking the corridor, and even some traversing the parking lot could see into this showpiece. At night, the library shined out on the neighborhood, displaying racks of periodicals and books, computer stations, and students and researchers walking around or seated in cubicles.

But the library wasn't visually open this night. It was totally dark. And this was not expected.

Monday to Thursday, 8am to midnight: Hugh had seen those posted hours scores of times. Tonight was Wednesday. It should be open. Except it wasn't.

It had never crossed Hugh's mind that the library might have closed early due to the viewing. He had wanted unhindered access to the building. But not this empty. Not so empty that he stood out like a fully grown Bengal tiger strolling New York City's Times Square on a winter afternoon. If he wasn't going to the library, what exactly was he doing on this floor?

And he might not have much better success than the tiger in offering a believable excuse to security. Not here. Not now. Not him. If he stuttered, he'd probably be marked as someone who didn't belong. The British accent would be equally problematic, especially if he ended up being taken to the security station or asked to surrender ID. Which would be two IDs, Thomas Fleming and Hugh Holiday, neither British, the first stolen and the second matching the person the Pittsburgh Police had no doubt been inquiring about.

Hugh was now walking slowly down the corridor clockwise. Listening. Watching. The darkened library merged with the low corridor lighting to enhance the deserted feeling that permeated the building. Yet, Hugh couldn't help but worry that a security guard was just around the bend, silently but alertly relaxing in a comfortable chair in one of the many alcoves.

Hugh's nervousness was increasing with each step he took down the darkened corridor, and the closer he got to his planned destination, the nearer he was to a full-bore panic. He passed closed office doors and various seating areas on his left. No one was in the alcoves. No one was in the corridor.

Hugh reached the foyer outside the library entrance. Here the corridor split off to the East Wing on his left, the library on his right, one stairway straight ahead, another behind. An elevator used to access the Complex's seven floors was located near the passageway to the East Wing.

And in this foyer, as conspicuous to his eyes as the tiger would be to those sharing the sidewalk in Times Square, were two darkened half moons, each five inches in diameter and set in white bases on the ceiling. CCTV. Closed-circuit television. Two fixed dome surveillance cameras designed to cover the foyer, the library entrance, the two stairways, and the elevator. Impossible to avoid, as Hugh knew from past glances at the monitors in the security station, itself one floor almost directly below.

And this was his risk, the reason he tried to talk himself out of this backup plan. And even then, he had counted on the library being open, and that eyes one flight down wouldn't be drawn to the isolated sight of a man walking across two otherwise dormant monitors.

Hugh figured he had a hundred feet to traverse to reach the East Wing corridor, where he had never seen a surveillance camera. He covered the distance in twenty seconds. Twenty seconds in which he needed security to be reading a magazine or dozing or surfing the net.

Reaching the East Wing, Hugh had no idea whether he'd been seen. Or whether anyone even cared. Or if they cared deeply and were now coming up the stairs or elevator to check on him. He tried not to think, since his only thoughts were of panic, of a desire to abandon his plan, to get out of the building. He picked up his pace, moving quickly. He reached his destination halfway down the corridor on the left side, two hundred feet short of the juncture marking the head of the East Wing's T, where the corridor split left and right.

In contrast with Faccon's comparative fortress, DuPont's office was vulnerable, secured only by a single, interior door lock. But Hugh already knew that. He had been here many times. And he knew that breaching it should be straightforward and easy, as uncomplicated as unlocking a car door without a key. Particularly since it wasn't unlike those used for the rooms within his own office. And those were locks he had experience with.

It wasn't a lot of experience. Just a couple of hours late on the Friday night of a long holiday weekend. A night he had stayed to finish off a report and discovered, after the last person had left the office, that his tablet was still in the boardroom, now locked. Adverse to calling Bridgewater, unwilling to wait until Tuesday, Hugh took getting into the boardroom as a challenge, a puzzle to engage his mind. If everyone and her sister could do it on TV crime shows, then he surely could figure it out.

And it was an easy task. Assumedly. That is, if one were to use as a measuring stick the plethora of self-appointed experts on internet videos demonstrating how to use the "pick and wrench method" to open pin and tumbler locks. They made it seem like child's play, even accomplishing the task with bobby pins.

For Hugh, not so much. He understood the principle, he followed the instructions, he got nowhere. It seemed that without some focused practice time, perhaps honed on some of the transparent locks being hawked on those videos, he wouldn't be able to crack the lock to the boardroom.

What eventually worked for Hugh, he didn't learn in any video. He just looked at an identical lock on the open file room door and discovered an easier method for this style of lock: he simply had to use a firm but bendable wire to push the latch far enough to open the door. Later, he realized that this was just his own variation on the common credit card method that some used.

Now, months later, he wished that he had practiced more the pick and wrench method, that he had bought the transparent locks and developed the skill. Then he might've been able to enter Faccon's office and laboratory. But with his inexperience, with two locks and three locks securing those doors, he might have been standing outside Faccon's rooms for an hour or two figuring it out. If that quickly. If at all. He'd have to be content with noising into DuPont's office.

But DuPont's lock didn't turn out to be straightforward and easy. There was an additional complication: a rubber insert in the doorframe positioned right in front of the latch. It was in the way, frustrating him. With each failed effort, standing exposed in the hallway, Hugh found himself increasingly unnerved, until his hands began shaking and he had to place his left hand over his right to steady it as he worked the wire. He paused and breathed deeply. He tried to relax and start anew. He again failed. He was panicked. It was taking him too long.

And then the quiet feeling of isolation was shattered by the sound of a door being shut.

Hugh looked up. The sound must have come from one of the doors on the arms of the T.

And it wasn't an isolated noise. It was soon followed by the faint sound of dress shoes stepping heavily on ceramic tiles. A sharp clacking noise, still in the distance and only noticeable because the building was so quiet and Hugh so attuned to every sound. But the person was clearly moving closer, not further away. Perhaps moving to the East Wing elevator, less than two hundred feet away from where Hugh now stood trying to break into the office of a murdered professor.

Hugh worked feverishly. As soon as the person reached the junction of the T, Hugh would be visible. And on this night, with no one around, he wouldn't be overlooked. He felt an intense desire to bolt. To be seen walking away would be a lot better than to be seen trying to enter DuPont's office. Hugh took out his pocketknife and cut off the rubber door jam. He tried the wire one more time. The door opened.

No one was yet visible at the T, but a scuffling sound of a misstep indicated the person was right near the juncture. Hugh entered DuPont's office and closed the door behind himself. He stood next to the door, with his ear pressed tight to the wood until he heard the sound of the elevator.

****

Karsten continued cruising the streets of Pittsburgh, familiarizing himself with places Holiday might visit, routes he might take, and now hotels where he might stay. Karsten had hoped to be out of the area by now. But there was never a script that came with his job. There was always the element of unpredictability, where he would have to think on his feet.

But generally Karsten's quarries followed patterns. Predictable patterns. Patterns like Holiday had followed so far in showing up to his office every day.

But then Holiday hadn't parked that morning in the office parking lot. Karsten had watched the lot since early in the morning, only to see Holiday show up on foot. Then Karsten, despite driving all around the area, couldn't find Holiday's car in order to put a tracking device on it. And so he had followed him from the office, only to lose the trail at a restaurant that Holiday entered but never came back out the public entrance.

But, predictable again, Holiday had shown up at the viewing.

But then he hadn't parked in the lot, nor gotten off the nearby bus station. Karsten had been watching both, using inconspicuous, remote cameras he had placed. Holiday instead had appeared suddenly, and before Karsten could do anything, he was in the viewing line. And a drive around the area again had failed to uncover his Ford Taurus.

Only when Karsten started poking around did he figure out why he couldn't find the Taurus: Holiday had used his credit card at a car rental company. And that Karsten had not foreseen, just as he had not foreseen the kid leaving his phone off all the time, making it impossible for him to track that way.

And he certainly hadn't anticipated Holiday leaving the viewing with a police lieutenant. Nor his being dropped off at a mall. Nor his not coming out of the mall for so long that it dawned on Karsten that Holiday had slipped by him some way. A review of the video footage from the cameras he had painstakingly placed to observe each exit point—there were eight counting the individual stores—revealed that Holiday had changed his appearance.

Karsten could understand why they had brought him in.

Karsten now was driving by The MacArthur Medical Center. But it was just an exercise in crossing his "t"s and dotting his "i"s. It was very unlikely Holiday would come by here. Faccon had made it clear to the security staff that Holiday wasn't to be allowed in the building and had informed Holiday's boss that the Bioscience Center's contract with TMMC was terminated. Karsten wished that Faccon hadn't done that. It would have been one more point of predictability, another place where Karsten could have found Holiday.

Chapter 31

DuPont's office wasn't completely dark. Light from the parking lot and the night sky filtered in through the window just enough for Hugh to make his way across the room without bumping into the desk or tripping over chairs. But then again, he was familiar with the layout.

He stood to the side of the window and glanced outside. The lot visible from this vantage point was devoid of cars. Hugh found the cord for the blinds and shut them. And now the office was pitch black.

Hugh turned on a penlight. It was one of three items he had purchased purely for this evening. It was small: about three and one half inches long. And it wasn't very powerful: it ran on a single AA battery and produced but a weak beam of light. From three feet away, it made a four-foot diameter circle, but in reality only a narrow radius of two inches was well lit. The rest of the circle was a diffuse bluish light that barely dinted the darkness. Hugh hoped it was dim enough that no one outside would be drawn to a light shining out of an office that had belonged to a just murdered professor.

He sat down at the desk. DuPont's desktop computer was still there. This wasn't surprising; Hugh expected it. The police would have wanted to take the computer to thoroughly search its contents. TMMC officials would have insisted it stay, on grounds of protecting confidential medical information.

DuPont was, after all, a medical researcher. Records of medical exams and patient histories, analyses of DNA: these were all part of her purview. And this would have triggered rigorous rules regarding patient confidentiality, overseen by institutional review boards demanding exact and strict protocols on how subjects' health-related data was protected. No doubt this was impressed on the police investigators, who, rather than deal with the labyrinthine imbroglio, would have agreed, at least in the short-term, to the computer staying in place and being looked at under TMMC supervision.

But even if DuPont didn't keep confidential information on her computer, even if it were on secure servers in a locked TMMC room, or in paper files in a locked cabinet, or encrypted on electronic media, it wouldn't matter: Faccon would have fought tooth and nail to keep the TMMC computer where it was. He wouldn't allow unfettered access by some police technicians who might end up looking a little too closely and retrieving something that could lead back to him. And she had something. Hugh was sure of it. This hit was a professional set up, not a crime of passion.

An image of Dr. DuPont crowded out his thoughts. In his mind's eye, she was sitting even now in the desk chair, in her black skirt and white blouse, learning slightly forward, smiling warmly at him, speaking softly and sweetly. Giving him her full attention, time stopping in her presence.

He shook his head, trying to dispel the image. He sat down, reached into the inside pocket of his suit jacket, and pulled out the second item he had bought for this evening: disposable exam gloves. He pulled them on and started the computer. The monitor lit up the desk and office space enough to make his penlight unnecessary.

Hugh wasn't sure what to search for. He knew it was pointless to look for the email implicating him—the one that Faccon claimed he received from DuPont and that the police would have tried to verify from her side. Hugh was intensely curious about that email. But it wouldn't be found on some readily accessible email application on this computer. Simply because DuPont didn't send it, and thus the timeline wouldn't work: it had to have been sent after DuPont was already in trouble. A murder as planned as this one wouldn't have been tripped up by sending an email that a yet free DuPont might herself stumble across, nor from an office computer when she was elsewhere. It must have been sent after she was immobilized, or dead, and via the medical college's online system, where someone like Faccon could gain access. Or maybe DuPont herself coughed up the login information under duress.

Actually, Hugh wasn't confident of finding much on the computer. Faccon and his ilk would have scrubbed it of incriminating information. Hugh was fishing. And probably with a bare hook, in an empty pond, sitting in a leaky boat.

But, then again, he figured he just might know more about her habits than Faccon or the police. He spent a lifetime observing people.

Hugh was well aware of his knack of keenly observing the world around him. It was, he presumed, a byproduct of conversations that had more dead zones than speech. Or, he had told himself on more than one occasion, maybe he was just gifted in this area.

Or maybe not. Maybe it wasn't anything to get puffed up about. Maybe it was, as a psychologist once deflatingly put it, a function of his always being on the bottom in power relationships.

How had the psychologist expressed it? Something about "people compensate for their lesser position, their inequality, by scrutinizing more carefully those with more vested power." Thus the abused spouse better knows the abuser than vice versa, the children better their parents, the jailed better the jailer. Simply put, Hugh was displaying an ordinary social mechanism to gain an edge to manage his powerless situation.

Whatever the reason, DuPont had been in Hugh's small circle of people he saw regularly and close-up. And he had observed her closely. He was counting on this "gift" of his tonight.

As such, the need for a password to unlock the computer was an expected and not daunting task; Hugh came prepared with educated guesses. Conjectures borne of observation, but also fortune and trust. For he'd had the fortune to arrive several times at DuPont's office just as she was returning from a break, and then, trusting him, logged into her computer as they sat together, facing the monitor.

She had not hidden the movement of her fingers over the keyboard. He could see those fingers now— long and feminine and graceful—and only moving on her left hand as she typed her password, an obvious economy move that allowed her to keep her long and feminine and graceful fingers of her right hand on the mouse.

Hugh himself had copied her practice for his own password and created a three-word, eleven-letter combination using just his left hand. She had been even more economical: Hugh had counted eight key strokes prior to her shifting awkwardly and hitting a single key with her index finger on the top row of the keyboard.

He didn't know her exact combination of letters and numbers. The mirror in his mind was good; it was not infallible. Good enough to discern the pattern, not good enough to remember the exact keystrokes.

Hugh was confident that she wouldn't use random letters and numbers for a password. Not on a personal computer in a private office. No need to be tricky. She would want something easy to remember. Whole words or combinations of whole words.

Still, this left a lot of permutations, depending on whether DuPont used a single word password or blended two or three words, or substituted ones and zeros for the twelfth and fifteenth letters. The permutations would become particularly unwieldy if one included three-letter combinations, like art, cat, car, rat, gas, or four-letter combinations, like star, wart, agar, cart. The addition of "s" or "es" could turn single words into plurals, like stars and gases. It could be dispiriting to think about all the possibilities.

Except it wasn't dispiriting to Hugh. She had started her password clearly using an "a" and she had used her little finger a second time to strike this key. He remembered a couple of "t"s from her quirky way of lifting all her fingers when she struck that key. Just the kinds of things that Hugh tended to notice—whether inequality in power relationship, or conversational dead zones, or . . . a gift.

If she kept the same password—and the pattern was the same each time she had logged in while he was there—then the possibilities were narrowed down quite a bit. Eight letters, all with the left hand. One symbol, also with the left hand. An initial "a." Another "a" and two "t's." And for five-letter and above combinations the number of meaningful words was greatly limited. Hugh planned to start with one word combinations of eight letters and work his way down to two-word combinations like artcraft and atstraws, then three-word sequences like atcatweb and atwetcab.

It didn't take long. She had used a single word, "artefact," and the percentage symbol, "%." Artefact. The British variant. A good medical term, to be sure, Hugh told himself, whether she intended it for spurious results on medical tests or something extraneous introduced into a sample prepared for DNA analysis. Soon the word would disappear as the gateway to opening her computer. The TMMC administration would change her password and recycle her desktop. But not yet. To Hugh's fortune.

Or, maybe not all that fortuitous.

Ten minutes of intense searching revealed . . . nothing. No interesting files, an empty recycle bin, browsers cleared of histories, icons that were a waste of time to click on. There were files dated for last Wednesday, and Thursday, and Friday, and Saturday. But very few and all innocuous. It was as if DuPont had been wasting time on each day—or someone deleted virtually everything, unsure of what was important.

Even as Hugh was fishing in what indeed was turning out to be an empty pond, a part of his mind was contemplating a more promising pursuit. While her sensitive research data was no doubt stored on an encrypted server—one he lacked the knowhow to breach—DuPont's work for the Bioscience Center had always been presented to him on a USB flash drive. Whether this was some ethical issue related to using a server provided by grant monies, or whether she kept it on both and the flash drive was just a convenience for passing on information, he had no idea. But it was quite possible that whatever she had that troubled Faccon was also kept on a flash drive.

Hugh didn't bother to look in the desk drawer. In the unlikely event that a thumb drive had been overlooked, it would be brand new, unused. He could see her, standing up near the bookcase, holding a flash drive and explaining that those with medical data weren't casually left around, where a mistake, or the "borrowing" by a colleague or secretary, might allow sensitive information to escape. This was, after all, an institution where a professional staff's cell phone was programmed to automatically delete its contents were a wrong password typed in three times in a row.

She had shared a lot with Hugh. As he sat in her desk chair, memories of her flitted in and out, hovering now and then on recollections of the faith she had shown in him since early on. She had spent hours advising him.

Not like a professor. Or even a mentor. More like a protective big sister, who had taken little brother under her wing. She had talked to him about the medical profession as if he actually would go to medical school someday. She had lent him copies of interesting medical articles and one of her research protocols. She had tutored him on methods to keep medical information confidential, on how she encrypted data and stored it securely. Hugh's own work required that he complete ethics training regarding confidential data; she had shared from years of experience.

To her, Hugh wasn't a charity case; he was someone worthwhile in whom to invest her valuable time. Even if his words didn't come out like those of her professional colleagues.

And what was important now was she hadn't disguised from Hugh where she kept flash drives designated for the Bioscience Center. And those thumb drives didn't come from her desk; she would fish them out of a decorative cup from Peru that she kept on her bookcase, each drive labeled "BioSci."

Piercing the darkness once again with his penlight, Hugh found the Peruvian cup, reached in, and found a flash drive on the bottom. It had no identifying marks.

Hugh inserted the drive into DuPont's computer. There were only two files, one labeled A1201872, the other A1202872. Hugh brought up the first record. It showed an extensive DNA sequence, similar to what he would receive from DuPont. But only the codings. Nothing else. No name or other identifying information. No associated notes or description. Nothing of obvious use.

He brought up the second record. Again, an extensive DNA sequence but nothing more. Hugh minimized this second document and brought up the first document alongside it, so he could look at the two images on the same screen.

A1201872. A1202872. Hugh was familiar with DuPont's labeling system. Per confidentiality protocol, records with medical info were kept separate from those with the personally identifying information. The linkage was these seven numbers and one letter. The labeling system she employed used the last three digits for the particular research project—318 was always used for her work with the Bioscience Center. The initial letter and first four digits were used to identify specific subjects. Hugh needed to find in her files research project 872 and subjects A1201 and A1202.

A quick search of her computer failed to yield any files containing these two digit-letter combinations. The identifying information either was on a server or in her hard files. For Hugh, there was only one option: the hard files in her locked cabinet.

Hugh looked for a key in the desk. It had been the place she had normally taken the cabinet key from when she pulled the Bioscience file. There were no keys whatsoever.

He stood up and reached behind her file cabinet. He retrieved a magnetic key holder. And from this he extracted the cabinet key.

And he smiled. Not because he had made an astute guess and was right. It wasn't a guess: he'd seen Dr. DuPont do this once before, when she had pulled a cabinet drawer and found it locked. Even now, he could see her in his mind's eye, her tall frame, with its invariably erect posture, near the file cabinet, her left hand on the cabinet as she reached behind with her right, her bosom pressed tight against the metal. Hugh's smile now was because her action again confirmed a trust, a kind of special bond. One apparently not offered freely or the key would be gone by now.

Hugh unlocked the file cabinet. He clicked on the penlight. Near the back of the middle drawer, Hugh found a green hanging file folder labeled 872. Within it were two beige file folders, one labeled A1201, the other A1202.

Hugh pulled the first one and laid it open on the top of the drawer's contents. It had a name, Edward Gleason, and the notations DOB641123 and CODRAR. Nothing else.

Hugh pulled out the second folder and laid it open on top of the first. It also had a name, John Morris, and the notation DOB660314, as well as some brief notations scribbled with a pen.

Two folders, two single pages inside, very little content.

Hugh committed what he saw to memory. And then, not trusting his memory under its current stress, He grabbed a pen from DuPont desk and a piece of paper from the printer and wrote the information down. He replaced the folders.

Hugh continued his search, looking through the file cabinet. He found file 318: the Bioscience Center. Nothing out of the ordinary. No references to him. Just the usual information. He replaced the folder and closed the file drawer.

An unease he had suppressed since entering the office now moved from the edges of his mind to the forefront. He was the suspect in a murder snooping inside the victim's office. This realization, no longer held in check by more pressing matters, was amplifying by the second. He noted his hands were starting to shake, and he swore he could taste the acidic bile from a stomach now beset by queasiness. Time to go, to get out of the office and out of the building. He could almost feel Dr. DuPont herself, his big sister, advising the same.

Hugh reversed everything he had done since entering the room—locked the cabinet, returned the key, replaced the flash drive, shut off the computer. He went back to the window, clicked off his penlight, and went to open the blinds, grasping a horizontal slat with trembling fingers as he looked through the opening.

Outside, on the near side of the parking lot, sat a TMMC security vehicle, the driver's side facing the office.

It was so unexpected, Hugh reflexively dropped the slat, causing the entire blind to sway. He stood frozen for a full minute, until he could bear the curiosity no longer. When he cracked a slat open again, he saw that nothing had changed. The car was still there, and although parked in an unlit spot, he could discern there was a figure in the front seat. *Is the person looking up here right now? Did he see the flash of my light? The moving blind? Is he notifying security in the building?*—these were questions racing each other unanswered through his mind.

Hugh waited. Five minutes passed. The car didn't move. No one got in or out. The only thing that changed was Hugh's queasiness had been joined by a feeling of unreality and an irrational fear that he was trapped, that security was gathering outside his door. He waited five more excruciating minutes. During which time the security vehicle sat, the person in the front seat didn't move, and Hugh became more certain that security, if not already outside the door, was on its way.

Hugh's anxiety overrode his caution. He left the blinds down and made his way to the door. He listened. No sound. He took off his gloves and eased the door open a crack, using his stripped off gloves to turn the knob. No security guard. Or two. Or three. No one was there. He glanced one last time at Dr. DuPont standing near her desk, smiling at him. He then moved into the hallway and closed the door behind him. He headed back down the hall toward the De Angelis Complex.

Hugh was feeling pretty good. Almost elated. Things were going well. Right up until he ran into the security guards.

Chapter 32

Joey and Salvatore had a change of plans. The call came in while they were on I-95: continue to Philadelphia that evening for an urgent pickup. The New Jersey job would go as scheduled tomorrow, but the Philadelphia one couldn't wait.

They were used to sudden changes; their itinerary was never set in stone. This trip fit a particular pattern of unpredictability. New Jersey had been planned. Boston had been a late addition to the schedule. Philly was now a last-minute addendum.

Fact is, at any time a cargo run from point A to point B could have points C and D added, and in any particular order. Or in no apparent order. Not long ago they had a run that started with only Delaware on the schedule, but after that they were first redirected to northeastern Pennsylvania and then later all the way down to Northern Virginia. Crazy from a logistics point of view. Their present trip, Boston to Philly and back to northern New Jersey, looked to be an easy run. They would still get some sleep.

And anyway, they liked what they were doing. And it paid handsomely.

The security guards were at the bottom of the Kardashian Stairway.

Hugh had moved quickly along the second floor corridor to the stairway—and then started down slowly. He had decelerated to a snail's pace not because he was wary and had his antennae up. Quite the contrary. He felt safe where he was: he but had to go down one flight of stairs and out the nearby exit to the parking lot.

It was exactly because he felt safe that he began thinking ahead to his next step, when he actually exited the building. Preoccupied with how to avoid suspicion from the security he assumed was watching from the vehicle in the parking lot. Visualizing himself walking casually. Contemplating whether he should go left and walk to the street, and thus avoid cutting so visibly across the lot, or if it would look more natural to be traversing the lot, as if going to his car or taking a shortcut to one of the nearby apartments.

He was like the woman who turned off the engine of her car while it was still traveling fast on the highway—because she had wanted to remove her key chain in anticipation of unlocking her home's front door. Not focused in the moment. His mind five minutes ahead of where it needed to be.

Or maybe he was just being blissfully oblivious that he was still at risk where he was. Like the man who walked into an open elevator shaft and after falling eight floors thought, "Hey! This is going well so far!"

It was a few steps past the landing between floors when his contemplation was broken by a gruff male voice. Startled, he halted, every muscle immediately tensing.

There near the base of the stairs stood two men. Or at minimum two men. Hugh could only glimpse the pant legs, which were black with a gold stripe. TMMC security guards.

It took a few moments of dread before Hugh registered that the voice he heard wasn't menacing. It was muted and not directed at him. At the same time, he realized that the men, who were facing away, seemed to have not even noticed his presence on the steps.

A second voice broke the stillness. It also was subdued, but with a joking, congenial tone.

With every utterance from below, Hugh retreated a step back until he reached the mid-floor landing. The conversation halted and Hugh wondered if they had heard his footsteps, if they knew he was just above them, if they knew all along and now were finding his behavior odd. Frozen in place, he mentally kicked himself, more than half expecting the two men to call out to him or come up the stairs.

But then he heard another gruff voice, answered by another joking comment. These were men that were wasting time. And smoking. No doubt about it. The smell was unmistakable.

Hugh slowly, quietly backtracked, moving at the start of every remark. Marveling at the men's audacity. Or stupidity.

Smoking in the medical school building? It wasn't just prohibited: even the smell of smoke on an employee's clothes was enough to draw a warning. Three warnings and one would be fired. Even from second-hand smoke. Or third-hand smoke. Even as a consequence of traces of odor left from eating lunch with a smoker or getting a lift to work in a smoker's car. These men had found a corner out of sight of the security camera on a deserted night. A corner where they never expected someone to be that night. Fortunately for them, it was someone who could never expose their secret.

Hugh moved again along the darkened second floor corridor and down a stairway. This time he took the Northeast Stairway, placing him for the third time in sight of the library foyer surveillance cameras, although this time only briefly, a few seconds as most. The Northeast Stairway exited close to the security station on the first floor, but also near a place Hugh would be more comfortable being spotted, the student lounge.

The student lounge was an expansive, open space with elements of a mall food court mixed with hotel foyer and coffee shop. It took up nearly the entire space on the ground floor between the north side's two stairways, with the corridor effectively running through the middle.

On its outer rim were many small, single- and two-person, elevated round tables with tall chairs, as well as some larger rectangular tables and booths. Scattered here and there among these were sofas and easy chairs and coffee tables, as well as two TVs, which were now off, but during the day Hugh knew would be tuned to news stations or medical talk shows.

The inner side of the corridor—to Hugh's left as he entered from the stairs—had some tables as well, but its dominant feature was a small cafeteria with a variety of food stations, where Hugh could see signs for sandwiches and soups and pizzas. There was a separate salad bar, now closed, and some vending machines for coffee and snacks and soft drinks. Unlike a mall food court, or hotel foyer, or coffee shop, the room also had a number of lockers, all on the far wall from Hugh, and a mailroom area, near where Hugh entered.

Why it was called student lounge was lost on Hugh. It was a place frequented just as well by faculty and staff. And, between the students, faculty, and staff, it was place normally bursting with activity even late at night.

Except now. Now it was empty save for two figures. To Hugh's relief, they weren't security guards. They were, quite apparently, students. Only two, but Hugh found comfort to know others around his age were in the building. The students were sitting together at one of the rectangular tables on the right side of the lounge, looking at textbooks and drinking coffee.

One glanced up when he saw Hugh enter; he quickly returned his gaze to his textbook. The other student had his back turned to Hugh and never looked up.

Hugh strolled into the mailroom area, allowing the space to provide a natural feign while he calmed his nerves and composed his next step. It was a substantial hub, including a staffed mailroom, now closed of course, and partially encircled by an inner passageway lined with student and faculty mailboxes. Nearby, a large bulletin board was filled with postings, announcing upcoming seminars, faculty presentations, apartments for rent, requests for roommates.

Hugh wandered into the inner corridor, as if checking his postal box, and then drifted to the bulletin board to read some of the postings.

His nerves now under control, feeling not totally out of place with the two students in the lounge, Hugh meandered across the floor to a vending machine, where he got a bag of chips, and then to another machine, where he purchased a bottle of water. He sat down in a booth, near the window. The security vehicle was no longer visible in the parking lot.

Hugh looked over a rack of magazines and newspapers and retrieved a medical journal and sat back down. He couldn't remember the last time he actually read a magazine article that wasn't online. But he didn't plan to read now, either. He just needed to fit in until he felt it likely the security guards near the exit were gone. Soon, the two students would leave and he would once again stand out—unless he walked out with them.

Not a bad idea, he thought. But, for now, he would wait and relax.

It was hard to relax. He was positioned between the security station on one side and two security guards on the other, near the exit he needed to take. He figured he had walked at least four times in front of security cameras, three on a floor where he had no business being other than to visit the office of a murdered professor. And he had gone to the office of another med school professor, Faccon, who was somehow in the middle of this. And he couldn't piece any of what was happening together.

Hugh took a sip on the water and closed his eyes.

An image came full form into his mind.

Something he had noticed on his earlier trek to Faccon's office. Something that, at the time, seemed irrelevant. Now, he wondered.

It was the image of a ladder extending upright in the first bend. It had been inside a short hallway that had branched off the main corridor, providing access to some rooms on the Complex's outer edge. A ladder perhaps placed there to fix a light or one of the ceiling tiles or to gain access to one of the air conditioning ducts. But maybe…?

Hugh once had seen a small, squirrely guy in an old building walk up a ladder and then disappear into the ceiling. In whatever manner that building was designed, the man had found some way to move around above the ceiling tiles.

The reasoning part of Hugh's brain told him that getting into Faccon's office by such an approach would be fruitless. It reminded him that in his own office, when he had gotten locked outside of the boardroom, he had moved one of those ceiling tiles to see the possibility of gaining access via the ceiling; it hadn't been possible. The metal frame was very fragile and supported only by some light wires. Hugh wouldn't have been able to move above without collapsing the structure.

The caution part of his brain added that to even attempt such an approach would be an unnecessary risk. He needed to get out of the building. Now.

Still….the squirrely man had success. And Hugh was already in the building.

As Hugh sat there, he saw the two security guards stroll into the lounge area. With their dark shirts sporting broad, shoulder patches of bright yellow gold, and their black pants sporting an equally highlighted gold stripe, they stood out, their clothes alone shouting, "We have the right to question anyone we come across on this property." Hugh held the magazine higher, propping it up to cover his lower mouth area, trying not to seem like he was hiding. Yet hiding.

The guards moved slowly through the lounge. And then they were gone.

And the self-preservation part of Hugh's brain said to hell with reason and caution.

Chapter 33

It was a combination stepladder/extension ladder, set up in the stepladder option and rising a good thirteen feet, bringing it within one foot of the first floor's high ceiling. Hugh noted it was positioned under a bank of lights. Whether an arbitrary placement or whether the lights were malfunctioning was impossible for Hugh to deduce; only the corridor's recessed lights were on this night.

Hugh pulled the ladder under a ceiling tile. His ultimate ambition was to break down the ladder, carry it outside Faccon's office, and use it to try and gain access through the drop ceiling. But he knew that no matter how vacant the building seemed, it would take just one security guard wandering down the hallway to see Hugh hauling the ladder, or climbing up, and he would be trapped, as if the ladder were one large glue board and he were the mouse. Albeit a mouse with a sheepish smile. He didn't exactly look like maintenance staff in his suit and tie. And so, a preliminary excursion to see if what he was planning was even doable.

Hugh climbed to the top of the ladder and pushed up on the mineral fiber tile. One corner easily lifted out of its frame. He peaked inside.

It wasn't what he was expecting.

Hugh pushed up the entire tile until it was nearly out its frame. Holding it aloft with his left hand, he shined his penlight inside.

Definitely not what he was expecting.

Hugh could see huge, rectangular structures made of sheet metal ranging through the above-ceiling space. Joining these were shiny, flexible, rounded ducts, some large, and into which he could easily fit, but also branching to smaller tubes, probably only fourteen to twenty inches in diameter. This assortment, Hugh assumed, comprised the heating and air conditioning and ventilation system.

But none of this was what surprised Hugh. Those structures were expected. What surprised Hugh was that the above-ceiling space was perhaps five feet or more in height and there were walkways snaking through the area. Metal walkways that looked to be a good two and a half feet wide and extending as far as he could see.

Hugh stared open-mouthed. The building designers seemingly had thought of everything. Including a crawl space where one could easily do repairs on the HVAC system and lights and hot water heaters and myriad other devices. A crawl space that on this Wednesday night might also serve another purpose for a man in a suit and tie.

Hugh let the tile drop. It failed to fall completely back into its frame.

Within a few minutes, Hugh had moved the ladder closer to the walkway, slid away that ceiling tile, climbed to the ladder's top rung, hoisted himself onto the walkway, and replaced the ceiling tile. He held onto a pipe and reached across to the original tile and pushed that back into its frame as well. He was now secluded in the space between the first and second floors.

This zone wasn't entirely dark. There were some dim commercial-type nightlights along the walkway and visible far into the distance. There was also an extensive lighting system; Hugh could discern that from the uncovered fluorescent light bulbs revealed in the sweep of his penlight. But the system wasn't on, and Hugh wasn't planning to turn it on even if he knew how.

There was much more up here than Hugh first imagined. As he shined his light to and fro, it exposed not just sheet metal structures, and metal tubes, and flexible tubes, but quite a number of larger structures, most of which Hugh had no idea of their function. Hugh remembered as well talk of plans to eventually add a clean room to the building. This would require yet additional above-room equipment to control airborne microbes and particles—equipment that could easily be installed via this crawl space.

And the walkway was itself extensive, branching regularly. It occurred to Hugh that with a plank placed between branched walkways, one could traverse over every conceivable space, doing repairs or installations relating to all the fixtures and equipment in the area.

A "false floor?" Hugh had heard the term used for those small spaces below floors, where one could hide electrical and computer cables. But maybe the term also applied here: this was like a floor hidden between the first and the second.

But, then again, Hugh considered, maybe *floor* was an overly optimistic term. It was not a comfortable space. He might have overestimated the height when he saw it from below. In order to walk he had to bend over considerably, even more so when his path intersected that of various ducts and tubing.

Yet, cramped and back strain and all, Hugh was feeling something akin to euphoria. He was now trying to calm himself, not from anxiety, not from fear, but from the thrill of adventure, of achievement. For the first time since he entered the building, he was in a place where he felt shielded, safe, confident… and clever. Yes, definitely clever.

For ten minutes, Hugh inched along the straight section of walkway over the main corridor, trying to judge where Faccon's laboratory might be. Finally, he reached down to lift a ceiling tile and gain his bearings. He couldn't grip the tile; its supporting metal frame was too tight, his fingers too thick, the fingernails too trim.

He reached out to a nearby flexible air duct for balance and found some give where it attached to the square metal facing, where floor met ceiling. In no time at all, he had tilted it out of the grooves holding it in place. The grating below was equally easy to move. He now had a broad field of vision—enough to know he had jumped the gun. He had farther to go.

Twice more Hugh repeated this. Twice more he found himself looking at a dim hallway short of where he needed to be. The fourth time he moved an air duct, he found it positioned between two doors. One non-descript door led in the direction of the corridor. The second door's location was evident from the signs Hugh could see: "Restricted Area: Authorized Personnel Only," "No Entry to Cleaning Staff," and "Room 112: Innovations Lab." Faccon's lab.

The walkway near this spot branched into two, separated by about fifteen feet and paralleling one another for more than fifty feet. The right walkway ended at some massive metal units that hummed and occasionally clicked, buzzed, and whooshed, and extended below the tiles. Hugh selected the left walkway. This one he figured traversed the length of the left side of the laboratory, near Faccon's office.

Hugh strode a third of its length before kneeling on the walkway and contesting with a ceiling tile. Once again, his fingers proved too thick to remove the tightly packed tile out of its edge molding. He reached out to an adjacent air duct, wiggled it free, squeezed his fingers through the opening, and pushed up and removed the tile from the laboratory's drop ceiling. He shined his light down.

He closed his eyes. He breathed a sigh of relief. Below Hugh was the raised part of a laboratory workbench, a place where normally one might put reagents or small boxes of chemicals or supplies. Now, it looked to be a solid, and unobstructed, and convenient place for him to land.

Still, it looked intimidatingly far down for someone who was invariable selected last, or nearly last, for gym class teams. Even now, even here, that haunting memory flashed into his consciousness: his standing on the gym floor, hoping against hope that he will not have the shame, the embarrassment, of being the last sorry choice in front of all his classmates, the one selected only because they had to select everyone.

He removed his tie, fastened the thinner end to the walkway, and dropped its five-foot length into the space below. It came up short of the bench. It was quite a drop. Hugh pulled the tie back up, gripped it, and then, with all knees and elbows, and about as graceful as a seal descending a ladder backwards, hung over the walkway and lowered himself onto the raised part of the bench.

He let go of the tie. He felt smug with his ingenuity. If those gym classes could see him now. He managed a smile.

And promptly lost his balance. He tipped forward, his toes on the edge of the shelf. He waived his arms in an attempt to regain his balance. He rocked backward. And then forward again, reaching futilely for the tie. It was no use. He barely had enough illumination to glimpse the countertop below and the outline of a black chair and he leaped out, hoping to avoid both and not land on some other unforeseen object.

He landed with a loud bang on the tile floor. But upright. He had not crashed into any boxes or glass tubes or microscopes or chemicals. He stood motionless for a minute, breathing heavily, smiling.

He looked around. It was impossibly dark. Save for an exit sign, the only lights came from various instrument panels, shining like crocodile eyes in a river on a moonlit night. The laboratory didn't seem to have any windows; there was no light from outside at all.

Hugh switched on the penlight and surveyed the room. There was indeed no window. There were two doors. One was in the direction of the corridor: a solid wood entrance door to the lab. The one near the lab workbench no doubt led to Faccon's office.

Hugh worked his way to the light switch and the banks of bright fluorescent lights lit up the laboratory. With no clearing staff allowed in, with no windows or light getting out through the door, he felt like he was in a safe cocoon. He had accomplished his goal of getting into Faccon's lab.

The laboratory was much more impressive than what he'd been expecting.

Chapter 34

When Hugh switched on the lights, he was standing in a narrow entranceway near the door. Ahead of him was the main part of the laboratory, some fifty feet long by forty feet wide.

The workbench onto which he had descended, rather poorly, would have been the attention-grabber in most laboratory settings. It was about ten feet long and bisected by a double-shelved, epoxy-coated reagent rack that rose to seven feet above the floor, separating workstations on each side. There were dissecting microscopes, and bottles of chemicals, and electronic equipment, and sinks, and storage spaces. And now it was highlighted by a single red tie, which hung down over the reagent rack from an opening in the ceiling.

But in this laboratory, the workbench wasn't the most prominent feature, not even with the tie. The real eye-catcher was the isolated surgical station set right in the middle of the room.

The station looked similar to those Hugh had seen in a surgical suite on the basement floor. However, in that case, there had been several operating tables in one room, set up for training purposes. Here was just one hydraulic table, maybe seven feet long and a foot and half wide, complete with overhead LED surgical lights, monitoring and anesthesia equipment, a ventilator, and an instrument table. Surgical headlamps lay on a nearby table, as did suction pumps and clamps. There was patient monitoring equipment set at the head of the apparatus and, further away on racks, monitors to show the surgery.

Nearby, mounted on a wheeled apparatus, was a moveable arm with an attached microscope.

The surgical station didn't have all the equipment he had seen downstairs. It didn't have the robotic surgery equipment or a laparoscope. But it was visually arresting.

Hugh was familiar with most of the items. He had studied surgical equipment with great enthusiasm once. It was when he had gotten his first big break: to be able to shadow a surgeon. Until then, he had been frustrated when all his efforts to find a physician to shadow had failed repeatedly. Then, through a chain of email correspondence, he had lucked out and found a surgeon willing to let him observe him during surgery. It was to be the lynchpin for his medical school application.

Hugh prepped for days. The surgeon had told Hugh he could stay for as long as he wanted, warning him that surgeons sometimes had to stay on their feet twelve to fourteen hours during a surgery, without any breaks for food. Hugh wanted every minute. He studied the equipment, read up on surgical procedures, and prepared himself physically.

But then it had all fallen apart. When he met the surgeon face to face shortly before the big day, the surgeon explained that he was too busy to take on another shadow. And then he encouraged Hugh not to go into the medical field at all. Communication skills were just too essential for the field, or so he said.

Hugh moved past the surgical station. There were other interesting accoutrements in the lab, some reminiscent of features he had seen on his tour of the lower floor. In the far right corner was a large refrigeration unit with double doors. The metal structure rose to the full height of the room, but its actual dimensions were unclear as it was built right into the walls.

There were two dials on the front of the unit. One read four degrees Celsius. The other read minus four degree Celsius.

Hugh understood what he was looking at: a cold room where inside would be access to a freezer room. It was simply duplicating on a smaller scale the morgue room downstairs, where cadavers were held for the gross anatomy laboratory.

Despite an initial sense of wonderment when the lights went on, Hugh realized that none of what he was seeing was all that surprising. Not given Faccon's position. He was a surgeon and researcher, who studied and published on experimental surgical techniques. He had a job teaching students—and probably other surgeons as well—on the complex, high-risk procedures he was renowned for, particularly his specialty of spinal surgery. Here in this laboratory, they could hone their skills before venturing onto real patients. Here, Faccon could conduct his research.

And clearly, the surgical suite notwithstanding, this was a laboratory, not the highly sterile environment one would expect of an operating room. On the one hand, there were scrubs and shoe coverings evident, and Hugh spotted used masks and gloves in a bin. But there were also two bookshelves along the wall close to the entrance, with all kinds of reference manuals and equipment catalogs and dust. There were some remnants of food brought in from the student lounge and even an umbrella stand. Sterility, while evidently of some importance, didn't have the same priority as in a hospital operating room, where the leading cause of death from surgery was sepsis from infection.

Here there was no pretext of anything other than a laboratory for teaching and research.

Fitting into that teaching purpose was the large metal cabinet standing by itself along the wall opposite the lab entrance. About four feet high, three feet wide, and two feet deep, it had two doors. The first, a solid metal door, had been left unlocked. The second layer of protection, a glass door, was locked. Through this, Hugh could see a startling diversity and quantity of analgesics for relieving intense pain: codeine, hydrocodone, **dihydromorphinone**, oxycodone, and diacetylmorphine, some labeled both under their trade name and common names, like morphine/sevredol.

It was a narcotics cabinet, bigger than Hugh had seen, or could imagine for a med school laboratory. But, what did he know? He never made it to med school. Perhaps Faccon was the main teacher in terms of administering these drugs. After all, this was one of the many areas in which in which he supposedly considered himself an expert.

Hugh went to the large refrigeration unit in the far right corner. It was locked. So too were the several small refrigeration units on the floor. Each was a little bigger than a chest cooler and were also marked with temperature gauges, each displaying different settings: twenty degrees Celsius, fifteen degrees Celsius, four degrees Celsius, minus four degrees Celsius, minus eighty degrees Celsius. The ones that weren't locked were empty.

One large glass cabinet took up a quarter of the wall on the office side. This one had been left unlocked. There were racks of chemicals here, most in amber glass containers. Only a few items had common names, such as glycerol and proplylene glycol. The others were labeled only by their chemical formulas: HCl, H_2SO_4, $CHCL_3$, $F_3CCHBrCL$, $C_4H_3F_7O$, $ClCHCCl_2$, $C_3H_2F_6O$, C_3H_6, $C_3H_2ClF_5O$.

Hugh completed his circle of the laboratory, arriving at the door leading to Faccon's office. Its single lock was oriented to prevent access from the lab. That it did poorly, as Hugh had soon breached it. Light from the lab poured into the room and Hugh stepped inside.

The office had a large, picture window to the outside, but the vertically slated blinds were shut. On the other side of the room was another glass pane, this one small and occupying the top of the door to the hallway; it likewise was obscured by a blind, a single, solid shade. Hugh left the lights off. The illumination from the lab would be enough.

The office was long and somewhat narrow. It did billow out near the entrance door into a type of antechamber with a sofa and easy chairs, explaining the narrowness of the laboratory's two-door entranceway. It was the walls of this antechamber, rather than the bookshelf-lined ones near his desk, where Faccon had deigned to display his degrees: New York University, B. S. in Biology; Yale School of Medicine, M.D., Ph.D. There were pictures of him with various dignitaries: U.S. senators and congressman, CEOs, entertainers, some in hospital settings.

Hugh moved to Faccon's desk near the window. Here the laboratory light spilling in through the door barely cut the darkness. Standing behind the desk, Hugh gently slipped a vertical blind to the side and saw that directly outside was a grassy area with scattered trees, including two somewhat shielding evergreens; the sidewalk and parking lot were some distance away. He switched on the penlight and rifled through the papers on Faccon's desk, then the desk drawers, the filing cabinet, the bookshelf. He saw nothing of any interest. He started a second time through the desk drawers, going more thoroughly this time...

There were three knocks on the office door.

Hugh looked up, rattled.

A student? Security guard? Cleaning staff? Had the laboratory light spilling into the office attracted attention? Did they think Faccon was here? Hugh stayed frozen in place.

A second set of three knocks came. Hugh remained immobile. His mind raced to the possibility of cleaning staff or security walking in, only to see him standing at Faccon's desk. He switched off the penlight, gingerly shut the open desk drawers, and soundlessly, like a rapidly advancing shadow, moved across the carpeted floor toward the door to the laboratory, ready to enter it and close it at the first sound of a key turning.

There was no turning of a key. There were no more knocks. Hugh entered the laboratory and closed the door to the office, making sure it locked behind hm.

And then he cursed himself. He cursed himself for nosing around the rooms before first taking care of his main business, the reason he'd purchased the third item.

Either bookshelf would work. Both were of the tall, eight-foot variety. Both were filled with large volumes that jutted out near to the edge. Both had a layer of dust on the top shelf, indicating the books were rarely consulted. Either would be a pretty good place to position a camera that showed most of the laboratory and could go undetected for at least a few days.

The camera was cheap and plastic. It was overly large: just smaller than a can of soda and highlighted by the large cow's eye of a lens. It had no night vision. It had no audio.

But it had a lot of what Hugh wanted. He could turn the annoying LED light off. He could access its feed on his phone and tablet. It offered Cloud storage. It worked by WiFi, and thus he could connect it to the building's student network, whose password Hugh had seen posted enough times that he had used it himself when in the building.

And its remote feed was reasonably protected from prying eyes. The setup required the camera's serial number, so that it could be found across the Internet, and it used a personal identifying password as well.

And it only required a few minutes of setup. Most of those few minutes were spent positioning the camera on the top shelf of the bookshelf nearest the entrance. Hugh then turned on his phone just long enough to run the setup program and test the operation.

He liked what he saw. At least what he saw on his phone. What he saw in terms of the visibility of the camera was somewhat disconcerting. He walked around the room; from every angle he looked, the camera seemed to stand out.

Faccon would eventually find it. Of that Hugh was sure. Hugh just hoped it would last long enough. And that Faccon wouldn't know who placed it.

Hugh turned off the bank of lights and mounted the lab bench and reagent shelf to exit through the same opening he entered. He grasped the tie.

Then he got back down off the lab bench and turned on the laboratory lights.

How the hell am I going to get back up through the opening?

It had seemed like a good plan. He would grab the tie and pull himself back up. But he wasn't a good climber. He was the guy in gym class who barely got a foot off the ground in the rope climb. The kid who couldn't do a pull up. Sure, he had changed a lot since then. He had lost weight. He exercised. But going up wouldn't be anywhere near as easy as it had been coming down. And it hadn't even been easy coming down, not with a stretchy fabric tie that was a far cry from a thick rope. In struggling to climb up, he might well damage the ceiling tiles, or the metal edge molding and hanger wires that supported them. Maybe even dislodge a ceiling tile to break into pieces on the floor.

Going out one of the doors wasn't an option. At least not a good one. He couldn't secure the dead bolt behind him, a dead giveaway of an intrusion that night. Not to mention he would still have to get his tie and replace the ceiling tile.

Hugh went to the lab bench and lifted a box on the reagent shelf, then another, and yet another and another. Most were lightweight, probably filled with packing peanuts and glass tubing or chemicals. One wasn't. Located near the far end, it was heavy and solid, as if filled with books or a solid piece of lab equipment. Hugh placed it in the vacant spot he had descended, turned off the light, and, using his penlight, again mounted the lab bench. He stood on top of the box. He now had the leverage he needed.

He grabbed the tie and wrapped it around his right wrist, hoisting himself to where he could grab the walkway with his left hand. Now he was like a seal climbing up a ladder—if the seal was also trying not to dislodge ceiling tiles or break edge molding or hanger wires. When he finally hauled himself onto the walkway, he lay prone, breathing heavily.

Once he got again to his feet, he worked quickly. He removed the tie and crumpled it into his inside suit jacket. He replaced the ceiling tile. And he headed back to where he had entered the crawlspace. Somewhere up here there was a more natural egress. Somewhere equipment could easily be moved in and out. But he was anxious to get out of the building; he took the route he knew.

The tile over the ladder, which he had so meticulously pushed back into its frame in order not to create suspicion, was difficult to remove from above. This time he took the bent wire used for DuPont's office and worked the tile free enough until he could get his fingers underneath, chipping off small pieces of the mineral fiber in the process. He was soon back on the ladder and replacing the tile.

Which again didn't fit neatly into the frame. One recalcitrant edge wouldn't fall in place, no matter how many times Hugh lifted and dropped the tile. He again used the bent wire, this time to wrap it around the tile and pull it down. Which promptly broke the edge of the tile.

Hugh finished pulling down the tile, retrieved the broken piece, and squeezed it back into the open space. Until now, the whole evening had been a masterpiece. This was like smudging one's name on the painting at the very end.

Hugh dragged the ladder to its original location and headed back down the hallway, toward the entrance he had entered earlier that evening. Ahead, he could see that the student lounge had the lighting turned way down. The students must have left. Hugh reached the exit and started to open the inner glass door.

A TMMC security guard stood between the two doors of the entrance.

It was one of the guards he'd seen in the student lounge earlier. This time, Hugh spotted him too late. He couldn't retreat.

Hugh opened the first door nonchalantly, and headed toward the second door, nodding his head in pleasant acknowledgement toward the guard as he passed.

The guard looked very perplexed to see him.

"Excuse me," the guard said, somewhat commandingly, somewhat obligatory. "May I see your ID."

Hugh regarded him, as if he hadn't heard what he was requesting but was suddenly recognizing him.

He then made a half-smile, brought his right hand to his mouth, placed his forefinger and thumb together, and pretended to puff slowly on a cigarette, exhaling slowly. Then he waived an index finger forward and back in the direction of the security guard, with a "I-caught-you" look, and then side to side, like a mini windshield wiper, in the universal "no, no, no" finger wag.

Hugh then walked out, the stunned security guard letting him pass out of the building. Hugh turned left to the street and took the long way to his car. Soon he was driving out of the area.

Chapter 35

Hugh was exhausted. For several blocks after leaving TMMC, the adrenaline from the flight or fight response had kept him emotionally high. But as the evening's excitement and stress dissipated, he began to crash. He was mentally and physically worn down. He may not need much sleep any given night, but he needed some now. And the pace of the evening hadn't allowed him time to consider his options for where he would sleep.

Hugh began to work through those options as he drove aimlessly out of the city. Obviously, the apartment and house were out of the question. But so too was a hotel. If the mafia was on the lookout for him, and at least some of the police were targeting him, any sleep in a hotel room might end up being permanent. Walmart parking lot? Truck stop? His car would be exposed and might well stand out.

Perhaps I should just leave. Just drive out of town and keep on driving and start a new life somewhere else. I can use my British accent and find a job and make a life for myself.

It was an intriguing thought. Who didn't want at times to just leave everything behind and start again? He envisioned a new life. It could be anywhere. A city perhaps, where he could blend in. Or maybe a small town. It could be out west, or down south, or Canada even. He could pick anywhere he wanted. Maybe he would get a chance to find love and have friends. He could get rid of all the troubles, all the complications, all the corners he felt backed into. A fresh start.

But then, Hugh reasoned, he might as well wear a sign that said "I am guilty." He would be a wanted man, a man with a past that he had to hide. Kelly and the police would track him down, and he would be facing charges of murdering Dr. DuPont. Or the mafia would track him down first, and he would disappear for good. And he certainly couldn't leave behind Holly.

And besides, he had begun to feel some optimism about figuring things out.

Hugh was now outside of Pittsburgh, driving aimlessly on a two-lane through a rather hilly and sparsely populated area. He had no idea where he was, other than north of the city, having some time ago crossed the Allegheny River on one of the area's numerous bridges.

He was feeling so tired, his memory so fogged, that he scarcely remembered what bridge he had crossed or how many he had crossed since then. Most of the bridges he wouldn't even have noticed. Four hundred and fifty bridges. That was how many there were near here, making Pittsburgh the "city of bridges." Only some crossed the Allegheny, Monongahela, and Ohio Rivers; the others traversed ravines and connected hills in this steeply sloped, undulating region, a place dotted with neighborhoods carrying appellations like "hills" and "heights."

Hugh noticed the houses in this particular stretch of road were few and far between, separated by wooded areas. He wondered about the possibility of finding a deserted road in the woods where he could crash. Or maybe a parking lot behind a closed business, possibly a used car lot or a car repair garage, where no one would notice another car parked for the night.

Hugh neared a house ahead on his right with a "For Sale" sign in the yard near the two-lane. He had, for some time, been driving slowly, well below the speed limit, as he fought off sleep. Now he slowed down even more.

It was an old house. Not dilapidated, but it had seen better years. It was set well back from the road, with a driveway that stretched about a hundred feet. It was isolated from nearby properties by woods and further cloaked by some evergreens in the front yard. There were no lights on.

Three hundred yards further up the road, and only a handful of houses later, Hugh reached a stop sign, where the blacktop intersected with another two-lane. But this new two-lane was an obviously busier road: wider and straighter, with large shoulders and both edgeline and centerline pavement markers—everything the narrow, winding rural road was lacking.

And there was a business at the intersection. Just one small building, with no windows, but even at this late hour there were a lot of cars in the lot. A sign with the silhouette of a naked woman bent over at the waist was painted on the front. It probably was open to 2 am; later dancers and workers would come out. Not a place Hugh could get a night's sleep.

Hugh turned around in the establishment's parking lot and drove back down the winding road. As he neared the house for sale, he slowed to a crawl and then stopped on the road.

There was no indication that it was inhabited. The lawn had been trimmed, but the house itself was completely dark. Maybe not unusual for this time of night, but there also were no cars in the driveway and no garage to hide them. It looked like no one was home.

Hugh continued down the rural road a full mile before he felt comfortable turning around, there being no streets, just driveways. Finally, he came to a place where there was dirt pull off, wide enough to make the U-turn.

On this return trip, Hugh made a right into the home's driveway. He waited to see if anything would happen. No light came on. No movement.

He drove further in, to the back of the driveway. No lights from the house. No sign of life.

Hugh quietly got out of his car, left the motor running but turned off the lights. He looked in the windows in the back. The shades were drawn, but imperfectly. He took his penlight and shined it through the window of a room at the corner of the house.

He sucked in his breath. There was no furniture in the room.

He went to another window on the side of the house. Again, no furniture.

Hugh got back in the car and moved it off the driveway to behind the house. With the house surrounded on three sides by trees, many of them evergreens whose boughs went close to the ground, the back of the house was pretty well hidden.

Hugh was pleased to find a back door leading into the basement. Not one of those sloped, double-doors near the ground so common on houses in the Pittsburgh area, and which if locked he would have to force open and end up splintering. This was a simple unlocked metal and glass door set in the left side of a narrow concrete entranceway. The wooded steps lead down to the basement level. Here Hugh was confronted with another door, this one wooden and lightweight and old, with the white paint mostly peeled off. It yielded enough to Hugh's pull that he was able to pop the simple hook and eye latch and enter the basement.

The basement was very dark and very chilly. Hugh used his penlight to look around. It was a large space, extending the length and breadth of the house, with a concrete floor and concrete walls. Save for an oil furnace in one corner and a water heater in another area, it was empty. Hugh went to the furnace. It was running.

There was nothing else to see. There were three tiny windows set at the very top of the back wall, light fixtures, and pipes everywhere, but the place had been cleaned out.

Hugh walked up the interior wooden stairs. They squeaked loudly as he walked. The door at the top of the stairs was unlocked. Hugh entered the house, confident that it was empty.

And it was. The kitchen, the living room, the bedrooms, the sole bathroom, all empty. There was only one floor for living. There were narrow stairs going to an attic large enough to have two small windows, but there was no indication that it had been used for anything more than storage.

Hugh tried the light in the bathroom. It worked.

The reason for the house being devoid of furnishings wasn't at all clear. What was clear was that someone had removed them, and they were now in another house or maybe in many houses. Only the blinds and light fixtures had been left; the thermostat was turned down to the minimum. Maybe a sale had fallen through at the last minute. Maybe something had happened at the closing, or the new buyer had died, or maybe the owner had been overly optimistic about selling the property. Or maybe the owner had died.

None of this mattered to Hugh. All that mattered was the house was unoccupied and still had heat and water and electricity. And tonight it would provide a good resting place.

Hugh retrieved his backpack from the car, took a hot shower—the water heater obviously not having been turned down—and left his phone off, but plugged it into a wall socket to charge. He then did the same with his tablet.

He selected the bedroom into which he had first peaked with his penlight and crawled into a corner to sleep. As he drifted off from exhaustion, he felt a twinge of melancholy about Holly, as if he had abandoned her.

Chapter 36

Joey and Salvatore spent the night in the van. Not at the same time. They had gotten a room in the hotel they always frequented when in the area. But they took turns using the room. They were only there for a few hours anyway. The trip to Philadelphia had gone without a hitch but had taken them into the early morning hours. They were due in northern New Jersey at noon. They would make Pittsburgh no problem by 9pm, the time they were scheduled to arrive.

The hotel was outside Philly, across the Delaware River in New Jersey. It was modest but benefitted from the fact that it was in a small town, and Zanini had a good relationship with the owner and the local police. They wouldn't be bothered, and they had a secure spot to park the vehicle.

Joey and Salvatore had been doing this East Coast route for some thirteen months now. They knew that they weren't the only such cargo vehicle—they heard talk about West Virginia and Ohio— but Zanini kept and demanded silence. The other major rule was to obey the traffic laws: make sure not to get picked up for speeding, keep the van registration and inspection current, no drinking and driving, and don't road-rage shoot anyone that cut them off. Zanini had added that last one as part humor, but also looking at Salvatore when he said it.

Their cargo runs hadn't always gone smoothly. There had been a few unscheduled hiccups over the last year. They were stopped once by the police for a routine insurance/registration check. There was a fender bender, which Salvatore had almost made way worse by threatening to punch the offending party, until Joey calmed things down. And there was the time they were stopped for speeding—this cost them both one thousand dollars from Zanini on top of the cost of the ticket.

Perhaps the most serious snag was when they had a flat tire on the interstate. A police car had shown up and the policeman had dutifully parked behind them and flashed his lights to warn the traffic. Salvatore was sure that they needed to unload the cargo to change the flat. Joey was adamant they had to do without. Salvatore had won part of the argument—half the cargo was unloaded and kept on the side of the van, in full sight of the police officer, while they changed the flat.

None of these incidents got them in the least bit of trouble with the law. It didn't matter that they were trafficking in contraband and doing it interstate. They had all the paperwork that the police needed. Even a call-in by one policeman to check their paperwork just led to an "all clear, everything in order." They were safer than a tractor-trailer that was hauling too much in weight.

For Joey and Salvatore, the job had its thrills. They got to connect to the big-time crime families in New York and Boston and New Jersey and Philly. And they got paid handsomely. They just had to obey the two major rules. And rule one was clearly the important one. A word to even their spouses or any other soldier and they knew their lives were forfeit. They wouldn't get any glory in the organization for what they were doing. But that was more than compensated by the money they earned.

Hugh worried about oversleeping and being caught in the house. But he also worried about leaving his phone on in order to set an alarm, pretty certain it could be tracked by the police and the mafia.

And so he woke up sporadically throughout the night, checking the time. The first time he woke up he was completely disoriented, wondering where he was. When it finally clicked, he ate a snack out of his backpack to settle himself. He fell back asleep. After that, he woke up with just enough alertness to glance at the illuminated dial in his watch and then fall back asleep. When he woke again at 5am, he decided it was time to get up.

It hadn't been a lot of sleep, but he felt surprising refreshed. He moved quickly, his mind rapidly processing and planning every step of the way. He was out of the house and out of the driveway by 5:20.

Work was no longer an option. Once he got closer to Pittsburgh, Hugh turned on his phone just long enough to leave a message with his office that he was sick. Most of his Internet research he would do in a library later, using a public computer with its IP address. But he wouldn't spend a lot of the time in the public in general. Today, he figured that mostly he would spend the daytime driving to various de Angelis properties, not sure what he was looking for, but bidding his time until the night when he wanted to be outside the medical school, anticipating and hoping that the delivery mentioned Tuesday night in the park would take place at TMMC.

Chapter 37

Karsten relaxed in the back booth of the sandwich shop. He was in the South Side, and the restaurant was crowded during this Thursday midday. Even if it weren't crowded, even if he was the only customer in this Primanti Brothers shop, no one would recognize him. Not even among the de Angelis group.

The way he figured it, de Angelis himself wouldn't know him if they were sitting opposite one another in the same booth. Karsten made it a policy to never conduct business face-to-face. The people that hired him knew him only by reputation. And only by the name Karsten. Not his first name—or his real name. But he knew the faces of de Angelis and Zanini and every mob boss from New York to Los Angeles. It was just that few had ever met him. He treasured his anonymity.

Karsten finished his sandwich of knockwurst, provolone cheese, coleslaw, tomatoes and French fries. He supposed that when visiting Pittsburgh, one had to have a Primanti Brothers sandwich with the coleslaw and French fries placed between the slices of bread. It was a unique and, he thought, quite enjoyable combination. In fact, this was Karsten's second trip to a Primanti's in the last twelve hours. He had been at the one in the Strip District at three in the morning.

Karsten ordered a black coffee and spent a few more minutes reflecting on his task at hand. He was impressed by his adversary. Just a young kid, but this Holiday had been wary and mixing things up. He seemed to be a quick learner. Switching cars, changing into different clothes at the mall, leaving the phone turned off, and now he hadn't even showed up to work. Here was someone who had a habit of either keeping his dog with him or dropping her off while he worked and picking her up afterward; now the dog was left at the neighbor's.

Karsten was confident that Holiday was still in the area. His possessions remained in his apartment and his parents' old home. He seemed attached to the dog. He had called in sick to work rather than just abandon work. And then there was Holiday's old car that Karsten had located in the rental car lot: he was pretty sure that Holiday wasn't stealing the rental.

There also had been some sporadic usage of his cell phone. Not consistent enough to find Holiday—a few minutes from a street location, an odd signal from the area of the medical college, another few minutes from a fast food parking lot—but all three times still in the general vicinity. He was making himself a needle in the haystack right now. But he would be found.

Karsten grabbed his tablet computer and left a generous tip. Not enough to make himself memorable, but enough to make up for monopolizing the booth. He hoped he wouldn't be back this way for a while. He was being pushed to finish this job right away, and he had a reputation to maintain.

Salvatore glanced over at the passenger seat, where Joey was sound asleep. Normally, Joey liked to stay awake while riding shotgun. To be a good co-pilot. But it had been a long night and they were on a boring stretch of highway. They had taken I-80 out of New Jersey, and once they had crossed the bridge at the Delaware Water Gap and passed Stroudsburg, the traffic had thinned out considerably. It was a half-hour after Stroudsburg that Salvatore had replaced Joey as the driver, and Joey had drifted off.

Not much really to look at. Two hours of mostly driving through forests until they would hit Route 220 and pass through State College; then another long stretch of driving through mountainous areas; and then Route 22, where the initial stretch was also desolate. Salvatore couldn't fault Joey falling asleep.

Things had gone well in Philly and New Jersey. The Philly group initially had been quite agitated that someone higher up their food chain had involved Joey and Salvatore at the last minute and without their input. And Joey and Salvatore bore the entirety of their anger. But Joey had a knack of disarming people just by listening and nodding his head and smiling close-lipped with an agreeable kind of "yeah-I-know, I've-been-there" look. By the time he was done, they were glad that Salvatore and Joey had shown up.

New Jersey: that was the same group as always. They liked both Salvatore and Joey and enjoyed their company. They tried to coax the two to stay and spend some time, have a few beers at the local club. But Joey and Salvatore had to beg off. They had a schedule to keep.

Joey was a good asset on these trips, thought Salvatore. He was funny and witty and bright eyed. And emotionally upbeat and steady: Salvatore never saw him lose his temper. In another life, he would have been a good psychiatrist, thought Salvatore. He certainly was a patient listener, who always seemed genuinely interested in the lives of the person he was talking to, whether it was Salvatore, or a client, or the waitress serving their table.

Whereas if I was a psychiatrist, Salvatore reasoned, *I would probably shoot a guy if he started whining about life. Or at least tell him to shut up, that he was a loser.*

But they weren't psychiatrists. They had found themselves in a job that was even more specialized and probably paid just as much, once one subtracted the cost of an education, which the psychiatrist needed and they didn't. They figured there were just two key qualifications: a reputation for silence and a clean record, driving and otherwise. "Keeping the Omertá," as Joey liked to say about maintaining silence of their mob activities. "Unbranded farm animals," as the more earthly Salvatore pictured their role, repeating a phrase he had heard someone use for those not having a criminal record.

Not that either lacked a history in criminal activity. Salvatore had been in loan sharking; Joey had headed up a small gambling operation. But they had been careful. So careful that Joey's family didn't have an inkling he was involved with the mob.

Salvatore woke up Joey when Route 22 intersected I-376. There was just twenty minutes of driving left before they hit Pittsburgh. They were ahead of schedule and would need to wait somewhere outside of Pittsburgh. Their instructions were to show up exactly at 9:00pm. Not a minute sooner. Not a minute later. And not to wait around long inside Pittsburgh.

There was a place they often stopped, where Salvatore could lay back in the driver's seat and get some rest himself. Then they could get some coffee before the home stretch. When the night was finally over, Salvatore would sleep in his own bed in his townhouse in Pittsburgh. He liked the city and the flow of the people and the choices of places to eat and company to keep. Joey would have a bit more to go, having moved his family to a sparsely populated township outside of Pittsburgh.

Chapter 38

Right place. Right time. Right strategy.

Of the three, the most nebulous was the place. He had control of the third. The second had a window in which it could occur. The first, however, was truly unspecified. But Hugh had to make a conjecture and felt the one he made was reasonable. It felt right.

The strategy, for the most part, was simply to wait patiently and covertly.

Being patient was no problem for him. And he felt he was pretty well hidden. There were suction-cup-held shades on both the driver's and passenger's side front windows of the rented sedan, just as he had employed earlier. To these he had now added a folded sun reflector for the front windshield. As long as he slouched down, he was hard to see from most directions. He could peer out through a crack between the shades without drawing attention.

The time had been in-the-ballpark vague.

He had heard "Thursday evening" for the delivery. Zanini had mentioned Thursday twice when he had spoken to Faccon in the park; he had mentioned evening once. But when does evening begin? Dusk? Six o'clock? Hugh had read that in some parts of the United States, notably the South, it often started even earlier. And how late does evening go? Midnight? Till after dinner? Till one went to bed?

The vagueness meant that Hugh had to arrive early. And he had. He had arrived well before dusk—five o'clock, actually.

After all, this was the only thing he had been waiting for all day. And he had plenty of time on his hands anyway. His only concern was arriving too late.

It was the unspecified location that made him the most anxious.

Still, Hugh had a fairly confident sense it would be at the medical school. It was a logical supposition, given all that he knew and that Faccon was the center point for the delivery.

And so Hugh waited just beyond the back parking lot of the medical college, on the same side street he had parked on Tuesday night. But, if anything, he had a better vantage point now. It was a bonus of arriving early. He had moved farther up on the left side of the one-way street as cars ahead of him had driven off. He was now closer to the intersection of this street and the main street that bypassed TMMC. This location not only let him see the parking lot, and the entrance to the De Angelis Complex, but he also had a clear line of vision to Faccon's office and the loading dock.

And so he sat and sat and sat, as daytime gave way to dusk. Not moving. Not getting out of the car. And not seeing, since his arrival, any sign of Faccon. Neither the person nor the Jaguar.

As he waited, Hugh was aware of one clear advantage over Tuesday night. And one clear disadvantage. The advantage was that Holly wasn't there on the front seat, attracting attention through the uncovered windows or the spaces left between shades. The disadvantage was that Holly wasn't there on the front seat, providing him any companionship. Keeping his spirits up. Keeping him focused. Keeping him awake.

Since his arrival, Hugh's mind had drifted off in varying directions. But it kept being drawn back to two particular intersecting lines of thought: Holly and friendship. Holly and he had been together every day since the time Hugh returned with her as a puppy. He had left her with a good person for now, but the neighbor was elderly, and Holly could require the investment of a lot of energy. Maybe the neighbor took Holly for a walk now and then, but most likely just gave Holly the run of a fenced-in back yard. And maybe Holly wondered why Hugh never returned. He had heard of dogs getting depressed when their owners packed up their bags and left on a trip. Maybe Holly was depressed now.

Hugh missed seeing Holly. Holly was Hugh's only true friend, as sad as even that thought made him feel. Holly was always delighted to see Hugh, always loved to jump into his lap, and was excited by the smallest attention he showed her.

Hugh had heard that if you had one true friend, then you are lucky guy. Well, he'd never had one true friend. Not of the human variety. He didn't even have people he could call casual friends. In high school, Hugh had tried hard to fit in. but his efforts were always awkward. It became so important to him that he tended to make mountains out of mole hills, and his stammering grew worse the more he tried. He could think of clever things to say to prospective friends; it was just that what sounded witty in his brain sounded odd when he vocalized them.

Like the time he heard a group of kids in the hallway talking about songs, and one mentioned Eric Clapton, and Hugh clumsily tried to interject a comment about one of Clapton's covers. "I love *Cocaine*," he had blurted out in disjointed words that took forever to verbalize. Only to be mortified when he realized how it sounded, and the odd stares and derisive comments it had elicited.

On another occasion, he found himself in a group of students at their lockers when the school jock passed by, having had an awe-inspiring basketball game the previous night. Hugh tried a witty, "Matt and I combined for 50 points in last night's game." It sounded good in his head. Sure to elicit chuckles. It took so long to deliver that the only kids who hadn't looked at him as if he were strange had been those who had already moved on to ignoring him.

That fact that Hugh was such a good student had offered some social interaction. It was just that it wasn't the kind he wanted. Students would sit next to him to try and copy his answers to tests and would intimidate him to give them his homework so they could copy it. For a while he compiled, thinking this might be a way to make friends. But it didn't lead to any friends. And when he realized that he was just being bullied, not befriended, he stopped helping the other students, which made things worse.

His love of learning really had provided Hugh his only solace in getting through high school. He delighted in discovering new things, felt pride in the way he could grasp concepts quickly, and enjoyed the chance to express himself through written assignments and even tests. But he couldn't break through the social aspect. By his senior year, when students in twelfth grade normally have the run of the place, Hugh dreaded going to school.

This nostalgia wasn't helping, Hugh surmised. *Not a good time to start feeling sorry for myself.* But it was hard to focus, to stay alert when sitting hour after hour motionless in a car while absolutely nothing was happening. He couldn't get out and stretch, because he might be seen. He didn't even want to shift around in his seat, because someone might realize he was there and wonder why someone was sitting so long in a car in their neighborhood.

And he didn't want to risk turning on his tablet or cell phone and connect with the Internet. Because whoever was the "top professional" mentioned in the park, the one who apparently tracked him to the hotel, he probably was savvy enough to find him that way. For this reason, Hugh had only viewed the footage from the cam in the laboratory a few times and only from some distance away. Never in a place he planned to stay long.

At any rate, Faccon had never showed up. And his car wasn't there now and his office light wasn't on. So Hugh stayed slumped down in the seat, looking out at the same scene. Hour after boring hour.

And then he did just what he didn't want to do. He nodded off.

When he woke up, it was dark. The medical school parking lot was nearly empty. He perked up: Faccon's Jaguar was in the lot. And some light was escaping through the heavy shade in Faccon's office.

And there was a large white van in the loading dock. Two men were standing outside of it. Hugh lifted his the binoculars and took a look. One man was short and wearing wired-rimmed glasses, the other large and with a substantial midsection.

Chapter 39

The loading dock was nestled inconspicuously in the southwest corner of the De Angelis Complex. The grassy area with trees and shrubs that separated the Complex from the surrounding road and parking lot also served to conceal the loading dock, its concrete platform standing only slightly higher than ground level.

The ramp to this platform, although long and wide enough for an eighteen-wheeler, was similarly masked. This was a result both of its incline to below ground level—it descended at a fairly sharp angle from the parking lot road until it was more than four feet below the platform—and by the fact that it was bordered on either side by concrete walls that reached to just above the grass and were topped off on both sides by tall, overhanging hedges.

The actual doors of the loading dock were unobtrusive only by nature of their dull gray color, which matched the muted gray of the walls into which they were set. There were two doors, five feet back from the edge of the platform and about three feet apart. One was a large bay door; the other a single steel door.

The single door—to the left from Hugh's vantage point—not only led out onto the platform, but also provided close access to a six-step stairs cut into the platform, leading to the pavement below. Opposite the stairs, on the side nearest the single bay and just inside the concrete wall on that side, a three-foot-wide ramp gently descended to the pavement. It had a handrail on both sides and was reminiscent of a wheelchair accessible ramp but likely employed for hand trucks.

The entire platform was protected by a dull gray canopy overhead that jutted out its entire depth.

If Hugh hadn't been positioned where he was, he might not have been able to see the two men. They were standing alongside the van, which was backed up in the loading dock. Fortunately for Hugh, they were standing to the left of the van, near the platform's steps, and thus within Hugh's narrow line of sight between the van and the concrete wall and shrubs.

However, even with binoculars, Hugh couldn't see the men well. It was simply too dark. The only illumination, beyond that from the distant parking lot lights and even more distant night sky, was from a yellowish light set between the metal door and the single bay. The men, vague forms as they were, appeared to be doing very little beyond enjoying the pleasant evening. Not talking. Not moving. Just standing. Waiting.

The waiting ended. As Hugh watched through the binoculars, the single metal door on the left side of the loading dock opened and light poured out. Into the light stepped Faccon.

He was dressed in jeans and polo shirt, a far cry from his sharp dressing style of the previous night. He held the door open while he maneuvered an apparently heavy object, about two feet high, to act as a doorstop. Only then did Faccon acknowledge the two men, nodding a quick greeting as he walked down the stairs.

And straight to the rear of the van. No handshake. No exchange of pleasantries.

The larger of the two men opened the back door and Faccon disappeared from sight. The two men stood idly by.

It was a good five minutes before Faccon reappeared. He stretched his back a little, hands on hips, as he spoke to the two men, and then the three walked to the rear of the van, Faccon and the shorter man disappearing from sight. A minute later they were once more in view, and Faccon and the shorter man were scampering up the stairs to the platform and into the building. The doorstop was moved, the door shut, and the loading dock again enveloped in near darkness. The big guy walked behind the van, out of Hugh's line of sight.

Hugh lowered the binoculars. He abruptly brought them back up: the larger bay door was opening. Out came Faccon and the man, each pushing an empty cart: Faccon a gurney, the shorter man a flatbed hand truck.

But even with light spilling out through the bay door, the area where van met platform remained too dark for Hugh to be sure of what he was seeing. When it had been daylight, he had noticed floodlights set just below the canopy; they remained off. Binoculars provided some help: things were much brighter and clearer than the naked eye. But Hugh was too far away, the binoculars of too low power to provide the clarity he wanted. He was straining to see any details at all.

Straining so hard that he didn't see the man and woman until they were almost on top of him. The tiny portion of his visual cortex responsible for peripheral vision finally was able to get its message across, "hey, got something important here," and Hugh turned. And then all kinds of systems woke up.

It was a young couple, walking hand in hand down the sidewalk in his direction. Looking at his car. Looking at him. Both of which he suddenly realized were well illuminated. Lit up by something he hadn't considered when he had pulled into this spot in the daylight. He was parked right under a street lamp.

Hugh folded his hands around the binoculars and brought them to his lap. He studied the pair through an open space left uncovered by the sun reflector and the left window shade. Neither was talking. Both were staring straight at him through the same space.

For a brief moment, the man's eyes met Hugh's straight on, then averted away. The piercing gaze of the woman remained even when Hugh looked at her head on. Which miffed him.

What is their problem? Hugh said to himself. *I'm just a guy sitting in a car, lady.*

Just a couple of thoughts, which in quick succession were followed by some others along the lines of: *a big guy, in dark car, at night. Hiding behind suction-cup-held shades and a folded sun reflector. In a quiet residential neighborhood. Looking through binoculars.*

He frowned. *Yeah, maybe their curiosity has a point. Particularly if this is their neighborhood.*

Hugh leaned back. He tried to look as if he were resting. To appear nonthreatening and nonchalant while they passed by. Hoping their imaginations, if not dulled entirely, at least leaned more along the lines of Walt Disney than Edgar Allen Poe or Stephen King. Imaginations that conjured up more Joey from *Friends* sitting in the car than serial killer *Dexter*.

The couple strolled by. Silently. Even through the shade, Hugh could sense the couple staring in his direction and again after they passed the car and had unhindered visibility through the back side window and rear window. Hugh waited a couple of minutes. And then, not seeing them any more in the mirrors from his crouched position, turned around in his seat to look out the back windows. They were in a mirror blind spot, preparing to cross the street. The woman had her head on full swivel, glowering at him as she said something to the man.

Hugh turned back in his seat. He waited. And then waited some more. *They hadn't been on their phones. That ought to be a plus. Would they call the police about this odd man in a car?* He didn't think so. But he didn't dare bring the binoculars back up right now. He looked with his naked eyes at the loading dock. There was activity.

The shorter man and Faccon were disappearing back into the building, their carts now loaded. Hugh reached for his binoculars. He didn't bother using them. He was too late. The two men were already out of sight and the loading dock door was closing. The van and the lone man outside were again shrouded in darkness.

They were more in darkness than he was. Hugh slowly pivoted, peering through each available space in the car's windows. The light from the lamppost, now that he was aware of it, made him feel like an insect under a dissecting microscope.

And there were other lights compounding his worry, those shining in the houses and apartments across the street from him. That meant people were home in those apartments and houses. And some Nervous Nellie might look out and, like the couple on the street, find him worth being concerned about. Hugh hoped he wasn't attracting the kind of attention that would result in a call to the police.

Which, he realized, might just make him the Nervous Nellie.

When Hugh again looked back at the loading dock, it was just in time to see the bay door opening. This time only the shorter man came out, pushing his flatbed cart. It had something on it, heavy enough that he was laboring. He made the short walk across the platform. Soon the back of the van was again blocking Hugh's vantage point.

Hugh was curious about Faccon. He hadn't returned.

Hugh picked up his tablet computer from the passenger seat. He reached to power it on. He hesitated. It would add a new variable to his desire for invisibility. It might attract attention from those in the apartments on his right and on the sidewalk to his left. It wasn't odd for someone sitting in his car to be looking at a tablet—but sitting in a car at night with shades on the side windows and a sun reflector in the front? Whether they could see the light through the shades, Hugh had no idea.

Hugh looked back at the loading dock with his naked eye. The shorter man was on his way back through the bay door, again with his cart loaded. The bay door closed behind him.

Hugh wondered why he was even considering to look at the tablet. Everything that the camera was recording in Faccon's office was being saved to the Cloud for later viewing. He didn't need to look now. He could be patient and do this later.

Except he very much wanted to see what was going on in Faccon's lab. And he wanted to see it now. *I probably won't attract attention*, he mused. It was a rational thought, but too weak to move the dial from tentativeness to action.

Hugh again scoured the area around him. A car was driving up the street behind him, moving very slowly, as if lost. Hugh waited for it to pass. If anything, its pace seemed to slow. Maybe it was trying to find a particular house, trying to read the house numbers. But it didn't stop and when it got to the intersection, it continued on through.

A thought deferred came back: The couple on the street. He guessed they probably lived close by. He began anew to wonder if they deemed him enough of a threat to the neighborhood to call the police. If they had, how much time before the police would arrive? Should he start the car and be ready to pull out at the first sign of a police cruiser?

And then the bay door was once more rising, the shorter man again returning with his flatbed cart. Hugh picked up the binoculars. This time the man's flatbed hand truck had two cases on it, so seamlessly placed that Hugh at first thought it was one massive case. Both cases disappeared behind the back of the van. Soon the man and his flatbed truck were again headed back through the bay door and the bay door closed.

Hugh decided to forego the tablet. The phone—that should be discreet enough. He pulled the phone out of his pocket.

But before he had time to turn it on, he saw two things.

One was a man with a dog on a leash walking down the sidewalk towards him.

The other was a TMMC security vehicle, which stopped in front of the van in the loading dock.

Hugh had a fierce impulse to watch what happened next with the med school security. He was in equal measure apprehensive about himself being watched by this man with the dog.

In the end, disquietude won out. Hugh leaned back in the seat and closed his eyes, feigning sleep. He counted the time until he figured the man was past. Then waited another agonizing thirty seconds and looked out.

The man on the sidewalk had passed by. At the loading dock, a single security guard was talking with the big man, standing near the front of the van. It was too dark to see much, but judging by the big man's hand gestures, and what seemed to be a big smile on his face, there was the impression of an amiable conversation going on.

Then the side door of the loading dock opened up and the shorter man was positioning the heavy doorstop on the side door. He stopped when he saw the security guard. He smiled broadly, and waved, and came down the stairs to greet him. The three talked. Then the shorter man motioned back towards the platform, and the big man started walking to the back of the van and the security guard went back to his vehicle. Soon the guard was driving off, the shorter man pushing his flatbed through the side door with one case on it, the larger man opening the back of the van.

For what turned out to be the last time, the man and his flatbed cart disappeared into the building. When he came back into view thirty seconds later, he removed the doorstop, stepped out onto the platform, closed the door, and headed for the passenger seat, while the other man got into the driver's seat.

Hugh scrambled to fold the sun reflector in the front windshield. He pulled down the shades on the left and right, throwing them all to the passenger seat floor. He started his own car, nearly simultaneously switching on his phone with his other hand. *What was Faccon doing?*

The van pulled out of the parking lot and made a right turn onto the main road. An advantage, thought Hugh. It would pass in front of the street he was on.

Hugh began pulling his car out, following the van with his eyes.

This time the few millimeters of visual cortex involved with peripheral vision sent a message that was instantly received, loud and clear. Of course, it would have been hard to miss. It was bright headlights. And they were getting brighter by the second.

Hugh turned his head and saw the car barreling down the street. The driver seemed to be in a hurry. Hugh yanked the steering wheel…and pulled out in front of the car. The driver abruptly braked, so suddenly he seemed not to have time even for the obligatory blast of the horn.

The angry blast followed almost twenty seconds later. Which was when the driver had recovered himself and jammed on the gas pedal to pull right behind Hugh.

Hugh disregarded the car. If the car had reached the intersection only to wait for traffic as it made a left or went straight, then Hugh would lose the van. As it was, Hugh reached the intersection as the van passed by. He executed a right turn and followed.

And then he remembered to turn his car lights on.

Following the van by itself was simple. It stood out from other vehicles on the street. It was keeping to the speed limit. It was stopping at every stop sign, signaling every turn.

The complication was following the van while trying to first access, and then view, the image coming from the camera in Faccon's lab.

It wasn't, it turned out, the only complication. The driver he'd cut off, who had gotten stuck at the intersection as other cars drove through, who then got stopped a red light, had raced and passed cars and finally caught up to him, and now was sitting on his bumper, blowing his horn. Obviously, the earlier horn blowing had done little to mollify the driver's rage.

The horn blowing wasn't so prolonged as to necessarily attract the attention of the two men in the white van ahead. Probably because the furious driver didn't want Hugh jamming on his brakes while he was on top of him. That was something he intended to do right after he passed Hugh and cut him off. Probably with an accompanying hand signal out the window.

Hugh shook his head. *Can't the guy see that I am busy enough already looking at my phone while trying to stealthy follow a van?*

The car pulled up alongside Hugh and the driver glared over. What he saw was Hugh, his right hand holding a lit phone with three fingers lightly gripping the steering wheel, while his open left hand was tapping his chest and his head mouthing a submissive "I'm-at-fault, I'm-sorry" gesture. It worked. The driver didn't do more than offer his solitary finger salute and shake his head. He drove on and soon turned left down a street.

The problem with viewing the image on the phone while driving wasn't as easily resolved. From observing drivers in the Pittsburgh area, one would assume that it didn't take all that much skill to balance driving and electronic devices. Driving while talking on a hand-held phone was ubiquitous. He had seen people texting and driving, using tablet computers and driving, using laptops and driving. He had seen women driving while talking on the phones and putting on makeup. He had even seen one man in a truck reading a newspaper stretched over the steering wheel while looking at the phone in his hand. And a woman with a cell phone in each hand, driving with her elbows.

But Hugh wasn't one of those drivers. If there was skill involved, he was likely to be one of those eliminated by Darwinian selection because of lack of such a skill. He was finding it difficult to view the cam's low resolution image on his phone's screen while trying not to lose the van and trying not to get too close. A few times Hugh found himself drifting halfway into the left lane and more than a few times dangerously close to cars parked on his right. Once he nearly rear-ended a car in front of him that had slowed to make a left turn.

When the white van finally arrived at its destination, Hugh never got to experience relief from being able to stop his shaky multitasking. That was because he went right from anxiousness to surprise. The van pulled down the long driveway that led to the back of an eccentric-looking, Queen-Anne style, Gothic-flavored house, topped with pointed arches and rounded towers and one rectangular tower crowned by a fence of sharp points and crosses. The DeSandis Funeral Home.

Hugh slowed as he passed, then found a spot to pull over next to the curb. He turned his lights off. For a while, he couldn't see more than the vague outline of the van. Then a floodlight was turned on and the back parking lot lit up. The two men got out of the van. Shortly, they were joined by two other men, coming from the back of the funeral home. One had a very distinctive appearance: short in height, wide upper body, broad shoulders, thick neck with gold chain—Zanini. The other man looked like DeSandis himself, the man Hugh had seen at the DuPont viewing. Hugh watched as the men unloaded the van.

He had a clear line of sight but felt a little exposed where he was. There were no shades on the windows, he was but a block away. Nonetheless, he wanted—no, needed—a better view. He reached for his binoculars.

Hugh stiffened. A bone-chilling unease rippled through him.

He had used software to see if anyone else were accessing his feed from the laboratory. He now found that he had been joined by another viewer. With all the security measures—camera's serial number, personal password—it didn't seem likely, even possible. Clearly, he was dealing with someone with unique skills.

Hugh logged off the webpage, turned his phone off and threw it onto the seat next to him, and headed out of the area, driving away from the funeral home as quickly as he could.

Chapter 40

Karsten had finally gotten the break for which he had been patiently waiting. He knew Holiday would slip up sooner or later. It was a matter of when, not if. And the when was now.

At first Karsten thought this was probably an intermittent signal like he had detected in previous days from static locations too far to reach before the signal would disappear. These had been like some kind of ghost transmissions given how short they were in duration. But this time the signal didn't disappear. And Karsten could trace Holiday's phone over the Pittsburgh streets, starting from near the medical school.

As he drove, Karsten looked at two monitors on the dashboard, which were receiving information from the computer system in the back of the van. The first had two colored dots superimposed over a street map of Pittsburgh, with a red dot signifying Holiday's phone location and a blue dot Karsten's own vehicle. The second monitor displayed a visual feed of what Holiday was looking at. It was a grainy image from some kind of webcam feed. Clever guy, thought Karsten.

But the second image was irrelevant to Kasten's task. And it soon disappeared.

But then the red dot also disappeared, indicating that Holiday had turned his phone off. Clever guy, indeed.

It shouldn't matter, thought Karsten. He had another advantage. He knew the make, the model, the color of the car Holiday was driving. And he had gotten close enough to the location that he ought to be able to find it. If he had to, now that he had narrowed the search area, he could access the city's street cameras to help find the car. But that would require pulling over and going into the back of the van, and he didn't want to stop. He was too close to where Holiday had been when the signal had died.

In the end, he didn't need the extra help. The red dot lit up again. Holiday was back on his phone, first looking at the webcam image, then bringing up a map of Pittsburgh, then a list of bus routes and schedules, and finally again the Pittsburgh map. Still irrelevant as long as Holiday kept the phone on long enough. And he did. It stayed on long enough for Karsten to spot the car in the distance.

Clever, but not clever enough.

Karsten eased back and kept his distance. He relegated the second monitor to showing the same image as the first, but magnified to just the streets around the two cars, without the larger map of Pittsburgh. It provided him a much easier visual on any potential obstacles to tracking Holiday.

Karsten kept Holiday in visual range, well aware that he might turn off his phone at any moment and make that tracking worthless.

But Holiday didn't turn it off. Karsten remained back just far enough to not alert Holiday to the fact he was being tailed. Karsten would wait until Holiday stopped for the evening, and then he would complete his job and get out of Pittsburgh. Well, maybe one more stop at the Primanti Brothers in the Strip District.

Karsten watched Holiday turn onto Liberty Avenue and then over the 31st Street Bridge, crossing the Allegheny River. He was now north of the city. As he followed Holiday, he noticed the area growing progressively more rural, until finally they were on a two lane with only himself and Holiday on the road.

And then the drive was over. Karsten saw Holiday make a final right turn into a driveway. Karsten slowed considerably. The red dot stopped moving. Karsten pulled to the side of the road and switched off the monitors. This had worked out perfectly.

Karsten stayed parked on the side of the road for a couple of minutes. He then began to drive again, past the property where Holiday had pulled in, scoping it out. He spotted the car in the driveway.

It wasn't exactly the same shade of color as he expected. But that wasn't what was most disconcerting. What was most disconcerting was that it sported a license plate with a different number than he had listed, and that there were two people visible through the living room window.

As Karsten continued on by, it took twenty seconds for the scene to fully register in his mind, the first nineteen occupied with the thought that Holiday was staying with some acquaintance whom Karsten had failed to uncover.

He gritted his teeth.

It was okay. Karsten would go over the images from the street cameras and bridges and tunnels and get a bearing on the route Holiday had taken.

Surprisingly clever, yes, but he was still in the vicinity of Pittsburgh.

Holiday settled back in his "house for sale." He was now short one pretty expensive phone.

When Hugh first noticed that someone had joined him online, it had unnerved him. He knew how easy it was for someone knowledgeable to track a phone. People who had their phones stolen could see everywhere the thief went if the phone remained on. Those skilled could track the phones of others. He just had no idea how long they had been monitoring him and how close they were.

For a couple of blocks, he just drove, his mind darting through possibilities. It was obviously not Faccon doing the monitoring or the camera in the lab would've been disabled. The odds of it being a random hacking was too minuscule. There was one logical suspect, and that was the person Zanini had referred to.

To the forefront of Hugh's thoughts came the memory of the hacking of his apartment cam and a man showing up at his hotel in a van soon thereafter. Hugh had called the hotel the next night asking whether anyone had been looking for him. After an initial hesitation on the clerk's part, and Hugh's stuttering insistence on an answer, the clerk had blurted out about an AFT officer.

But it wasn't an ATF officer. Not in that van. Not coming by himself in the middle of the night. Whoever it was, the person had a special skill set, or resources to a special skill set, and was probably close on his trail right now. He probably knew his phone location up until Hugh turned it off. And a professional worth his salt to be brought in by the mob probably knew what car he was driving now.

For a while, Hugh considered dumping his car and his phone and taking a bus. He just didn't want to be spotted waiting at a bus stop. And the Pittsburgh buses won't stop, especially at night but even in the daytime, if you're not clearly waiting and clearly looking like you want the bus to stop. Get distracted and the bus flies on by. Stand in the shadows and you might as start walking to your destination.

And then opportunity knocked. And it didn't need to knock twice. Hugh saw a man get out of his car at a gas station and walk into convenience store. A similar looking car to Hugh's rental and one the man hadn't bothered to lock. Maybe the car was driven by someone just getting off a late shift at work.

Maybe someone leaving a bar or heading to work. But mostly, driven by someone who could be used to unwittingly throw off the Zanini hire for a while.

On a nearby dark street, Hugh sat in his car and watched the gas station. He had barely settled into his spot when he saw the white van, the same one at the hotel with the curtains in the back, drive by the gas station, following the same route as the car with his phone

Chapter 41

Hugh had a tough night trying to sleep. He tossed and turned, his mind racing and unable to rid itself of concerns that crowded out the possibility of more peaceful thoughts. He figured that if he could file the disquieting thoughts in a remote part of his brain and get a good night's rest, his unconscious brain could process the problems while he slept, and then in the early morning, his mind clear, he could think of a way out of this mess. He was always so much sharper when he first woke up.

But there was no "first-wake-up" period. He just couldn't sleep.

Everything in his life seemed to have cascaded, rather remarkably quick, and getting worse and worse with each passing day. He was sleeping in a stranger's house, without their knowledge, without furniture. His job was in jeopardy. His life, maybe not that high quality to begin with, was at risk of being forfeit completely. Holly was virtually abandoned.

Morning arrived and he was tired. The stress, the lack of sleep, the fact that he was the hunted and the hunter, left him worn down, weary. He had no one to share with, no one he was close to for advice.

Hugh got out of the house in the pre-dawn darkness and drove a half-hour before stopping for some breakfast at a diner. Rather than refresh, the meal left him with an overpowering desire to sleep. *Sure, now I'm sleepy*, he thought.

Hugh drove across the Allegheny and to Highland Park in the northern part of Pittsburgh. He had been there many times with Holly and knew the area well. He parked along Reservoir Drive, placed his shades and sun reflector, and went to sleep.

It was a good sleep. Sound and deep and needed. And there was a dream about being back in his old house. His dad was talking to him. His dad was saying some nonsense about how Hugh had messed this up like everything else he did, that he should have gone to the police. And then there was a knocking. Hugh looked at his dad and wondered where the knocking was coming from. Upstairs? The window? The front door?

Hugh awoke. The knock was coming from the front door. The driver's side door. Hugh popped it open and the sunlight blinded him, and he turned his head down for a second, glimpsing dark blue trousers through half-closed eyelids. He looked up squinting and could make out the dark blue uniform of a police officer, some flashing lights in the background.

"Hugh Holiday?" the voice asked.

Hugh nodded.

"Please come with us."

Hugh slowly exited the car, eyes blinking and watery from the late morning sunlight pouring from behind the officer. He made out the outlines of two officers. Hugh rubbed his eyes and shuffled along between the two, the direct bright sunlight joined by that reflected off the pavement and shiny, white hood of the patrol car.

Hugh noted it was parked on the far side of this one-way road in the middle of the bike path, flashing its warning of red and blue and amber lights. It was a sedan, basic white, but with the word *POLICE* written in big, bold, yellow-orange letters inside a wide black stripe along its side. Below it was the words City of Pittsburgh. Soon the wording and stripe were broken up, as the officer opened the back door, and Hugh got in.

Hugh was still adjusting to having been soundly asleep. He felt groggy. He considered that he should be more jolted by the experience. That the lizard part of his brain should be shouting a warning to his body. But somehow he felt resigned to his fate. He wondered whether one of these officers was the one he glimpsed in the park, the one working with the mob.

Soon the patrol car was on Route 8, but not proceeding south, as one would take to go to a police station in Pittsburgh. Hugh had been to the nearest two stations, those in zones 4 and 5. The former with his dad to deal with a stolen license plate. It wasn't all that impressive, a two-story brick and stone building that also housed fire trucks. The police station in zone 5 was more imposing and with a beautiful backdrop of trees. Hugh had stopped by there in a largely failed attempt to file a report on a theft he had observed a year earlier in Highland Park. It not only encompassed a separate building for the fire trucks, but even a building where firemen could practice their craft. That one was much closer. Probably five minutes away.

But the patrol car wasn't going in the direction of either police station.

The patrol car was going north on Route 8, not south. It soon was passing over the Allegheny River, out of Pittsburgh. Hugh felt he would not mind going to a police station. Better than to some field or empty building or wherever they were taking him. He felt powerless. A lamb to the slaughter.

He began wondering if they were hoping he would try to escape, and they could kill him for resisting arrest or would try to say he went for a gun. Or maybe they didn't even care how it went down.

Then the car exited 8 and was soon on Route 28, back towards Pittsburgh, but traveling north of the Allegheny River. No one in the car spoke.

Hugh's mind was just a shade more engaged than blank, closer to a dream state than an awake one. Or as if he were watching himself on a movie set, following set lines, with a director choreographing the scene.

He wondered whether he would get one last look at Heinz Field and PNC Park, whether the car would go that far south, to the North Shore.

The car did, and he got his look. The driver exited Route 28 and went onto I-279, where Hugh could look at PNC Park to his left. And then the car turned onto Route 65, where Hugh could see Heinz Field.

But then they exited onto Western Avenue, and this Hugh noted seemed to be a warehouse area. He passed buildings with hardly any windows, or opaque windows where they did exist. Some had tractor-less semitrailers parked in otherwise empty lots. One lot had been abandoned so long nature was re-establishing itself in the form of weeds and small bushes.

Hugh wondered in which building he would meet his demise. And still, the reptile part of his brain failed to spur his body into flight or fight. He felt . . . detached. Resigned to his fate.

And then the car slowed near one warehouse and made a right up a road. As it entered, the cop in the passenger seat gave the call sign "3-5-1-1" and said, "We're here with the suspect, outside." And the car rounded the turn and pulled in front of the Pittsburgh Bureau of Police Headquarters.

Chapter 42

The Pittsburgh Police Headquarters was in a large block indeed dotted with old warehouses. Fittingly, it was renovated from a warehouse and a bottling plant. These were conjoined by a brand new construction that served as the lobby.

Hugh stood outside the police car and looked at the entrance to the lobby. In contrast with the two mundane buildings on either side, Hugh found it captivating. It was a two-story concrete structure, with a glass awning over the glass doors. Rising above the awning was a sort of decorative, twin-tower facade that fronted the second floor and extended beyond the roof, which was itself folded inward toward the twin structures, rather than sloping downward from the center.

The buildings on either side were unimpressive. In particular, the yellow-gray brick building to the left was virtually without any distinguishing feature—or windows for that matter. Well, technically there were windows, but they were few, tiny, very high on the building, and each shielded by a metal cross frame. The two-story structure on the right was much larger and had plenty of large windows, at least on the side with the parking lot where Hugh was. But its top portion of brick still conceded a history as an old building.

It was the left-side building into which Hugh was ushered, after a brief excursion through the lobby. The entire adventure became somewhat of a blur, as Hugh moved like a steer through stockades, soundlessly enduring the wave of new experiences: the two officers—from Zone 5 it turned out—passing him off to another officer in the lobby. The emptying of his pockets to show pretty much nothing but car keys and a wallet, both of which they returned to him after verifying he matched his driver's license photo. Standing at a desk where they pressed one finger after another into ink. The officer leading him past rows of paperwork-piled desks, each set in an open cubicle with partitions that rose no more than eight inches above the desktop. His getting a chance to go to the men's room, accompanied. His then being placed in a small, windowless room, equipped with a small metal table and three wooden chairs.

And then nothing for ten minutes.

Hugh reflected on what had transpired. The police had taken a set of his fingerprints. But so far no handcuffs, no formal charges, no reading of his Miranda rights. Maybe this wasn't as bad as it looked.

Then two police officers walked in the room and stood before him, and one read the Miranda warning. No introductions. No advance notice. Just "You have the right to remain silent. Anything you say or do can and will be used against you in a court of law. You have the right to an attorney. If you cannot afford an attorney, one will be appointed to you."

The officer who read the rights, an older man with graying temples and sergeant insignia, looked up and added: "Do you understand each of these rights I have explained to you?"

Hugh nodded yes.

"I need a verbal confirmation. Do you understand each of these rights I have explained to you?"

"Y-y-yes."

The officers turned to leave. Hugh blurted out: "Uh, uh…am I under under ah-ah-arrest?"

"This doesn't mean you're under arrest. We simply need to ask you some questions."

They pivoted to walk away again, when the sergeant turned around and said, rather formally Hugh thought, as if preplanned,

"Having these rights in mind, that I just read, do you wish to talk to us now?"

"O-o-ok."

"Is that a yes?"

"Y-y-yes."

"Someone will be with you soon. Just stay here."

The officers left.

No one was with him soon.

He waited five minutes. Ten minutes. The younger officer returned, but only to bring him a glass of water.

Another five minutes passed. It had been fifteen minutes since anyone had talked to him; about a half-hour in this windowless room without anything more than hearing his Miranda rights.

In another place, or another time, he would have been consumed with an overwhelming boredom. But not here, not now.

Hugh got up to look at the large mirror that took up much of the back wall. It was set right into the wall. A one-way mirror, he thought. Although as soon as his mind said *one-way mirror*, he knew this was a misnomer; if it led to an observation room on the other side of the wall, then it would be two-way. The room would just be darker on the other side. There, someone could see him clear as day through what looked to be transparent glass, while he was seeing himself also, due to the bright reflection off the thin metal making the mirrored surface.

He wished that he had a flashlight and the ability to turn the lights off in this room. Then he could see who was on the other side watching him. Perhaps Kelly? But even the light switch was outside the room.

He wondered why a one-way mirror would even needed these days, when one could put a camera in the room with him. Maybe it was just a holdover from the original setup. Maybe not even a one-way mirror.

Hugh rapped the knuckles of his right hand against the surface and cocked his head to the side, listening. It sounded hollow, not solid. He cupped his hands and placed them on the mirror, making a dark tunnel, and he began to lean his eyes in to see what he could discern…

The door opened and a strong woman's voice said, "Take a seat, Mr. Holiday."

Into the room strode two people. The woman who had spoken to him looked to be in her thirties. She was thin, with long black hair, and was sharply dressed in a light blue shirt, navy blue suit jacket, and navy blue pants. She was wearing high heels and still was more than half-a-foot shorter than Hugh. With her was a heavy set man about six feet tall, also wearing a dark suit jacket and pants and light blue shirt, but with a dark blue tie. The woman carried a black satchel, the man a manila file folder.

There was something out of place about the woman's looks. Hugh couldn't place it.

He sat down. The woman continued speaking as she and the man took seats opposite Hugh, the man to the woman's right. The woman's eyes never left Hugh as she set her satchel down at her feet. The man placed his file folder on the table in front of him. The file folder was stuffed with papers.

"I am Detective Phoebe Feliciano. This is Detective Edward McPherson. We are with the Homicide Squad of the Major Crimes Division." If she had an accent other than that of a native of Pittsburgh, it wasn't perceptible.

Hugh nodded. There was something about the woman. She was definitely pretty. Very pretty in fact. High cheekbones, clear skin, narrow face, big and shining and captivatingly beautiful brown eyes. Luxurious and wavy hair that she wore swept over her left shoulder. The perfect shade of eyeliner and lipstick. A well-proportioned figure.

But something was out of place.

"We have a few questions for you."

Hugh nodded again. He noticed that she had an authoritative manner, but a kind of saucy smile, one that would creep up the edges of her lips at the end of her sentences. She enjoyed interrogations. But that is not what he was finding different in her.

"You know, we'd thought you'd skipped town."

Hugh nodded a third time. The two detectives looked at him. The women continued.

"Where were you the last few nights?"

"I-I-I, um, uh, well, in the p-park."

"Yeah. That's so not true. We know you weren't in the park overnight."

It was the Adam's apple. She had a prominent Adam's apple.

"Holiday. Are you listening? We know you weren't in the park last night. Where were you?"

M-m-my ... ah-ah-apart-apartment."

"No. We checked that. You haven't been staying there. Want to try again?"

A prominent Adam's apple on a beautiful woman. A flaw? No. Just something different for critics and haters and competitors to label a flaw and make themselves feel better by tearing you down. He had thought a lot about, and become very sensitive to, society's tendency to judge. And in this age of photoshopped images, and plastic surgery, and the perfect selfie, and supermodels, it was so easy to compare others to some artificial standard—and even to be your own worst critic. But everyone had something, he figured, that if examined closely enough could be fodder for judgment. *My feature just happens to be very public and prominent. Like hers.*

"Holiday?"

"H-h-huh?"

"Where have you been staying?"

"I-I-I did s-s-s-tay in …um, uh…hotel."

Hugh took out his wallet and opened it. He took out the receipt for the hotel he had stayed at Monday night and put it in front of the woman. He'd thought it might be a good idea to keep one where he'd stuttered. Just for Kelly.

Feliciano looked at it for a while and then asked the man to go make a copy of it. She didn't wait for him to return to continue speaking.

"This receipt is for four nights ago. And it doesn't even have your name on it." She paused. "If this is even yours, where were you Tuesday night and Wednesday night and last night?"

Hugh shrugged his shoulders. She waited. Hugh just looked at his hands on the table.

"Why not at your apartment? Or your parent's house?"

Hugh shrugged his shoulders, then answered, "T-t-too many, uh, well, m-memories."

A prominent Adam's apple. Too many people spend time dwelling on where one of their features fits in the Bell curve. Even if they are within what they assume is society's top half, they often compare themselves to those in the top ten percent. Or five percent. Or one percent. *Except when someone like me comes around. If nothing else, I make them feel good about themselves. The problem is those who like to point out my problem. Probably masking their own insecurities in other areas. I wonder if she does better than me and blocks out the haters, the critics, those who annoy with their expressions of pity. The "I am so sorry that…"*

"Holiday. You paying attention?"

He nodded.

"Lieutenant Kelly said you gave the impression that someone was after you. Is that true?"

Kelly. I guess it was a matter of time before that name came up. Where is he anyway? Behind the mirror?

Hugh just shook his head. He had already spent enough time moving the pieces on this question. It would be of no help to him to answer. To say the mob is after him and tying to kill him? This would just lead to him saying he was set up, and then to the fact that he had been at DuPont's house, and then to his arrest. After that it was anyone's guess, but it wouldn't end well.

"So no one is after you?"

Hugh shook his head again.

McPherson returned to the room and put the original receipt in his file folder and gave Hugh back a photocopy on 8 ½ by 11 inch paper. Hugh didn't bother complaining. He folded up the paper and put it in his pocket.

McPherson addressed Hugh. He had a low voice, somewhat gruff. "That receipt says the person paid in cash for the room. Do you always pay for your hotel rooms in cash?"

Hugh nodded.

"When you traveled to Cincinnati and Columbus and Indianapolis, you paid the hotels in cash?"

Hugh nodded. They wouldn't find any record of him in those cities either—other than the ATM machines from which he withdrew money. He was just traveling through.

Feliciano spoke again. "So where were you sleeping the last few nights. In a hotel?"

Hugh shook his head. "N-no, in in m-my c-c-car."

The man interjected. "Sleeping in your car? You are one strange guy."

The woman winced. Hugh just shrugged his shoulders. If he didn't have to speak, he wouldn't. Maybe this Miranda thing was right up his alley.

The women cocked her head, seemingly sympathetically. "We can help you if you're in trouble."

Hugh didn't trust her. He could sense she was playing to an audience. Not just him, not just McPherson, but whoever was behind the mirror.

"N-n-not in in t-t ...um, uh... trouble."

"You left your dog with a neighbor and haven't returned. You didn't show up for work today. You're sleeping in your car. It sounds to me like you're in trouble. Why don't you tell us what's going on. We can help."

A thousand times. Hugh had been through this a thousand times in his head. He had replayed in a loop every key action since fleeing the DuPont house on Sunday. He needed the continual reminder, to reassure himself of the route he had taken. And so again he replayed everything. The obvious setup at the DuPont house and his apartment, his apartment being broken into more than once, the man showing up at his hotel, the conversation in the park, the appearance of the policeman in the park at night with Zanini and Faccon.

The conclusion was always the same: there was no way that confiding in the police would work out. The way he figured it, he actually had made all the rights moves, as odd as they might seem to others. He had only himself to trust at the moment. He just had to buy more time until he could work this out.

McPherson interjected again. "You're not going to say *anything?*" He sneered this final word. "*No explanation* about this *strange behavior?*" The smugness, the way the man leaned in bothered Hugh. The way he tried to intimidate was vexing.

What if I don't answer questions? Will they have probable cause to hold me? Hugh decided it wouldn't hurt to put on a show of cooperating without actually saying anything. And in his own inimitable way.

"M-m-my my p-parents um, uh, died. T-t-too many, well, m-memories."

"But you already took three weeks to yourself," the man countered. "Maybe it's something else that's bothering you? Maybe something about *Sunday?*"

Feliciano interjected again. She seemed not to be very impressed with the other detective's manner. "Listen, Mr.

Holiday. If you've anything you want to share, it'd be a good time." She spoke softly, quietly, sweetly even. She thought the "mister" was a nice touch. It would make Holiday feel respected, like an equal partner with the police. Put him in a place where he would want to cooperate.

Hugh shrugged his head no. This "you have a right to remain silent" seemed tailor-made, he thought. He felt comfortable not speaking.

For fifteen minutes, Feliciano and McPherson went over the same tired territory: Why has he been sleeping in his car? Why isn't he staying in his apartment? Why did he have a rental? Why didn't he show up for work, is he in trouble? With each question, Hugh was feeling more awake, engaged, even invigorated. They didn't seem to have any more than they ever had. Why had they even bothered bringing him downtown?

Feliciano looked at him and asked, "Where is your phone by the way, Mr. Holiday. It wasn't among your possessions today."

Chapter 43

"Ph-ph-phone?"

"Yes, your phone. Did you leave it in your car?" Feliciano raised her left hand, palm up, as she asked, softly, sweetly.

She looked nonchalant. Hugh couldn't read any expression from her face or detect anything from her words other than genuine interest in why it wasn't on his person. His mind clicked through possible scenarios. He chose one.

"M-m-may-maybe."

"You're not sure where it is? Could it be in the apartment? House?"

"N-n-not sure. ...um, uh ... may-maybe in c-c-car."

The woman paused. McPherson went to speak, but Feliciano gently put her right hand on his arm.

"No, Mr. Holiday. Your phone isn't in your car."

She reached into her black satchel and took out a plastic zip bag. Inside the bag was a phone.

"Your phone was turned in this morning by a man from north of Pittsburgh, in Ohara Township. He found it on the floor in the back seat of his car." She paused for effect. "Can you explain how your phone ended up in the back of his car?"

Hugh shook his head. He shrugged his shoulders and generally tried to seem mystified. Which he failed at miserably.

"His name is Robert Kittering. Do you know a Robert Kittering?"

"N-n-no."

"Have you been up in Ohara Township."

"I-I-I ……..DON'T know wh-where it is."

The explosiveness of Hugh's "don't" brought stares from Feliciano and McPherson. There was an awkward pause. Then Feliciano continued, "It is north of the park you were found in today. Across the Allegheny. Above Sharpsburg."

Amazing. The general area that I've been staying.

"N-n-no. N-not not up th-th-there."

"Well, he worked in Pittsburgh. Maybe you put it in his car in Pittsburgh?"

Hugh smiled. He shook his head.

"Do you know his wife, Marilyn?"

Hugh shook his head.

"Well, they claim they don't know you either, Mr. Holiday. I can't think of any explanation how your phone could end up in the back seat of some stranger's car. Can you?"

Well, someone was trying to kill me, and I suspected they could be tracking my phone, and I had to get rid of it, so I threw it in the back of this man's car, because, well, I didn't want to die. How about that?

"N-n-no."

"The car was a blue Ford sedan. Does that help?"

He shook his head.

"You can't think of any reason that your phone ended up in the back seat of a stranger's car?"

Again, Hugh shook his head.

"Nothing? No explanations?" injected McPherson. Loudly. Commandingly.

"I-I-I g-g-guess, uh, um, l-lost it. O-o-or, well, stolen."

"Why didn't you search for your phone on the computer?" countered McPherson. "Kittering said the phone was on when he found it. You could have tracked it easily. Why didn't you?"

And, this, Hugh smiled inside, *is why I took this line of response about not realizing it was gone. How possibly to explain not searching for a $600 phone? Not plausible.*

"I-I-I didn't know was l-l-lost."

"Didn't know? That's your answer? How do you not know your phone was lost?" McPherson looked exasperated.

Hugh shrugged his shoulders. "D-d-don't use much."

"Don't use much?" McPherson's tone indicated just how incredulous he considered Hugh's response.

"S-speech, well, problem." Hugh smiled broadly. Feliciano broke out into an equally wide smile.

McPherson didn't smile. "There were no other fingerprints on the phone other than yours and Kittering's."

Hugh looked at his hands. Then he took a sip of water.

"It sounds like maybe you broke into his car. That's breaking and entering. That's grounds for you being arrested."

Hugh looked up, startled. He began to speak. He thought better of it. It would be an outrageous charge for holding him.

"You've nothing to say?" continued McPherson.

Hugh shook his head. For a phone? For a phone that the Kittering guy ended up with, not something taken from him? It certainly seemed like a ruse. Still, even an honest police officer must wonder about Hugh's odd behavior in recent days.

"Well," said the woman after a long pause. "We'll be giving your phone back to you. We've no need for it. And you're right. It seems to have been barely used."

Hugh shrugged his shoulders. He took another sip of water.

"You don't even seem grateful that you'll be getting it back," snapped McPherson. "Why is that? It's an expensive phone."

"I-I-I am g-g…"

McPherson didn't let him finish. "Doesn't look like to me."

There was a awkward silence. The detectives looked at Hugh, then at each other. Finally Feliciano said, "Just stay here. We may have some more questions." They left the room.

Five minutes passed. Then another officer cracked open the door and said, "If you give us your keys, we'll pick up your car for you at Highland Park and bring it here."

Finally, some optimism. For a moment, Hugh considered telling the man to just drop him off at the park. But traveling alone with a police officer to Highland Park, or being dropped off in the park alone, might not work out so well for his long-term prognosis. Hell, a policeman must have been involved in the scrubbing of his phone. The "barely used" was not Hugh's doing; he had dropped it into this Kittering car on the spur of the moment. Someone could easily see what websites he visited, his phone log, even the app to the webcam in Faccon's office.

Hugh reached in and got his rental key and gave it to the man.

Hugh's optimism went up yet another notch when a civilian member of the office staff came in and said that she would pick him up some lunch. That there was a McDonalds and a Taco Bell just a block away. Hugh selected a burrito and a taco.

She was back in less than fifteen minutes with his food.

And something else. She handed him his phone back. Said the officers were done with it. She added, "The part of the building you are in blocks cell phones. Do you want access to the building's public WiFi? I can get you access to play some games or browse the Internet while you're waiting." Hugh nodded and she took out a piece of paper and a pen and wrote out for him the password for the wireless network. And then she left and he was alone again.

Hugh started up his phone. He looked through his call log. Empty. He looked through his browser history. Empty. Emails, texts. Everything was empty. Someone had done a thorough job on his phone.

And then Hugh started to log into his Cloud account to access footage from Faccon's laboratory.

He stopped. Not because he suspected that the police had provided his phone and network access so they could track what he looked at. No, he didn't suspect that—he was sure of it. But he was willing to accept the risk if it might help take the infernal attention on himself and redirect it, even a small amount, onto Faccon.

The problem was he couldn't explain how he got the video feed. It couldn't be the fortuitous picking up of a signal on his tablet while outside TMMC, driven by his suspicions of Faccon. A person needed to know the camera's serial number to find it across the Internet. And knowing that was something Hugh couldn't explain.

Hugh turned off his phone and sat back.

His ordeal in the station seemed to be coming to an end. They had been fishing and didn't even have much bait to fish with. It had been somewhat of a surreal experience. They had found his phone is a stranger's car. He was driving a rental car instead of his car. He had been sleeping in his rental car. A bunch of odd things, for sure, but nothing of any real substance. Did they think bringing him to the station would crack him? They didn't even have enough for Kelly to show up to interrogate him.

Hugh felt no ill feelings about the process. The police were just doing their jobs. After all, he was a likely suspect. And they had been pretty decent to him; the "interrogation," if one could call it that, hadn't been that bad.

If anything, he was going to be walking out with more respect for the police. There was still that nasty fact that someone on the force was working for the mob. And he wasn't naïve about police corruption; it wasn't all that long ago that even Pittsburgh's Chief of Police was sentenced to federal prison for corruption.

But, in comparison to all the good that officers were doing? Many at daily risk to their lives? Hugh wondered what it had been like for people in this office when they heard about the three officers who died in the Stanton Heights neighborhood from answering a 9-1-1 call about a domestic violence issue—stemming from, of all things, a dog urinating in the house. And, on a more personal level, what was it like for the policeman, when Hugh couldn't be reached, who had to come to his door to personally deliver him the news about his parent's fatal car accident? What a tough job and how amazingly compassionate that officer had been toward him.

Hugh felt tears welling up from the last thought as the door to the interrogation room cracked open. A uniformed officer entered and firmly, but politely, asked Hugh to come with him, that they were headed back to the lobby where he had come in.

Hugh shook off the excitement of being released as a new set of thoughts took precedence. He needed to strategize, to weigh his options. When he left the parking lot, he would no doubt be followed. How would he deal with this?

Hugh looked at the officer who had come to get him, a black man who was probably in his early forties. Hugh thought he had one of the sharpest, most wrinkle-free uniforms he had seen among the lower-ranked men at the station. He led, Hugh followed. Hugh rounded the corner, immersed in thought, and started to walk down the aisle between the rows of cluttered desks.

That is when he saw him. The old man he had encountered outside DuPont's house was walking right towards him, down the same aisle.

Chapter 44

The aisle—and the entire row of desks along the aisle—were cleared of people, save the five making their way toward one another down that narrow passageway. There was the old man, who was walking behind one uniformed officer and followed by another. And there was Hugh, following a uniformed officer. It was going to be hard to avoid being seen by the old man.

The room was laid out like an L-shaped Tetris block. Hugh had entered into the wide portion, where the bottom one-third of the room jutted out to his right. The old man was ninety feet straight ahead, in the top of the I-portion. At the slow rate the oncoming group was proceeding, they would meet in that I-portion.

And there, in that I-portion, the narrow five-foot aisle would afford no cover. Although the room had an open feel to it with a high ceiling and cubicles with but low, three-foot-high partitions, the aisle was very focused. The desks on both sides of the aisle were back to back, such that the cubicle separators on the sides of the desks formed a type of short wall along the aisle; the only spaces off the aisle was where one entered a cubicle. There was one exception to this: there was one aisle jutting off to Hugh's right in the wide, bottom portion. But now that aisle was behind him.

Hugh looked at the old man. He hadn't yet seen Hugh. He was shuffling with his eyes glancing at the desks as he passed.

Hugh could think of no excuse to alter their present collision course. There were no windows to pretend to want a look outside. No bathroom to excuse himself. He might be able to reverse himself and walk back to that aisle he had passed, but that would give cause for the policemen to make a scene and draw attention to Hugh.

While the aisle was cleared out for the two groups, the room was far from empty. Policemen were standing at scattered points along the walls. All seemed to be watching him and the old man. To see how the old man reacted. To see how Hugh reacted. Hugh surmised that there were probably cameras recording the scene as well.

A heightened awareness of his own physical features rushed by in rapid succession: What should I do with my eyes? Should I look at the ground to avoid the old man? Maybe to the right as if interested in something? What about my hands? Should they be in my pockets? Should I use them to partially cover my face? Should I slow my pace and try to hide behind the policeman in front of me? Should I slouch down to look smaller?

What was happening internally only added to his self-consciousness. The constricted chest was back, accompanied by concern about his heart trying to beat its way through that vice. He was breathing rapidly. He felt faint and his legs weak.

My God! He's an old man. This isn't an encounter with a grizzly bear.

Maybe the old man won't even look. Or, if he looks, maybe he won't recognize me. People often don't recognize even familiar faces in places they don't expect them. And then he remembered just how well this reasoning had done with the med student Emily.

No, it was impossible to relax. Whatever Hugh was trying to sell himself, now the reptile part of his brain wasn't buying; the body was in full fight or flight mode. He knew in the core of his being that the old man would recognize him. The police had carefully choreographed this "chance encounter," and the old man was no doubt fully prepped. He wasn't walking in blind. He was here as a witness to the DuPont murder. He might've been told there would be a lineup, and that the man he met in the street might be here in the building.

Hugh would be in the front of his mind. The old man's senses would be attuned. Nothing left to chance. No escape.

They were thirty feet away now. Other than some sideways glances at the desks as they passed, the old man had mainly looked into the back of the cop in front. He hadn't made eye-to-eye contact with Hugh.

Twenty feet away. The old man still hadn't looked at Hugh. Maybe his eyes weren't all that good.

Ten feet away. The old man was still looking straight into the cop's back. *Maybe he won't notice me.*

Five feet away. The cop in front of the old man moved more quickly, leaving a space between himself and the old man. But still no eye contact. The old man was being polite. Or maybe just a learned response to not look at strangers.

Three feet away, the cop in front of Hugh slowed down and moved to his right, blocking the space between desks. And the cop in front of the old man then suddenly veered to his left and bumped into Hugh.

Hugh looked at the old man. He was staring right at Hugh. Recognition crossed the old man's face. He lifted his head and started opening his mouth to speak to Hugh.

"Aw-aw-officer, are are we g-g-g-going to g-g-get my my k-k-keys f-f-for my my c-c-car?" Hugh broke the silence, rapidly blurting out disjointed consonants and syllables to the officer in front of him. To the exaggerated enunciation, he added a foolish look for good measure.

The old man looked down and away. The recognition passed from his face.

Hugh averted his own eyes. And in so doing, they came across those of Lieutenant Kelly, watching from across the room.

Kelly looked . . . disgusted.

The two groups continued their walk down the aisle. Hugh watched Kelly turn away and walk out of the room.

Hugh's thoughts were so clear they were almost audible. *If Kelly puts me in a lineup, I'll ask for a lawyer. Otherwise, I'll end up in a lineup standing in the middle of four short people. Probably four leprechauns. Maybe even four women leprechauns if there's such a thing.*

Hugh felt rising indignation at being manipulated. No, it was more than some righteous indignation. It was more than anger. Maybe not the level of rage, but it was passionate and it was fierce and it was burning. He tried not to show it, telling himself that he didn't have the luxury of even looking annoyed, not with cameras probably recording his every twitch.

When they reached the front desk, Hugh was asked to sign a paper, a paper that simply noted the police had picked up Hugh's car with his permission, a paper that easily could have been brought to him to the interrogation room to sign.

Then, unsurprisingly to Hugh at this point, he was escorted back to the interrogation room.

Chapter 45

Another interminable wait. I'll have a full-fledged beard by the time I'm out of here. Even Kelly won't recognize me, let alone the old man.

Hugh's hackles were raised. If they thought this long wait was breaking his spirit, they were wrong. He had spent a lifetime waiting in silence.

And he had been through enough. Set up. Hassled by the police. Hunted by the mob. This full-on police interrogation. The asinine stunt in the hallway.

And now this wait. Alone in the interrogation room with the one-way mirror. This time Hugh didn't wander around, looking at the mirror. He stayed seated, fuming, and let his mind do the wandering. And it landed on another time when he had been the unwanted focus of everyone's attention.

It had been a college class in research methods. A class where they had actually discussed one-way mirrors—or two-way mirrors, as the professor called them—as part of observational research. A class in which a major part of every student's grade was an oral presentation in front of the students, who were encouraged to critically evaluate each presentation.

Hugh dreaded the day when he would have to give his presentation. He signed up for the last day of classes, with the hope that maybe he would be saved by a class-cancelling December snowstorm. But he prepared. He certainly prepared. Every week, anxiety ridden or not, he slowly advanced toward his goal. And he had a workable plan: a PowerPoint presentation with some short embedded videos and much of what he wanted to say written on the slides. With that kind of game plan, he fancied that he might skate through with minimum words and yet make a good impression—on the professor and the students.

But nothing went as expected. Or as hoped. The snowstorm did come. For days Hugh tracked a major storm headed his way, his expectation growing daily. It was massive, it was snarling traffic and closing schools in its path—and it shifted south at the last moment. Some students in West Virginia were no doubt delighted. Hugh, not so much. Only two inches fell in Pittsburgh. Still he spent the evening and morning refreshing the Duquesne University website and checking the portal; the expected cancellation of class didn't happen.

But the snowstorm did have one major impact. As he made his way to class, he slipped on the little snow there was—and the laptop crashed to the ground, dying on the spot.

And with the laptop also died his presentation and any confidence. He hadn't used Cloud-based presentation software. He hadn't backed up the presentation online. His flash drive backup was left at home; no time to retrieve it or a copy from his desktop. He stood on the college quad, broken laptop in hand, fighting despair.

Hugh slogged through the presentation. Without visual aids. Just his voice. His fifteen minutes passed like molasses on a cold winter day—for him, for the students, and for the professor.

The professor was a kindly man. But also one wholly inexperienced with someone with a major stuttering problem. In fact, his words during and after the presentation didn't even seem to indicate he had any awareness that the problem was a stuttering problem versus someone who was scared of speaking in front of a class. There were the same old clichés: "Slow down. Take your time. No need to be nervous. When one is nervous, it is good to have a PowerPoint or Prezi presentation so the audience has something to look at." The professor tried to encourage with "this is a good presentation" and afterward "that was very interesting," whereas his lack of any questions whatsoever indicated he had been so distracted he hadn't even understood the talk. Or was simply too embarrassed to prolong Hugh's misery.

Hugh sent a copy of his presentation to the professor later, and clung to the hope of "this is a good presentation." Until he got the grade for the class: a B-. The presentation and class participation grade had overridden the grades on his tests and paper and reduced his grade from an A to B-. A grade that could damage his chance of getting into medical school.

The door to the interrogation room flung open, dramatically. Into the room strode Lieutenant Kelly.

No big surprise, thought Hugh.

"Hello, Mr. Holiday," started Kelly.

Great. So Kelly is picking up pointers from the lady detective.

Hugh nodded. A wry "I-am-the-innocent-one, stop-hassling-me greeting." But he was soon to find out the hassling had just begun.

In his Internet searches, Hugh had seen pictures of Kelly in a suit and tie. This wasn't such an occasion. He was, as twice before when Hugh met him, dressed in his neatly pressed uniform, with the white shirt with embroidered name and the dark blue pants. If he meant to be more intimidating in full uniform, then, Hugh agreed, he was probably right. He was an imposing figure.

This time, Kelly was unaccompanied. He pulled out a chair directly across from Hugh, and sat down, back straight, eyes on Hugh.

"It's nice to see you are still in the area." Kelly began with a matter-of-fact tone. Hugh noted that he didn't bother with a dramatic pause. Perhaps he was now clear that such pauses would just be met with a patient stony silence, not nervous chatter. "When you didn't show up to work the last two days, we thought you'd skipped town."

Hugh shrugged his shoulders, more defiantly than sheepishly.

"Why'd you skip work?"

It was Hugh who paused. Finally he said, with an almost exasperated tone, ""S-s-sick."

Kelly looked at him closely, his eyes not leaving Hugh's face. He was surprised that Hugh was not looking down. His eyes were locked on Kelly's, unwavering.

"You're obviously not sick today. And you didn't call in sick today."

Long pause. Hugh just sat there.

"Why didn't you go to work today?"

"S-s-sick." Hugh again met Kelly's gaze.

"Mr. Holiday. Two of my detectives tell me that you claim you've been sleeping in your car the last few nights. Is that true?"

Hugh nodded his head slightly, as he looked unflinchingly at Kelly.

"But your car was empty. Nothing in the trunk, nothing in the car. Where are your possessions, your clothes, your toothbrush, anything?"

Hidden in an empty house that I broke into and entered. Maybe up in this Ohara Township area.

"A-a-apart-apartment," he answered.

He was stammering, but the look in his eyes was steely. Kelly was having trouble adjusting to this new attitude. Gone was the nervous kid he'd seen before.

It gave Kelly pause. Maybe the kid wasn't going to fall apart in this police headquarters like he thought.

"We've been watching your apartment, Holiday. We haven't seen you there the last couple of nights. You left your dog with your neighbor."

Hugh didn't answer. Kelly was unconcerned. It was only an opening, a diversion.

"Okay. Well, let's take one night. Wednesday night. Wednesday night, you asked me to drive you to your apartment. But you had me drop you off at the mall. We know that you got this rental car on Tuesday and left your own car at the rental lot. Why didn't you drive your rental to the viewing?"

"I-I-I, um, um, like b-buses."

"Where was your rental car? "

"A-a-apart-apartment." Hugh gazed straightforward at Kelly, eye-to-eye, unwavering.

"Why even get a rental if you like buses?"

"C-c-car, well, easier for some p-p-places."

"Yeah, like going to the viewing." Sarcastic. Abrupt. Hugh's stuttering already was again getting under Kelly's skin.

"I-I-I like b-buses when d-d-don't, um, uh, know wh-where g-going."

Kelly didn't respond. Not immediately. He just looked at Hugh.

Finally, he said, "Did you sleep in the rental car Wednesday night?

"Y-y-yes."

"Where did you park at when you slept?"

"I-I-I th-think, well, Walmart."

"What did you do before that? Where did you go after the mall?"

"P-p-parent's, um, uh, house."

"And after the house and before Walmart. Anywhere else?"

"Wh-wh-why?"

"I am asking the questions here, son."

"N-n-no p-place in in par-par… ticular."

"How about to your office?"

Hugh shook his head.

"How about back to the area of DuPont's house?"

Hugh shook his head no.

"No?"

"N-n-no."

"How about to where she worked, MacArthur Medical College?"

Hugh tried not to look shocked. *Does Kelly know something?*

Hugh shook his head.

"No?"

"N-n-no."

"How about Tuesday or Thursday, did you go to the area of DuPont's house?"

Again, Hugh wondered. *No, he wouldn't have asked about Tuesday* and *Thursday.*

Hugh shook his head.

"On Tuesday or Thursday, did you go to the area of TMMC?"

Hugh shook his head.

"So, on none of these days you went to either place, correct?"

Another shake of the head.

Kelly shrugged his shoulders. He paused. And then he developed a conciliatory tone.

"You had us worried, son. You get a rental car, when you already had a car. You don't stay in your apartment or your parents' house. Yeah, I know, 'memories.' Now, you don't show up for work for two days. You're living in your car."

Kelly paused again. "We can help you. I can help you. You can trust me. You know you can trust me. You showed that when you asked me to drive you from the viewing. But you need to come clean with us. Then we can help you."

This again? Really? Yeah, Kelly, I can sure trust my life in the hands of the police. Your former Chief of Police is in federal jail. Someone in your department just erased my phone. Someone on the force was meeting in a park at night to discuss my demise. Guess what? I think I'm better off on my own. You just want to place me at the scene of the crime. Then there will be no way out, other than the way intended by those that set me up.

Kelly waited. When he got no response, he stood up, "Okay. Well, we gave you a chance." He then walked to the door, opened it and went out.

Is that it? Hugh shook his head, this time not a "no" answer, a gesture of incredulity. A half-smile crossed his lips, even in an empty room.

Kelly walked back in. This time carrying a file folder.

"You had your chance to be honest, Holiday." Gone was the *Mr. Holiday.* Gone was Kelly's sympathetic tone. He didn't sit collegially next to Hugh. He didn't offer him any help. Instead, he stood on the opposite side of the table, towering over Hugh with a glowering look. And then he let the folder fall to the table with a resounding bang.

Hugh winced slightly, simply from the jolt of the sound.

"Now you're caught in your web of lies. This is *not* going to look good to a jury."

He opened the folder just enough to remove two 8 x 11 photos, which he kept shielded from Hugh's view. He walked behind Hugh. He put one of the photos in front of him.

"Take a look at this picture. It was taken Wednesday night."

It was a clear shot of Hugh entering TMMC via the De Angelis Complex entrance. The time stamp showed the date and time.

"It seems, son, that you were indeed at TMMC Wednesday night. And that you used someone else's ID to illegally enter. This is a still from the video we have of you entering."

Kelly took the second photo from his folder. He placed it on top of the first. It showed Hugh departing TMMC via the same doors, in the presence of a TMMC security guard. Although the still was from the rear, it was obviously Hugh.

"This was taken about two hours later. And the security guard confirmed seeing you in the building as well."

Kelly looked at Hugh. He paused for dramatic effect. "It just so happened, son, that a student noticed his ID had been stolen and reported that to the medical school security. And, wouldn't you know it, the TMMC security found out that someone had used it. They found *you* on the video footage."

Kelly walked in front of Hugh and put both hands on the table, with a slow nod of his head in an "I-got-you" look.

Hugh laughed.

Kelly tilted his head, quizzically.

Hugh smiled broadly.

This wasn't the response Kelly had in mind. He moved his face close to Hugh's. When he spoke, he was loud and he was irate.

"You're laughing about this? This isn't just catching you in a lie. Not just a pattern of deception. We've got you for breaking and entering. And not just any place. The building where DuPont worked. Are you too dense to understand that these are nails in your coffin?"

Hugh chuckled.

Kelly felt himself getting red in the face. "What's so damn funny?" he demanded.

"I-I-I, well, simply, well, went to r-return the I-I-I-ID ….found at at v-viewing."

"What do you mean *returned the ID*?" Kelly hated this kid's stammering. It broke his concentration. He had trouble being effective.

"I-I-I, well, went to, uh, um, mail area and and d-d-dropped I-I-I-ID there for s-s-student. Uh, um, in p-p-postal b-box."

Kelly looked up at the mirror. A someone-go-check-this-out look.

"You stole the ID."

"F-f-found on on g-ground. S-student p-p-probably g-grateful."

"You were there two hours. Where'd you go?"

"A-ate in l-lounge. R-r-read, well, m-mag-magazine. W-w-walked around."

"Did you go to DuPont's office?"

"S-s-sure. Uh, uh, m-mem-memories."

"We found fingerprints on the outside doorknob." Kelly instantly kicked himself internally. The emotion paraded across his face. He had blown a major reveal. It wasn't how he had planned it. The stammering was annoying the hell out of him.

"S-s-sure." Hugh replied. With a confident, matter-of-fact look.

For the next twenty minutes, Kelly stayed on the topic of DuPont's office. Had Hugh broken in? Was that why he went to TMMC, to get into her office? Did he do something there? Kelly showed stills from security camera footage that indicated Hugh had been there on the second floor for quite some time, and had passed three times through the area. He noted the discrepancy between the police notes on the blinds being left up and the fact they were now down. He referenced a piece of rubber the police found near the door and its matching part from the insert in the doorframe, "obviously cut because it was blocking someone's jimmying the lock."

All to no avail.

Kelly had indeed botched his line of attack. With Kelly's seven simple words, "we found fingerprints on the outside doorknob," Hugh was confident they had no evidence that put him inside DuPont's office. His explanations, even if delivered in spurts and stops, were flawless in content: An expectation that the library would be open and he could do some reading, memories, wandering the hallway. None believed by Kelly. All plausible to the ears of a judge or jury.

Then a policeman entered the room and whispered into Kelly's ear. Hugh didn't have to hear what they were saying. The look on Kelly's face told him everything he needed to know. That the mail clerk had discovered the student's ID.

"Why didn't you mail the student's ID or give to a security guard?"

"D-d-didn't want s-s-student to g-get in t-t-trouble."

Kelly blurted out, exasperated: "At any rate, we got you on breaking and entering into TMMC. *At minimum* illegal trespass."

Hugh smiled. A broad, confident smile. "F-f-for, well, being a G-Good S-S-Samar-Samaritan?"

In the room behind the mirror there were smiles and some muted, but undisguised chuckles among those gathered. Gathered ostensibly to watch the great Kelly dismantle a twenty-three-year-old kid. Delighting in seeing Kelly get his comeuppance.

Hugh sat with steely determination. Where could Kelly possibly go with this? Hugh had been to TMMC many times. A lot of non-students go in and out of college spaces all the time. Hugh could easily feign confusion about the original question whether he'd gone to the medical college that Wednesday night.

Kelly, still standing, opened the folder. He took another photo out and pushed it over to Hugh. It was a bloody picture of the scene at the DuPont house.

"Do you think *this* is funny?"

Whether it was said in exasperation or honest disapproval or enmity was impossible to discern. But clearly Kelly had lost his composure. Somehow, he had thought Hugh would be the panicked kid he had met five days ago and that he would confess everything this time.

Hugh looked at the photo. The image of Dr. DuPont in a pool of blood brought up strong feelings. But not so much of sadness as of outrage. A passionate anger towards those who killed her. Anger toward those who set him up. Anger at Kelly's tactics.

"B-b-but. I-I-I. D-didn't. D-do. T-t-that." He spit his words out staunchly. Authoritatively.

Kelly's face turned red. His eyebrows lowered. His nostrils flared. The twenty-three-year-old kid and his stuttering were aggravating enough. Now he was arrogant? He almost spit his words at Hugh.

"The old man puts you at the scene."

Hugh meet him head on. "Wh-who now is n-n-not g-going to, um, look g-good to to a j-j-jury." Hugh spit out the words with a sardonic twist.

It set off the already-on-edge Kelly. He blew. He was well aware that this kid got under his nerves. He just no longer cared that others knew it. He forgot the observers, the cameras. He forgot the reputation that he had carefully cultivated, often at the expense of the work of others. A twenty-three-year-old kid who couldn't even speak right, challenging him. Kelly slammed his fist on the table.

"You're *going down* for the DuPont murder. And don't think you can run. You might think because you *lost your job* that you have an excuse to get out of town. But we'll watch you wherever you go. You can't pretend stuttering your whole life. And we'll expand the search for where you used the British accent now that we know you were using cash."

Hugh looked shocked at the mention of his job and turned pale.

Kelly raised his face in awareness. And smirked. When he spoke again, it seemed to Hugh as if Kelly were speaking from a long distance away, the words barely piercing his consciousness.

"You didn't know about that, did you? Yeah. Don't show up to work for two days, and what do you expect? When we called Bridgewater this morning looking for you, he told us you were through. That's what you get for not even calling in sick today."

Kelly had gotten his last shot in. He picked up the photos, stuffed them in the folder, turned his back on Hugh, and left.

A whole lot of small nothings. That's what Hugh decided. A lost phone. Images of him at TMMC and some fingerprints on a doorknob. Sleeping in his car. A search of his car. He guessed maybe their big gotcha was going to be the old man. Or maybe Kelly thought bringing him to police headquarters would scare him. That each of those small nothings would break him, rather than inoculate him. But Hugh was pretty sure that nothing worked the way Kelly had envisioned.

They kept Hugh another hour sitting there alone. Then they escorted him out of the building.

Chapter 46

For the last hour, sitting alone in the interrogation room, Hugh had been able to think about little other than the loss of his job. Funny, he realized, if Kelly or Feliciano or McPherson had led with that, things might have gone terribly bad for him. At minimum, he would've been totally off his game. Quite possibly, he would've lapsed into a debilitating depression where he wouldn't have cared about his fate. He was close to that now.

The moment he found out he'd been fired, Hugh felt devastated beyond measure. For others, such a development might not have been all that disconcerting, not in light of just walking out of a police station unscathed by a murder accusation. The job wasn't that lucrative and most would think of the day-to-day work as boring. Just move on and get another job.

But Hugh liked the work. And it paid well enough that he could make ends meet in his paycheck-to-paycheck existence. And where could someone like Hugh Holiday get another position like that? Or any position in his field for that matter? It wasn't as if he made a good first impression in interviews. And with Kelly watching him, perhaps more determined than ever, he didn't dare speak in a stutter-free accent.

Hugh had already received a financial blow when it had turned out, to his astonishment, that his parents' mortgage exceeded their home value and they had left virtually no savings. And no life insurance. The funeral alone had taxed his resources. Now he was in debt and jobless.

I just screwed up bad, he commiserated. *If I'd just called in, then my boss might've forgiven me.* But Hugh knew his boss had already been overly patient.

Hugh wasn't escorted to his car. He was just given the keys and pointed in its direction. It was parked along the wall of the larger of the two renovated buildings.

He sat for a long while in the car. He had nowhere to go. Except the "for-sale" house and it was too early to go there.

He drove up Western Avenue and found the McDonalds on the next block. He went inside and ate his food in a booth. He toyed on his phone and even picked up a discarded newspaper from another table to look at. From Mickey D's, he stayed to public areas until it was dark enough and late enough to go to the vacant house he'd been occupying.

Karsten sat in his van watching the red dot of Holiday's car superimposed over a street map on one monitor. And the red dot of Holiday's phone superimposed over a map on the other monitor.

Karsten was in Pittsburgh's North Side. He'd spent the better part of the day in the North Side at various locations: the parking lot of a Giant Eagle store, a residential street, a strip filled with a number of fast food joints, and now a park not far from the National Aviary. Mostly near to the police station where Holiday was being held. Moving the van just enough to avoid suspicion.

He wasn't about to lose Holiday this time. He had planted two devices on his rental car. One under the back seat. One under the car itself. The earlier call from Zanini that a Zone 5 police contact knew the location of Holiday's car had been superfluous: Karsten had already picked that up on police scanners. By the time he got to Highland Park, the police had already hauled off Holiday, but Karsten had been able to plant the devices before someone had come back for the car.

Karsten hated getting calls from Zanini when he was working. But Zanini had insisted he be on call. And it had proven useful on this day. Karsten had been kept in the loop on what was happening in the police station. And the exact time when Holiday was to be released. And in coordinating that the phone made its way back to Holiday.

By the time Holiday was finally released from the police station, Karsten was ready for anything.

Anything except the one thing that happened. Holiday had given up.

Karsten had been prepared for Holiday to abandon his car. To look for tracking devices. To take the bus or a cab. To ditch his phone.

Holiday had done none of those things. He had spent a lot of time at eating establishments: McDonalds, Wendy's, Taco Bell. He had gone to the community college's library for a while and a Rite-Aid Pharmacy. He had checked his personal Cloud account to see if the images from Faccon's laboratory were still there. They weren't. Karsten had seen to that.

There had been no attempt to hide, to elude, to resort to tricks. All this Karsten could discern from the dots on the screen. But he also kept Holiday in visual range, to make sure he didn't slip out the back of an establishment or give his phone to someone. He hadn't. Holiday was . . . disconsolate. The long police interrogation had somehow unnerved him. Had broken his spirit.

Karsten had seen it before, when his prey simply gives up. Realizes the situation is hopeless, that he cannot escape. Just goes through the motions while waiting for the inevitable. Some had even taken their own lives before Karsten had the chance. Didn't matter to Karsten. He still got his pay.

Karsten was in no hurry. He was a very patient man. It would be finished tonight, but it had to be done just right. He couldn't exactly grab him off the street. What would he do with Holiday's car? What if he were seen? If it was supposed to look like a suicide, he had to wait until Holiday settled down for the evening.

Around 9:30 pm, Holiday began to move with clear intent. From the North Side, he got onto Route 28 and headed north along the Allegheny River. He was headed out of the city.

Karsten kept his distance. As long as the dot for the car didn't stop, and the dot signifying the phone didn't deviate far from that of the car, he didn't need to keep Holiday in visual range. But he had to remain close enough that should the car stop, he would be able to make sure Holiday hadn't ditched the car and the phone and was up to his old tricks.

Holiday did make two more stops—one a gas station, another a chain fast food restaurant. But those were quick stops, and Karsten had reached each soon enough to confirm Holiday wasn't making a run for it. Just some gas, some junk food. And then back on the highway. His last meal was going to be some kind of artery-clogging, gas-station Twinkies and drive-through cheeseburgers and fries.

Holiday mostly stayed on the move until he was well north of Pittsburgh. He slowed down as he drove through a rather rural area. Then the dots stopped moving.

Karsten drove past the location where the dots had halted. He got there in just enough time to see the brake lights as the car pulled behind a house. The house was dark. There was a "For Sale" sign on the lawn.

The clever devil, thought Karsten. *Staying in an empty house.*

He now had Holiday's hideaway. Karsten drove past twice more, turning around both times in driveways where the houses were set so far back the occupants probably wouldn't bother to look out their windows. Holiday was being careful: no lights were visible from the road. One would have to be deliberately looking to see the very back of the car jutting out from behind the house. They would have to be looking for it like Karsten was.

Now it was just a matter of waiting until Holiday was asleep. Until he had gouged himself so much on all the carbohydrates he had been buying that he couldn't help but sleep.

Karsten laughed. With the visual image of a sleeping Holiday, the words "to sleep, perchance to dream" popped into his mind. But it wasn't that line that had made him laugh. It was another one that came after it in short succession: "The undiscovered country, from whose bourn no traveler returns." Holiday would soon be headed to that undiscovered country.

Karsten figured that, like a good angel of death, he actually would be helping Holiday, who had suffered for so long in his life "the slings and arrows of outrageous fortune." And Holiday had given up. He seemed to be almost welcoming Karsten as his "arms against a sea of troubles."

To Karsten, it had never been only about the money. Sure, he got paid considerable. Indeed. But he recognized his job as more about the strong and fit weeding out the weak, the unfit, the maladjusted. Those who polluted the gene pool with their very existence and got in the way of real men and women of strength.

And he enjoyed the challenge. Immensely. He knew that his combination of brains and brawn put him above those he would meet. These types of jobs allowed him to exercise his full repertoire of skills. Made him feel important. Alive. He would have been bored in any other line of work. Holiday had been an interesting challenge—for a short while. But, in the end, he proved a weaker challenge than most.

To sleep, perchance to dream. Too bad, Holiday. You won't die in your sleep. That would be the easy way to go. But I need you to be awake in your final moments. Just immobile.

Chapter 47

Karsten sat patiently in the back of his van. Waiting until he felt the time was right. Resting himself mentally and physically so that he would be at his peak when the time came. Soon he would be as alert as the stealthiest ambush predator the animal kingdom had to offer.

He was parked in the lot of a strip club just up the road from where Holiday was staying. It was the perfect spot to wait. And the ideal place to leave his vehicle when the time came to stalk Holiday. The club's size had proven deceptive; a Friday night, its lot was crowded with cars. No one would think twice about his van, one of many parked there; the driver they knew would be one of the nameless faces inside. And being a building without windows, the only ones who would see him when he ventured outside would be those patrons going in and out and maybe the workers taking a break outside.

If they even could see him clearly at all. The parking lot was huge and largely un-illuminated, a wide semicircle of hard packed ground mostly well out of range of the building's lights. Karsten was able to park far from the building. Darkness would be his ally this night.

Karsten waited until after midnight. And then he waited some more. Finally, he put on a jacket with the tools of his trade and the suicide note tucked into an inside pocket. He was grateful for the cool spring evening, when wearing a jacket wouldn't be unusual.

The walk to the house didn't take long. He had been concerned about being seen on the road; a lone man walking at night might be memorable. But his concerns were unfounded. The traffic was almost nonexistent, and what cars did come had headlights spotted so far away he was able to get well off the road and out of sight, one time taking refuge in a concrete culvert on the side of the road. No dogs announced his passing their owners' homes. No strangers walked the road with him. No police patrol made any rounds. He made the quarter-mile to the house undetected and in little time.

Karsten's mind was trained to stay in the moment. Still, a part had moved on—to reflecting on how perfect this setup was. Patience and time had won again. Holiday would die of a suicide in an empty house he had been sleeping in for days. It would occur the very evening after a police interrogation, where he had felt police closing in on him for having killed DuPont. Holiday's body could be left to be naturally discovered, even if several days. Already the attention was on him; the police had no other suspects.

Tomorrow, being Saturday, Karsten figured was a likely day for someone to come by: the owner to check on the property, the realtor to show the house. Maybe he could leave a light on in a front room to prompt an earlier discovery, or move Holiday's car out where it were more visible. Once the body was found, the case would be closed, the clients once again satisfied.

Karsten looked one last time at his phone. The red dot of the car, even under high magnification, was nearly superimposed over the dot of Holiday's phone. He hadn't moved during Karsten's trek to the house. Karsten turned off his phone. He didn't want anything to go wrong.

Karsten stopped first at the car to make sure Holiday wasn't sleeping there. It was empty.

He went through the unlocked glass and metal door and down the concrete entranceway to the basement. The door was unlocked. No need to pick a lock.

Karsten moved slowly. Very slowly. The patience of a hunter sneaking up on a prey that he knew wasn't moving and was oblivious to the danger.

No, more like a cat stalking prey. For although Karsten was moving in pitch darkness, without aid of a flashlight, he had a similar advantage as a cat. In the feline's case, there was the more elliptical eye shape, the larger corneas and tapetum, and the greater concentration of rod cells. Karsten's advantage was artificial: night vision goggles. Although they restricted his field of vision, he could see in the near total darkness in which he found himself.

The basement was large, with many areas concealed from first sight by concrete block pillars and partially jutting walls. Karsten slowly and methodically searched each area until he was sure that Holiday wasn't sleeping in some corner. He searched behind the stairs, near the furnace, in the root cellar. The basement was empty.

But at least the basement, with its concrete floor, was soundless. As Karsten headed up the stairway to the first floor, he found that the wooden stairs were anything but soundless. With each step, a creak assailed the stillness. He tried stepping on the edges of the floorboards. He tried taking two steps at a time. Still, the creaking was unavoidable. He hoped that Holiday was in a deep sleep. He hoped that the distance to Holiday was so great that the noise would be muffled.

He was even more fortunate. There was a closed door at the top of the stairs. Karsten was confident that it had entombed the sound within the basement.

He turned the knob and slowly opened the door. It swung silently and Karsten stepped inside an empty kitchen. To his right, he saw a doorway to the outside. To his left, he could see into what must be the dining room and the living room beyond. It was just conjecture on his part: The lack of furniture required speculation as to what the rooms' functions were. But the important detail was evident: they were empty. Holiday must be in a bedroom somewhere.

There was another important detail that quickly became evident. Whether dining room or not, with his first step into the space it was as if the house was rejecting his presence. The wooden floors, either because of poor construction or simply age, creaked, announcing his arrival. Not every floorboard. And not all loud. But to Karsten, even the slightest creak sounded like the crack of nearby lightening reverberating all around. It was impossible to tell which steps would elicit the creak or how loud it would be. He tried long strides. He tried short strides. He tried moving closer along the wall. Nothing worked.

With each emphatic complaint from the floorboards, Karsten froze, staying immobile for a few minutes, a seeming eternity, before venturing another step. But as he stood motionless, he felt some comfort in the fact that the entire house was filled with sharp noises and squeaking noises and clanging noises. Now and then, here and there, he would hear the sounds that spawned as the cooling and windy night air set nails and wood to shrinking, and joints to shifting, and water pipes to clanging against floor joints. His creaking floorboards were likely lost in the cacophony of night sounds of a very old house.

His cat-like stalking finally brought him to the living room. A hallway ran to his left and then, ten feet down, bent again to the left. On the right side of this hallway, at the bend, Karsten could see the first bedroom. Its door was slightly ajar. Karsten approached the bedroom with the same practiced patience. The opening was just wide enough for Karsten to look inside.

Karsten saw three things at once. One was the sight of a phone plugged into a wall, charging. To the left of that, in the far corner, was a figure lying prone under a large blanket. He even had a pillow. Holiday had made himself at home.

The third thing was a scattering of fast food paper bags, just out of reach of Holiday. McDonalds, Burger King, Wendy's, Taco Bell. The guy was an equal opportunity artery clogger. He really had given up.

Karsten stealthily slipped into the room. He raised his gun and took aim. Not an ordinary gun; a handgun specially developed for jobs like this. A tranquilizer gun whose darts contained a powerful, quick-acting sedative.

But it wasn't to be the method of execution. And there would be no need for autopsy bloodwork to hunt for a cause of death. The cause of death would be obvious: Asphyxia by hanging. Oxygen cut off from body and brain as the airways and carotid arteries were compressed. And Holiday would be very much alive and awake and able to move when it occurred. The sedative would slow Holiday down to make it much easier to stage. Nothing more.

Yet, if bloodwork were done, if the sedative were discovered in his bloodstream, it would set off no red flags—just mimic pills Holiday could have purchased on the street, something extra to take as he despondently, inexorably plodded toward his suicide. Just in case Zanini's guarantee of the coroner's support wasn't as lock-tight as promised. Every angle covered.

Karsten moved closer. And fired the gun at the sleeping Holiday. The dart hit its target with a dull thud.

He expected more of a reaction. The tranquilizer was quick acting but not instant, and anyway would only make Holiday sluggish. Karsten realized he must have shot somewhere the dart didn't penetrate. Perhaps in a space between the arm and the torso. Certainly it got through the blanket.

Karsten reloaded and moved closer. He fired higher this time. Direct hit.

Still, the mass never moved. *How sound is this guy sleeping? Is he dead already? Had he killed himself?*

Karsten moved closer. And with that, he suddenly felt dizzy.

This is no time to have a heart attack, he told himself. He felt the world spinning. And he noticed an odor in the room, a kind of sweet odor.

Karsten fell to the floor with a heavy thud.

Chapter 48

Karsten woke up. Groggy. Disoriented. And with a dry mouth and a wicked headache. He had trouble focusing his eyes. Although maybe that was the darkness. Wherever he was, it was very dark.

He went to stand up. He couldn't. His arms wouldn't move. He could move his legs, but not much and only as a unit.

He began to understand. He was propped up against an old metal radiator and his upper body was fastened to it with ropes. His legs were tied together. In the dim light, he could see that he was stripped down to his t-shirt and shorts. His clothes and shoes were nowhere to be seen.

His eyes caught a movement on the opposite side of the room. Someone was in the room with him. Someone hidden in the darkness, moving closer.

The form began to differentiate. It was a large man. A large man who appeared to be wearing Karsten's night vision goggles.

"Awright, mate! Blimey! Finally wakin' up." Stated in a strong British accent.

Well, there's no doubt whom I'm dealing with, thought Karsten.

"You might want to have some water and take these painkillers," said Hugh. "I picked them up for you at the Rite Aid yesterday."

Karsten indicated with a nod of his head that he would take the aspirins and drink some water. Hugh placed one pill in his mouth and gave him a sip of water. He waited for him to swallow and then repeated it with a second pill.

"What happened?"

"An anesthetic. Well, two really. One is bloody fast acting. But I combined it with another to try and avoid that blinking small margin between knocking you out and depressing your system too much." Hugh smiled and added, "At least that's what I read in the bloody library."

"How long have I been asleep?" asked Karsten.

"A long time, mate. To be honest, I was worried you wouldn't be waking up."

Karsten raised an eyebrow. "Did you know what you were doing?"

"Ah…Sure. Knocking someone out with anesthesia is actually quite easy." He paused. "The challenge is being able to wake the person up afterward. At least according to the medical school adage that I read." He laughed.

Karsten looked at him with amazement. This kid's gall surprised him. Then he realized that with the night vision goggles the kid could see his expression. He retreated to a poker face.

"The word on the main anesthetic was that it had a quick recovery time," Hugh continued, unprompted. "When you didn't come to, I thought you might be in a bloody coma. This isn't the typical method of administering; I had to do a lot of guessing and hoping. But it worked out. Maybe I can get a job as an anesthesiologist someday."

Karsten silently marveled how Hugh had mastered the subtle difference in how anesthesiologist was enunciated in the two dialects. Indeed, he seemed to have the British accent down, at least from what Karsten could tell. If it weren't for his annoying habit of using *bloody* so bloody often.

"As it was, you only fell arse over tit."

Hugh laughed at his own use of slang. He had no idea if this phrase worked for men or just women. Maybe if he ran into someone from England, he'd come across as the village idiot. But he loved so many of their expressions: "shag" and "snog"; and "salad dogger" for someone overweight; and "shake hands with the unemployed" for a man urinating.

Karsten's tone showed that he wasn't all that entertained with the "arse over tit" quip. "Where'd you get anesthetics?"

"Borrowed them from a laboratory I visited a couple nights ago."

"You mean stolen. I don't think you plan to return them," said Karsten with a sneer. He was feeling more recovered minute by minute.

"Well, that true. But it's okay. I think the professor was trying to get me bumped off anyway. ...And I think by you, Mr. Karsten."

Karsten lost his poker face, which now had astonishment written all over it.

"Well, I guess if that *is* your name. The person that called you on your phone when you were sleeping started out the conversation calling you that. He said, 'Karsten, this is Zanini.' I had barely turned on the phone when it rang. Does that name of Zanini ring a bell?" said Hugh, with a laugh.

"What'd you say to him?"

"Well, nothing. I just turned off the phone. What was I supposed to say to a mob leader, 'Karsten's tied up right now and can't come to the phone?'

"But then again," Hugh continued, "the name Karsten? Hard to be certain. You seem to have a lot of aliases. You had all kinds of IDs and names in that van of yours. And disguises too."

Hugh noted Karsten's surprise. He continued.

"Yes, I found the van down the road. Not many places you could've parked around here. And I didn't think you lived around here," Hugh added with another laugh.

"You have a real cute British accent," Karsten said, dripping with sarcasm.

"Like it? I can do Irish, too."

They sat there is silence for a while. Hugh sat down, propping himself up against the wall to Karsten's left, but a good five feet away. He removed the goggles and leaned back against the wall.

"You seem tired, Holiday."

Hugh leaned forward and faced Karsten. "Well, I did have to stay awake all night. First to be ready for you. Then to watch you sleep so you didn't wake up and slit my throat in the night... Oh, beg pardon. Help me to commit suicide. At least according to my suicide note in your jacket."

"Nothing personal."

"I'm sure not. From the look of your van, you were for hire. Just Zanini, or did you deal with de Angelis too?"

"None of your damn business."

"But it is my business. It's actually my throat on the line. Well, now yours too."

"If there is one thing I know, Holiday, it's that you're not going to kill me. It would weigh *way too much* on your conscious. I studied you, collected information on you from sources the police don't have. And I know you didn't kill that lady. And I know you couldn't kill someone in cold blood."

Hugh leaned his head back against the wall. It was certainly true. And it did pose a dilemma. Eventually Karsten would get away.

"I could turn you into the police."

"That would just get you in more trouble than you're already in. You see, my record is completely clean."

"What about your van and all those IDs, the weapons, the surveillance equipment?"

"Listen, kid. I have it covered every which way. You don't think I have prepared for being stopped by the police or a car accident or any other possibility? All the IDs there? You won't find a single one that's been used in the past. Just a hobby of mine. The weapons? All legal. The surveillance equipment is all legal. The van traces to a sham home I keep that is clean."

Hugh wondered if Karsten was protesting too much, covering up a vulnerability. He had no way to know.

"But," countered Hugh, "Zanini and de Angelis would probably have you killed just to be sure you didn't lead back to them."

"They're not worried. Not in the least. There's been no direct contact between me and either one. Just some phone calls from Zanini using unregistered phones. Neither one even knows what I look like. They have no reason to kill me. But if you turn me in, they will help me to be released within minutes, not hours."

Hugh remained silent. Karsten then continued.

"But your having kidnapped me would just give the police another reason to consider you deranged and kill you on the spot. An innocent man grabbed at a gentleman's club and drugged from stolen chemicals and then tied to an old radiator? Probably fit right in with the police psychologist's diagnosis of delusions and paranoia that led you to kill DuPont."

Hugh looked at Karsten. He had no idea if what he was saying was true. But he was right about two things: Hugh had no intention of killing him or turning him in to the police.

"Well, at any rate," said Hugh, "you don't have to worry about your bloomin' van and all its bloody weapons and disguises being discovered. I made the front tire quite obviously flat to give an excuse for it still being in the lot after the bloody closing. And, if anyone looks, they will see that the back tire is bloomin' flat as well. They'll just figure the driver got a ride home and will come back to fix the van later."

Karsten stayed silent. His headache had nearly dissipated and yet he was feeling something not right. Not exactly groggy, but his mind a little confused and his heart palpitating, like a combination of a caffeine-high and being drunk. He wondered if it was the aftereffects of the anesthesia and the supposed painkillers Holiday had given him. He would have to be more careful, to think things out, plan things out more before he spoke. But still, if he knew Holiday's psychology, gaining his trust would help. And as Holiday was a person who didn't have a lot of social interaction, or people to confide in for that matter, gaining his trust might not be so hard.

Hugh pressed further. "What is it with the dart gun? Some kind of tranquilizer?"

"Something like that."

"How long was it going to make me sleep?"

"You wouldn't sleep. Just slow you down. Make you easier to handle."

"For how long?" Hugh pressed.

Karsten looked at him. He guessed there was no harm in letting him know. "An hour or two."

"But you shot two darts?"

Karsten stayed silent. The conversation died.

Hugh was feeling tiredness creeping in from the long day and night. The initial rush of energy from when Karsten had arrived was long gone. Also gone was the extra coffee he had picked up at the last fast food stop. He'd been careful not to leave those cups around the room for when Karsten first entered. But their impact had worn off. Even the cold one he had saved and then drank only two hours ago.

The room was getting lighter. Karsten could distinguish Hugh now. He was no longer just a dark object in an even darker room. The sun had quite obviously made its way to just below the horizon. It would soon be sunrise, maybe a half hour at most, and the uncurtained windows would have even more light streaming in.

He was nearly recovered. The painkillers, or just the anesthesia wearing off, was bringing back his old wits. And he sensed some weakness in Hugh. If he understood correctly, he might be able to exploit it. And he had Hugh's undivided attention now. He decided to start by lightening the mood.

"Listen, kid, if you use that word *bloody* again, you won't have to worry about me. I might just kill myself."

Hugh chuckled.

"Listen. As I said, it wasn't personal," Karsten continued, emphasizing the past. "Walking away from this is easy for me. But I studied your life. Rather intensely, I might add. I know your options. And they are few and not good."

"Go on," Hugh said.

" One option is to run. Now that you have me, there's a window of opportunity for you to get out of town unnoticed."

Karsten paused to let that sink in. Only to shut the door on it.

"But you're up against the mob. And not just here in the Pittsburgh area. Not just de Angelis and Zanini. My sources say that the Philly mob and the five families of New York want you dead as well. You can't hide long from the mob. At most, you will carve out a few more days of life. And if they have to hunt you down, believe me, they will make you suffer greatly before your last breath."

Hugh stayed silent. It was still not light enough, Karsten thought, to see the subtleties of his expression. But he seemed immersed in thought.

"Then there's also the matter of the police. Soon as you run, the police will use that as evidence that you're guilty. Pittsburgh has always been your home. You just renewed your apartment lease a few months ago. You can't sell you parent's home that quick. There's no way you wouldn't look guilty. There would be a manhunt for you. From what I'm told, once you are in jail, you're going to commit suicide there as well."

"And how would you get a job anyway? You couldn't use your social security number. You couldn't use this British accent, or the police have all the evidence they need to put you away for murder. No, running is not an option. At least not a viable one."

Karsten could see Holiday's head join his back in resting against the wall. He felt as if he could also see the wheels turning in Holiday's mind. Holiday may have already thought this out somewhat. But he didn't have the details Karsten had. Not about the Philly mob and the New York mob and the prison "suicide." And he lacked the certainty that Karsten could offer.

Karsten chuckled, but only on the inside. On the outside, he was a sincere man with concern for Holiday, helping him think things through.

"Let's go to option two. That is, to speak to the police. To tell them everything."

Again, Karsten paused.

"But, as you know, that *everything* puts you at the scene of the crime and under arrest again. They also will never believe you versus either Faccon or de Angelis."

He paused, then continued. "I know you were in Faccon's lab. And that you placed a cam there. But I also know something you probably don't know: that anything you saw in the lab, at least anything incriminating, is no longer there. At least nothing Faccon doesn't have a right to have in a laboratory. Because I already reported to Zanini what you were up to. The cam is gone. The images you recorded are gone. You have no evidence for the police, just your word against a respected professor and a very respected benefactor. And if you think you have something of interest to the police, believe me: it will disappear, either right before or after your confession and in-jail suicide."

"Hugh," Karsten continued, slipping in the use of the first name, "the only thing you accomplished is to make yourself an even greater target of the mob. The last that I spoke with Zanini, he gave me until the end of tonight before he was calling in even more people."

Karsten paused, letting the hopelessness of Holiday's situation sink in. He could see his face a little better now. Holiday was clearly deep in thought. Karsten fancied himself an excellent logician. It was now time to take this to the next logical step, to take this to a philosophical conclusion.

"I would like to suggest a third option."

"Go on."

"Let's look at your life through the lens of reality, so to speak. You don't have any friends, any girlfriends, any family. I don't think you have ever had a girlfriend. Is that correct?"

"Yeah . . . That'd be . . . accurate."

"Well, you have one friend in the world. And that is a dog. A dog that, to be honest, would be just as happy with most any other family, one with kids perhaps. So really, it's a one-way relationship: you need the dog, the dog doesn't need you. But you don't have any friends and with your stutter, you're not confident of getting any friends you can share your heart with."

He paused again before continuing. "Your one goal, medical school, fell apart. You lost your only hope of a job, one that came after numerous failed interviews. And on top of this, you're being hunted by the mob and by the police. And the latter will never believe anything you say, because it contradicts their evidence and the testimony of respected leaders like Faccon."

Another pause. He had Hugh's rapt attention. "You did learn how to speak without a stutter. Congratulations, kid, and I mean that sincerely. But it requires you to use an accent. But, as we already went over, once you use that accent, it places you at the scene of the DuPont murder. From which you fled. And again, if held for the murder, you would never make it to trial.

Although you might have a lot of prisoners treating you as their girlfriend in the meanwhile."

Karsten paused, and then continued; "To be honest, kid, you are on a kind of endless Penrose stairs, with each step cut from Hell."

Karsten detected a momentary look of confusion. "You know, the impossible staircase. The one with a continuous loop, such that you can climb forever and never get higher. Holiday, you think you are making progress and getting out of Hell, but you're going nowhere."

Karsten noted the look in Holiday's eyes, the tilt of his head. The kid seemed to be showing a greater appreciation of him; he was not quite the brute expected. Karsten softly added. "I've a lot of time to read in this business. I've enjoyed Roger Penrose's insights on cosmology and consciousness."

Karsten let everything sink in. The lack of response suggested that it was now time for Karsten to press his line of argument to its desired conclusion. He felt that Holiday was most of the way there anyway.

"The point is, Hugh. The point is. . . well, as Shakespeare said, 'take arms against a sea of troubles, and by opposing, end them.' A lot of people end their toilsome, struggling existences for a lot less. Be the one in control. Get it over with on your terms. To be honest, your future is even more hopeless than the bleak past."

Hugh looked at him seriously, with a reflective look on his face. "Pretty hopeless, huh?"

Karsten went for it all. Even if Holiday weren't ready, his resolve could be weakened. It would put him in a state of mind where he would make bad decisions.

"Look at what the future holds for you. Already you wake up mornings to face another day with no friends, no prospects of a girlfriend. Another day where the only thing to look forward to is being on your computer or reading about other people's lives or watching videos or movies alone. But now you will also have to look over your shoulder every minute. Your bills are only going to get worse; you are probably one step from being homeless. You're going to be ridden with constant anxiety and so much depression you'll find it hard to even get out of bed. And there is no way out. Except one. Take things into your own hands, Hugh. End the misery."

Holiday nodded his head, thoughtfully.

Then he laughed.

Paused. And laughed again. A hearty laugh.

"Is this how you justify yourself? Listen, Karsten, if that is your name: I much prefer to be on this side of the dirt."

Hugh leaned forward from the wall and met Karsten's eyes.

"Bollocks. Total rubbish." Hugh said it with a smile. And then retreated to yet another British slang of incredulity: "Are you having a laugh?" And then he chuckled. But his tone was serious.

"You know, Shakespeare actually made a pretty good case against suicide in that same soliloquy. Something about trading the known for the unknown. If I remember correctly, the 'dread of something after death, the undiscovered country... makes us rather bear those ills we have than fly to others that we know not of.'

"Yeah, my life has been balls-up. And it may look like a miserable life to you. I may have struggles in relating to my fellow man, and, sure, loneliness at times, and bills. I have my anxieties and my down times. And like everyone, I can be plagued by bad memories.

"But you seem to think I have no hope even outside of the present situation. Truth is, every day that I wake up, my first thought is not those negative things you mentioned. I think that I'm actually the *fortunate one*. Billions of people, billions, would feel blessed to wake up in my circumstances. Mine is just a First World problem. And even if I only compare myself to those in the First World, I still feel fortunate."

Hugh felt awake again. Engaged. Excited.

"You see, I get to wake up every day and see things that delight me. I love the outdoors. I love beauty. I enjoy the creativity of my fellow man. I love reading. I don't want to miss anything in life. It's not like I'm in an actual prison, just a virtual one from which I can escape just by changing direction anytime I want. And even people in actual prison, even in Auschwitz and Dachau, they kept going. For me, I've so much to focus on that brings me happiness."

Hugh began to speak quieter. "My handicap even has its advantages. I've learned to be better at listening and watching. And I think it has heightened my sensitivity to others. And as long as I don't dwell on the problems, as long as I stay in the moment, then things actually don't look dreary at all. You don't actually understand me. I could get delight out of watching an ant walk across a prison cell floor.

"And I'll share one more thing with you. To be honest, I am starting to enjoy life more than ever these last couple of days. I'm feeling alive."

"But nice try," he added with a laugh.

"It was worth a shot," countered Karsten.

"Also, Karsten. There's a fourth option. That's what I am going to do now, with the help of some things from your van. But, the sun has come up, and I really should leave." He smiled. "It's been a nice chin wag. But no more time to bugger about. I have to see a man about a dog. … That's British slang, by the way. I'm not really going to see a man about a dog."

"That's nice to know."

"But I am going to have to put you back to sleep. I think I know the amount to administer now."

Karsten showed a look of genuine concern. "Are you sure you aren't going to make a mistake and kill me?"

"I'd like to just leave you. But you seem to be a pretty talented guy. I think you'll be out of these ropes before long."

Hugh paused, as if mulling something over. "I could try your tranquilizer gun. That could buy me enough time. And there are the two flat tires you'd have to deal with if you get free. And the fact that your electronic equipment has had a major malfunction." Hugh laughed. "Meaning, it is going to need some major repair. Consider that my bill for your trying to kill me."

Hugh smiled. "And, I'm going to take your phone with me, if you don't mind. I also need to borrow your keys to get something from the van. Well, as you say, *not borrow*," he said with another laugh.

"And you should get checked by a doctor at some point. The anesthetic may cause some kidney damage. I don't know about the tranquilizer."

Hugh shot him with the tranquilizer. He looked at the reaction. And then shot him again.

Chapter 49

The man slid the identification card to the woman manning the TMMC welcoming desk. "Who do you want to see?" she inquired.

"De Angelis," the man replied.

The security guard standing nearby glanced at this man with the well-groomed black beard and mustache. The beard was a full beard, but the sides were thin and neatly trimmed— a short, boxed beard, as he mentally categorized it. It matched the color of the man's hair, although that was somewhat long and ruffled, yet in a style that said, "carefully coiffured." The guard noted that the stranger was also quite well dressed, with a rich looking tie, a suit jacket, and slightly tinted glasses. He was tall, the guard guessed maybe six feet four inches or so. And he had an aura of importance.

"He doesn't have an office here," the woman responded.

"At the board meeting," the visitor countered. "A matter of importance."

The security guard walked over and took a look at the identification card of the man, who sported a foreign accent, probably British he supposed. He nodded and added a "fine" and turned away.

"Sign here, Mr. Granger," said the women, "and then go to the first desk on your right in the main office."

And with this Hugh picked up his fake identification card and nodded a thank you. He added a pleasant and dignifiedly delivered "cheerio" as he turned right and went through the double doors leading into the TMMC administration offices.

It was a calculated gamble, but he was only halfway to being able to come face-to-face with de Angelis. This was the easy part. Hugh had expected to be able to get by the welcoming desk with this disguise from Karsten's van. He'd had a lot to choose from and this beard, mustache, hairpiece, and glasses fit the image he wanted. He hardly recognized himself. The addition of the platform shoes he purchased and the fancy tie from Karsten's collection helped further alter his appearance. The only concern was using the same suit jacket and pants that he wore when he entered the building on Wednesday night—his attire for the viewing—which were also wrinkled and not classy in the least.

Still the welcoming desk, he knew, didn't have a policy of stopping anyone that looked legitimate. And the ID, also from Karsten's collection but with Hugh's mall-machine photo substituted, helped to smooth that process and limit Hugh's need to convince them verbally.

But all of this only got Hugh to the main administration office—no big deal. The problem would be getting de Angelis out of the board meeting. For that there was the envelope Hugh carried.

De Angelis wasn't on the TMMC board. He was only a financial benefactor, a philanthropist who had made TMMC one of his major causes. But from what Hugh had read, de Angelis would be at this special meeting, called for this Saturday morning to deal with the shocking death of TMMC's beloved professor DuPont. It was big news that de Angelis would fund an endowed chair, to the tune of one million a year, in DuPont's memory, and that he would formally present his generous offer at this meeting.

Now, the trick would be to get de Angelis to agree to meet Hugh.

The ID was the first part of this plan as well. It identified Hugh as the Assistant to the Director of the Division of Technology, Industry, and Economics (DTIE) of the United Nations Environment Programme (UNEP). It is said that the longer one's title, the less important the position. But it was the only ID of Karsten's many that fit with a foreign accent. The ID itself wouldn't be enough to get de Angelis out of the meeting. But, Hugh hoped, it should give the receptionist enough of a reason to agree to his request, to take the envelope he carried into the meeting and deliver to de Angelis.

To that she did agree. It was de Angelis' assistant, a burly guy who no doubt doubled as a bodyguard, who carried the envelope to de Angelis.

Hugh's big concern was that he would be kept waiting until someone decided to check him out further. And he was kept waiting. But no one showed up to escort him to the waiting arms of the police. Or the mob. Instead, he enjoyed some tea prepared by the receptionist as he waited.

When de Angelis did step out of the board meeting, he first talked to his assistant just outside the meeting room door. He then glanced at Hugh and proceeded to an empty conference room down the hall. Shortly thereafter, the assistant escorted Hugh to the conference room.

The burly assistant now transitioned to burly bodyguard. He frisked Hugh, but only lightly, knowing that Hugh had already been through the metal detector—a TMMC precaution developed in light of a fatal shooting that once took place at the University of Pittsburgh Medical Center.

As Hugh walked into the conference room, followed by the bodyguard, he saw de Angelis standing ten feet in. He didn't ask Hugh to sit. Instead, he said abruptly: "You don't look like Hugh Holiday."

"I borrowed a disguise from Karsten," said Hugh.

"You're pretty tall."

"Platform shoes."

De Angelis gave a brief nod. He gave the envelope and note to his bodyguard and indicated with a flip of his hand to give it back to Hugh.

"Your note," de Angelis continued "said you had information on Zanini and Karsten. You have five minutes. Start talking."

Hugh put the note back in the envelope and placed the envelope in his jacket pocket. The note had been simple: "I am Hugh Holiday. I need to meet with you right away regarding Karsten and Zanini." A UNEP business card was paper clipped to the envelope, courtesy of the receptionist. Simple, but it had done the trick.

Hugh exhaled slowly and began his explanation.

"I know that Mr. Claudio Zanini and Dr. Michael Faccon were involved in the murder of Dr. DuPont and are working together on…"

He got no further.

De Angelis abruptly raised his hand. Only to just above his waist and accompanied only by a flip of the wrist, but with such authoritativeness that Hugh halted.

"Stop. No more. Not even five minutes." De Angelis turned to his bodyguard, "Gino, escort Mr. Holiday to Joseph's car and have him take Mr. Holiday to my house. I have to finish this board meeting. I will come to the house soon." He turned to leave.

Hugh was astonished. De Angelis was almost to the doorway when he found the nerve to respond. "No, I think I would prefer to just meet here."

De Angelis half turned. "We will meet at my house."

"I don't think so," said Holiday, a lot less firmly than he was intending.

De Angelis turned to face Hugh, slightly tilting his head. "You don't really have an option, *Mr. Granger with the British accent.*" At the same time, his bodyguard, perhaps not recognizing what de Angelis had already conveyed, that Hugh was boxed into a no-win situation, moved his suit jacket to reveal a weapon. Together, the logic was unassailable.

Chapter 50

De Angelis left the room. Hugh followed the bodyguard out of the building, using a door that permitted exit from the back of the administration offices; from the outside it was nondescript and without a handle.

Two identical Chrysler 300s were parked together near the exit door, the first with just a driver, the second with a driver and another man in the front passenger seat. They walked to the second car and Hugh waited outside while Gino spoke to the occupants through the passenger side window. He then opened the back seat for Hugh.

The drive to the de Angelis house was long and quiet. Neither the driver nor the man in the front passenger seat spoke to Hugh, nor to each other. The driver looked like a younger clone of de Angelis himself: bespectacled, thin, probably below average height, and with a placid demeanor. The other occupant was quite large, with a muscular upper body and a thick neck. His square jaw made him look like an Adonis. He was, Hugh thought, the prototype of a personal bodyguard: intimidating to see, with an alert look, and obviously not very talkative.

The silent ride gave Hugh time to wonder about his early morning talk with Karsten and whether he would be waking up again to see things that delighted him. And that thought transitioned to a regret. A melancholic remembrance, not of his mistreatment at the hands of a cruel world, but of when he had been cruel. One of many for sure, but one that filled his mind at the moment. Something that he couldn't take back. A case where someone with misfortune had passed his way, and he had looked the other way.

In this case, it had been a student in high school who was in special education classes due to a quite severe learning disability. Someone whom he had befriended in a quiet moment. A boy who saw him in the crowded lunchroom, who came happily to Hugh's table to sit with him, and who was being mocked by others in the lunchroom, just as Hugh was always mocked. But then Hugh, torn between his compassion for the boy and his desire himself to be accepted by the lunchroom insiders, chose the latter and ignored the boy, who, rejected by even the shunned, dejectedly walked away.

The emotion generated by the flashback washed over Hugh. He realized he had just made a speech to Karsten about his positive outlook in life and here he was flooded by a sad memory.

He chided himself to move off the past, to do good with what time he had left, to make better memories from here on out.

But the high school recollection was only replaced in his consciousness by anxiety over what lay ahead. Whether there would be a "here on out." He felt like he was heading into a lion's den. His concern only heightened as the car left the city and drove, via a winding, two-lane road, up and up and up a mountain. Here houses were far apart and mostly hidden from the road by trees and tall shrubs, only the driveways and gates giving evidence of their existence. For those that Hugh did see, these were, for the most part, expensive houses and mansions.

And then the car slowed and turned into one of the driveways. It went seventy feet until it reached a metal gate, with a small, stone guard house just beyond. Other than via the gate, Hugh was pretty sure the property couldn't be viewed from the road: the eight-foot stone wall assured that, as did the forested area near the stone wall.

The car stopped at the gate, but only momentarily. After a few seconds, the gate move inward, the car moved to just beyond the gate and stopped, and a security guard came out to look in the car.

Hugh was told to get out. He was ushered into the gatehouse and then into a backroom. Here he was "asked" to strip to his underwear. His clothes were taken to another room. A metal wand was moved around him and his body was searched. The disguise—fake hair, fake facial hair, fake eyeglasses—all were roughly removed.

The discovery that he had two phones led to pointed questioning. Why two phones? Hugh shrugged, to which he was informed the two phones would be keep at the gatehouse.

Hugh relented without objection to his personal phone. Not so with the Karsten phone. That, he insisted, he would need. A guard disappeared with the phone for ten minutes while Hugh waited. Then his clothes were returned. As was the Karsten phone—but handed to the large Adonis that had accompanied him this far. The back seat of the car was searched for good measure before he was allowed to continue on.

Once past the gatehouse, the car made the winding journey up the driveway, which continued to climb the mountain, passing a huge, rolling lawn on the left that covered a football field in size, dotted here and there with massive oak, maple, chestnut, and elm trees. At the top of the hill stood a mansion that overlooked a valley.

The main part of the mansion was made of gray stone, rising three stories in height, with a stone terrace encircling the second floor. Sharply arched windows could be seen, as well as a huge second-floor picture window.

The car came to a circular drive, the artistic center of which was a flower garden and statue of a woman holding a baby. But the car didn't stop in front of the house; it continued to the far end, to an attached garage, and then into the third of the three garage doors. There Hugh was escorted to a hallway and through a doorway that lead down to the basement. He was taken to a rather bland room and told to wait.

Chapter 51

The room looked like something constructed as a bomb shelter. It was about fifteen feet by twenty feet, with concrete walls, ceiling, and floor. The furnishings were sparse: five wooden, hardback chairs with thin seat cushions and a small, round table around which the chairs hardly fit. There were two lamps in the room, one on the table and one a standing lamp.

The room was otherwise empty. There were no pictures on the walls, no sofa, no bookcases, not even a single box being stored. It seemed like a room being wasted in the basement of a mansion, a mansion that probably had thirty rooms. Hugh could hardly see a purpose for the space.

He was kept waiting about thirty minutes, most of the time which he spent pacing, having nothing to do and too concerned that he would get sleepy if he sat down. He would need his wits now; that is, if de Angelis were actually going to meet with him personally.

De Angelis did. He entered the room, trailed by another man. A security guard looked in, saw Hugh standing on the far side of the room, and then, in response to a nod from de Angelis, reached in and closed the door, leaving Hugh in the presence of the two men.

Hugh thought he recognized this new figure. He looked like the person standing near de Angelis at the DuPont viewing.

If so, this was the first that Hugh was getting a good look at him. The man appeared quite a bit older than de Angelis, maybe even seventy or seventy-five, and was stockier and somewhat taller. Unlike de Angelis, who had a full head of hair, black and barely streaked with gray, this man was balding in front, and with the hair in the back and sides blending more gray than black, particularly graying on the sides above the ear, where it was somewhat curly. And unlike de Angelis, who had no facial hair, this new man had a thin mustache of the same mixed gray and black as his head.

Both men sported glasses, de Angelis with gold, wire-rimmed frames and the other of a thick, black, plastic variety. The older fellow was darker skinned than de Angelis but with the same five o-clock shadow and piercing eyes. Both wore suits, de Angelis with the black one Hugh had seen him in earlier, the other of gray.

De Angelis said nothing at first. He just looked at Hugh, scrutinizing his very different appearance from their earlier encounter. He then motioned with his hand toward a chair on the far side of the table, and Hugh sat down. De Angelis and the man took seats opposite him, after first pulling their seats a few feet out from the table.

De Angelis caught Hugh looking uneasy at the other man and said matter-of-factly, as a way of introduction, "This is my advisor. My right-hand man." Hugh noted de Angelis had a deep and clear voice and very alert eyes. Still, despite the solemnity of the situation, sitting in an isolated room in the presence of the reputed mob boss in the area, Hugh found himself chuckling inside: his right-hand man was sitting on his left. But . . . he was just glad it wasn't Zanini.

Hugh nodded.

Then in an authoritative tone, with every word carefully weighed, de Angelis said, "Okay, Mr. Holiday. Tell me what it is you think you know."

Crunch time.

"I know that Claudio Zanini and Dr. Michael Faccon arranged the murder of Dr. Megan DuPont."

It was how Hugh had rehearsed it in his mind, a strong opening in his flowing British accent. Except in this, his opening act, he lowered his eyes. He caught himself and looked back up at the two men. He couldn't make out any expression. At all. Of course, de Angelis had already heard this opening gambit.

Hugh continued, "She'd stumbled across a scheme they're involved in, and that's why they had her killed."

"*What* scheme?" demanded de Angelis.

Hugh could now detect an emotion. It was caged hostility, barely restrained. Hugh sensed it could break through the bars at his slightest misstep. The other man moved ever so slightly forward in his chair, his eyes trained on Hugh. Hugh met both their gazes full on, but his confidence was threatening to run out the door. He turned to some British slang to hang onto his accent and mask his nervousness.

"Some might say I bloody sound as mad as a bag of ferrets. After all, Dr. Faccon is a respected professor of surgery at a top institution." Hugh resented using the honorific "Doctor" for someone who didn't deserve any esteem, any respect. And it wasn't how it played in his head. Ever. But from the moment he'd found himself in the presence of de Angelis, Hugh squeezed it out, somewhat because he was cowed in the man's presence, but also to avoid appearing rude. If Hugh had gleamed anything from his years of failed social interactions, it was the importance of first impressions.

He continued, "But the main piece is trading in body parts. Dr. Faccon is stripping cadavers of body parts…"

"Body parts" repeated the older man, slowly and without inflection. He clearly felt free to speak. But the two words he spoke were so toneless that Hugh couldn't discern their intent. He took it as an opening to elaborate.

"Yeah, harvesting body parts is bloomin' lucrative. From a single human body, one might harvest more than a hundred thousand dollars in organs and tissues. A spine can bring three thousand, a knee seven hundred dollars. Even toenails and fingernails can bring thousands of dollars. Bloody heavy demand. Tendons and ligaments can be sold for knee repair. Bones, cartilage, teeth are harvested for orthopedic purposes, dental implants. Ribs, elbows, knees, eardrums, teeth, heart values—all can be used. Corneas. You can get six square feet of skin off a hu…"

"Of course," said the older man, interrupting, "We know one can make a lot of money from body parts, but…"

"You have our attention, go on," said de Angelis, himself interrupting, but politely towards the other man. Hugh could see that he did have his attention.

"All these parts," Hugh continued, "can be used for transplanting to people or even sold for research or training. Just a bloomin' huge demand. Much greater than supply.

"At any rate, where does one get these parts? Hospitals and morgues, of course. Funeral homes, crematories. All of these deal with corpses. Alistar Cook, the broadcaster, had his bones stolen before cremation to be sold for bone grafts.

"But other institutions dealing with cadavers are *medical schools*. UCLA medical school had a scandal dealing with body parts, and the Irvine campus had a scandal involving the sale of spines."

His looked at the two men, but he couldn't discern what they were thinking. He plunged on.

"This is one thing Dr. Faccon and Zanini…Mr. Zanini…are doing: harvesting parts for sale. Well, actually "recovering" is now the "in vogue" term. Organ *recovery* was one reason, I suspect, Dr. Faccon pushed for a clean room at TMMC."

"One thing they are doing?" said de Angelis, picking up on Hugh's cue.

"The second thing, I think, is that Mr. Zanini is running a cleanup operation for people being killed by the…"

He paused wondering, in vain, what term would be inoffensive.

"by the mob. They run murdered and disappeared people through the process as cadavers that …"

De Angelis raised his hand off his lap and to just above his waist level, signaling Hugh to stop. He seemed to be bothered, but trying not to show it. With all the authority of the most powerful man in the area, he spoke slowly, deliberately.

"*Exactly* what *evidence* do you claim to have?"

His voice revealed that the caged hostility, if it ever truly left, was clearly back, pushing on the bars.

"I-I-I k-know t-t-that…" Hugh twitched and stopped. *The stutter. Now?* His mind went blank. Unnerved, a thinking of unreality overtook him. He stared at the two men, unable to remember where in the conversation he was.

"The *evidence*," repeated de Angelis.

Hugh wiped the sweat off his hands onto his pants. He took a breath. He calmed himself. *Accusatory. Privacy. Laboratory.* He said them in his head. He started again.

"Arrh. Blimey! The laboratory. The bloody laboratory. I bloomin' know that in Dr. Faccon's bloody laboratory"—he was looking down now, putting himself in character, his voice lowering, the accent returning, the pronunciation of laboratory confidence-building—"he keeps bloomin' refrigerated coolers with the temperatures of some set at minus eighty degrees Celsius, some at a bloody minus four, some at plus four, and others at fifteen degrees. Each of these bloody temperatures is designed to preserve different tissues. The coldest temperature is preferred for long-term storage of bones, tendons, skin, and heart value tissue—you know, for blinking grafts, like skin for a bloomin' burn victim. The four degree temperature is good for short-term storage of things like a kidney or skin."

Relief was washing over Hugh with each perfectly enunciated word. And there was something more. Not only had he regained the accent: In his entire life, he never remembered a conversation, at least with a non-canine audience, where he had been allowed to speak so long without being interrupted.

But before him were two totally indecipherable faces.

"Some bloomin' things don't last long, of course. One should harvest...recover...skin from a refrigerated body within twenty-four hours of death. But there is a longer leeway for things like bones and heart values. Same things with storage. I-I-I."

Hugh paused, started anew. Just a blimp. He was rolling. He'd be okay, he told himself. *Accusatory. Privacy. Laboratory.* He continued.

"Bloomin' eye tissue can only be stored up to about a week. But heart value tissue can be stored for *ten years* and bones and tendons and skin for *five bloody years*. And I found glycerol and propylene glycol in the laboratory. These are used for banking skin for allografts. Then..."

"And you know this how?" said de Angelis.

"I read it in the library on Friday. I was..."

"No. How do you know Professor Faccon has these coolers and these chemicals?"

"I snuck into his laboratory one night, after the viewing."

"How?

Hugh hesitated. There were things he didn't want to reveal, but de Angelis' tone indicated he was going to get his answer.

"There is a walkway above the first floor. I used that to drop down into the professor's lab."

De Angelis cocked his head a little and stared at Hugh.

"You do know that Dr. Faccon is a medical researcher," interjected the older man. "Dealing with tissues is hardly unusual."

"Of course. But there also is the matter of a large refrigerated white van that showed up Thursday night. I watched from the street. There were two men in the van, a short guy with glasses and a very large man with a docking big gut. They unloaded at least three bodies that"—he couldn't stomach it any longer, the honorific title for someone he loathed—"Faccon took into his laboratory."

"You could see clearly that there were bodies," said the older man.

"Well, not really from the street. But I could tell when I looked at the monitor that I put in the laboratory."

"You put a monitor in Dr. Faccon's lab?" continued the older man. "When you snuck in?"

"Yes."

"At any rate, none of this is unusual, Mr. Holiday," said de Angelis, with palpable frustration. "Professor Faccon is in charge of procurement of cadavers for the medical school. He's also in charge of the Willed Body Program for the college."

Hugh persisted. "Cadaver procurement and the Willed Body Program are for getting cadavers for medical students. But I also saw him cut up tissues and put them in the refrigerated containers. He may be good at teaching anatomy class or laparoscopic surgery or arthroscopic surgery or repairing heart values, or whatever else he teaches. But he's also good at removing tissues from cadavers for sale. I suspect this is also why he's not doing spinal surgery on the students' cadavers—instead students are observing surgeries remotely on cadavers at other institutions, involving other doctors. He says he needs them for his research but in recent years he has published little on spinal research. He is getting good money for the spines."

"You have this recorded?" asked de Angelis.

"No. It was erased."

A silence permeated the room. When de Angelis spoke, Hugh felt it was in line with a patient inquisitor, with all the time in the world, probing a man suspected of being a heretic.

"Again, there is nothing unusual here. A research professor of surgery in charge of procuring cadavers for the college is actually procuring said cadavers and doing research on them. "

Hugh persisted. "There is more." He felt emboldened by the fact he had gotten his far. "The refrigerated coolers were loaded into that white van late at night and hauled off. As well as at least one body taken from the lab to the white van. And you know where that white van ended up?"

"Go on."

"A crematorium. It stopped at the DeSandis Funeral Home and Crematory."

"A crematorium," deadpanned de Angelis. "You mean where medical colleges normally dispose of their bodies after they are done being used. What did you think happened to the bodies, that they're put in a dumpster?"

Hugh felt if they were outside, de Angelis would have punctuated his remarks by spitting on the ground.

"But I saw one more body taken out of the van at the crematory than went into the van at the medical center. There must have been a body in the van that Faccon rejected for some reason, and it went straight to the crematory."

"That's a stretch."

"And what about the refrigerated coolers. Why were they loaded into the refrigerated van other than for delivery someplace?"

"Where were they delivered to?"

"I don't know. I didn't have time to follow the van after the funeral home."

De Angelis was too dignified to roll his eyes. But that was sense that Hugh got as de Angelis stated, more than questioned, "So you didn't actually see whether the coolers were unloaded, and their contents were possibly cremated also."

"No, I didn't see...I got busy.'

De Angelis wasn't too dignified for a sneer. "So, in essence, you saw nothing, you have nothing. You don't have any recorded images or sound. You saw a professor doing what professors in Faccon's position do, and then the expected cremation of discarded body parts or cadavers."

The older man spoke. "And so far you have spoken a lot about Dr. Faccon. Your claim was that Zanini was involved."

"I saw Zanini at the funeral home when the refrigerated van arrived to deliver the bodies."

"You do know that Zanini is one my most trusted friends." De Angelis did nothing to hide his contempt for Hugh.

"L-l-look." Hugh caught himself and paused. He felt sweat had dripped into his eyes. He rubbed them. He continued, betrayed by the stutter, but acting as if oblivious to de Angelis' words. "I'm godsmacked, but this is a bloomin' smashing plan for trade in parts and bodies and also as a bloody cleanup operation. One can transport bodies easily if they are treated as cadavers being donated to medical school. They probably have all the necessary papers to not be stopped. Some bodies aren't suitable for parts and are just cremated, to disappear forever. Some are scavenged for parts. Some may be used for the medical school to keep up the illusion of donations as med school cadavers. No one is going to question anyone."

"You have nothing," said the older man. "An overactive imagination. And not very interesting or important. No one would take you seriously."

"Except," replied de Angelis, looking coldly at Hugh, "you are accusing a great professor of a crime and speculating about one of my trusted associates—and, I guess by extension, accusing me. And I do find that interesting. And important. And serious. That is, in a kind of 'here is an annoyance that needs to be taken care of' kind of way."

"Th-th-there...," he paused, then continued. "There is bloody more. Much more," hastened Hugh. "I haven't gotten to the issue of Dr. DuPont or what else I know."

Chapter 52

"So, your claim is that Dr. DuPont was murdered by Dr. Faccon and Mr. Zanini. Is that correct?" scoffed the older man. "What, was she sneaking around like you, Holiday?"

"No," said Hugh. "I think she was just being nice. It seems an anatomy student took a sample from his cadaver and asked Dr. DuPont to do genetic testing. When students get cadavers, they're only told the cause of death and the age. Perhaps this student thought he'd impress his instructors by discovering another factor contributing to the cause of death. Perhaps he thought he spotted something that didn't seem to match the cause listed. If there were a gene abnormality discovered, it might support another illness, you know, like the EGFR mutation suggests a type of lung cancer. This chain of events led Dr. DuPont to finding something alarming."

"Go on," said de Angelis.

"As you know, Dr. DuPont's expertise is genetic testing. She has access to bloomin' large DNA datasets from all kinds of research projects and screening programs, those either she's part of or on the review board. For some reason, she ran the DNA markers for this cadaver against those in a database. Probably she found something in the cadaver's DNA that pointed out a particular medical condition where she had a lot of screening data. What came back must've stunned her."

Hugh paused and looked at two inexpressive faces. He figured that getting this far was nothing short of a miracle, but he was rolling now, words flowing from his lips, with a pleasant tone, an intriguing delivery. He felt no need to interject much slang. He was adding dramatic pauses like a storyteller. He had someone's undivided attention for the first time in his life.

And Hugh felt something more: de Angelis was showing patience with Hugh's obviously contrived accent—something his own father wouldn't have done.

De Angelis made a motion with his hand for Hugh to continue.

"Dr. DuPont found that the DNA of the cadaver in the anatomy class was identical to that of a known person who'd been screened. But there were some major discrepancies in the records. Students aren't given cadaver names, but TMMC has them on file. The name on file was Edward Gleason. He was listed as having a birth date of November 23, 1964 and the cause of death on the death certificate was listed as RAR—meaning respiratory arrest. The one in her DNA dataset had a different name and a different DOB: March 14, 1966. And he didn't have a COD listed. In fact, she made a notation that he had "disappeared" and referenced a recent newspaper article to this fact. I looked up the article. This person, a John Morris, had indeed disappeared and to date hasn't been found."

"John Morris?" said the older man. He looked at de Angelis, who nodded.

"Yes. Apparently John Morris had been part of a medical study that Dr. DuPont had some involvement with, and they couldn't locate him for the follow up survey and treatment. From what I can discern, he actually had a treatable form of lung cancer, and there's a drug targeted for his particular gene mutation. But, in the meanwhile, he'd disappeared."

"How do you know all this?" added de Angelis.

"I found the files in her office," replied Hugh. He noted their look. "Yeah, I had to break into that also. I found that she had a flash drive with two DNA samples. The DNA markers were identical. They came from the same person. But the disappeared person, this John Morris, was mysteriously a cadaver in the TMMC lab. Dr. DuPont must have brought this to Faccon to explain. This was her fatal mistake. Her going to him only brought Faccon some time and DuPont her death."

"I am pretty sure she didn't suspect Faccon," Hugh continued. "If she had, she would have better secured her computer. She could have required a flash drive to unlock and lock her computer, overriding the system password that TMMC administrators and Faccon would know. She also could have encrypted the USB flash drive. It seems that when she left her office, she really wasn't expecting the level of trouble she soon found herself in. She probably told Faccon she would take it to the police, but never really realized what she'd stumbled across. Just an innocent snag in the plan."

A silence fell upon the room. For a while, no one spoke.

De Angelis finally broke the silence. "Mr. Holiday. I commend you. You seem to have been pretty ingenious in figuring this out."

"I was motivated. And with the advantage in knowing Faccon was involved, since he'd set me up to go to Dr. DuPont's house and take the bloomin' rap."

De Angelis learned forward. He spoke bluntly, "Have you told your theory to the police?"

Hugh ignored the use of the word theory.

"No," he replied.

"No, I would imagine not," said de Angelis. "You seem to have little hard evidence. No recordings, right?"

Hugh shook his head. Any thought he might have entertained of de Angelis as a kindly, father figure, based on his patience in listening to Hugh's contrived accent, vanished. Before him sat the mob boss who could give one word and Hugh would be in the trunk of a car at the bottom of the Monongahela River.

De Angelis continued.

"Any evidence has likely been incinerated. It's just your word against Professor Faccon. You have nothing that would stand up against the professor and any honesty on your part would only put you at the scene of the crime. Am I correct? Not to mention breaking into two professors' rooms at TMMC."

"Very weak evidence," concurred the older man.

"Well, I'm not presenting in a court of law," said Hugh, a lot more timidly than the words had played in his head.

"Why *have* you come to me with this," said de Angelis.

"I'm hoping you can help me solve a problem, that being that Faccon and Zanini have been trying to kill me."

De Angelis leaned back in his chair. He looked relaxed. His words were anything but: "What makes you think that we're not going to kill you."

There was a long nervous pause before Hugh could respond.

"Because we have a common interest," Hugh finally said.

"Go on."

"First, I don't think you're involved in this scheme. In fact, it seems certain that Faccon and Zanini were trying very hard to keep you from knowing about it." Hugh smiled, awkwardly. "I have bet my life on it."

"Indeed you have."

Hugh looked at de Angelis. There was no smile, no emotion on his face. Hugh continued.

"Tuesday night, I saw Faccon and Zanini and a Pittsburgh policeman having a clandestine meeting in a park outside of town. At first, I couldn't think of a reason why Faccon and Zanini would meet in this park. Sure, they own fancy cars and would want to meet somewhere where the road was paved. But you have hundreds of properties in Pittsburgh, and Zanini manages a number as well. There are many excellent places they could've met, over which you have control. I know. I drove to many of your properties. Despite this, Faccon and Zanini and a Pittsburgh policeman drove outside of the city to meet."

"Finally, it dawned on me. They weren't keeping their meeting from the police or FBI. They were keeping it from you and anyone that might report to you that they were meeting. Even at the DuPont viewing I noticed that when around you they acted like they were but casual acquaintances. And in their meeting in the park, their words made it clear there were very worried about someone discovering what they were doing. That someone was you."

"Continue."

"Also, why would Zanini and Faccon need a scapegoat? I think it was more because of you than the police. I doubt any operation you ran would even need to set up a fall guy. You've the police and everyone else it seems in your pocket. Why complicate matters? Zanini and Faccon were more worried that if this was not tied up nicely, then you might become interested."

"I appreciate your confidence in me," de Angelis said with a wry smile that suggested his remark was more dry wit than sincerity. He continued to draw Hugh out: "That's it?"

"I would add that Lieutenant Kelly, he indicated to me that you were a person of some character. I'm banking my life on it."

De Angelis remained silent. He nodded ever so slightly.

"As for why this is in your interest. When I was observing Zanini and Faccon in the park, they talked about Dr. DuPont getting in the way of their scheme and about killing me. But that wasn't all they talked about. They also talked about the five families in New York, about the Philly . . . group, about New Jersey. They seemed to be working together with them. This left me with the suspicion that Zanini is running a cleanup operation to dispose of people that were killed in those places. Of course, they might have just been collecting corpses from funeral homes. I really don't know.

"But it seems clear that Zanini is not only doing something without your knowledge, he's also doing something that has risk for you. He is ingratiating himself to various people in other . . . mob families because he might be planning to make a move."

Hugh paused, expecting to be interrupted. He wasn't.

"But even if he's not, you could well get ensnared in this because he's using the medical center as a cover. Already Kelly has been alerted to a connection between Zanini and Faccon." Hugh left out the inconvenient fact that it was he who had tried to draw Kelly's attention to that connection. "And Kelly, as you are no doubt aware, is very clear on the relationship of Zanini with you.

"You know that you will be implicated if they catch Zanini and the professor. The professor, for one, will 'turn states evidence' and implicate you for a reduced sentence. Maybe he can maneuver into the witness protection program since you are the big fish, not him. Even should they not implicate you, the medical school's reputation will be ruined. And your legacy rubbish."

De Angelis sat there. The older man started to speak. He stopped. He sat back and waited for de Angelis.

"Look," continued Hugh. "I know you aren't sure whether I can be trusted. I'm a stranger who just showed up with some stories. But all of this is easily proved. First, you can find those two drivers, the short one with glasses and the more rotund fellow. I am sure you can be very convincing to have them talk. Then there is the policeman who was in the park with Zanini and Faccon. I heard him referred to as Scott. I also got his police car's license plate number. They all may be very surprised to find out they weren't working for you anyway. And then there is Karsten."

"What do you know of Karsten?" said the older man.

"I know he's a contract killer. And I know he was trying to bloody kill me, well *suicide* me, on orders from Zanini. And I know he is now tied up in a house."

"Tied up in a house?" interjected de Angelis, with a look of genuine surprise.

"Well, he may be out of the house by now. He could be at his van, although I left it with a couple of flat tires and dumped the keys. It was a bloody amazing van, with a lot of disguises and high-tech equipment. Although he is now minus one phone. A phone on which Zanini called him. Your security guard has the phone. If someone called back the number from the middle of last night, I am sure that Zanini would answer. I understand that he is very anxious to hear about my demise."

"Captured a hit man." De Anglis nodded his head up and down. "You're quite the interesting young man."

"My guess is that Karsten would be very surprised to find out that he's working only for Zanini, not both Zanini and you. I certainly got the impression he never met you personally. That was the one detail that I was trying to get out of him."

Hugh looked at de Angelis and continued: "But maybe you would like to meet him? I can give you the address of the house where he is. If he's not there, then he's probably at his van parked a few hundred feet away at a strip joint."

"Why don't you write the address down," ordered de Angelis.

The older man pulled out a small notepad and ripped out a sheet. He added a pen and pushed both toward Hugh.

Hugh wrote that address of the house down, a notation about color and type of van, and added the license plate of the police car. He pushed the paper back across the table.

The older man got up and walked toward the door, where he was joined by de Angelis. They spoke quietly for less than a minute. Then the older man left the room and de Angelis sat back down in his chair.

"Who else have you told about these things?" inquired de Angelis.

"Just you, really."

De Angelis scrutinized Hugh. "Stay here for a while longer. Someone will be back for you. If you need something, let the security guard know. He will be just outside the door."

Hugh nodded. And with that de Angelis also left the room.

Hugh stood up after de Angelis left and began to pace, breathing heavily. His first thought was to wonder whether he should have stood up when de Angelis went to leave. What is the proper etiquette with a mob boss?

His second thought was whether the entire meeting had been a big mistake. He had been very confident when he had thought it all out. But even now, after the long meeting, he still wasn't sure where he stood. De Angelis had a poker face. Other than the surprise he'd shown about Karsten being tied up, de Angelis never gave away what was going on in his mind. For all Hugh knew, he had blundered, and now de Angelis was figuring out the best way to have him disappear.

For a half-hour, Hugh was left with his thoughts. Then the door opened, a security guard looked in and stepped back, and de Angelis entered the room alone. He didn't sit but stood opposite Hugh.

"Mr. Holiday. To whom did you report about the body parts scheme? Kelly? Anyone else?

"N-n-o." He paused, reset. "No. I didn't tell anyone but you."

"Did you report about Karsten to anyone?"

"No."

"Did you report to anyone about why Dr. Megan was killed, or about Faccon's involvement or Zanini's?"

Hugh hesitated. "No."

He wasn't sure he liked where this might be going. He hastily amended his remarks. "Well, Lieutenant Kelly has reason to suspect about Zanini and Faccon, and he has his eye on me. He's keeping close tabs on me."

"But did you give Kelly any specifics about Zanini and Faccon?"

"No."

A small smile broke on de Angelis' face. "Mr. Holiday. Hugh. Don't worry. You're going to walk out of here alive. For now, I'm going to have you wait in my house. Then we'll take you home."

They exited the room. The security guard was there, but the older man was nowhere to be seen. De Angelis took Hugh up a different set of stairs from the one he had descended. These stairs led into the house.

He escorted Hugh into the living room, where his wife Violetta was seated. She rose and de Angelis greeted her with a warm kiss on the cheek and introduced Hugh as "this is the person I told you about." And then he left to "take care of some unfinished business."

Mrs. de Angelis showed Hugh around part of the lower floor of the house: the vaunted ceilings, stained glass windows, dining room, large swimming pool. All beautifully decorated. All immaculate. And then she had him wait on a large sofa in the living room while she fixed something for him to eat. She expressed surprise when her offer of tea was rebuffed with an "I don't actually like tea," but brought him a water while she went off to fix him lunch.

When she returned, Hugh was sound asleep.

He remained so until hours later when a car came for him and took him back to his apartment and a joyous reunion with Holly.

Chapter 53

Karsten did much better with his three new jobs.

His first was fulfilled when Michelangelo Prospero Faccon failed to negotiate a curve going 110 mph in his Jaguar XKR-S coupé. Faccon had been on the road to a resort in New Jersey at the time. Had it happened in the Pittsburgh area, it might have merited a much bigger notice in the newspaper.

As it was, it was dismissed as the unfortunate accident of a person who was known to drive at reckless speeds. No mention was made of failed brakes or an accelerator that seemed to stick. The accident was soon forgotten and, given that de Angelis opposed any special chair or wing or monetary grant in his honor, Faccon's name would soon fade out of TMMC's collective memory—other than those ex-wives clamoring after a portion of the estate or scholars who had occasion to reference one of his articles.

The second job merited even less press attention. It was fulfilled when Claudio Zanini disappeared while apparently traveling out West. His wife, ever the trooper, had maintained a stiff upper lip and, combined with his boss's unconcern, and the police's apparent relief, not much was made of this disappearance.

The third job was just an ironic footnote. The undertaker DeSandis died of a heart attack and ended up cremated in his own crematorium.

Three jobs. All for free. All consecutively for one client. And so Karsten paid his debt and moved on, although he could no longer claim the same anonymity as he did before, now being a recognizable face to de Angelis.

Officer Bill Scott was determined to have been unaware that he wasn't also working for de Angelis. He did his penance. Pittsburgh police were allowed to moonlight on second jobs. None worked for free as Scott found himself doing and quite willingly given the options. The planned trip to Europe and the property in the Caribbean were soon distant dreams.

Joey and Salvatore also paid their debt. They'd been judged to have been as unaware as Scott. But they still did penance, making one last delivery, this time to Arizona.

It was in Arizona that a first-year medical student had the honor of dissecting a donated cadaver that had an interesting feature: the tattoo of clenched fist on the wrist, above which was written the words, "Lucky." The student thought it a particularly interesting moniker given that the cadaver seemed to have suffered some abuse or torture.

Holly sat at Hugh's feet, snuggled there as her master played a game on his computer.

Tomorrow, Hugh would be back at work at the Bioscience Center. De Angelis had called Bridgewater personally and said he had some business for the Center. His philanthropic efforts, he had noted, involved lending support to a nonprofit that reunites families, particularly those separated by war and human trafficking. He wanted the Bioscience Center to do the necessary DNA work to prove family relationships for immigration purposes. And he had a personal request: he wanted Holiday hired back to do this work. Bridgewater had called Hugh just two days earlier with the good news.

Even better for Hugh, the police saw their leads in the DuPont case dry up, and with pressure from the mayor and TMMC rapidly dissipating, the case moved to a back burner.

Hugh finished his game. He playfully patted Holly's soft coat and got up to stretch. He looked out the window. It was dark outside. Still, he could make out the vague outline of a policeman sitting in an unmarked car, the same car and same vague outline as the last two nights.

As de Angelis told Hugh when he last saw him, he wasn't a miracle worker.

Lieutenant J. P. Kelly looked up at the apartment and thought he saw someone looking back through the window.

This Holiday kid may have slipped through the raindrops until now. But he couldn't evade them forever. Another man was now dead, the professor that Holiday had mentioned. And another man who Holiday had referenced had disappeared. And Kelly had informants who said they saw Holiday leaving the de Angelis property.

This kid, he thought, *is in this deep*. Someone with power was able to waylay the investigation. But Holiday will eventually slip up. He will speak with a British accent or speak stutter-free or in some other way be exposed.

And, thought Kelly, I will be watching for that moment.

About the Author

Professor, high school academic dean, scientist, author—Richard Straws is used to juggling positions simultaneously the way Hugh Holiday has to juggle accents. He is the author of both academic works, from scholarly journal articles and books to encyclopedia articles, and fictional short stories and books. He currently lives and works in Connecticut, but has also lived and worked in northern and southern California, Colorado, Wyoming, New York City, upstate New York, and Pennsylvania, in addition to having traveled to over 40 countries for nonprofit and educational programs.

Check out richardstraws.com for his humorous short story *Running with the Curimbata* and the science fiction short story *Future Jau*, both of which will be made available for a time free of charge.

The journey of Hugh Holiday will continue in the next book in the series as he travels to Bridgeport, CT, compelled by mob boss Anthony de Angelis to investigate the murder of the Angel's son-in-law and disappearance of his daughter. In addition to recurring characters Holly (of course), Lieutenant J. P. Kelly, and Karsten, the book introduces a humorous, quick-witted Bridgeport lieutenant, two potential love interests for Hugh (!), and a mystery blonde who may (or may not) hold some of the key to unraveling the murder and disappearance.

The publication date for this forthcoming book has not yet been set at the time of printing of *Hugh Holiday*.

www.ingramcontent.com/pod-product-compliance
Lightning Source LLC
Chambersburg PA
CBHW020653110726
47901CB00001B/168